APOLLO

Bosnian Chronicle | Ivo Andrić

Now in November | Josephine Johnson

The Stone Angel | Margaret Laurence

The Lost Europeans | Emanuel Litvinoff

The Authentic Death of Hendry Jones | Charles Neider

The History of a Town | M. E. Saltykov-Shchedrin

The Day of Judgment | Salvatore Satta

My Son, My Son | Howard Spring

The Man Who Loved Children | Christina Stead

Delta Wedding | Eudora Welty

Heaven's My Destination | Thornton Wilder

The Hungry Grass

Richard Power

APOLLO

Apollo Librarian | Michael Schmidt || Series Editor | Neil Belton
Text Design | Lindsay Nash || Artwork | Jessie Price

www.apollo-classics.com | www.headofzeus.com

First published in 1969 by The Bodley Head Ltd

This paperback edition published in the United Kingdom in 2016
by Apollo, an imprint of Head of Zeus Ltd.

1 3 5 7 9 10 8 6 4 2

A CIP catalogue record for this book is available
from the British Library.

ISBN   (PB) 9781784977412
          (E) 9781787977405

Typeset by Adrian McLaughlin
Printed and bound in Denmark by Nørhaven

Head of Zeus Ltd
Clerkenwell House
45–47 Clerkenwell Green
London EC1R 0HT

We are not Angels from Heaven that speak to you, but men, whom grace, and grace alone, has made to differ from you.

—CARDINAL NEWMAN

Introduction

Everyone's life is a ruin among whose debris an artist may be able to deduce what that person might have been. That injunction pressed heavily on Irish people in the aftermath of the Great Hunger of the 1840s. According to folk tradition, whoever walks on the grass where a Famine victim fell dead risks a similar affliction: hence the 'hungry grass' of the book's title. Perhaps it is a fear of seeming famished which causes Father Tom Conroy to refuse offers of food at various moments. But the novel also engages with a wider sense of emotional and cultural starvation: of the tragedy that is underdevelopment and of the underdevelopment that is tragedy. Every so often the celibate Father Conroy imagines scenes of conjugal love, not as a grand passion, but in terms of the kind of warm fire which seems to be missing from his own life. Of course, he curbs these reveries for the sake of his vocation. The hungry grass could never be ploughed by farmers, who feared infection from it; and the parish priest of Kilbride confronts a related problem, in that he is expected to supply the spiritual nourishment that his flock needs, but there is nobody to nourish him.

The book was published in 1969. It was acclaimed for breaking free of saccharine depictions of the Irish priest, that 'soggarth aroon' beloved of nineteenth-century novelists and twentieth-century Hollywood movies. Its central character is sardonic, even to the point of being caustic, about those trendy clerics of the 1960s who call for a revival of rural Ireland. In his world (just before the changes unleashed by the Second Vatican Council) the mass is still said in Latin, a language whose aphorisms are often quoted with urbane approval by Tom Conroy. His Catholicism is as much rule-bound as it is visionary. For example, he suffers from 'scruples' not just about wet dreams, but about being late with his daily reading of the Holy Office.

His initial vocation seems to have been dutiful rather than Damascene. He simply took the place of his brother who had suddenly abandoned the seminary, as if he were a volunteer soldier substituting for one who had deserted an army. Never sure as to exactly why he joined, he lives an inner life too deep ever to risk vulgar self-definition. He is the sort of man who would have understood the Ulster poet John Hewitt's answer to the question 'What is the religion of all sensible men?' – 'They are far too sensible to define it'.

Father Conroy outrages colleagues who realize that he has not troubled to compose a last will and testament, as if such things were a matter of the sordid letter rather than the inner spirit. Yet his negligence also bespeaks the crisis of a rural Ireland with little sense of its own future. More than once in the narrative, as his powers wane, he finds himself expected to deliver a homily for which he has not prepared, as if in his ideal church, the altar would take strong precedence over the pulpit. He is shrewd enough to intuit that the moral and religious impulses are very different things and may even destroy one another in the end. Hence his indifference to his curate's social programmes and to his uncle's partisan campaigns, for as a man of God he must seek the spiritual, rather than political, kingdom.

The disinclination to write a will suggests an inner suspicion that the Catholic Church will not be central to shaping the Irish future. Ten years after *The Hungry Grass* was published, Pope John Paul II visited Ireland, the first pontiff ever to do so. On the surface, that visit seemed an example of the Church Triumphant, with more than a million people attending each mass he celebrated; but deeper down, his coming registered an immense crisis. Ever since 1967 there had been a sharp decline in vocations to the priesthood, and the official teaching on contraception was widely disregarded. An urbanizing laity was more likely to practice à la carte Catholicism, or none at all.

Read against this wider perspective, *The Hungry Grass* might be taken as an elegy for a doomed way of life and for a priesthood that did little or nothing to arrest its decline. As a young priest during the war of national liberation, Tom Conroy acquires a reputation for favouring socialism and is transferred by a nervous bishop to a poor, out-of-the-way parish. Even after this punishment, which he humbly accepts, Father Conroy continues to harbour sympathy for dissidents, silently endorsing the actions of a poor boy who stole the silver of another priest in order to give himself a start in life. He notes with dry asperity the emergence of a new kind of party hack in politics after independence: a coalition of large farmers, publicans and ward heelers sailing, like new recruits to a pirate ship, under a flag of convenient pietistic nationalism. Landless labourers, once welcomed without stint at the food table of families for whom they worked, are now made to eat at a separate bench, as members of a lower order, and the cost of that food is deducted from their wages. Father Conroy is not, in the end, a social radical, but all around him he notes the hidden injuries of snobbery and respectability destroying the new state.

The old Latin rituals persist and the priest says mass at an altar facing a crucifix, but already – before the shift in furniture ordained by the Vatican Council – Tom Conroy has a tendency to confront that final puzzle: his own congregation. Its members may take him for granted, as he may sometimes take them. 'What do ye want a church at all for?' is a question that may trouble him even as he puts it to his people. He is alert to the absurdities of a subsistence economy, which calls men in their forties and fifties 'boys' simply because they are still waiting to inherit their families' land. He can mock the obsessive-compulsive religiosity of elderly men, while recognizing that many old men he encounters may be versions of himself as he prepares to die. His inadequate speeches are increasingly followed by a clued-in, turbo-charged alternative, tossed off with fluent insincerity by one of the men of the new order. In that ambiguous context there is a certain nobility to be found in his refusal to pontificate or to state what he doesn't truly feel. This priest is too honest for self-assertion.

The rising cadre of switched-on priests speak in the same language as that of soap advertisers on television; however, Tom Conroy is something of a latitudinarian on postmodern culture and, while not deigning to purchase a TV set, he likes occasionally to eavesdrop on the absurdities of some of its programmes. He seems to sense, however, that most of the Father Trendies will not be long in the priesthood. And he can sense the deadlock in a society where most of the youth were compelled to emigrate to a life of hard labour in Britain, while large farmers tighten their hold on the land. Between the year of independence in 1922 and 1969, one in every two people born in the country left it. That missing middle generation, which might have refereed the conflict between tradition and modernity, thus achieving an intelligent balance, has gone forever. As Antonio Gramsci remarked of the rural communities in southern Italy – also devastated by emigration – the haemorrhage of a middle generation caused the old to elaborate fantasies of a reactionary conservatism, and the young to submit to a heedless, depthless consumerism.

A certain kind of priest might once have filled the vacuum left by that lost generation with an alternative kind of leadership, but Father Conroy cannot do so. He ministers in the years after ordination to the migrant community in England, fretting ever afterward about the fate of his brother Owen, who died in his twenties leaving two young sons whose names the man of God never knows.

That deficit of knowledge hints at a certain coldness in his character, perhaps even some incapacity for primary experience in the living stream of persons. 'A true priest is never loved', wrote Georges Bernanos. However, the quality of this priest's solitude, though at times almost chilling, can bring out a loving tenderness in others. His loneliness is so deep and invincible as to cause many people to offer him bank notes that he neither needs nor desires. He stores the money up over a lifetime, intending to give it to some worthy recipient but never quite managing to do so. It is as if, like an over-ripe potato, it is forever sprouting pointless and uncontrollable shoots.

If bank notes represent a form of human labour that has never been materialized, they may be a fair image of their owner's condition: alienated from his original home at Rosnagree, to which he hopes one day to return. He is haunted by letters sent decades earlier by another priest of the family from a mission to South America. If such writing is a metaphor for going into exile, then exile is the condition of much of Richard Power's writing, which in *Úll I mBarr an Ghéagáin* (*Apple on the Treetop*, 1959) and *The Land of Youth* (1964) had taken estrangement for theme. Even the language in which the characters achieve expression in this book seems like an estranged form of Irish ('and she munching slowly as she read') of a people still half-thinking in Irish while using English words. The dialogues which drive this novel are rich and flavourful, the Synge-song of a kind which – like the community itself – is still hanging onto old ways, but near to the moment of its erasure. The younger priests do not speak in such phrases, although the narrative itself often does, as if in tacit endorsement of jeopardized tradition. The lines of farewell in which the 'last of the bards', Aogán Ó Rathaille, spoke about going into the clay which held his pre-Christian ancestors, seem to spread like a dye across the final pages.

The novel begins with Father Conroy's death and the revelation that neither his brother nor sister managed to attend his funeral. This foreknowledge adds a poignancy to accounts of his fumbling encounters with members of his family in the ensuing narrative, while also raising a question as to whether some emotional blockage was a strong element of the family inheritance. There is something rather withheld about Tom Conroy's very presence in the most central of the novel's scenes. However, against that must be set his capacity for unexpected moments of passing grace: 'he'd see a pain inside you'. This is what makes him a vessel of God, yet that very empathy is disabled by a self-protective wit that deflects deep feeling at just those moments when it may become both lucid and intolerable. The loneliness endured by Father Conroy is that of a man who knows more than it is decent to know about the lives of his community. That community finds him essential to its self-definition, but displays remarkably little interest in his priesthood: he is simply part of the givenness of things. He must embody a holiness that ordinary parishioners cannot afford to admit in themselves, but also a clarity of vision found more often in artists.

Richard Power's portrait is of a good man blocked by the very culture that makes him possible, and disabled by that very sensitivity which makes him such an honest minister. James Joyce had once written of the priesthood, whose vague acts pleased his protagonist, Stephen Daedalus, by reason of their semblance of reality and, at the same time, their distance from it. If Joyce anticipated John McGahern in offering compelling portraits of the artist as frustrated priest, Power has offered something that is even more unusual – a depiction of the priest as the 'removed' artist.

The money saved and never used becomes a symbol of a life lived at a remove from the well-springs of emotion, a life often fearful of committing itself to the here and now. For the Famine had not only destroyed people's trust in nature, but it had also left them fearful of living with full relish in the present moment. Such an incapacity for primary experience was frequently notable in people of high intelligence, who might have what Flann O'Brien once mordantly called 'a memory and no experience to account for it'. The fear of submitting to the sacrament of the present moment became also a fear of the future, causing terrible, shoddy compromises (such as panicky marriages based on convenience rather than on true feeling). To people of Power's generation, the whole of life could seem like a preparation for something that never finally happened. For stay-at-home peasants, the saving of money in a stocking was one way of evading experience in the here-and-now; for richer people, that might involve the adoption of a profession which proofed them against real adventure. And the priesthood, as George Bernard Shaw said more than once, was like all professions: 'a conspiracy against the laity'.

It took its harshest toll not on that laity but, as Power shows, upon the priests themselves. Tom Conroy remains at all times stoic and unsentimental: unlike the sugary padres of preceding popular novels, he knows it would be sentimental to invest his own life or world with more significance than God would give them. Some readers have found the novel's diminuendo a little less compelling than the passages at its centre, but that, surely, is exactly as it should be: the kind of denouement in which people are dismayed not only by fate, but saddened by the fact that they are saddened so little. For this really is a story of emotional underdevelopment, in which the worst must ultimately return to laughter. There is no other position possible for those who believe in God than to find the antics of mankind hilariously funny and touching, 'as if bubbles of pure laughter were trying to break through'.

Patrick Kavanagh once said that tragedy is underdeveloped comedy, comedy not fully born. Behind its somber moments and chilly witticisms, *The Hungry Grass* is a supremely divine comedy:

God's laughter at the shattering of a world. In the end that world proves too strong for one mortal man to sustain, and so he must feel himself set free of life rather than deprived of it.

Richard Power died in his early forties in 1970, not long after the acclamation of this book as a masterpiece.

Declan Kiberd, 2016

Prologue

At the funeral, several priests remarked how appropriate it was that Father Conroy should have returned on his last day to Rosnagree, the parish in which he was born. They had been touched by his return, by the way he had limped in expectantly among them, like an emigrant returning to seek nourishment at his roots. They had never thought of Conroy having roots before.

One or two – Father Mahon, for instance – saw no cause for sympathy. Conroy's return, to them, seemed a final example of the man's genius for causing trouble and inconvenience. That he should have timed his death during the dinner at the parochial house in Rosnagree was more than upsetting; it was deliberately destructive, for that annual dinner – which Conroy had never bothered to attend before – would never be the same again.

It meant a lot to all of them, that dinner. It was the one occasion of the year which reunited them, the fifteen priests who had been ordained together for the diocese of Kilcloyne.

Arriving every year in Rosnagree always gave them a feeling of holiday. Just as one becomes suddenly aware of the onset of spring, so they noticed everything at once – the hedgerows opening out to distant blue hills, the Scotch pines behind the steeple, the rooks that sailed across the front of the parochial house. On the road below the gate, the car roofs of some firstcomers gleamed in the sunlight, and on the top step – his saluting base, they called it – Father O'Hara, the parish priest of Rosnagree, waited to welcome them once more.

His hostliness beamed down the length of the tiled path between the rows of newly staked dahlias. It made each of them feel he was being welcomed individually, that his failings as a guest would be overlooked and that any little graces he might have would get full appreciation. The strange thing about Father O'Hara's dinners was that these promises were fulfilled. They always left, looking back as happily as they had looked forward in anticipation.

Dinner was late, for Elsie, the housekeeper, was not to be hurried. Anyway, nobody minded the delay; it seemed only to lengthen the day pleasurably in their anticipation. They were all of an age when a good time must be taken slowly and with a minimum of waste.

While Father O'Hara moved among them with the decanter, they stood chatting and sipping their sherry, conscious of the aroma of roast lamb from beyond the green baize door down the hall. They were waiting until it was time to move into the dining room. Elsie never had to sound the gong on the hall table, for they knew by some kind of sixth sense when their number was complete. And this year, although none of them knew that Father Conroy was coming, they were waiting for him.

Two of them had slipped out for a stroll in the garden. The sun was shining. A cool, resinous breeze idled up the valley, stirring the leaves. Hands in their pockets, feet crunching the gravel, they strolled around the side of the house. Bat Cullen, who had seven dogs of his own, went on up to the yard to cast an eye over Father

O'Hara's setter, which was suffering from some distemper. Father Mahon preferred to turn away onto the path that led under the apple trees.

He was a professor in St. Declan's, the diocesan seminary down in the town of Castlemore. Being the only one present who had never been out in a parish, he always felt at a loss during the initial exchanges when his colleagues met – not that he had a lot to say when the conversation became general. He had long ago resigned himself to being rather a "dry stick" to his students and friends.

An old man was scything the long grass beneath the trees, his head down and his back bent so that the wide-brimmed hat seemed like a fulcrum for the arms that swung the scythe. Father Mahon called hello, but the slow, rhythmical strokes continued without a pause. The air smelled of new-mown grass, and the first bees buzzed in the blossoms overhead. Soon it would be summer.

He walked on, head tilted back to watch the blossoms pass like clouds across the blue sky. The scything ceased behind him and, next moment, the air was rent with the scraping of stone on steel. Irritably, he turned to look back, but the man's head was still hidden. All that he could see were the two bent arms moving around the circle of the hat.

Standing there, vaguely put out by his inability to see the face of the old man, he noticed a faint trail of dust rising along the line of the road. Next moment, a car came into view. It emerged from between the hedgerows and recklessly took the old humpbacked bridge without slackening speed. On it came, dusty as the road itself, with that squinting, rodent look of the Volks hastening up and over the contours of the ground. He did not recognize whose it was, until in the sudden silence after it stopped at the gate, he saw through the dusty windshield a head of gray hair bent over the wheel. For a moment the head lifted and he glimpsed the powerful, arched nose of Father Conroy; then it sank again, as if Conroy were reading or searching for something on the floor of the car. Thinking perhaps that he had not yet been seen, Father Mahon turned quickly away between the trees and toward the back of the house. There was a surprisingly long delay before he heard the car door slam and then the creak of the gate.

He was timid, Father Mahon, and he had never been at ease with Conroy. All his life, ever since his student days, he had avoided Conroy's eye, fearful of drawing some judgment on himself, one of those Conroy remarks which were remembered forever in the diocese. And so he waited awhile by the yard gate until Bat Cullen returned from ministering to the setter. They talked for a while, or rather Bat talked about one of his dogs which a parishioner had entered for him in a race and which had not been given a "fair do." It was his only trial, as a priest, that he was not allowed to attend the dogtrack himself and see that his dogs were given fair dos.

He stumped off at last when Father Mahon's sympathy proved too contrived even for his comfort. At the corner of the house, he halted at the sight of the gray Volkswagen parked across the gateway. "Tom Conroy! Well!" He turned, grinning with delight. "Why didn't you tell me he was here?"

Father Mahon gave a deprecating smile and a shrug, as if to say, I kept it as a surprise, Bat.

"Come on in, then, and we'll see what the oul' scoundrel is up to!"

"Go on in yourself," said Father Mahon. "I'll stroll around a bit. Work up an appetite."

Bat hurried on, trousers flapping over loose green socks (he always seemed in danger of wading out of his clothes). He was halted by a sudden hoarse cry from the direction of the house.

"What's that?"

They waited a moment, listening, but there was no sound, only the steady swish of the scythe, somewhere between the trees.

"Must be O'Hara, calling us in." Father Mahon was trying to persuade himself. The cry had frightened him.

"No, he'd have Elsie sound the gong."

"Oh, I don't know. Only O'Hara's brazen lungs…"

"It wasn't O'Hara," Bat said irritably. He left the footpath and ducked under the branches until he got a view of the gable end of the house, "Sounded more like…" As Father Mahon joined him, he called out, "Hey Tom! Tom Conroy!"

There was no reply. The gable end had two small windows, both frosted. The one below, presumably that of a scullery, was closed. The bathroom window above was ajar, and the edge of the white curtain stirred lightly within. The only sound was the distant swish of the scythe.

Bat turned away abruptly. "Ah, some cod-acting he's up to, ye may be sure." He grinned suddenly, in relief. "Though they've hardly reached that stage yet inside, the clamor… how's this it goes, the signs of a good dinner?"

"Silentium, stridor dentium, clamor gentium."

"Ay. About time we went in and let the old dentia have a go."

"Dentes."

Bat gave an exasperated wave, "Come on in, Pete, for God's sake."

The hall was cool and dark. Beyond the dining-room door, they could hear voices and the clink of cutlery. Unobtrusively, they entered and were passing down the table, when Father O'Hara turned to them from the sideboard, where he was carving the joint.

"Sorry, men," he called. "I never noticed... And damn it, we've just said grace." He seemed put out that he had been caught napping. "Bat, where'll we put you?" He saw a vacant chair farther up the table and motioned Bat to it with the carving knife. "Now what about you, Peter?"

Father Mahon had stopped by a vacant chair.

"Who's..." he began and looked at the plate of soup which steamed there, the half-empty glass of sherry, and the crust of bread crumpled on the side plate. "Where's Tom Conroy gone?"

The priests chatting on either side looked up. "I didn't notice," said one.

"He was there a moment ago," said another, "but you wouldn't mind that. Sure, he's always on the wing."

"I wouldn't stand for it, Pete," somebody laughed. "You were expected, he wasn't. Why should you have to move?"

"The bathroom!" Bat said in a low voice. He scraped back his chair and rose to his feet. With the haste of premonition, Father Mahon remembered the cry, the bathroom window ajar, the stir of the curtain. He hurried up the stairs to find Bat already knocking on the door. They waited a moment; then Bat seized the knob and rattled it. "Father Conroy," he called, nervously formal, then, "Tom!" He threw a single scared glance over his shoulder at Father Mahon. "Tom, d'ye hear me?" And almost at once, he swung his heavy shoulder at the door. It gave way at the second blow, the bolt splintering away from the jamb so easily that Bat stumbled forward into the room, fighting to keep his balance. He went down on his knees at once. Over his shoulder, Father Mahon could see a length of black trouser-leg on the red tiles, and a boot twisted against the pedestal of the lavatory. Then he was on his knees too, helping Bat to lift Father Conroy very gently and turn him over on his back.

The eyelids stirred, as if he were trying to force them apart.

Father O'Hara, summoned from the dining room, knelt by his head and whispered the act of contrition into his ear, all the time feeling for the small throb of the pulse. Some of the priests crowded in the doorway, until Father O'Hara looked up suddenly and, as at a word, they withdrew, all except Father Mahon and Bat. Somebody was at the phone downstairs, trying to get through. Out at the gate, a car engine revved up, then roared away into the distance.

The eyes opened at last. They stared up, their smoky blue flooded by the black iris. Then they turned, seemed to reach out and find Father O'Hara and stay upon him. The lips moved several times in silence, as if rehearsing the name which came suddenly, "O'Hara" and then, low but clear, a frightened invocation. "Christ, O'Hara, am I done?"

Father O'Hara smiled, patted the wrist, and looked across at Father Mahon. "We'll see, Tom, we'll see."

The eyes searched him a moment longer, but he kept looking obstinately toward Father Mahon. Slowly, with frightening deliberation, they followed his gaze, overhauling it, reeling it in until they had Father Mahon captive. The lips parted – it seemed, at first, in a grimace – but the eyes, the whole face, was sweetened by the smile, and the head nodded several times, as if bubbles of pure laughter were trying to break through. Suddenly the intensity went out of the eyes, leaving the lips still parted, so that the whole face had a stricken look. The head fell sideways, a heavy lump half-turned to the wall, all the buoyancy gone out of it. It did not move again.

Laughter at what? The question troubled Father Mahon, who felt that laughter must have some object, some butt. Yet, it hadn't been that kind of laughter, not the sharp Conroy kind; it had come welling up from some deep, inner spring which had lain hidden all Conroy's life.

But why? What had Conroy discovered in that last searching moment? What could he have found to laugh about?

The question gave Father Mahon no peace in the days that followed, all the more when he was summoned to the Bishop's House and told that Conroy had appointed him executor.

"But why, my lord? I mean, we were classmates, yon might say, But I didn't know him, not that well. In fact, I'm the one he had least to do with."

"I don't think there'll be much else, Father," the Bishop said. "As for the papers and so forth, I'll leave all that to your discretion. You needn't consult me." There was a delicate pause. "You might check with the different banks in town. I don't know if he had an account."

"Yes, but I can't understand why he wanted me to—"

"You may also find there's some livestock to be disposed of." The Bishop smiled. He had a very pleasant way of dealing with questions which should not have been asked. "A couple of bullocks that he grazed on a bit of land belonging to the parish. He also, I'm told, let them out to graze on the long acre, where they were a menace to passing traffic."

"Yes, my lord. But Father O'Hara, Father Cullen even – They were much more..."

The Bishop's hands moved firmly to the arms of his chair. "That's the way it is, Father." He rose to his feet and watched with a smile as Father Mahon, taken unawares, floundered to kiss the ring. "Good-bye, Father, I know you'll do the best you can."

That wasn't the only arrangement that disturbed Father Mahon. The funeral itself had been most unsatisfactory. Father Conroy's family hadn't turned up. His brother Frank (who had the farm), was over in Aintree for the Grand National and couldn't be contacted in time. No one knew where he was staying. "Not a man of much substance," remarked Father O'Hara.

The sister, Kate, and her husband, who had a farm up near the mountains, didn't arrive until everything was over; their car had run out of petrol. "And why wouldn't it," said O'Hara, "when they never put anything in the tank? And because they can't buy petrol, they can't take the milk to the creamery. And because they can't sell the milk, they can't buy the petrol. So there they are, spreading butter on everything."

Then someone, no one seemed to know who (it was probably the undertaker), had decided that the remains, instead of being interred in the family grave nearby, were to be brought to Kilbride, where Father Conroy had been parish priest. It all seemed so settled that no one thought of questioning the arrangement.

The funeral left Father O'Hara's house, slowly at first. Farm laborers and foresters, cycling home from work, dismounted and touched their caps or walked a few steps with it. Once out of the valley and on the main road, the sleek, bulging black hearse picked up speed rapidly; it was wanted for another funeral later in the evening. The long line of cars sped after it, up the winding road into the hills.

The best of the diocese lay behind, the uplands of Rosnagree, good farming country with comfortable old farmhouses and big red barns, the wide parklands of the plain beyond watered by the river and its streams. Down there, among copses of oak and beech, was the cathedral town of Castlemore, where all the affairs of the diocese had, if anywhere, their meaning.

The Kilbride country was drawing near, bare hills peopled with sheep and boulders. Small fields had been ironed out of the fern and yellow furze, which thronged back again against the loose stone walls. From the doorway of a thatched cottage, an old woman made the sign of the cross as they passed. The houses were small, the yards dungy. The hay was ricked in the open, pinned down by central stakes, and eroded by the grazing of the cattle into the shape of toadstools.

Conroy had been priest here for seven years. He had sat in these stuffy parlors, under the faded photographs of priests and bearded grandfathers. He had fitted himself into these interrelated, clotted lives, into the smell of damp and turf smoke.

"They're a difficult people, right enough," said Father O'Hara suddenly. "Inbred, you know. But Conroy could handle them. He always said Kilbride was a fine, airy parish."

Or the dunghill of the diocese – he had said that too!

Beyond the crossroads which was Kilbride – the three houses and the pub – the road led on through a few backward hamlets and petered out on the bare slopes of the mountains. It was a place halfway to nowhere.

They passed the school, a new one, all concrete and glass. Conroy had plotted years to get it, besting the men from the Department who had wanted to close the old school and commute the children down the valley to the big school in Donore (that bloody, big infantarium, Conroy had called it). The Department's statistical forecasts had proved to be better than Conroy's; already the population had fallen so much that the new school was only two-thirds full. The teacher's residence alongside lay derelict, and the teacher commuted every day from Donore. Conroy hadn't liked that; he had always put his parish first, right or wrong, and expected everyone else to do the same.

As the hearse slowed to walking pace, the figure of Father Conroy's uncle, James Conroy, the T.D., could be seen moving through the crowd, accepting condolences with practiced hand, now and then drawing a sympathizer in close to give or receive a whisper. In spite of his eighty-six years, James never missed a good funeral. Following someone's coffin afforded him the perfect opportunity to conduct some little bit of political business in a decent and dignified way, as well as to pick up any floating votes. Although he still headed the poll in every election, he collected votes as a boy hoards chestnuts.

He came toward the priests, bearing his Anthony Eden hat on his chest like a great funeral medal.

"Ah, Father O'Hara, and Father Mahon!" He reached in to receive their hands. "Very good of you to come. Yes, very sad, yes indeed, yes, yes. Of course, poor Father Thomas had been failing for some time – he would never admit it, but it was quite clear to me." He began to move on at sight of the Canon in the car behind. "It's turned out a nice day for it, thanks be to God. He should bring a big crowd."

And they could hear him continue at the window of the car behind, "Ah, Canon Fitzmaurice, how are ye? Yes, very sad, yes indeed, yes, yes."

"Ever notice," asked Father O'Hara as he rolled up the window, "that James has one ear bigger than the other? It's always the one facing away from you – it picks up the background noises."

The farce continued. The hearse came slowly through the gateway of the churchyard, its curved wings almost touching the stone pier on either side. Behind it came a black limousine with blue-tinted windows through which several white faces peered dimly. On it came, in steady, imperturbable slow motion, for a moment carrying with it a chilling presence of death. But only for a moment. As it rolled to a stop, the undertaker hurried to open the rear door. Out came Elsie, Father O'Hara's housekeeper, massive in black. After her, dabbing at her eyes with a little handkerchief, came the woman who had been Father Conroy's housekeeper a few years back. She threw a glance around to see who was present, then, with a whimper, buried her face again in the handkerchief. Her husband tagged behind her, respectfully attending her. The local women came forward to shake her hand or kiss her tearstained cheek.

"Peg!" muttered Father O'Hara. "A dreadful cook, but a great actress." And Father Mahon understood his resentment that there was no one else to mourn Tom Conroy.

As the coffin was shouldered across the porch, Father O'Hara nudged him and whispered, "If a spider wanted the quietest spot in this church, where would it hide?"

Father Mahon looked startled, and shook his head. O'Hara nodded to the collection box, marked BAPTISTRY FUND. "There! According to Tom. He used to tell them that a spider could be warm and snug in there. Undisturbed from one week's end to the next!" And with a grin at Father Mahon's discomfiture, he passed into the church.

The congregation was very quiet while the priests recited the prayers over the coffin. A stolid lot, Father Mahon thought. Then a sob surprised him, quite close, and he saw an old man slumped in the first pew with hands hiding his face. There were others, yes, quite a number were crying, but it was getting so dark that it was hard to see them; he could feel the emotion spread from one to another. Fortunately, Father O'Hara launched straight into the first decade of the rosary. The congregation, of its own accord, began the second, forcing Father O'Hara to go on to say the whole five, though only one was usually said.

"A true priest is never loved," someone – Bernanos was it? – had said. The syllogism formed itself before he could stop it. "Father Conroy was loved. Ergo, he was not a true priest." His tricks of logic often disconcerted him, and now he shrugged the conclusion aside to join in the prayers.

And at once, he was caught in the tide that flowed strongly between priest and people – what kind of tide, he wasn't sure, but it seemed to carry him toward a dissolution, a chaos which threatened him, threatened them all. Even O'Hara seemed conscious of how close was the threat; he cleared his throat several times and tried to set his voice on a steadier course. What was it? What was wrong? It couldn't be Conroy, that shabby old baluba of a parish priest with his boxful of spiders. It must be the twilight hour, the old church like a well-scrubbed kitchen from which the light had faded; it must be that shy, violent crowd, overstressed now with emotion that the formality of the prayers barely held in check. Whatever it was, Father Mahon found it distasteful. He was to find that peculiar distaste in all his last dealings with Father Conroy.

A few days after the funeral, Father Mahon took the bus out from Castlemore to see to the effects. It seemed more of a place now, a destination. The sound of the bus dwindled away, and it grew very quiet; there was only the distant, vague bleating of sheep on the hills.

The ring of a shovel on stone held him on his way past the churchyard. Between the tilted crosses and the leaning head-stones, he saw a clod of earth flying in the air. He went in, through the long grass which had been trampled by the crowd on the day of the funeral. Just beyond Conroy's grave, a man's cap bobbed back and forth on a level with the ground.

"Evening, there!" he called.

The man looked up. He wiped a large, red face with his sleeve, drove his shovel deep down into the clay, and slowly climbed up out of the grave. Then he lifted his cap, for a moment meeting the priest's eye. When he spoke, he seemed to be addressing the far distance, a dark blob of forest on the mountain. "'Tis hard to get the depth, Father."

"'Tis, I suppose. You'd need some help there."

"No, Father."

"No?"

"I'm the digger of graves."

"I see." Father Mahon wasn't used to this; Castlemore people were usually more accommodating in conversation. "I suppose it's very rocky."

"'Tis not, then. Not a bit rocky." The small eyes flickered over Father Mahon's face, then returned to rest on the mountain. "The way it is, the place was never rightly sounded."

"Sounded? I didn't know these places had to be…"

As if Father Mahon hadn't spoken at all, the man went on to explain. He spoke with a sort of restrained impatience, each word slow and precise, as if it were in a foreign language. "When you'd go down now, a fair depth, you'd meet a coffin maybe, or bones, and you'd not be deep enough at all. You'd have to take up that coffin or what remained of it and put it aside. Then you would dig deeper and get the depth."

Father Mahon looked around at the headstones and shivered slightly. "It doesn't look…" What was the word? "…overcrowded," he said at last.

"Well, no, Father, it wouldn't be, for the one that's to go into it." He let his gaze wander nearer, panning slowly over the hills of the parish. "They're a fair few families to go into it yet."

Thank God, thought Father Mahon, that I'm in a reasonably civilized town, where people have some regard for the decencies. He half-turned to move away, but the fellow glanced at him, so that he felt compelled to find a suitable remark to depart upon.

"It's strange," he ventured, "that the next is to be buried there, right beside Father Conroy."

"Well indeed may you find it strange."

"It's some relation, perhaps?"

"Oho! We can relate ourselves to anybody, Father, if we pay enough."

Some cryptic, peasant phrase, perhaps? Father Mahon had had enough; it was time to bring the conversation to a close.

"Shall I need a key to get in?"

"No, Father, he never had a key. No one's been in there since."

Father Mahon looked at the house with some aversion. "It's very exposed, isn't it?"

"He liked it open, Father." The eyes swung up suddenly in a raking glance. "The kind he was, Father, he'd see a pain inside of you."

"I didn't know him well, not very well."

The man hitched his cap impatiently and turned back toward the grave. "If you didn't know him, Father, there's no use in me telling you."

"No." Father Mahon made another uncertain move to go. "I suppose not."

"He had brains to burn – that was his trouble – brains to burn."

"Yes," said Father Mahon, grudging praise to Conroy even now. "Yes, I suppose."

"Yes indeed, Father!" He paused as he lowered himself into the grave and looked up at Father Mahon defiantly. "There's no man hates more to be shuttered up than him." He plucked the shovel out of the clay and spat on his hands. "The light will be going fast, Father, and there's a share of work to be done."

And though Father Mahon called good-bye, he was already too absorbed in his task to reply.

More than the hedge had been leveled. On either side of the drive were the stumps of trees which had been felled. Why? he wondered. Surely Conroy couldn't have wanted to burn them all?

The back door gave easily when he lifted the latch. A pair of

Wellington boots stood apart under the scullery window. In the kitchen was a big, old-fashioned range and a single kitchen chair facing it. Out of the range protruded a charred stump of wood. He was just about to move on when he noticed on the floor some broken lengths of mahogany and a chopper beside them. Surely he couldn't have been burning the furniture?

The kitchen garden, outside, was overgrown with nettles and ragwort. It wasn't just neglected; it was spoiled with small heaps of cans and bottles among the weeds. My God, what a way to live. Like a tinker!

But tinkers would not have been so deliberate. The man seemed to have delighted in ruining the homeliness of the place. He seemed to have had a talent for destruction. (That was a good phrase; he might use it, if he had to report to the Bishop – and he might well have to report the damage, for the sake of Father O'Leary, Conroy's successor.) But why, the Bishop would want to know, why should he fell trees, rip up furniture, scatter rubbish? What was the meaning of this – yes, another good phrase that the Bishop would appreciate – this scorched-earth policy?

He went down the hall, past the hall stand, crowded with coats and hats, and into a room with bookcases and a large dining table littered with papers. Several pipes lay about, with the ash spilling out of them.

He found the stipend book on the table and put it aside. He also found baptismal certificates, school forms, letters asking for marriage clearances, a thank-you letter for a job recommendation. Well, he would have to start tidying them up – that was his job. A pity O'Leary hadn't been stuck with it! By rights, he should have been expected to take the rough with the smooth.

He got a shopping bag from the kitchen, the kind of brown leatherette bag that countrywomen used. It would be embarrassing to be seen carrying it through the streets of Castlemore, but there seemed to be nothing else in which he could take the stuff home with him.

He began to tidy the papers, sorting them into bundles to make them easier to deal with later. Among them was an old letter, cracked along the folds. Intrigued by the address – Casa del Cura, Santa Orosia – he took it up. It was dated the first of February, 1920, the year Conroy and he had been ordained, and it began, "Dear Frank." Frank! Conroy's name was Tom. And then he remembered that Frank was Conroy's brother, the farmer in Rosnagree.

St. Brigid's Day has come – and I haven't written to thank you for your letter at Christmas. Or was it Tom's? I forget; I'm confused, and time passes so fast, it seems only yesterday since you were both little lads in Rosnagree, the last time I was home. Anyway, you're the one who's to be ordained, so that keeps me right.

Frank, I had been hoping to let you know that I would be planning the journey home to be with your mother and brothers and sister for the big day, perhaps even been on my way already, like Blind Raftery in the poem. Do the old people still quote Raftery? I hear the Gaelic is going out, but how can they manage without Raftery on St. Brigid's Day? "Anois teacht an Earraigh…" Sure, that poem of his would make the cripple rise up out of his bed and walk!

Anyway, Frank, it's a bitter blow to me, but this year I shall not be going home. God has his reasons, no doubt, but now after another twenty-one years this side of the Andes, you'd think I'd be given some hope of seeing my own people and the old neighbors I knew, I ask myself why should I be let go home, what right have I to see them, why should they mean so much more to me now than ever?

I know the people here better than I've ever known my own. I've ridden my parish from end to end. I know every tree and hill, every track of the oxcarts, the twists and turns of every cañada. Why, then, should my own mean so much to me now, and these people nothing? That's just one of the questions which keep my night's sleep from me. So little light is given to us. Why are we told in the scriptures "If any man come to Me and hate not his father and mother and wife and children and brothers and sisters, yea and his own life also, he cannot be My disciple"? I know the scholars would explain what He really meant, but all the same, isn't that a terrible way for the God of Love, "Rí na nGrásta," to be speaking?

Don't mind all this. It's an old man rambling, and he after living too much on his own. The doctor tells me I must give up the reading and the pondering over problems that will never get anyone anywhere. He doesn't tell me what else I'm to do with myself. I'd be better if I could eat, but I suffer badly from wind on the stomach (they've come against me now, all those Sundays I spent riding from one pueblo to the next without breaking my fast). I'm not complaining – it's God's holy will – but when I eat one of those damn tortillas and think of a good feed of bacon and cabbage in the big kitchen, at home in beloved Rosnagree... Frank, I could take it all and more, if I wasn't tormented by so many things that Christ left...

The end of the paragraph was heavily crossed out. The next paragraph began:

I'm enclosing something to help you over these last couple of terms and to lighten the expenses of your mother. I'm sorry it's not more. I haven't helped you as I should have, all these years in college. Say a prayer for me on that day, and may God direct you and bring you safely to His altar. May He grant also that you'll be a better priest and a better man than your idle and complaining old uncle. Give my love to the family and especially to Tom, that little schemer with all the talk.

Yours in Jesus Christ,
JOSEPH CONROY

Father Mahon refolded the letter grimly, What an unsuitable letter to write to a senior student in sight of ordination! Things must have been pretty lax in those days. If it happened now, he would see to it that the letter was stopped and sent back to whoever it came from, or better still, burned straightaway. The man's wits were wandering, judging by the way he had mistaken Frank for Tom. Frank had, of course, been at the seminary for a time, but he had left the year before Tom came. That must have been at least six years before the letter was written.

But why had it been kept? Why should Father Conroy have been reading it lately? It was a question he would have liked to mention to the Bishop, but he knew he would be told it had no connection with the matter in hand.

He had a quick look through the drawers of the desk. There

was no sign of a bank book. He looked through the bookcase – nothing very exciting, Dickens, Shakespeare, some old college textbooks. O'Leary might keep some of them, and the rest, O'Leary's housekeeper might be persuaded to pack into bundles for the auction rooms.

He noticed a little door in the wall above the fireplace. It was wedged with a piece of cardboard, and when he tugged, it opened easily. Inside, a cupboard reached deeply into the wall – one of those cubbyholes in old houses for storing odds and ends. He struck a match and saw the light glint on glass far within. His hand hesitated a moment, stayed by some premonition. Was drink Conroy's vice? Hardly likely. Firmly, then, he reached in and drew out, not a bottle, but a two-pound jam jar. It was dark in color, filled seemingly with a dirty wad of papers. He was about to shove it back when the rounded shape of the wad caught his attention. He tugged at it, but it was wedged so tightly in that he couldn't get it out. Impatiently he twisted it this way and that, and when it finally came with him, he found that it was made up of one-pound notes. There must have been several hundred of them, mildewed, grimy with dust and soot. He put them down on the desk and watched them jack themselves out of their roll and sprawl over the edge of the desk onto the floor. Even when they ceased to move, he stood staring down at them, rubbing his hands against the legs of his trousers.

Then he turned to the cupboard and peered in. When he lit another match, the light glinted again on glass. He raised the match, reaching it in, and stared with horror on three, four, five more jars, each filled with the same kind of dirty, tight-packed wad. His movements had stirred up the dust, which caught at the back of his throat. He wanted to cough, to spit out whatever was catching at him, but his tongue seemed to swell and fill the space of his mouth. He realized he was going to be sick and began to run, out through the hall and the kitchen, reaching the yard just in time, with breath gone and mouth agape. Crouching forward, holding himself out from the wall, he vomited, When it was over, he leaned in against the wall, pressing his head to it so that the rough pebble-dash bruised his temple. The silence gradually bore itself in on him, and he opened his eyes, wiped his mouth with the back of his hand, then searched hurriedly for his handkerchief.

The back door stood open behind him. He turned to stare at it, afraid to go back in, But what if someone came and found the money there, coiled on the floor? My God, what a scandal there would be! No one must know. O'Leary must not know. No one else, not even the Bishop, must ever know.

He forced himself to go back through the kitchen and into the study to face that black hole in the wall. Could he slam the cupboard door, nail it shut? No. O'Leary was coming, would settle down unsuspectingly to live here. It would be wrong to leave the money in the house; it would be like leaving a curse. Quickly he pushed the papers down into the brown shopping bag and stuffed in the money on top of them. He took the other jars out of the cupboard, one by one, and emptied them into the bag, not touching the bundles of notes but levering them out with a paper knife he found on the desk. Then he folded down the top of the bag. He was just securing it with a piece of string when there came a knock at the hall door.

Fumbling in his haste, he knotted the string, then took the bag with him when he went to the door. An elderly woman in a black straw hat stood on the step. From beyond her, Father O'Leary advanced with his hand outstretched. "Well, here I am," he said, "and this is Mrs. Delany, my next-door-neighbor-to-be and my chapel woman."

Mrs. Delaney nodded her head, not smiling, and said, "Evening, Father."

"Mrs. Delany saw you getting off the bus, and she's convinced you're the new P.P. That's why she's so suspicious of me."

Mrs. Delany smiled slightly and glanced from one to the other. She had the compressed look of one who is seldom spoken to. "Oh, no indeed, Father," she said, and added with a titter, "Indeed and I'm not now," But her neck had flushed.

"Well, what are you up to, Father? I'm told you're here to make a clean sweep. I hope you've left me a bed for the night."

"I haven't gone upstairs at all," Father Mahon said. He became conscious of Father O'Leary's eyes on the bag in his hand and drew it back a little. "Come on in."

He led the way toward the kitchen, but Father O'Leary paused at the study door and peered in, "Jam jars! Good God, what next? I hope you're clearing them all out?" And his eyes moved again toward the bag in Father Mahon's hand.

"Oh, yes, Father... that is... The Bishop said if there's anything you'd care to have..."

"No fear! The sooner you have it all shifted out of here, the better. You can auction it or give it away or send it to a jumble sale, whichever you like. My own furniture is coming in at the end of the week and I don't want it to catch the worm."

"It's not giving me much time."

"No, I suppose not." He moved jauntily through the hall, whistling. "Yes, the worm is here. No doubt about it, They say that if you took the roof off this house, his furniture would levitate. Of course, they'd say anything in this diocese!"

He pointed to the grandfather clock. "Oh, there's that famous clock that he bought at Lord Dunboy's auction for fifteen bob. It never worked. His glugger, he called it."

Father Mahon looked askance.

"The glugger is the dummy egg that keeps the hatching hen on the job. Well, now, how about showing me over the rest of the establishment?"

They stopped at the foot of the stairs, each giving way politely.

"After you, Peter," said Father O'Leary. "It's your house at the moment, officially."

Father Mahon went up first, still holding the bag. He strode boldly enough into the bedroom. It was the other man who came slowly in, for the first time hesitant.

There was no carpet on the floor. A washstand stood against the wall, on it a plain white jug and ewer. There was a black crucifix over the bed. The blankets had been folded neatly beside the pillow. There was no sign of his clothes in the room. Everything seemed to have been tidied away for good.

They both stared at the bed, both considering whether Conroy had known that he would not be returning from O'Hara's dinner that day. Father Mahon broke the silence at last, "You'll sleep here tonight, so, Father?" and there was a noticeable pause before Father O'Leary replied, "Ay, I suppose so."

On the way downstairs, Father Mahon saw the woman heading toward the sitting room with a tea tray. Immediately, he stopped in the hall and hoisted the bag under his arm. "Well," he said, "I'd better be going."

"What's your hurry?"

He muttered something about the bus back to Castlemore.

"Don't worry about that! I'll drive you home. Come on in."

He wasn't forceful enough to get away. Father O'Leary pushed him triumphantly hack into the sitting room. "Sit down, can't you? You're nervous as a cat."

He tried to smile as he sank into one of the armchairs. He didn't know what to do with the bag. At last he pulled it into his lap and saw Father O'Leary's eyes following it.

"What's in the bag?"

"The bag?" He looked down at it. "Just some papers I thought I'd take."

"Papers, huh?" He waited till the woman cleared a space on the table and set the tray down. When she began to pour out, he abruptly waved her away, and she hurried off in relief. "Letters?"

Father Mahon nodded his head and clasped the bag closer.

Father O'Leary seemed to accept the reply. He sighed as he lifted the teapot. When he handed the first cup to Father Mahon, he said in a very subdued voice, "I suppose, Peter, there isn't a spare bed?"

"Why?"

"Well, I mean, if you'd like to stay..."

"Oh, no, thanks, I have to get back. The Dean is, I mean... anyway, there's seven-o'clock Mass in the morning for the nuns."

Father O'Leary took up his own cup and saucer and looked at it moodily.

"It'll be a fine house," Father Mahon tried helpfully, "when you've had a chance to get at it."

"Ay," Father O'Leary said listlessly. "Seems a bit damp, though."

"Oh, well, any house would need a good airing…" Father Mahon began, then decided it was better to let the sentence trail away.

In the silence, they could hear the woman moving in the room upstairs, probably changing the sheets. Father O'Leary cleared his throat suddenly. "One of the big farmers, I believe, has bought the grave space next to his."

Father Mahon looked up, bewildered.

"Conroy's!" Father O'Leary said impatiently. "The man's father is to be buried in it tomorrow. They paid a lot of money for it."

"Oh, I see," said Father Mahon, realizing the meaning of the grave digger's remarks. "But isn't that common enough in the country?"

"Isn't what common enough?" Father O'Leary's choler had not altogether been cured by promotion.

"Being buried next to a parish priest. It's a peculiar form of class distinction, I believe."

Father O'Leary considered the suggestion morosely. "I don't know. No one around here would pay a bob extra unless they felt that Conroy had some… some remarkable qualities…"

"Conroy?"

"That's what I'm saying!" He glared now. "How'd you like that? How'd you like to spend the night in the bed of a bloody saint?"

"Good God!" Father Mahon half-rose from his seat and slopped the tea over his knees. The bag slipped to the floor. He bent quickly to retrieve it and found that it too had been soaked. "I'm sorry," he murmured, "I seem to have messed things up."

Father O'Leary rose impatiently and went to the door. "Bring in a cloth, ma'am, will you?" he called. "We've spilled our tea."

He stood by, waiting sullenly while Father Mahon wiped himself down, watched by the anxiously sympathetic woman. "You're all right," he burst out at last. "You'll do!" But Father Mahon over-scrupulously kept on wiping, until at last Father O'Leary seized the cloth, gave a couple of perfunctory wipes, and handed it back to the woman.

"Now," said he as she left the room, "what d'you think of that? D'you think it's true?"

Father Mahon looked up, trapped, and then, as by a miracle, was saved by the blare of a horn down in the village. "The bus," he said, starting forward.

"Oh, to hell with the bus. I'll run you home."

"Not at all." Father Mahon had a head start toward the door. "There's no need."

"I'll run you..." Father O'Leary called, in something like desperation, but Father Mahon was safely in the hall and heading for the front door. "Good luck, Father," he called as he got the door open. "I'll be in touch."

Looking back, as the bus pulled away, he saw that one of the upstairs windows was lit up and the blind drawn. The bedroom, was it? Conroy's room! The blank, yellow space seemed to be waiting for some shape to fill it. Yes, it had that waiting look, and as he watched it grow small and dim, he thought, I didn't know him, thank God. I knew nothing about him and never will. My job now is to dispose of this money. As soon as I have that done, I can forget all about him. He's got no claim on me.

The money was disposed of, and Conroy proved quite easy to

forget. Father Mahon was helped by the routine of seminary life, by his daily chores – seven-o'clock Mass for the nuns, his lectures which he knew by heart, his walk around the track, and his evening games of patience. Once, however, in the refectory, he heard a reading from the life of Saint Theresa of Ávila; it was the saint's description of how she dreamed of hell in the shape of a muddy path leading to a cupboard in a wall. For a moment Conroy seemed somewhere there, just a brief, indistinct glimpse of him, with head lowered, as if he were searching for something.

Apart from that unpleasant moment, Father Mahon was not bothered by Conroy again.

Chapter 1

On one of the ember days of Lent in the year of his death, Father Conroy had a strange encounter – at least, looking back on it in the light of the weeks that followed, it seemed to gather a strange significance. He was walking at evening among his beasts. It was cold. He wore a bulky black Aran sweater that rolled up under his chin and a pair of old corduroy trousers tucked into his Wellington boots. A short pipe was stuck in his mouth; it was hardly ever lit, for it was always in need of either tobacco or the light of a match – not because he begrudged the cost of tobacco or matches (as some people said), but because he found in the lack of them an excuse for stopping people he wanted to talk with or indeed any people going the road. In his job, it was important to keep tabs on everyone.

This evening, the pipe was empty. He turned from inspecting his bullocks and blew gently through it as he looked at the pony, which a horse-loving old spinster had bequeathed recently to the parish building fund (in fact, he was all that was left when her estate had been sold and all the debts paid off). Father Conroy looked at him now regretfully. He was a fine animal – as the radio commercials put it, slim, trim, and brimful of energy – and Father Conroy had had to put him up as a prize in the draw for the Baptistry Fund.

It was bad enough not being able to keep him. What was most galling was the fact that he had been won by an Englishman called Drewitt, a new arrival, who had bought up some good, much-coveted land, who knew nothing at all about horseflesh and, by all accounts, had jibbed at paying half a crown for a ticket.

There were several possibilities to be considered: Drewitt might be persuaded to relinquish him as an ecumenical gesture; the draw could be declared invalid – it would be easy to do that on a technicality, since a wad of sold tickets had been found next day under a furze bush near the schoolhouse – but such an admission would have a bad effect on the proceeds of future parish draws; as a last resort, the animal could be stolen some night – Troys, the tinkers, would soon be passing through, buying for Donore fair, and they would hardly refuse him, if he was, so to speak, put in their way. But that would hardly be honest.

No, he thought, this won't be easy, but I'm damned if Drewitt is going to have him without a fight.

As he turned back toward the house, he heard a tentative human cough from the direction of the road. It was getting dark and he could barely make out a white face looking in at him between the dark clumps of the furze bushes. Quickly he strode nearer, but he could not recognize who he was. "Good evening," he called inquiringly.

The man ignored the greeting and simply called, "Am I on the road to Donore?" He had a strange voice, lifted to carry far; his vowels were cockney, slackened into Dublin.

Father Conroy was so intrigued that he made for the ditch and scrambled agilely out onto the road. He found himself looking down on a small figure in a shabby, overlong gaberdine, holding a little fiber case under his arm. A tramp, he thought, and then, no, maybe not; there's some authority here, a dull metal that's not easily bent.

"The road to Donore!" the man said. His tone, close up, was not unfriendly, just cold.

"D'ye know anyone there?" asked Father Conroy. The man shook his head. "Come on so, and I'll see you as far as the cross below."

They walked down the road in silence. And salute no man by the way, thought Father Conroy, around whom phrases gathered continually, like gnats. Now, where did that one come out of? Frowning, he looked down on the little man who had engendered it.

The fellow was looking at the house. "That yours, then?"

It was a big house; it looked impressive now in the half-light, when one could not see the paintwork, the drooping gutters. On an impulse Father Conroy said, "Ah, no, I'm only the boy there."

The man looked at him curiously. "D'you work there, you mean?"

"Ay, I keep the place in order, trim the our hedges and all to that. 'Tis hard to keep up with all they want done." He hesitated, then lowered his voice, "The boss is a bloody divil."

The man nodded in sympathy. "'e's got money, I can see that."

"Don't be talking!" said Father Conroy, and stretched his hands out to encompass the wealth of the world. "Will ye come in? Come on in to the kitchen and I'll get ye a cup of tea."

The man shook his head. "I got business to do."

Father Conroy looked at him. He wasn't a traveler, that was one sure thing, unless he was in a very small way, pushing holy pictures, perhaps, or out-of-date Latin missals. Only for his accent and the little case under his arm, he might have been a tinker, buying for the fair. But a tinker would have been bolder.

"The business of one greater than I," the man said, and suddenly, ingratiatingly, smiled.

Father Conroy began to rub his jaw slowly. He had seen that smile before, more uncertain than a salesman's, an evangelizing smile. Lord, this had gone far enough. It would be just his luck to be caught in such a situation by Phil O'Hara, or Bat Cullen, or worse, someone like Peter Mahon, dropping in on him out of the blue. He could imagine the remarks the diocese would pass – Tom Conroy, Secret Agent – Kilbride, a nest of Jehovah's Witnesses – sure, we might have known!

And yet, it was the kind of situation he could not bear to walk out of. Damn it, wouldn't it make a good story? Conroy's conversion! But no, that wouldn't be fair – the poor devil was cold, he looked as if he could do with a good bite to eat. Ask him in, then, why not? Tell him who I am and send him on his way – that would be the decent thing to do.

But the man held back, shaking his head. There was an obstinate, leaden streak in him.

"What's the matter?" asked Father Conroy.

The man glanced toward the house, as if he were afraid of being watched. He slid his hand into his case and fumbled out a small pamphlet. "I have something here I'd like to ask you to…" But he held the pamphlet limply, as if he did not really expect Father Conroy to take it from him.

Father Conroy looked up and down the road to make sure there was no one coming. He didn't want any unauthorized versions of the scene circulating in the parish. "Well, come on, man, show us it," he said, and almost reluctantly the man handed it over.

It was them, all right – on the cover, the dark tower outlined against a sunburst. Father Conroy thumbed through it, his impatience growing as he read, "… today, after nineteen centuries of selecting, there is yet a small remnant of the 144,000 on earth… The call for the heavenly inheritance is now closing, but the Bible makes plain that Jehovah is now separating to his side of favor a great crowd of sheeplike ones…" Oh, Lord, he thought, suddenly weary of the encounter, I'm not in form for this sort of thing.

The man was watching him. "As you see" – he gave an apologetic little gesture – "it's the good news I bring you."

Father Conroy looked at him as he stood there, smiling his broken smile. There wasn't a single door in the parish that would not be shut in his face. He would be lucky if nothing worse happened to him. In some parish up the country, they had assaulted a Witness, broken a couple of ribs, bashed in his teeth, then had him charged in the district court with causing a breach of the peace.

"Look, do you want a bite to eat, or don't you?" he asked, impatient to get the man off the road, out of view.

"I haven't time. I must get the bus to Donore and then go back to Castlemore later tonight."

"Well, I haven't time either," Father Conroy said, and handed back the pamphlet.

The man made no attempt to take it back. He looked along the road on which the bus would come. "You've never thought, then," he hesitated, "about the future."

"What future?"

"Your future, your children's…"

"I've no children. Here, take this, will you? I don't want it." But the man still did not seem to have heard him. "The time may be very short, for the last days are at hand." A Bible had appeared suddenly, as if out of the air, and he was shifting the dog-eared pages, hurrying through the small print. "And there shall be signs in the sun and in the moon and in the stars…"

"I know. Luke. Men withering away for fear."

"Yes." The man stared. He shut the book and began to push it back into his case. His eagerness to get away made Father Conroy want to play him a little longer.

"Hold on! Aren't you going to try me?"

The man looked around, as if afraid of a crowd emerging from the darkening hedgerows and tiptoeing in to surround him.

"Oh, come on, you can't announce that news to me and then leave me here. What are we waiting for?"

The man looked down at the book in his hand; he could hardly have read it now, it was growing so dark. For a moment, rain flaked the roadway, very lightly, then the cloud thinned out. A star showed briefly in the evening sky. It was bitter cold.

The man stirred and looked suddenly into Father Conroy's face. Poor divil, thought Father Conroy, let him alone! He's only doing this for a job. But I don't know what to say; I don't know how to stop this now.

The man opened the book and again began to push through the pages, back and forth, like a dog which had lost the scent. Mother of God, thought Father Conroy, he doesn't even know what he's looking for. No wonder he's doing this for a job.

But the man had a text at last. He held it with one close-bitten nail, while he laboriously spelled out, "If anyone wants to come after me, let him disown himself and pick up his torture stake and follow me continually."

"Take up his cross and follow me."

"No." He inspected the verse carefully and shook his head.

"His torture stake."

"An inferior version," said Father Conroy. He saw the man look at him and then look at the book in alarm. "Well, I must go," he said, and began to turn away.

"I'm sorry." The man smiled again. "You owe me fourpence."

"Fourpence?" And then he looked down at the pamphlet.

"I don't want it," he said and thrust it into the man's hand. "To tell you the truth, I wouldn't read it anyway."

He turned his back on that painful smile and hurried to his gate. There he paused, feeling his back exposed, but the man was walking away, his figure moving into the darkness between the hedges with a lame, slovenly gait, which yet impelled him steadily forward.

He never saw the man again, nor heard how things had gone with him in Donore; in fact, no one there remembered having met him. Perhaps he had walked right through the town and out the far side – that would not have been difficult.

Only later, when he woke one night in pain, was he bothered by the phrase, "And salute no man by the way." He lay for a while trying to place it, and at last remembered the man who had passed him on the road in the evening. Or had the man passed him? Could he have been a figure in one of those strange dreams that had begun to plague him? Father Conroy was never sure, but the doubt was enough to cause him another restless night.

Later still, after returning from his desperate visit to England, when he knew and had accepted that he was going to die, he thought again of the man. By that time he could laugh at his fate, and he laughed now at his encounter with the harbinger of his pain. "Who but a cursed Conroy," he asked himself, "would have a Jehovah's Witness for a banshee?"

Chapter 2

It was the watershed in Father Conroy's life. Looking back, the vista seemed wide and flat as a bogland, sunny for the most part, with shadows moving over it here and there – like the trouble about Drewitt's pony. The country ahead declined steeply into mists and darkness; it was broken by chasms, which when the light glinted on them were rivers carrying reflections of the past; it was the country in which he was to spend the last weeks of his life. Between the two was the night the Witness passed, the night the pain began.

It began suddenly in his sleep. He had been dreaming of a horse which he was trying to harness in the stable of his father's place in Rosnagree. Slowly he circled it in the darkness of the stall, and slowly it withdrew from him, eluding him with a cautious violence which struck terror into him. He was conscious of breathing close at hand, of a hoof striking softly on the floor. At last, when he could wait no longer, he moved in to where its eye gleamed, and at once pain thudded sharply in his leg. He woke up trembling, to find the pain there just above the knee, still so sharp that he rolled over in agony on the bed. Holding the knee doubled up to him, he gradually became aware of his whereabouts and waited, not knowing what to do, just sweating it out.

Noctis equi, he thought, as if he were naming a disease, noctis equi! And he tried to place the quotation, as if by doing so he could assuage the pain. Who, in God's name, could have been troubled by the horses of night? Not Horace. Vergil, perhaps? But where, which book? Even when the pain eased away, he lay racking his brain until the cocks of Kilbride began to crow and the window blind grew yellow against the light.

By the time he vested himself in his oratory for the morning Mass, the pain had gone altogether, leaving only a slight numbness, as if he had been lying with the leg doubled under him all night. Was it only a dream, and if so, what was the meaning of it? And where had noctis equi come from? Damn it, he thought, as he began another search through the ruins of a classical education, that's going to bother hell out of me now. He had long since given up hope of success when he set out on his searches; most of them had to be given up in facetiousness, as now, when he shrugged his shoulders and said, "It's the celibate's nightmare," at which he began to chuckle, "Must tell that to Phil O'Hara."

The back door slammed and the heavy footsteps of young Gabriel, his Mass server, sounded in the hall, hurrying as usual, for Father Conroy was very strict about starting on time. (There were only two points of his day pinned down – the Mass at 7:30 A.M. and the reading of his Office at 11 P.M. The time between flapped fitfully in each day's passing.) The boy came into the oratory with a smell of new milk. He ducked on one knee, then wriggled himself onto the prie-dieu, his steel-tipped boots scraping at the floor. He shone all over, cheeks moistly red, hair brilliantined and brushed flat by his mother, who was ever conscious of his privilege in serving the parish priest's Mass.

Vested and ready to begin, Father Conroy paused to take a squint through the slit of window. "How's that pony?" he grunted.

"I dunno, Father."

"Didn't you take a look at him?"

"No, Father."

"And you passing right by?"

"I never thought to, Father." There was no apology there, nor pertness either. It was a reply shot back like a catechism answer.

"You didn't!" Father Conroy knew as he said it that the sarcasm was wasted, and he launched at once into, "I will go to the altar of God."

"The God of my gladness and joy," rang out the boy's brazen catechism tone.

Between them, they set about the Mass, ping-ponging the responses back and forth in the little oratory, like two cool, sure-handed professionals. As they straightened up from saying the Confiteor, Father Conroy's glance strayed again toward the window.

"Oh, God, renew Thy life in us."

"And Thy people will rejoice in Thee."

Strange I can't see the pony from here, he was thinking; maybe he's lying in the shelter of the hedge. Suppose he's dead, or, better still, stolen – wouldn't that be a way out? Or would it? Drewitt might demand the price of him. That would be awkward, especially with a Protestant involved – just the sort of thing that might reach the Bishop's ears. But supposing…

There was a silence in the oratory.

"Go on," he said impatiently.

The boy looked up in surprise. "It's your turn, Father."

"Lord hear my prayer," muttered Father Conroy.

"And let my cry come to Thee," Gabriel shot back.

Say the Mass properly, anyway, Father Conroy told himself as he went up the step to the altar. Don't be giving scandal to the young fellow – God knows he's only waiting for the chance to be scandalized.

Or was he? Turning around to say "The Lord be with you," and to wait for Gabriel's, "And also with you," Father Conroy looked down suspiciously at the eyelids lowered over the missal, at all that shining innocence exposed to view. Please God, he thought, let Gabriel's piety (if it is piety) be set against my carelessness, and so, accept this Mass from us.

From then on, the mechanics of the ceremony came easily, the offering of the bread and wine, the washing of the hands. He went through the motions simply, as something necessary like shaving, whose doing he had never questioned. Only once did his attention wander, when, genuflecting suddenly, he found his left knee was gone stiff. "That cursed pony," he muttered, and though the pain was no longer there, felt it was waiting inside him, ready to strike again.

After Mass, when the boy had gone clattering out of the house, he went down to the kitchen and looked in the shopping bag to see if he had anything for breakfast. There was only a loaf, a bit hard, which he had bought at the shop because nobody had been in with homemade bread. He set it on the table and took a half-pound of butter, still in its wrapper, from the cupboard of the dresser. There were no eggs either; it was time for him to do some foraging. Gabriel had brought the milk; he poured it into a jug and took a good, long, thirsty drink of it. He lit the primus, and when it was well pumped, set on it the kettle for tea. As he waited for the water to boil, he prowled around the kitchen. It was the time when the day usually shaped itself, the calls, the interviews, the visits, but now his mind waited in case the pain should strike again.

He switched on the radio. "The soft, creamy lather of Marley soap," came a Dublin voice, deepened in slightly adenoidal sexiness. "Cuddle yourself in a cocoon of it, so smooth, so soft, so little extra cost…"

He threw himself on the radio, killing the voice. And as he did so, the memory of his dream flashed into his mind, so that he stood for a moment appalled by the pent-up violence that had faced him in the stable. What did it mean? What could have prompted it? And then he relaxed, thinking that it must have been the pony. Yes, that was it, the damn pony.

There was just time, before the kettle boiled, to see whether it was standing or lying down or whether the curse-of-God thing was still there in the field. He hurried out, pulling the back door shut behind him.

It was a relief to be in the open air. Just up the road from his gate, a gang of roadworkers was about to start the day's work. They had been drawing chippings there the last few days with horses and carts, and now the tar-spreader had arrived. While the fire was being stoked up under the machine, the men squatted beside their bicycles and smoked. One of them was feeding sugar to the pony, which had its head through a gap in the hedge.

Ned Foley, council worker, grave digger, and Father Conroy's right-hand man, had made a small fire by the roadside and was gathering the blackened billy cans together to make the morning tea. As Father Conroy approached, he looked up and drew the priest toward him with a secretive, in-curving gesture. It was the same gesture which accompanied always his phrases in Gaelic, "Cogar i leith chugham"; in English it had no equivalent, not even, "Come in here, close, till I tell you." Yet all he had to say, when the priest stooped conspiratorially over him, was, "He's a right pet, Father."

"He is, Ned. Easy known an old woman had the minding of him."

"'Tis a damn shame, Father, to have him going where he's going. And all the breeding he do have."

Father Conroy nodded, his eyes on the men, who were touching their caps to him. Ned glanced at them too and said aloud, "Sit down, Father, and take your ease. I'm just wetting a sup of tea for the men."

Father Conroy needed no urging. He hunkered down in the shelter of the hedge as Ned selected the cleanest of the billy cans and wiped its lip with his sleeve.

"He'll have to go there, Ned, all the same. That's all there is to it."

"Oh, that's all," Ned hastened to say. "Fair's fair. Still…" And he began to spoon the tea thoughtfully into the billy can.

"'Tis a damn shame," agreed Father Conroy, "when the fellow wouldn't know a good pony from a tinker's nag that you'd pick up at the tail end of a fair for a fiver."

Ned's eyes met his for a moment. "Wouldn't he, Father?"

"Of course he wouldn't," Father Conroy said impatiently, "but the question is…" He stopped at that secretive gesture from Ned. The other men were drawing near, one by one. "Mornin', Father," they said, as they squatted down and reached for their billy cans. From their lunch bags they produced small bottles of milk with which they colored the tea. Then they held up the cans between their cold hands, pursing their lips over the steam. The pale sun shone on the smoke of the boiling tar, so that they seemed enclosed in a transparent blue tent.

Father Conroy knew them all and sat back to amuse them. "A fine morning in early spring, sitting by the roadside, drinking tea in the council's time. No wonder the country's broke."

"Whose time are you drinking in, Father?" asked a young fellow. He winked at the others, as if asking them to back him up, now that he had taken on the challenge.

"God's own time, but He knows what I'm at. Which is more than your ganger knows about ye."

"Ah, sure, we've a long, hard day ahead of us," laughed the young man.

"Ye have," said Father Conroy, and he took a long, caustic blow at his tea.

"We can't start, anyway, till the ganger gets back. He's gone up the road to get orders from the engineer."

"I'd need no orders, then. Sure, I'd have that stretch of road tarred and graveled before I'd sit down to my breakfast."

"You would not, Father," they declared, nudging each other.

"Wouldn't I, then?" He leaped to his feet, as they half-hoped he would, and picked up a shovel. He spat on his hands and held it out before him, like a hurler waiting for the ball. "Spill out the tar there, some of ye, and I'll show ye how to work."

"Sit down, Father," said Ned, who had been sipping away, unsmiling, "Here's the ganger back now."

Father Conroy put down the shovel, as the ganger's dusty old Anglia drew up. "Only me leg's a bit stiff, I'd show ye all up. Where's me tea?"

The ganger got out carefully, looking askance at Father Conroy, sitting with a billy can under the hedge. Father Conroy ignored him. So too did Ned, who fumbled out a pipe as the others rose hurriedly to begin work.

"We'll be having a long rest soon enough, Father," said Ned placidly, lighting the pipe, "when the council gives out the contract for the roads."

"The contract?" said Father Conroy. Then, to cover up (for he never admitted ignorance), he said, "Who d'ye think is behind it?" Whatever the business was, it was bound to look dirty – and to have someone behind it.

Ned's pipe was working easily; only the volume of smoke showed that he was hard-pressed.

"Ah, sure, you should know yourself, Father. I wouldn't like to be telling you."

"The uncle, is it?"

Ned inclined his head in a gesture which only the most practiced eye would have taken as a nod. As if he hadn't answered the question, he continued, "They do say there's a big company from Castlemore got it; they're to open up the old quarries and bring in the machines. Sure, two men will mend a mile of road."

'I'll speak to him."

"Ye might as well, Father." Much good will it do, the tone implied. As if outraged by his resignation, Ned's pipe began to billow out smoke, and coughing, clutching at his chest, Ned burst out, "He might as well have us all shipped off to England, while he's at it. But we won't take it from him, Father, I tell you that straight."

"I said I'm going to speak to him," Father Conroy said, and his tone implied that the attack on his uncle James had gone far enough.

"Ay, Father," Ned said, the smoke quite gone now. He sighed as he changed the subject, "And what about this pony?"

"Never mind about that. I'll fix it, too. Anyway," he burst out ambiguously, "aren't ye entitled to it – what's the council for, only to get roads done and to pay for doing them?" He looked up as the ganger passed, and meeting the man's suspicious stare, he began to rise to his feet. "Well, I can see I'm in the way here."

"Do your best, Father, to get that pony into good hands!"

"Leave it to me. Leave it all to me."

But he wasn't so sure of himself, when he walked in the gate of the drive and stopped at sight of his house. There were too many things all at once. Where was he to start? He looked at the house. He could never go in when he was restless – it maddened him to be cooped up. Sometimes he would set off on a walk through the parish, so fast that it took a succession of items of interest, a new hay machine, a pheasant darting from the stubble, a prime bullock posing in a field, to slow his train of thoughts. Then he would stop, go into some house at random, and slouch down in a chimney corner with a cup of strong tea. Occasionally he kept going so fast that he overshot the parish boundary, and before he knew where he was, he was knocking on the door of Father O'Hara's or Father Cullen's house to give them the job of driving him home. Once he had ended up with his sister, Kate, up in Coolnahorna; he had to walk home again, all ten miles of mountain road, when Mikie's car wouldn't start.

His leg spanceled him now. He sat in his car, parked before the inhospitable face of his house. Where in hell could he go? There were a few visits to be made, old people in bed or living on their own. God, he wasn't in form for any of them; all the same, he might as well get the job over and done with, but which of them? Whose turn? Hennessy's, was it? And then he groaned, "Oh, no," thinking of the cottage window at which old Hennessy's face would be watching. Most of the day Hennessy watched for him – there was nothing much else to watch for in the Bohernascorna Gap. At sight of his car, the old jaws would start working, the rosary beads would be pulled out, and as Father Conroy went up the path between the wet fuchsia bushes, he would hear the long-drawn-out moans of "Hail Mary – Holy Mary!" echoing in the kitchen. What irritated Father Conroy most of all was that when Hennessy came down every week to collect his pension money in Kilbride, he could entertain the regulars in the pub for hours on a couple of pints of stout. Only with the priest did he talk in pious exclamations and roll his eyes up to the interceding saints. After suffering for years his conversations with Hennessy, Father Conroy had got his own back at last by naming him "Watch and Pray."

Still, old Hennessy wasn't the worst; in a way, Father Conroy enjoyed their exchange of pious nothings, each trying to outdo the other in the art of humbuggery. An hour or so with Watch and Pray would kill the morning nicely. Yet, as he leaned forward to switch on the engine, a tenable lassitude descended on him. Am I not well? he wondered, looking at his fingers on the ignition key, unable to turn it. He disliked illness, so much so that he had to force himself to enter a sickroom, which he did practically every day of his life. An expert in fixing things – a dispute over a boundary fence, a dowry, a job on the council – here was something he could never fix. He got his revenge by never admitting illness in himself. He regarded minor pains as a bluff his body was trying on him, and he showed it that he wasn't having any. He never had recourse to a doctor in his life. No thanks, he would say, I'd sooner call in a plumber to mend the hall clock (he had a thing about plumbers too; there was one in the parish who never paid his dues). Anyway, illness never bothered the Conroys; they never lingered and became a nuisance, but were struck down in the heat of the day, leaving no doctors' bills. His father died suddenly at the age of fifty after a foolish show of strength at the fair of Donore. His brother Owen had burst himself on a building site in England at the age of twenty-nine. Father Conroy was sixty-three and had always known that the family monster would get him yet; he didn't mind, as long as he was given immunity from all the lesser, tiresome illnesses. Fair's fair, he always said, with a vision of the Conroys like so many Samsons pulling the Temple down on themselves, in their own time.

He turned the key and the engine spurted into life. Had it really come suddenly for his father and for Owen? Or had there been a secret pain, a seeping away of strength? He wanted to know now, urgently, but there was no one he could ask – no one except his mother and Frank, and he couldn't ask them. God, Conroy, he told himself, you're a shaky! You get an imaginary kick from an imaginary horse and you wake up thinking you're dying. Cop yourself on, man! Off you go and do your morning's work!

Slowly he began to let out the handbrake. And then he thought of Kate, with enormous relief, of his sister, Kate, so near, so solid, so changeless. Christ, I must go talk to Kate.

No, I'm not frightened, he thought, as he let in the clutch too vigorously; all that's wrong is that I just can't take another morning with Watch and Pray. The place is getting on my nerves. It's time I broke out, took the morning, the whole bloody day off. Come on, he told the car, as he dug at the accelerator, get the hell out, go foreign!

He sped through the gateway, wheeling expertly, with the usual belated glance to confirm that the road was clear. But even as the roadmen downed tools to wave to him, doubts were setting in. How long would he be away? Suppose there was a sick call? Blast it, he thought, my bloody scruples! There was nothing for it but to call on young Farrell and tell him to take over. No harm to check up on the fellow too; rumor was that he was a bit of a bradaí, like those young bullocks which broke out in search of pastures new.

Not that one could blame him for breaking out. Murtagh's Cross was a small settlement, clotted around a railway crossing at the far end of the parish, its focal points being the crossing-keeper's cottage and the chapel, where the curate said first Mass on Sundays. Father Conroy came to say second Mass, arriving from the metropolis of Kilbride at the same time as the curate left to say second Mass there, all this sabbath journeying being intended to keep them both in touch with the parish as a whole.

The curate's house was a neat, suburban bungalow set in a wilderness of gorse and heather. There was a big car parked at the gate. Father Conroy eyed it carefully as he drew in behind it. A Dublin registration! Whose could it be? Farrell had his hand in a number of underground movements; it could be the car of an agricultural adviser, an engineer starting a group water scheme, a salesman of theological quarterlies. Or could it be – Yes, it looked big enough to be that of a mendicant order. Was it the Fras on the prowl? Well, he would shift those boyos fast – they weren't going to milk Kilbride as long as the parish clergy were living from hand to mouth.

Farrell was practicing with a golf club on the lawn in front of the house, watched by a young man in chunky white sweater and suede shoes.

"Morning, Bobbie," said Father Conroy, when neither looked up.

"Tom!" commented Farrell as he swung hard with the spoon and followed the imaginary ball with his eyes. He always played it just a shade too cool for Father Conroy's liking.

"When you find that ball, you might introduce me," said Father Conroy.

"Sorry, Tom." He handed the club over to the young man. "Dickie, this is Tom Conroy, my P.P. Tom, Dickie Walsh. Dickie's home for a month."

Dickie had already taken up his stance. He paused on a downward swing, said "Hi," and continued with the swing practically unbroken.

Holy God, thought Father Conroy, what's Ireland coming to? He wasn't one for tugging forelocks, but there was a limit.

"Home from what, Mr. Walsh?" he asked with a sweet solicitude.

"I'm sorry, Tom," Farrell said hastily. "Father Walsh is home from Sacramento."

"Ah, Father Walsh!" and Father Conroy bowed his head graciously.

"Yes, we were together in Maynooth, Father." He seemed to feel the golf had made a bad impression. "Dickie has some good ideas about setting up a parish committee."

"The country's full of committees," Father Conroy said, "clubs and committees! Like scrub bulls."

"I beg your pardon, Father?" said Dickie.

"Scrub bulls. The country's full of them, producing nothing but bullshit."

There was a long silence.

"Fine car you've got," said Father Conroy, and decided to continue with the Father business, "Father."

Dickie stopped swinging and turned to look at his car, as if he hadn't noticed it before. "Think so? I jes' picked her up for the month at the airport. First thing they showed me." How long had he been away, Father Conroy wondered – two, three years? Already his face had tapered into a New World shape. "Guess she's a little too good for your roads, Father!"

"They're not my roads." Father Conroy smiled. "If they were, of course, I'd have had the red carpet laid out on them."

"Tom is guardian angel of the road gang," said Farrell. "They're like civil servants – engaged for life."

"Yes, like us," said Father Conroy.

The idea startled Farrell. "Of course, they'll all be sacked soon, once this contract goes through."

"Oh, yes, the contract!" Father Conroy said sharply. It annoyed him that the young fellow should have such good sources of information (his father was a bank manager in Castlemore and moved in the right circles). "That won't go through so easily, I'm telling you."

"Oh, now, Tom, we could do with a little more efficiency…"

"Who's we?" Father Conroy exploded. "Christ, man" – he saw the American blench, but rode headlong on – "who are the roads for? Who's going to be left in this place? A few big farmers and ourselves?"

Farrell hadn't intended to bait the lion so far. Flushed, he looked at his friend and murmured, "I think you're exaggerating, Tom. I'm sure the employment aspect was gone into. In fact, I believe there was a cost-benefit analysis that showed..."

But Father Conroy had turned his back and was heading toward the gate. He did not stop until he stood by the car, about to get in. Suffering Jesus, he asked himself, did you ever hear the like? What in God's name are they teaching them these days? And yet, under his indignation, he was uneasy; he had never lost his temper with Farrell before, though the brat had baited him further than this. He had a feeling that he had lost a round.

After a moment or two he turned, and with his head bent a little, almost contritely, he retraced his steps. Farrell was still flushed, but Father Conroy caught his friend extinguishing a smile. So they thought it was funny! Well, he'd show them.

"I'm going to be away for the day," he told Farrell. "Look after things, will you?"

The two exchanged a quick look. Consternation, was it? They had probably planned to sneak off for a game of golf in the afternoon, taking for granted he'd be there as usual, holding the fort. "You weren't going out, were you?"

Farrell shook his head.

"All right, then." Even the approval sounded schoolmasterish when he spoke to Farrell. He looked from one to the other of them, their young faces downcast. You're a brute, Conroy, he told himself; look what you've done, spoiled the day on them. He waited for the parting words which would restore good humor, give them, all three of them, a boost. But instead an idea came to mind, so promising of comedy that he couldn't resist it. Now, he told himself in one of his catch phrases, might I do it, Pat.

"D'ye know, Bobbie, there's a little job you could be doing for me."

"Yes, Tom?" said Farrell warily.

"There's an old fellow called Hennessy lives up there at the far side of the Bohernascorna Gap." He saw Farrell begin to shake his head, "No, you wouldn't know him, I'm sure. He's a character, a very pious old man, a real saint. I was going to call in to see him this morning so would you..."

"All right, I'll try and get 'round to him."

"And bring your friend too," Father Conroy went on generously. "It will be an experience for you, Dickie, to find such," he took a deep breath, "real, Old World, Catholic, Irish piety here in our midst."

"Yes, Father."

"Sure, 'twill give ye a boost anyway." And he turned to leave the field, in reasonably good order.

"What's his problem, Father?" asked Dickie.

Problem? Watch and Pray with a problem? He laughed. "Oh, he just likes an oul' chat." And when he saw they weren't satisfied with that, he added, "I don't think he has any problem that the rosary won't solve. You just tell him that."

Chapter 3

K ate and Mikie Donovan lived on a hill in the shadow of the mountains. In winter, the tallest of the peaks cut off the sun from them soon after noon; that peak, according to Kate, was only the first of their troubles. "Ah, now, Kate," Father Conroy had told her more than once, "Sure, you can't blame Mikie for putting that there!"

The boreen down to the house was long and aimless. It wandered around the edges of the fields, sometimes diverging where Jimmy, the son and heir, had suddenly thought of cutting a corner. Father Conroy never saw these double lanes without chortling, "Just like the Donovans! They can't even decide on their way home."

The house itself had its back to the visitor, reminding him of Mikie turning away to open his purse. Roofed with thatch at one end and corrugated iron at the other, it was a disconcerting house to be in when it rained; in the kitchen, the rain drummed overhead and all outside seemed awash; in the parlor, under the thatch, an ominous silence gave the impression of waters pent up, ready to roll down in a mighty flood.

The approach to the house was through the cow yard.

Knowing the usual condition it was in, Father Conroy left his car at the gate and walked, or rather, leaped, stiff-legged, from hummock to hummock. The yard was strewn with electric cable, some of it sunk under the mire. He passed a tumbledown shed in which was an enormous harvester, red and shiny, with hens perched on top of it. No doubt several harvests had been mort-gaged to buy it, so heavily that Jimmy probably could not afford the necessary seed. The Donovans were like that, gambling on a great future.

There was a slow, creaking noise in the inner yard, a strain-ing of timber, a brief gush of water, followed again by the slow creak. Old Mikie was bent over the pump, one hand turning the great wheel, the other supporting all the effort on his hip. Most of his life had been passed at the pump, squeezing gouts of water out of the ground. Signs on, he was permanently bent over to one side. It was too late now to straighten him up; as Father Conroy remarked, he couldn't have reached the handle with his other hand.

Under his breath, Mikie carried on a continual, low-pitched monologue – his work song, Father Conroy called it, because from a distance it had something of an African rhythm. Every now and then a loud exclamation broke through, something between a groan and the self-satisfaction of a belch. Possibly it was his comment on the way the water was coming, grudgingly or otherwise, into his seemingly bottomless bucket.

Often before, Father Conroy had been tempted to steal up on that familiar figure and knock the hat down over his face (quite likely, Mikie would continue to pump, blindfolded, his worksong muffled, until he was suffocated inside his hat). Now, however, Father Conroy had no time for Mikie. All he wanted to do was to steal past unobserved and make his way in to Kate. She would be in there, he knew, on the old car seat under the window, one carpet slipper half-scuffed off, a book on her lap, and she munching slowly as she read, sometimes stopping for long moments with the slice of bread waiting in her hand. As a child, he remembered watching her read and thinking that her eyes, so huge behind the glasses, must be burning the pages blue. Dear old Kate, she never changed.

He was almost at the front door when he heard the clomp of a hoof on the flags of the yard. Under the ash tree, a pony was tethered; it was flicking its tail and, now and then, shifting its weight ponderously from one leg to another. There had always been a pony tethered under the ash tree, as far back into his childhood as he could remember. How many generations of ponies? Impossible to say. All the Donovan ponies seemed to reach the same sedentary middle age, at which they stayed indefinitely until they reproduced themselves. How had Mikie managed to excite that ambition in them? How, for that matter, had Mikie managed to excite it in himself? But that was a thought which Father Conroy put firmly away, not for the first time. Here was his chance to do a deal with that Drewitt animal, quickly, before Kate learned about it. Not that she would disapprove (that would be too much trouble); yet he would feel embarrassed if she knew. She would be sure to pick up his motives with that vague, generalized attention she paid to everything; like a slowly revolving radar screen, she missed nothing, great or small. Or did he exaggerate this talent in her? Perhaps the reason why she would swivel toward him as he spoke was because she was having trouble with her corsetry.

He went back across the yard and in a subdued voice greeted Mikie. Taking over the pumping, so as not to arouse Kate within, he broached the subject of the Drewitt pony. "Oh, a fine animal, Mikie, but sure it wouldn't suit the like of Drewitt at all. 'Tis something more sedate he'd want for Mrs. Drewitt – the like of your own there – for gentle exercise."

"Ay," said Mikie.

"So if you know of anyone who'd be interested, or maybe yourself…"

"Ay." Mikie pushed a hand in under his hat and began to forage there. "Sure I might."

"Now, what would ye think yours would…"

"Sure, I might take him, Father, if ye want me to."

Father Conroy realized that he had been moving too fast.

"It's not that I want you to, Mikie, it's up to yourself."

"I'll take him, Father," Mikie said obstinately, "to please ye."

"Right! Well, then, Jimmy can ride your pony down tonight and leave him in my field, and he can ride the other one back. So that's settled. All we have to do now is to make the bargain."

"Sure I told ye I'd take him, Father. I don't mind."

Father Conroy paused a moment to gather his wits. Mikie was one of the thickest men he knew; it was extraordinary how long it took to get an idea through to him. Father Conroy couldn't mention money; that would have been tantamount to selling what was not his to sell. He would have been quite satisfied with a contribution, even a fairly nominal one, to the parish funds.

"But he's a good pony, Mikie; he's worth a good few quid if he's handled right."

"To tell ye the truth, Father, I wouldn't be expecting much." Mikie gestured toward the pony under the ash tree. "I wouldn't say he's worth all that much, but sure he'd suit Drewitt's lady fine."

God give me patience, thought Father Conroy. He glanced quickly at Mikie, wondering, not for the first time, whether there might not be some slight glimmer of intelligence there, but he was reassured by the dull gaze that Mikie had fixed on him.

"Look, Mikie," he began kindly, "you know when you're selling a car?"

Mikie shook his head. "No, Father." He was quite right, of course. The Donovans had had only the one car, bought second-hand seven years ago.

"Let's suppose, then, you were to sell the oul' car. You'd bring it along to the garage, and the man would take it as a trade-in against a new car."

"Would he, Father?"

Well, would he? Any garage man that would take the Donovan car should have his head examined.

"D'ye think he would, Father?" There was a glint in the eyes at last. Mikie was interested.

"I don't know whether he would or not. I was only supposing. Anyway, I wasn't really talking about cars at all."

"No, Father." The glint faded.

"What I'm trying to say, Mikie, is that here you have a stumbling, spavined oul' nag that's maybe sixteen years..."

"Ah, no, Father, ah, no."

"That's long past his best anyway. And here you expect me to give you a fresh young three-year-old. Why the hell should I?"

Mikie took time to work it out. He sent a hand up again under the hat, cropping the bare pastures. His eyes roved the yard and lighted at last on the kitchen door. Turning, Father Conroy saw a gleam of white move within, his sister, Kate.

Mikie smiled. "Sure, I suppose, Father, it's because ye're one of the family."

Goodnight, groaned Father Conroy. He flung his arms up, acting out his despair. And with head bowed, he began to walk slowly across the yard as the calm voice of Kate sang out, "Have they come, Mikie? Bring them in."

He paused, looking inquiringly at Mikie, who answered simply, "Yes." Next moment, she came forth blindly into the light.

My sister, Kate! He always felt a twist of pain whenever he saw that vague, confident smile on her face as she stepped into a half-seen world. Had she never looked at herself, at her life here with Mikie? No, he told himself, watching her smile (she still hadn't recognized him), she had never knowingly settled for this, she a girl who had been taught to speak French, to play the piano, crochet, make sauce tartare, and keep accounts for a doctor or a dentist.

"It's you, Tom." Not exactly disappointment – she liked him too well for that. Was it a slight anticlimax? Whom could she be expecting?

She kissed him on the cheek as he passed in; he had to pause to let her do it, but suffered it with a certain grudging pleasure. There was a dry, warm feel to her lips which reminded him of the chimney corner in the old home in Rosnagree, of children's bodies pressed against his, washed and warm and ready for bed, of his father's voice giving out the rosary from the depths of the big armchair.

"How are you, Kate?"

"Oh, sure, same as ever, Tom, pulling the divil by the tail," and she laughed.

She was a fine-looking woman still, he noted with pride, her hair drawn back in an old-fashioned way that suited her – it was still brown, though she was a good deal older than he was. She was tall and moved slowly, as if allowing for a greater bulk than she had yet achieved. No, she was the same Kate, grown solidly all the way up out of his childhood. "Kate…" he began, then saw that Mikie was standing in the doorway behind her. "Well, Kate," he said, turning away impatiently, "Here I am."

"You didn't have your dinner, Tom," she announced in her stately way, "I suppose?"

That "I suppose?" brought Father Conroy up short. She usually issued the invitation when he was safely ensconced by the fire in the kitchen. Was it a hint that she didn't want him today?

"No, I didn't," he said defiantly. And then he brought his hand to his head. "Damn it, the primus!"

She looked at him blankly.

"I left the kettle on for my breakfast."

"Oh, well," she said soothingly, "it's too late now to have your breakfast. You'd better come on in, so."

The kitchen was tidier than usual. She ushered him through it, toward the parlor, a place to which he was not usually impelled – it reminded him, with the white sheets spread over the piano and the sofa, of the catechism picture of Limbo, "a place or state of rest, where the souls of the saints who died before Christ were detained."

He slipped aside as she pushed the door open. "No, no, Kate, I'll do here. Leave the room above for the visitors. I'll sit here by the fire and have a smoke." And he took a stool and sat down firmly by the kitchen fire.

To his irritation, Mikie lowered himself to the bench opposite and sat with hands on knees watching him, waiting upon his command. When he felt in his pocket, Mikie reached forward at once with a plug of tobacco and a penknife. "No, thanks, Mikie, I've forgotten the oul' pipe."

When Mikie rose to go to the dresser, he added quickly, "No, I'm off it, Mikie, I'm off it altogether." Usually he accepted other men's pipes as a matter of course (he was as unconscious as a child of some privacies), but there was something about the shape of Mikie's mouth which put him off. Yet, he felt ashamed of his refusal, as if he had said something snobbish.

In silence, both of them watched Kate lay a cake in the pot oven and heap burning sods of turf on the lid. She had an oil stove, which she rarely used, possibly because she was a good cook, but more likely because she never had enough paraffin. Father Conroy watched her movements jealously; these preparations were usually for him, and it seemed to him now that she was put out by his visit.

"You're very busy, Kate," he complained.

"You haven't been to see us for a long time," she said, as if she were counting how many months. Now, what did she mean by that? Was she saying, "It's a pity you had to come just now!"? If only Mikie would go out, he could talk to her. But what about? What had they ever talked about? God, he thought, with a feeling of urgency, have we never talked to each other at all?

"How's the family, Kate?"

"The family?" She looked up, startled.

"Our family," he said sharply. "In Rosnagree."

She was silent, busy raking the fire under the pot. Mikie was lighting his pipe, all his attention on the job. Only the match wavered uneasily over the bowl.

"I was over there last Sunday," she murmured. "Frank was out, of course, but…" She hesitated, trying out "my mother," "your mother," and finally coming out with the common name from their childhood, "Momma was there."

Father Conroy knew she wanted to be pressed further. For twenty years and more she had been waiting, the Conroy dove of peace. Well, she would have to wait longer – the message had to come first from them to him.

"Lovely family we have, Mikie," he burst out. "Just like the weather this time of year."

She got up quickly and went out to the back kitchen. He heard her rattling the cutlery on to the table, not a bit like her usual quiet way about the house. After a few moments she came back with a big dish onto which she heaped potatoes from the pot beside the fire. "Sit up, now, to your dinner, the two of you."

He wanted to explain that it was not what he had meant to say, yet all he could do was to shrug his shoulders defiantly as he followed her to the table in the back kitchen. As he passed the open door of the parlor, he saw that the sheets had been stripped from the chairs within and that firelight gleamed on the tray of bottles and glasses. Damn it, he thought, I don't care who her visitors are. I'd prefer bacon and cabbage in the back kitchen. And yet, he felt that she should have known he would call, that she should have been ready to talk to him, put herself altogether at his disposal.

As he sat down, bending his leg with care, he called, "Kate!"

"Yes." She paused in the doorway.

"I'll tell you what brought me. I was thinking of…" Of the Conroys, he wanted to say, of Papa and Owen and the way things used to be in Rosnagree. But he couldn't. With Mikie there, he couldn't bring himself even to say their names. "... of a good feed of bacon and cabbage. There's no one can serve it up like you."

"No, Tom," she said, as if she were agreeing with a child, and slowly she went out, leaving him alone with Mikie.

He looked at his plate, at the thick slices of bacon and the mound of cabbage. Mikie was mashing potatoes, mixing in a big dollop of butter, pouring on the cream. Father Conroy could not bear to watch him (what was wrong with the Donovans, he had always thought, was too high a butterfat content). He kept his eyes lowered and, slicing a potato, ate it dry.

It was close under the tin roof, though the day was cold outside. Somewhere flies buzzed, as in no other house Father Conroy knew; they seemed to winter at the Donovans. The pound of homemade butter was melting in its dish. Outside, under the window, a hen clucked a gentle, noonday clucking. Kate was working in the front kitchen; he could hear the pounding of the rolling pin, then a deep, vaguely dissatisfied sigh, her version of Mikie's groan.

A fly buzzed over the butter, and Mikie batted at it with his knife. He had taken off his hat, disclosing a gray cowl of hair low on his forehead. His whole face labored with the effort of mastication. Every time he licked his lips, a pat of butter on his chin evaded his tongue. His eyes cunningly followed the fly. He swung his knife again and this time knocked it into the butter dish, where it lay quite still. His face labored on.

Father Conroy was oppressed by a sense of time running on and on and on to no end. My God, he thought, what am I doing here? Yet what was he to do? Where else could he go? He rolled a forkful of bacon, and as its warmth slid on his tongue, looked despairingly at the thick slices still waiting on his plate. Is this what eternity is like, he wondered (trying to make a joke of it), eating with the Donovans, picking at a plate of bacon which won't diminish no matter how much you eat? Kate! he wanted to call out, breaking the long silence, can't we talk? It doesn't matter a damn what we say, as long as we talk. You're the only one I have left.

But, with Mikie there, he could not call her.

Then her voice sounded. "Tom!" A call out of the void, unsolicited, measureless in its reassurance.

He looked up eagerly. "Yes, Kate?"

"Did you hear about Maurice?"

"Maurice?"

"Maurice Connolly."

Who was Maurice Connolly? He had a bad memory for names; he could never attach them to faces, like phrases to their context.

"Don't you remember Maurice?"

"Maurice Connolly," he said, baffled, searching back through hundreds of faces glimpsed at communion rails, through confessional grilles, in kitchens, and on football fields.

"We went up the mountain once, up to the lake."

"Yes, Kate." When? He tried to prize out the face.

"One Sunday, Fraughan Sunday we used to call it." And her voice trailed away in her dreamy way, "Ah, but sure you don't..." And she drifted back into her silence.

But he had a face now. It tilted quizzically upward, eyes screwed up in the sunlight. Maurice Connolly stood half-in, half-out of the shadow of trees. He was addressing himself, with careful indolence, to two girls who sat on a grassy bank above him, their long skirts demurely gathered about their legs. Nearby, on the roadside, bicycles were stacked, leaning together, light shining from the spokes of the wheels. Yes, he remembered that tilted face, the thin, arrogant, whiplike curve of the body.

What day was it? He pushed the memory further back and felt a wave of light pass over him, just as a cloud passes over the sun and releases pent-up warmth. He caught a heavy, yellow smell and remembered walking through broken corridors of gorse. Who walked with him? Before him? He saw thighs moving in a strong, supple movement which later was to trouble him in daydreams.

The mountain lake in which they swam seemed black, unbroken. A body was reflected in it – thin, white arms folded, togs wrinkled around lanky legs – his own boyish body. And the girl – who was she? She sat on the short grass beside him where he lay. Now and then she glanced down at him, but her eyes were searching for the other couples lying somewhere near in the heather. They were greenish eyes, quartz-like in the sun, and he stirred now, again, uneasily, thinking of the movement of her thighs. Her name was Nan.

How well the experienced old censor of his memory had exorcised her! Not that there was much to exorcise – he was too young, too shy, and she had other interests in mind. But now that she had broken through the old censor's ban, she brought other memories of that day crowding in on him. He remembered the drowsy warmth of Kate's face, as she returned with Maurice's arm about her; had they perhaps been carried a little further than the censor had ever dared to consider?

It was the day, all right, for rolling in the heather, the old festival of Lúnasa, dwindled even then to Fraughan Sunday, the fraughans and the picking of their juicy black berries already a respectable euphemism. Nowadays, even the fraughans were forgotten; the feast of Lúnasa was just another Sunday in the year when the young and the gamy not-so-young crowded into the dance hall in Donore or twenty miles farther on, into the vast, reverberating, concrete ballroom of Castlemore, the Mecca of the diocese.

They had had their music too, that evening, when they dropped down the valley, sailing on their bicycles through the half-light. At the crossroads a man sat by the warmth of the wall, his cap down over his eyes, the accordion resting on his knees, and their feet hammered the dancing-board in time to his tune. Kate's face was uptilted, laughing, wide open to the light that was fading from the mountain, the silent trees, the rapt faces of cottage children.

"I remember Fraughan Sunday, Kate," he called. Yes, we really lived in those days. He turned toward the kitchen, toward the comfortable thump of her hands on the dough, He had been right to come; Kate and he had a lot to talk about. There suddenly seemed a great brimming reservoir on which he had never drawn, and it was she, his sister, Kate, who had led him to it. "I remember that Sunday well."

"And Maurice Connolly?"

"Oh yes." He smiled at her eagerness.

He wasn't sure if he had ever liked Maurice Connolly. As far as he remembered, none of the men had – Maurice's talent being a dangerous one in a community which liked its matches tidily arranged. But now he felt a surge of affection toward the man who had led her, when she came so blindly between the bushes of flaming gorse.

"Of course I remember Maurice!" He smiled, thinking how he was pleasing her and added, "But what about him, Kate?"

She didn't say anything; he could hear her thumping the dough. And suddenly, he wanted to recall his question, to keep everything as it was, but it was too late.

"He's dead," she called, in a voice that was pitched too loud. "Jimmy heard it this morning at the creamery."

Curse of God, he thought, what a stupid bloody fool I am. I might have known she wouldn't bring up Maurice only she had some news like that to tell.

"I'm sorry, Kate."

"Oh, he was a good age," she said firmly, and spoiled it by adding her usual afterthought, "I suppose."

No, she hadn't much to remember, poor Kate, but at least she had had that evening. He remembered the swift drop downhill from the crossroads, the way the stars wheeled in the branches overhead and the small arc of his headlight that fled before him along the road. Home was in the valley down below; here they were in flight. He felt they would sail right over the houses in the valley, over Rosnagree itself, borne up on the warm night air.

"I remember it well, Kate." He glanced at Mikie, chewing unconcernedly, and said, "That evening, I mean."

She thumped the dough a few times before saying, "I thought it would never end."

"Yes." It was how he had felt too, as if it would go on forever. That, now, was happiness, he thought, smiling, sure of his ability to have grasped it, even a single moment of it. "That's what I thought too."

"I must have cried all the way home."

"Cried, Kate?"

"All the way down from the crossroads."

Uncomfortably, he watched Mikie take a small bone from his pouting lips and lay it on the side of the plate. What was she talking about?

"The time we stopped in the demesne," she said.

Somewhere on the road down through the demesne, he heard the grating, hollow rattle of a wheel rim on the stones. He drew up, cycled back in consternation, to find Kate standing helplessly beside her bicycle. Someone swiveled a lamp around, and he had a brief glimpse of the faces around the upturned bicycle, of the spokes shining as the wheels spun.

"Didn't we mend it, though? With a nailfile to lever the tire off? Maurice and—"

"No, not Maurice." Quietly she said, "He had gone on ahead."

It was a fair-haired man who was bent over the wheel, whose name he could not remember. A bat swooped under the trees. He was choked with feelings of rage and humiliation.

"With – with that girl," he said.

"Yes, with Nan. He was friends with her too, for a while."

"He was a right bastard," he burst out, and glared at Mikie, who stopped chewing and looked up at him with mild inquiry. "To go on like that."

"Well, a friend of his, a fair-haired lad – what's this his name was? – waited behind to help—"

"No," he shouted, "I mean – the way he left you."

"Oh!" she said; then added her doubtful, "Yes."

Had she no pride, then? Was that her trouble? One evening he was crossing the fields with his gun, heading for the copse where the pigeons came in to roost. Through a gap in the hedge he saw her standing on the road; she didn't see him; she was facing toward the village, but he knew from her hunched shoulders that she was cold and that she didn't really hope any longer that Maurice would come. He hadn't spoken to her. He had turned back to the house, ashamed for her, knowing that she would not want him to see her waiting. Two, maybe three years she had waited, but when, at last, Maurice succeeded to his father's farm, he married someone else.

Mikie was shoveling in the last few mouthfuls, one eye fixed on the fly in case it showed signs of moving. When he paused to rest knife and fork on the table, he had the relentless, patient crouch of a beast of prey. Father Conroy felt he had never really looked at the man before. Christ, he muttered, why did we let Kate marry him?

There was that fair-day in Castlemore; he remembered standing in the doorway of the hotel, watching the herds of cattle go past on the wet street, being rushed by shouting drovers to the railway station and the butchers' yards. In a room upstairs, his father and the Donovans were making Kate's match. He hadn't been told about it – he was too young to be one of the company – but he knew what was going on. And once again, he experienced the misery of that day, watching the hooves go trampling past in the puddles of the roadway. Why hadn't he spoken up? Why hadn't he rushed upstairs and broken that cursed conspiracy apart?

Well, the answer was simple; it came to him almost at once. He had never thought about doing so, had accepted the match as foreordained because his father had said so – his father, the all-knowing, all-loving, omnipotent Tom Conroy. So much had he accepted it that even now, at the back of his repulsion for Mikie, was the feeling the match had been inevitable after all.

But how had his father justified it? Money? Hardly, for the Conroys at that time could afford a dowry that would have bought her far better places than Mikie's. Local gossip? No. Mikie hadn't the fire to raise that kind of smoke. Most likely, Tom Conroy was afraid that she would not marry, that one of his children would be less than perfect. Jesus, if he could see her now!

She came slowly into the back kitchen, as Mikie scraped back his chair, blessed himself, and reached for his hat. She made way in the doorway as, loutishly, he blundered past her.

Father Conroy watched her draw the plates together and stack them one on top of the other. She seemed so placid that he wondered if the conversation about Maurice had ever taken place. Perhaps, he thought, looking at the fresh cheeks, the untroubled brow, all she ever needed was to settle herself into this butterfat contentment of Donovanhood. She should have had more pride.

Yes, indeed, with a little more pride she might have won Maurice. She might even have held herself ready for him when his wife died after the first child. And then? How much of him was left to hold?

A picture formed itself of Maurice seen at a point-to-point meeting a year or two ago. The slight, straight-backed body moved stiffly across the grass, the bow legs, wrapped in stained jodhpurs, moving in a sort of creaky coordination, like strips of dried-out leather. A tweed cap was pulled down over the narrow face, in which only the eyes lived – a thin light in them as the horses were led past for the next race. One would never have thought that anything warm, human, had ever belonged to him. And yet –

"Kate!"

She was wiping the table with a damp cloth. She barely paused to glance up.

"He had a son."

She stared; what was he talking about?

"He had a son called Tomás. Maurice had." Made in his image, cast carelessly aside. "I knew him well, up in Slievenalua, when he was a little fellow. I often thought—" What? That he might have been Kate's? That he might have been remade in her image, in our image, as a Conroy.

She was wiping the table slowly, deliberately.

"I hope I didn't upset you, Kate." And when she looked up, he added, "About Maurice and all that."

"Oh, sha!" She looked up and laughed with an easy Donovan laugh. "That old foolishness."

And, chilled, he drew his arms back to let her wipe where he had eaten.

She hadn't asked him to move up to the fire, where Mikie had already settled down with groans of satisfaction. "Move on up, let ye," she should have said. Did she want him to leave? He stood up, jingling the change in his pocket, and looked at her uncertainly. He had never been wished out of her house before; he felt he had a right there – a small right, representing his small share in her. If he wanted to remind her of it, one remark would be enough, but he hesitated to make it, knowing that it might hurt because indignation would put an edge on whatever words he used.

He continued to wait, therefore, lifting himself up and letting himself down gently on his toes, wanting her to ask him to stay. But she said nothing as she wiped the table. Damn it, maybe she had just forgotten to ask him and that was all. Still, he waited to be reassured.

The sound of the approaching car made her look up suddenly. "Oh, thank goodness!" Her eyes were sharp with excitement. "I was afraid Jimmy wouldn't be back in time."

In time for whom, he wanted to ask jealously, but she hurried eagerly into the kitchen, leaving him on his own. Well, he wasn't going to rush to meet the great Jimmy. Stay here, he told himself, and play it cool.

"Good lad!" he could hear her at the kitchen door. "You got it, so?"

"That's the sherry," said Jimmy, "and that's the other. I got the twelve-year-old." His voice came nearer, his public speaker's voice, whose resonance he could turn on like a tap. Even muted, as now, it penetrated the house like a stage whisper. "'Twas safer to get it. He has a taste for the good stuff."

"Your uncle Tom's here," she murmured. And Father Conroy imagined her warning nod.

"Don't I know!"

"Sssh!"

"Just like him to turn up…"

Father Conroy moved forward hastily before any more was said. He could take direct abuse and revel in it. Home truths were different.

He stood in the doorway until Jimmy saw him.

"Hullo there, Uncle Tom. I noticed the tracks of your car in."

"Yes, I came in all right." How did the fellow think he came? By helicopter?

"You're not denying them, so?" Jimmy measured slyly how far he could take the joke. "Bald tires and all?"

Father Conroy did not reply. Jimmy, to him, had always been a furtive small boy who sat among their legs under the kitchen table and occasionally drew a sleeve across his smile at some piece of gossip from on high. He had never considered what Jimmy thought of him, or indeed the fact that Jimmy had any thoughts worth consideration. That was his mistake. Jimmy might still be the boy around the place, but, away from home, he was making a name for himself. The badges that flashed on his lapels were emblems of the various organizations in which he held office – a Young Farmers' Club, the Total Abstinence Society, the Gaelic League. He even wore the silver pelican of the veteran blood donors. Like a pirate ship, he sailed under any color which lulled suspicions for the moment. His own base color was charcoal gray, in various suits of which he milked cows, officiated at fund-raising dances, spread dung, and attended meetings of the county council to support his grand-uncle, James. And, of course, attended funerals.

Did he wear James's gloomy castoffs? Hardly, for Jimmy was tall, and though the butterfat diet was beginning to loosen his belt somewhat, he could carry his weight well. A fine-looking fellow he was, even with Mikie Donovan for a father. Now, how would he have looked if Maurice had been his father? Something like Tomás?

Father Conroy stared at his nephew, trying to refashion him as Maurice's son, whom he had last seen at the age of fifteen. Add twenty-five years, he thought, and subtract ten, for Jimmy's about thirty now... And then, in exasperation, he realized that there was no relationship at all between the two men, beyond the fact that Tomás, unfortunately, was not a Conroy and Jimmy unfortunately was.

"Well, Jimmy," he began, to break the silence, but at the intolerably avuncular quality of his voice, he knew he couldn't go on.

"Yes, Uncle Tom?" Jimmy's tone managed to convey solicitude. To hell with you, thought Father Conroy, and shot out, "Who's coming, anyway?"

Jimmy glanced up toward the parlor after his mother and made a small grimace, as if such a direct approach were in doubtful taste. "Uncle James," he admitted at last, "and some friends. Go on up to the room, will you?"

"I'm going up," said Father Conroy.

Kate was blowing at the fire in the grate, which had burned down very low. She pushed a few twigs between the coals and fumbled a sheet of newspaper up to make a draft. "Tom," she said, "would you ever keep an eye on this and get it going?" And she bustled purposefully out to the kitchen.

Left there on his own, half-kneeling, half-squatting for fear of bringing back the pain in his leg, he held the newspaper up to the fire and asked himself was this all they thought he was good for. Uncle James had something for the Donovans. The Donovans had something for Uncle James. What had he got for anybody?

Well, he had the few quid in the back of the cupboard at home. If they didn't even want that from him, he would find someone who would. He bent down and puffed at the faintly burning coals. An old bellows, that's all they thought him, full of angry wind. Now, who the hell said that?

*

The flames were spurting between the coals when he heard another car stop in the yard. A few moments later, Uncle James came bouncing into the room. "Ah, Father Tom!" The hand was extended, the old politician's hand, rubbed smooth by a half-century of shaking and being shaken. "It's a change to find you on your knees."

Father Conroy smiled. "My knees can take it." But he got up as quickly as he could, taking a chance on the pain in his leg.

James fitted himself into the biggest armchair. "Jimmy says you're not looking so well. Bedad, he's right. You're not! Not at all well!"

"Never felt better."

"Ah, well, I suppose none of us are as young as we were."

"I hope I'll look as fresh as you do, Uncle James, in my old age."

There was a truce while James got out his pipe and proceeded to fill it. This took a long time. He had a gadget for cleaning it and another for tamping down the tobacco in the bowl, but first he had to select the gadgets needed from the paraphernalia in his breast pocket – the row of fountain pens and pencils, nailfiles, and combs.

Even as a child, Father Conroy used to be fascinated by Uncle James's gadgetry – the gold chain across the waistcoat, the half-hunter watch that struck the hours, the plaques presented for various services rendered. One of his memories of the Black and Tan War was of the distant figure of his uncle squatting at the bottom of a field in Rosnagree, tinkering with explosives. He remembered James setting off at the head of an I.R.A. column with a row of bombs jangling from the handlebars of his bicycle.

From time to time, reports came in from different parts of the county as the bombs went off. One of them blew the thatched roof off a forge, against which the bicycle had been left leaning – a spectacular fireworks effect, as he had imagined it, hardly considering at all the aftermath, when a truckload of Tans coming to investigate were shot to death by James and his men.

When the pipe was filled, James fussed with it, as if it were about to explode any moment. Even when it was going well, he took it out of his mouth and looked at it, as if he suspected it of disagreeing with him – an agent, perhaps, of the opposition party. During the silence, Kate came in to pour him a half-tumbler of whiskey. As she bent anxiously to put more coal on the fire, she nudged Father Conroy and whispered, "Let ye be talking, anyway."

They sparked into conversation at last, almost immediately into an argument about the road workers and the council.

"No," said James, "I'm not ashamed, not one bit. Get this into your head, boy! The day of the tar bucket and the shovelful of chippings is gone for good. I'm older than you. Isn't it strange now how well I can move with the times?"

When the argument grew heated, Kate came hurrying into the room and, drawing back the curtain from the window, murmured, "Isn't it a lovely view from this window? It's one of the nice things about this house."

"Who's going to be traveling your superhighways?" Father Conroy demanded, echoing a phrase from a recent council meeting. "Your golden miles and your platinum half-miles?"

"I will, for one. And you will, for another. And what about the tourists? They're used to the best."

"Oh, God," groaned Father Conroy. "You'd sell us for the tourists."

"There's that little birch up on the hill," sighed Kate. "I think she's putting out leaves already."

Father Conroy stood up to go. He went in some ill humor, glaring at Mikie, who, nodding by the fire, wakened with a snort. Jimmy was in the yard, hanging around. Who were they all waiting for? What was James's visit in aid of? Father Conroy was tempted to wait, but he suddenly hadn't got the energy to be curious.

In spite of his protests, James accompanied him as far as his car. Even to go that distance, James had to clap on his black hat, for fear of being called to a funeral – as the Gospel says: "And he that is in the field, let him not go back to take his Anthony Eden."

They paused a moment by the car. James kicked casually at the front wheel.

"Time you got yourself a few remolds, Father; you haven't much left there."

"They'll do me a while yet."

"Oh, no," the Anthony Eden nodded earnestly. "'Tis never worth it. Next time you're in Castlemore, let ye go into Shea's garage and tell him I sent you. You'll get a good cut, I promise you."

Father Conroy fished out his keys in silence and got in.

"Mind you, Father" – James kicked out at the whole car now – "you got good service out of her."

"I've no complaints."

"Have a word with Shea – he'll give you a good trade-in. But be sure to tell him I sent you."

In other words, make sure of Shea's vote!

"There's plenty of wear in her yet," Father Conroy muttered. He started up the engine, but James was leaning on the window, preventing him from driving off.

"Speaking as one of the family, Father, and as someone like yourself who has to maintain a certain position in the county, I beg to differ with you. Now, I know you may think that these things are not noticed, but I say they are and that if you want the proper respect which is due to our class of people—"

"This car will see me out."

James's hat rose a little higher on his head, as it did at any intimation of mortality, particularly one referring to a constituent. He leaned forward and whispered, "My God, Thomas, are ye all right?"

"Of course I am. Why the hell shouldn't I be?"

"You're not your old self, at all, at all. You need a tonic or something." He still held tight to the window. "I'm feeling in great form myself these days. D'ye know why, Thomas?"

Father Conroy revved the engine, but at last had to ask: "Why?"

"Because I made my will. Yes." He stretched his arms out slowly, as if he were going to fly, then yawned luxuriously. "The best tonic you ever had. It's like a load off your shoulders; you wouldn't believe it. Of course, I'll be bad news with some people. I left nothing to the church, bar a few quid for Masses. It's my private opinion it has enough stacked away already, in spite of appearances."

Father Conroy shrugged carelessly, refusing to be risen.

"No, mine is all going into further production. It's going to the youth! And thank God" – he lifted his arms, pointing to the cowshed and the sound of milk pouring into a churn – "the Conroys have the youth to leave it to. D'ye know, Thomas," he murmured persuasively, reaching for the window, "anyone should make a will."

But Father Conroy had seen his chance. Before James could regain possession of the window, he released the clutch, and the car leaped forward and made its getaway as if it knew, faithful old doggy, that the bads were about, sixguns cocked, black hats rising out of ambush. All the way back through the fields it held to the shortest path and even gallantly took to the grass where the path could be shortened still further.

As it turned out onto the main road, a Morris Minor turned in. Both cars stopped, and after a moment the Morris gave way, reversing slowly to let the priest's car out, at the same time giving Father Conroy a good eyeful of the expected guests. He did not recognize the couple who sat sedately in front. He did not really see them, although the man saluted, for he was staring at the girl in the back of the car. She sat on the edge of her seat and leaned forward, peering straight ahead between the two gray heads. She did not glance toward him as he passed out; if she saw him at all, it was as something which had unaccountably obstructed her view for a moment.

What caught his attention was not her face – that seemed ordinary enough, even plain, so far as it could be seen in the interior of the car. It was her attitude, the eager, single-minded way she leaned forward, leaning so willingly toward that house, that loveless collection of Conroys.

Was it another deal? Was she another Kate being brought to market? By God, he muttered as he slammed in the gear, haven't we bought and sold enough human flesh in our time?

Chapter 4

He drove home fast; he had the feeling – a nervy feeling which nagged at him whenever he went beyond the bounds of his parish – that someone had been looking for him.

Sure enough, the primus had been turned off and the burned-out kettle put in the sink. On the table he found a message from his curate, Father Farrell; it was a request to attend a requiem High Mass next morning in Slievenalua for the soul of Maurice Connolly. He crumpled the note and tossed it into the grate. Maurice Connolly! Poor fellow, there couldn't be much left after him, hardly enough to pay the undertaker, never mind the cost of High Mass.

The kitchen was still full of the bluish fumes of burned aluminum. He took the kettle and the extinct primus and shoved them outside the back door. There was nothing left to hold him in the kitchen, nor, when he had traversed it several times, his study. He stood at the window, staring out at the misty light on the hedgerow and the fields beyond. He was hemmed in with greenery. The rhododendrons were coming on again; he would have to trim them, trim them away to hell this time. And with them, that bloody lilac – it brought nothing but flies in the summertime. Now, there was something he could be doing! But when he shifted his leg, he thought, no, I won't give them the satisfaction. I'll wait till I'm in good form; let them come on a bit more, and then I'll really do for them.

Got to cuddle yourself, he purred, in a parody of a sexy, adenoidal Dublin voice, caress yourself in a cocoon, wrap yourself in the lawther of what's-its-name's soap and you'll last forever. Well, if not forever, long enough to disappoint the Donovans.

A will! So they wanted him to make a will! Leave everything to the cool, nest-feathering Jimmy; yes, that would suit their book! Well, there was nothing much to leave; they all knew that. He glanced toward the cupboard door, reached mentally into the darkness within. How much? He hadn't looked in there for a long time. Maybe he should clear it all out and do a proper spring cleaning. Not just now, though! He'd give a day to it, sometime soon, when he was feeling in better form.

Briskly he turned from the window. What about a visit? he asked himself, like a host jollying along a shy guest. Whose turn was it? Who was the lucky man? Watch and Pray inevitably came to mind, but, thank God, he had done his duty there. Who was next?

Or rather, on whom could he call at this, the busiest hour of the day, between cow time and suppertime? Surely there was someone with whom there was business to be done? To his relief, he remembered that Drewitt had not yet been informed of the result of the draw. Well, there was an important piece of business that should have been seen to, had he a curate who showed any interest in the upkeep of the church and its buildings. He would have to see to it himself, then, without further delay. Gratefully he hurried out to the car and sat on the seat that was still warm.

*

Mrs. Drewitt stood at the back of the hall when the maid opened the door – he could see her shadow, thin, lonely, eager to be ecumenical with anybody. He leaned past the grinning Teresa McGrath (the seller of the winning ticket) and called out, "Ah, Mrs. Drewitt, how are ye?"

She emerged, showing all too obviously she had been flushed out. Gallantly, he lifted his hat, inclining his head as he did so; it was an old-fashioned gesture which always commended him to ladies of high degree. His pause of anticipation after they exchanged greetings left her no alternative but to ask him in.

"Yes, Padre? What is it?" Drewitt demanded. He had come out into the hall in jodhpurs and carpet slippers; he held an Agatha Christie in his hand as proof that he had been disturbed. Behind him, Father Conroy caught a glimpse of polished oak and deep-piled red carpet; above the flushed bald head, portraits of families more ancient than the Drewitts glowered down; they looked as if they knew they would end up with a scion like this, who had bought them with the furnishings.

Father Conroy was more than mild. They had had a brush before, over a right-of-way, a Mass-path which Drewitt had tried to close after centuries of use. A shotgun had been brandished, but Father Conroy and his men had walked toward it, maintaining their right-of-way even as the double barrels wavered wildly over them. Possibly the gun had not even been loaded.

Father Conroy waved the winning ticket in silence, as Drewitt made way for him into the sitting room.

"Another ticket, Padre?" It seemed he was going to play it cool, sarcastic, smiling.

"Ah, no, Mr. Drewitt. I doubt if I could persuade you."

"You're damn right, Padre." He chuckled, looked to his wife, forcing a timid smile out of her.

Father Conroy looked around for a seat. This was moving nicely.

"Sit down, Padre." If you must, the tone conveyed.

Mrs. Drewitt still hovered. It was important to keep her on the spot in case of difficulty.

"You've a nice airy room here, ma'am." Airy was right. Drewitt had a couple of screens around the back of his chair. The windows rattled, as if the wind were trying them one after the other. In the vast fireplace at the far end, the fire smoked away to itself.

"Yes," she said, looking around her with no sense of achievement, "but it's more or less as we got it. Mr. Drewitt bought everything, you know, just as it stood."

"Cleared out some of the clutter, though," said Drewitt. He began to fidget at the Agatha Christie, impatient to get back to it. "You're not selling another ticket, then?"

"I didn't think you'd be that keen for a pony, Mr. Drewitt."

"You're damn right, I wouldn't." This time his ferocious chuckle brought a smile hastening to Mrs. Drewitt's lips.

"Well, that's too bad now. There are plenty of people who would have given their eyeteeth to win it."

"You mean I've won it."

"Yes, indeed you have."

He took it coolly, with just a narrowing of the eyes. One could see how he had made his pile; even wealth and comfort hadn't done much to his self-control. "Why didn't Teresa tell me?"

This was an awkward one – Teresa had been warned to keep her mouth shut. "We wanted to keep it as a surprise." Father Conroy smiled.

"Where is it now?" he asked suspiciously.

"In my field below."

He got up, walked to the window, though he couldn't see it from there. He turned to Father Conroy with the next question – which Father Conroy forestalled.

"Ah, he'll be safe enough there. You'll be wanting to see him, of course. I'd say you'd be a great judge of a horse?"

"Well, not a great judge," said Drewitt, gratified.

"You'd like this one, anyway, though he has no mouth."

"No mouth? I don't quite understand—"

Father Conroy made Mrs. Drewitt smile faintly as he demonstrated with a tug of his forefinger on the unyielding side of his own mouth. "Bought off a tinker, I'd say he was, and then, well, you know the way he'd be abused afterward. You've seen the crotchety way an old lady would drive a pony and trap."

"Ah yes, of course I know what you mean." Mr. Drewitt half-turned to quell her smile. "A local expression."

"There's nothing you can do, once the mouth is gone. A great pity, because he'd have been just the thing for the good woman." And he tilted his head in his courtly way toward Mrs. Drewitt.

"Oh, no," she exclaimed in alarm, "I don't think I'd ever—"

"All the same, ma'am," said Father Conroy, "a little gentle exercise would have been excellent for the constitution. Ah well," he sighed, "so there you are."

"I see." Drewitt summed up. "A tinker's pony with no mouth."

"For a man in your position, it's not much of a prize, I agree, but sure 'twas only put up as a token anyway. The main thing was the parish funds."

"Why didn't Teresa tell me this" – the color was rising in that inflammable skull – "when she sold me that blasted ticket?"

"Oh well," Father Conroy smiled, glossing over the unpleasantness, "if it's only a question of the ticket—" He pulled the loose change out of his pocket and picked out half a crown.

"No, no, Padre, you don't get out of this so easily."

"Out of what?" Father Conroy stared blankly.

"Out of this – this infernal mess."

Father Conroy leaned forward and smiled as if he were encouraging a child that was striving to make itself understood. "But I thought you said you didn't want him?"

"No!" Drewitt burst out.

"No what?" Father Conroy encouraged.

"I won it – damn it, I won it!"

"Yes," smiled Father Conroy. "Of course you did." Watching Drewitt fume, he felt momentarily sorry for him. Exiled in a strange land, feeling himself at the mercy of rapparees, no wonder he didn't know what to think. Poor fellow, he had adopted the ways of a class whose vocation was the horse, and yet he couldn't even ride one. Rather than press him further now, in such a dangerous mood, Father Conroy inclined his head toward Mrs. Drewitt. "If you'll allow me, ma'am, I'll see to it that your pony gets a good home."

"Oh, Father Conroy, I'd be so glad if you would."

"No," shouted Drewitt.

Father Conroy and Mrs. Drewitt turned toward him in dismay.

"I'll see to it," he muttered thickly. "He's mine."

"But, dear, Father Conroy knows—"

"Will you be quiet!"

"Yes, dear." She gave him her small, appeasing smile. "Of course."

"I'm talking to this man here, you see," he blustered, "Father What's-his-name—"

Father Conroy's hat rested on his knee. He began to dust it slowly, with care. The game seemed lost; it had been a mistake to appeal to the woman. Yet something might perhaps be salvaged. He rose thoughtfully to his feet and took Mrs. Drewitt's hand.

"Good day to you, ma'am," he murmured, and pressed her hand sympathetically; then, while she stared in surprise, he began his dignified walk toward the door.

Behind him, Drewitt struggled to get out of the depths of his armchair, but so tightly did it hold him that Father Conroy was in the hall before he heaved himself erect. Viciously he flung the Agatha Christie into the chair. "Just a moment!" he shouted.

Father Conroy's voice could be heard exchanging pleasantries with Teresa. By the time Mr. Drewitt reached the hall, she had the hall door open and Father Conroy was outside, pausing at the top of the steps to don his hat. Drewitt would have shouted again, but there was something so practiced about the gesture with which the hat was fitted to the gray head, something so ceremonious about the slow descent of the steps in spite of or rather because of, the slight limp, that he felt that for once he had affronted more than a man. Deep down in his nonconformist subconscious was a feeling of ancestral awe that kept him silent just a moment too long. By the time the shout came, Father Conroy had got away.

Got away, at least, for the present. With the car door shut and the engine started, he knew he was not really getting away. Sooner or later, Drewitt would be after him for the pony. Sooner or later, the animal would have to be handed over. Was its mouth that bad? He sat in the car in the drive outside his own house and tried a little uneasily to recall what he had told Drewitt. Suppose there was a court case? Suppose its mouth was found to be fine? Ah no, damn it, how could it be when the old lady had been tugging at it for years, like a bell rope.

I'm losing my grip, he told himself, staring at the house. If I go in there now, I'll spend the evening worrying about the pony. But what else is there to do? Who is there to call on? He passed his hand over his scalp, feeling the length of hair, and fell, at last, as he knew he would, to the lure of Kavanagh's. He could do with a haircut, and if he hurried he might get the cartoons as well, at the end of *Children's Hour*.

With a sheet wrapped around him, he sat on a kitchen chair, watching *Paladin*, while Peter Kavanagh snip-snapped at his hair, careful not to block his view. The little living room of the cottage was crowded; Gabriel and the smaller children sat on the floor, absolutely still, their hands clasped around their shins, their faces intent. The sound was turned up full, drowning out the occasional banging on the wall (old Kavanagh lay within, staring at the ceiling in the half-dark and struggling to recall, so as to be word-perfect, a phrase of some old Gaelic song). Peter's wife worked away quietly in the background, setting out Peter's dinner on the table. She glanced occasionally at the snipping scissors, smiling, yet absorbed in what she was doing.

As Paladin and his men galloped into a draw, unaware of the ambush laid for them, Father Conroy's hands twitched under the sheet. "Steady, Father, steady!" whispered the barber, and he turned to wink at his wife, as Father Conroy reined himself in.

When the program was over, she began to bundle the children toward bed. Yawning, Peter turned away from the news toward where his dinner steamed on the table. He took a glance at his handiwork. "D'ye know what they say, Father? They say that you have the best-cropped head in the parish."

"Thanks to *Paladin*."

Peter laughed and waved to the other chair. "Sit in, Father, let ye sit in and have a bite to eat."

"No, no!" Father Conroy was adamant. He did not eat in road workers' cottages. A cup of tea, perhaps, he might take, and a scone or a slice of bread, but never a meal. It was too hard-won, he knew, and someone would have to go short, probably the woman of the house, who was always the last to fill her plate. "Sure, I have it all waiting for me above."

"What is it tonight, Father?"

"Roast duck, potatoes sauté, peas, applesauce – I'm a great man for the trimmings."

"Yes, Father" – the man was still smiling – "but won't you…" Father Conroy rose to go. The woman had returned, closing the bedroom door on the murmur of the children's voices. "The old man's very restless tonight, Father," she said.

"Lost another line of a song, I suppose?"

"You wouldn't know, the way he's wandering, you wouldn't know what's fretting him. 'Tis all mixed up with Peter's mother. God rest her, they were always very close." She moved to her place behind her husband, ready to refill his plate. "You ought to get the telly, Father," she said. "We were just saying what a comfort it would be for you."

Father Conroy glanced quickly from her to her husband and

ran his hand defensively over his scalp. Was it a hint that he was coming too often? But the two faces looked back at him, innocent of any stratagem.

"Yes, Father," the man said, "'twould be great company for ye in the nights! Wouldn't it now?"

"No, no, 'tis worse than the drink, for a man can take a pledge against drink. Ah no, I wouldn't stir out at all, then. Anyway" – he wheeled on them from the doorway – "isn't it the only thing I deny myself, that and a woman to warm the bed."

"Oho, Father." She laughed. "'Tisn't the women warm the beds at all. What with the amount of ironing and mending, sure himself does be turning over for his second sleep by the time I get in."

"Oh, ye get in all right! And you stay in, like a log." Peter planted his knife and fork firmly on the table. "Who has to get up in the middle of the night? Who, Father, but the poor man here. Yes, I have to get up to feed them and quieten them, ay, and even to…"

"Ssssh!" She clapped her hand over his month. And there, as they struggled joyously against each other, Father Conroy left them.

He had gone only a few yards up the road, in the dark, when the door opened and the woman called softly after him, "Father!"

He waited as she ran toward him.

"Father, I'd like you to say a Mass for her."

"For whom?"

"Peter's mother. She's on my mind, the way the old man does be fretting after her."

"All right," he muttered, and reluctantly he stretched out his hand, suffering the ten-shilling note to be slipped into it.

"Good night, Father," she whispered. "God bless you."

He watched her run back toward the lighted doorway. Then, crushing the note in his hand, he turned toward his own dark house ahead, toward that cupboard in whose depths the note would be stored.

Behind him the door closed, confining the light and the warmth within.

Chapter 5

High Mass for the high, he thought as he slipped into his pew in the chapel of Slievenalua, Low Mass for the low. He nodded to his colleagues on either side of him as they stood up to begin the chanting of the Office for the Dead. Two guineas a skull for fourteen of us, he calculated. He shook his head sternly toward the coffin in the center of the aisle – you're a terrible foolish man, Maurice Connolly.

He wasn't in favor of High Masses, or indeed of any liturgical luxuries.

Dum dee dum big bass drum
Fiddle, flute, euphonium;

he would hum when confronted with any ceremony that seemed to anticipate the majesty of the Church Triumphant. What kind of Mass was said on the first holy Thursday, high or low? And what color of money changed hands afterward?

More to the point, where was the money to come from here? Poor Maurice hadn't had it, not as a hard-living veteran "boy" in the service of the racing stables outside Castlemore. Or had he had it salted away, just for this? What about the son, young Tomás? Why hadn't the money gone to him? Ah well, he thought as he sought the place in his Ordo, ours not to reason why.

Canon Fitzmaurice began the Office, his delicate piping inundated in a moment by the whole ragged chorus – a Kilcloyne specialty, Father Conroy called it, the baying of the hounds of heaven. Four of them hadn't a note in their heads; the rest hit some key at random and doggedly refused to be pushed off it. As usual Father Conroy's baritone tried to impose order on chaos, but to no avail. He nodded wryly toward the coffin, let them at it, you'll be quiet in there long enough.

Mass over, the celebrant went to the vestry to put on the black funeral cope. Father Conroy sat back in the silence while the other priests adjusted their glasses, licked fingers, and flicked back through the pages of their breviaries. He stared at the vestry door. No matter how hardened he got, how little he noticed the whisper of last confessions, the hands fumbling for his, the coffins, shovels, all the paraphernalia of death, there was always one moment which struck him with chill – that was when the little procession came through the vestry door and down the aisle, with the priest in his black robe and the crucifix held aloft, beside the guttering candle. In that moment, he felt the finality of the soul's dismissal.

Always, it was a relief to get outside, to breathe the air, feel sunlight on him, know that he was alive. Two farmers stood looking at the top sods being thrown down on the coffin lid to deaden the sound of clay. "No, 'tisn't too bad at all," said one. "A good crop of spuds would clean the dirt out of it."

"Ah, 'tis heavy oul' clay, though," the other said; "'tis not fit for anything else."

The Castlemore undertaker had stationed himself at Father

Conroy's elbow, eager to exchange solemnities. "Poor Maurice," he began; "he wandered far enough, God knows, but he'll have to content himself with Slievenalua now."

"It could have been worse," muttered Father Conroy. "Wouldn't he be rightly buried in Castlemore?"

And the undertaker smiled behind his hand; it was the kind of joke he wanted from Father Conroy.

As the clay rumbled in, an old man said, "Tch, tch," a mild little protest against death. Then Father Cullen's voice rose sonorously to begin a decade of the rosary, and the crowd joined in. Father Conroy stood, hands clasped before him, head lowered. "And Lancelot at the ring rides well" – the phrase came to him from some long-forgotten schoolbook. It seemed like an unsolicited epitaph to Maurice.

But why be sorry for Maurice? He had knocked out a good old time, fame on the race courses in his youth, drinking, women, no ties, no responsibilities after the few years of marriage. As easy be sorry for an old dried-up harness hanging on a stable wall. No, Maurice never had feelings to spend on anyone, not even on his own son.

Father Conroy scanned the faces of the crowd as it drifted away. Tomás was only fifteen when he had last seen him. Would he recognize him now? Surely he had come back for the funeral?

Bat Cullen, the parish priest of Slievenalua, was looking after all the arrangements – he should know whether Tomás was there or not. Father Conroy moved toward him, taking off his surplice and rolling it up. But it was a bad time to ask. Bat was fussily urging the other priests, who were chatting in various parts of the churchyard, toward the vestry, where their breakfast was being prepared. As if to tempt them, the aroma of frying rashers and eggs floated out on the sunny air.

On his way in, he was accosted by Uncle James, holding his Anthony Eden on his chest.

"Ah, Father Thomas!" James shook hands formally – he had a great respect for "order and precedence" on public occasions.

"How are ye?" muttered Father Conroy, and made an attempt to move on.

"Very sad, yes indeed, yes, yes. He brought a fair-sized crowd, poor Maurice, but of course it's a good day, a lovely, sharp, spring day, thanks be to God. I always think that a fine day for a funeral gives you a great chance to get out and meet the people." He felt Father Conroy's impatient tug to get free and went on with a laugh, "I hope, Father, that ye'll have a sunny day for mine, and a good turnout, and that ye'll all enjoy yerselves."

"Please God."

"Oh, indeed, yes, I want ye all to be there. I want ye all to remember that day." He pulled Father Conroy closer. "Did you think over since, Father, that little matter?"

Father Conroy pointed toward the vestry. "I'm wanted in there, James. I'll see you again."

"Of course, Father." James released him at once. "You'll see me again. Faith, you will."

And Father Conroy hurried to catch up with the other priests heading for the vestry door.

In the doorway, a middle-aged farmer was filling tumblers and cups with whiskey and passing them around to several other respectable men of his class. As the priests stopped in surprise, Bat Cullen muttered, "My God!", strode forward, and growled out some reprimand. The man's face flushed with indignation. He slammed the cork deliberately into the bottle and turned away, followed by his shamefaced companions.

"You couldn't be up to them," said Bat, anxious that the other priests would not think that drinking in the vestry door was tolerated in his parish. "Last week I had a funeral, a young fellow killed by a tractor, and the poor father was so shaken that I let them have a few drinks here. And now they come along and set up a public bar in the place!"

"You wouldn't mind if it was a young man," one of the priests said in support, "somebody's son."

"Ay, that's what I'm saying," Father Cullen thanked his supporter. "Somebody's son, instead of poor Maurice, who had nobody."

What do you mean, nobody? Father Conroy wondered, what about Tomás?

But before he could get an answer to his questions, they were all being seated around the table and Bat was taking his place at the top beside the Canon. As the plates were passed around, Bat, as host, threw in the conversational ball – the shortage of hares for coursing – while the Canon, who was against blood sports, picked at his rashers and eggs with mild distaste.

You'd think, Father Conroy told himself, that Tomás would have come back from wherever he was for his father's funeral. Of course, he was a blackguard, always was. The first time Father Conroy ever saw him, he was bent over a school desk, a cane poised over him and two stripes reddening across his bare backside. The cane was put away hastily at Father Conroy's entrance (he had just come to the parish as senior curate, and the teacher was embarrassed at being caught so soon in the full flush of authority).

"What's he done?" demanded Father Conroy.

The teacher held up a stub of a pencil and gestured to another boy in the first desk. "He took that little boy's pencil."

"Little boy?" Father Conroy surveyed the owner of the pencil, who began to whimper with embarrassment. "Sure, he's twice as big as what's-his-name there."

"Tomás Connolly," the teacher said. And his cane twitched out of its hiding place behind his back. "He stole that little boy's pencil and took it home with him."

"Why did you steal the pencil, Tomás?" asked Father Conroy.

Still lying across the desk, Tomás turned his face up to the priest; he hadn't cried under the caning, but his lower lip was cut by his teeth.

"Well, Tomás?" The priest lifted him up and pulled up his trousers. "Why did you steal it?"

"I had no pencil."

"That's no reason why you should take his." Father Conroy looked down sternly at the small figure. "It's a sin to steal, don't you know that?"

"I had no pencil."

The teacher started forward. "Mind out, now, you! Mind how you talk to the priest." His cane twitched, as if about to take the law into its own hands. "I'll give it to him, Father."

"No, let him sit down."

"What, Father?" The teacher stared. He was a beefy young fellow, with a shiny face and muscles which bulged under the tight sleeves of his jacket. Father Conroy was seized with that rage which authority aroused in him. He glared at the teacher, who for a moment felt he would be physically assaulted.

"He needs it, Father," he murmured obsequiously, and he came closer, anxious to impart a confidence, to draw the priest into an adult conspiracy of reason. "A bad home he comes from, Father Fitzmaurice will tell you."

"Put away your cane, mister," Father Conroy burst out. And because he could think of no justification for his words, and because he was overmastered by his rage and there was no ground left between him and that shiny face, he turned and slammed his way out of the school.

Well, maybe there were better ways than the cane of compensating for bad homes, but he did not seem to have found one for Tomás. The burly young teacher (whom he had never pulled with afterward) was proved right after all. During the years Father Conroy came to that school and perched himself on the front desk to take the catechism class, it was Tomás's face he always addressed. Most of the time it was closed to him, but once or twice, catching it unawares, he found it had opened a little and was waiting for the thread of a story to unwind, a story from the Old Testament, Samson perhaps, or David and Goliath. At his look, the face would close at once, but the interest remained, betrayed only by an occasional impatient shift of the head on the cupped hand.

At fourteen, the boy was gone, and Father Conroy heard that he was at home on the farm, keeping house for his father. That setup did not last long. Maurice still lived up to his early reputation for leaving a rag on every bush. He racketed around in the company of jockeys, bookies' men, and other itinerants whose passing seemed to stir up likely women from the most unpromising countrysides. His lavish spending (his companions being half his age) soon wasted the farm for which he had waited so long. When he sold out and went to take a job in the stables near Castlemore, Father Conroy tried to get employment for Tomás from the local farmers, but they were wary of him; his troublesome reputation had preceded him from school. After some persuasion, Father Conroy managed to get Canon Fitzmaurice (plain Father Fitzmaurice then, and Father Conroy's parish priest in Slievenalua) to take the boy on, temporarily, as general help in the parochial house.

That parochial house! Father Conroy remembered with delight his formal weekly visits there from the curate's house in which he had set up his own untidy camp. The book-lined sitting room was waxed and shining as a convent parlor. On the hall stand was the cane – the massive, silver-knobbed cane – without which the Canon could not go walking. (It had belonged to the Canon's father, once mayor of Donore, the old cathedral town to which Fitzmaurice was later appointed canon, an appointment for which, even then, he was rumored to be keeping a canon's purple stock folded in mothballs.) Father Conroy's visits always made the Canon uneasy; he came as an interloper, with secret threats of anarchy. Perhaps that was why he had brought Tomás.

The boy was a good worker; even the Canon granted him that. He mowed the lawns, clipped hedges, and did all the chores which the sour-faced old housekeeper (ancilla mea, the Canon called her, my handmaid) gladly passed on to him. After breakfast, the Canon would patter down in his carpet slippers to the kitchen, where ancilla and boy were working away in silence. While he watched his own little boots being polished, he would question the boy about the place-names of the district.

"Kilnahorna! Now, what an interesting name that is!"

"Yes, Father."

"But it doesn't make sense, now, does it? The chapel of the barley!"

"No, Father."

"Isn't your father from that side of the parish? Surely you must have heard him explaining it? There's never been a chapel there (and I've looked up all the old maps), nor is there any tradition of growing barley. I understand the land thereabouts is not suitable for such a crop."

"No, Father."

"One would imagine he'd have told you these things. After all, that's how they're handed down."

The boy continued brushing, since no questions had been asked of him. After a while the Canon went away, shaking his head and sighing about how difficult the young people were getting and how the old ways would soon be lost forever.

"I wonder!" he mused to Father Conroy at one of their stilted Saturday-night interviews. "He's such a strange, quiet boy, I wonder, Father, if he's not thinking of a vocation."

Father Conroy looked up in surprise from the list of dues, then laughed. "Well, I suppose he's as likely to be thinking of that as of your ancilla inside."

"Father!" Fitzmaurice flushed and looked around nervously. "I do wish you wouldn't. It's not very fitting." He watched in some alarm as Father Conroy got up (he always seemed to be anticipating a physical assault), then relaxed as his curate merely stretched himself.

"In spite of what you say, Father," he went on, emboldened again, "I think I might have a word with the boy."

"Oh, do, Father, do! It's probably more than he'll have with either of us."

And picking up his hat, Father Conroy went sauntering off to his own house. Of course, it wasn't fair the way he was always baiting Fitzmaurice. And yet, he would start off every interview determined to be nice to the old man. Fighting with your parish priest, as he told his fellow curates, is like peeing against the wind; most of it comes back on yourself.

Fitzmaurice, in his way, was a kindhearted old fellow; he went to great trouble to build up the right mood in which to put the question. For days he took the boy with him on a course across the soggier reaches of devotional literature, from the C.T.S. pamphlets to the potted lives of the saints, with particular emphasis on his favorites, the boy-martyr Tarcisius and Saint Philomena (who was desanctified later, Father Conroy couldn't help remembering with relish). Only then, after much talk of prison bars and roses from heaven, with some obscure reference to the Sacred Heart, did he feel he had worked up to the emotional heights of his question.

Father Conroy was summoned for the occasion. The boy was in the sitting room, having as a pretext been given the job of cleaning the silver on the sideboard. His answer was flat and decisive, as Father Conroy knew it would be.

"Ah well," said Father Fitzmaurice, sinking back exhausted into his armchair. "You know best, I suppose. But, please God, you'll soon be shown what's in store for you." And he did not see, as Father Conroy did, the boy glance down at the entrée dish in his hand and smile.

Next time he called, Father Conroy found the boy sitting stiffly on a high-backed chair, while the Canon read from one of his first editions, his thin voice piping the most passionate verses with the same unabashed fervor with which he had read from the lives of the saints.

> And I think oft if spirits can steal from the regions of air
> To revisit past scenes of delight, thou wilt visit me there
> And tell me our love is remembered, even in the sky.

"Now, that's a lovely one, isn't it?" He turned to Father Conroy. "We're coming on with our English literature, Father."

"Good. That's the stuff." And when he looked to see the boy's reaction, he detected the slight lowering of one eyelid. At least, so he thought at the time. Later on, he was sure.

He came into the sitting room one day to be greeted with unusual warmth by Fitzmaurice. There was a letter lying on the sofa table.

"Read it, Father," Fitzmaurice said, barely sparing a hand from the book to wave him toward it. "I think you'll be pleased."

Father Conroy picked it up, recognizing the Bishop's handwriting on the envelope. As he paused, afraid to draw out the single sheet of paper, he looked up and found the boy tensely watching him. The few lines were more than he could bear. He had never thought of himself as deserving of promotion, and for a moment it seemed wrong that authority should be given to him, who had for so long fretted against it in the persons of the parish priests whom he had served.

"You have my best wishes, Father," said Father Fitzmaurice. "I'm very glad, naturally, for your sake..." The phrase seemed unfinished, as if the Canon felt it would not be charitable to show all his pleasure.

Father Conroy looked up to say – what had he been going to say? – something submissive or something arrogant? – and noticed that the boy had gone, slipped quietly out of the room.

He never saw Tomás again. That night the boy returned from whatever hiding place he had been in and took with him all the silver from the sideboard, as well as the box containing the Sunday's church door collection. The Canon dithered for a while about calling in the Guards and finally could not bring himself to do so. None of the loot was recovered, nor was the boy ever seen again. Some said he had come to a bad end and that it was the price of him, but Father Conroy was sure he would return someday. A clever young blackguard, he would say, half in admiration. Gave himself a start in life, and sent the bill to us. It was hard for Father Conroy not to admit some satisfaction at the loss of possessions, anyone's possessions, but, most of all, those so cherished by the Canon. In some way, he felt his own promotion had to be paid for and that the price of it would have to be high.

Yes indeed, he thought, but even that was not enough. I never paid the price. I don't deserve my place in the world. But who does? Cullen, O'Hara, the Canon? What have they done? Survived to the age of fifty-odd? Lost teeth or hair, or both, but kept – what? What lives in me, gives me continuity? The Holy Spirit, of course, my body its temple – so the catechism says – but suppose there is nothing there and that I am driven by my need to sleep, to eat – not driven, carried, rather, by the accumulation of what I have done, by the momentum of my habits…

They were looking at him, several faces turned to him to await his reply.

"What?" he asked.

Pheasants, they were talking about, having moved on logically from hares and coursing. What kind of a season had it been in Kilbride?

"Oh, good," he said, "quite good toward the end."

And they looked at him a little uneasily as he let the subject fall so lifelessly from his hands.

The conversation moved on to a controversy in the papers about the teaching of Irish in the schools. One of the young men asked what would happen if infants were left on their own, with no adults to bring them up; what language would they speak? The subject was tossed around with the kind of scholastic playfulness useful on such occasions.

"What would you say, Tom?" asked Father O'Hara.

"What?" Father Conroy found the faces once again turned upon him.

"The Canon here says that if they were left to their own devices, the little beggars would speak Irish, the language of their forebears – though whether it would be Old Irish, Middle Irish, or modern Civil Service Irish, he won't say. Probably all kinds would come bursting out of their consciousness, like Brussels sprouts. What language would you say they'd do their squalling in?"

"It's an interesting question." Father Mahon condescended to be helpful.

"Oh, let Tom speak," said Father O'Hara. "What language would you say, Tom?"

"Classical Greek!" said Father Conroy.

They laughed, mainly with relief – Conroy was back in form. One of the young men leaned forward, daring to act as feed to the great joker.

"On what premises, Father, would you base that conclusion?"

"On the premise that Greek is a perfect language."

"I see," ruminated Father Mahon and went on: "You'd agree, then, Tom, with Wordsworth's contention that,

Not in entire forgetfulness
and not in utter nakedness
But trailing clouds of glory…"

"Nonsense," said Father O'Hara. "Tom knows as well as I do that the kids would behave like my catechism class – in the three seconds my back is turned, they degenerate into a crowd of little cavemen."

"Classical Greek," said Father Conroy obstinately, "that's what they'd speak."

"You're generalizing, Tom, from your own particular case. You, of course, spoke Greek as a babe-in-arms."

"Yes," said Father Conroy, "and look at me now, conversing with my kind in grunts and asterisks." This time their laughter was made a little uneasy by the sharpness of his tone, the way his eyes irritably raked them.

"Grunts and asterisks," sighed Father O'Hara peaceably. "Ah well!" He began to rise to his feet, and at the signal, the others stood up to get ready to go.

"But trailing clouds of glory…" – Father Mahon was not to be done out of his quotation – "…do we come, from God who is our home." And then he looked around, at a loss, when no one found anything to say.

Poor Mahon! they were thinking; he always had a very heavy tread. It was left to Conroy's ingenuity to get him out of his difficulty.

"That's right, Peter," said Conroy. "Heaven lies about us in our infancy! Oh, it's true! Look what lies about us in our old age!"

"Oh, I don't know, Tom," Father O'Hara said; "I think you ought to take a course of liver salts." But he stopped laughing when Father Conroy's eyes fell on him.

"Tom!" Bat Cullen approached, opening his wallet and taking out two pound notes. "You're the only one I haven't got around to."

"No, Bat."

"What's wrong?" Bat stared, fingers arrested.

"I don't want it, thanks. It's… Give it to the relatives, whoever they are."

"But, Tom, there's nobody."

"Then where does that come from?"

"He had a son, I believe."

"Tomás!"

"Is that it? I never knew till just now. Apparently, he used to send the Canon money for the old fellow."

"To the Canon? But where from? Where is he?"

"Hold on, Tom! I can't tell you where he is. The Canon – why don't you go up and ask him?"

The Canon was rising to his feet, dabbing his lips genteely.

"Excuse me" – "Canon" was a word he found hard to say, but he managed to bring it out – "Canon!"

"Yes!" The Canon turned, eyes atwinkle for his interviewer, becoming suddenly guarded as he saw who it was. "Ah, Father Conroy, yes?"

The slight check enabled Father Conroy to hide his impatience. He came up close to the Canon, who backed away a little. Then, looking down at the little man, wrinkling his face in sympathy, he murmured, "How are ye?"

The Canon smiled his gentle saint's smile.

"I'm not so bad," he said gratefully, "not so bad, at all."

"Getting on, like meself."

"Up here I'm good" – the Canon tapped his head – "but the feet!"

"Ah!" Father Conroy looked down in great sympathy at the little handmade boots, wrinkled like a leprechaun's. "The feet!" And he made a note to tell the others sometime, "Poor oul' fellow! Gone in the feet!"

"Too bad about Maurice," he said, hastening to reach the Canon his cane. "I believe you're been hearing from that son of his."

"Yes, Father." The Canon was closing up.

Father Conroy pressed on. "A right blackguard he was."

"I'd be slow to judge him, Father, if I were you."

"Oh!" Father Conroy could no longer restrain his curiosity. "He was very good to the old man, I believe?"

"I don't know how you heard that, Father."

"Oh, I could have heard from him too."

"No, Father."

"Why not?"

"Because he couldn't bring himself to write to you." The Canon looked away, hesitated, then was forced by his own honesty to blurt out, "He seemed to – think something of you, Father!"

"I see." Overwhelmed that anyone should think highly of him, and even more, that the Canon should force himself to say so, Father Conroy wanted only to get away. But Father O'Hara and some others had drawn near, curious to know what the Canon and he had found in common. To divert them, he turned to them and said, "Maurice Connolly, the man we buried this morning, we were just talking about him."

"God rest him," said the Canon.

"Oh, rest him is right." And once more he fell to the temptation to play for a laugh. "Long enough he figured in the stud book of this parish, Canon, when you and I were here."

"It's hardly fitting to recall that now, Father," the Canon said nervously – but he was man enough to say it.

"You're right, Canon. I have to hand it to you, the way you behaved after all the trouble…"

"Don't bring that up, either." The Canon went pink in the face. "I don't want to hear any more about it."

"Ah, sure, I remember now, your silver!" said O'Hara. "So that was the fellow!" And then, when he saw the Canon's anger, he hastened to make the peace. "D'you know what you'll do, Tom?" Cood-humoredly, he laid his big hand on Father Conroy's shoulder. "To pay off this old score once and for all? You make over that famous pony of yours to the Canon!"

"What d'ye mean, make over?" Father Conroy asked sharply.

"Well, sure, whenever you're making your will."

Father Conroy glared. "I'm not going to make my will. Why should I make a will?"

The priests looked at him. They had never seen him lose his temper before; though his tongue could be rough enough, he had always seemed prepared to take as good as he got. Now they did not know what to say to him.

The Canon was tapping his way out of the room. "Good-bye, Canon," someone called, and in a moment there was a flurry of farewells. Father O'Hara was left alone with Father Conroy.

"Sorry, Tom," he said. Father Conroy was silent, looking after the others. "Why don't you give Doc Murtagh a call?"

"Murtagh? What for?"

"Well, you're not looking—"

"Look, Phil, if I had anything wrong with me, I'd go to Cullen."

"But Cullen?" Father O'Hara was a little slow on the uptake.

"Yes, for a ladleful of that stew he makes for his dogs."

"Oh, yes! Well!" He laughed it off dutifully. "Good-bye, Tom."

"Good-bye."

"And… look after yourself."

Outside the door, Father Cullen was waiting uneasily. He pulled out his wallet as Father Conroy approached. "Look, Tom, I wish you'd take this."

"No, I'd rather…"

"Go on, damn it." He pushed the two notes into Father Conroy's breast pocket. "For your trouble," he muttered. "The petrol, the whole morning gone." And as Father Conroy dug angrily for the money, he added, "There's plenty more where it came from."

Father Conroy paused, fingers still in his breast pocket. "Tomás, is it?"

"Yes, the son. He wasn't able to come, but he cabled the needful to the Canon, who passed it on to me."

"Where is he, Bat, tell us?"

"Well, the way it is, Tom…" Bat rubbed doubtfully at the

small bald patch on the top of his head, "I don't rightly know about that."

"You don't know about what?"

"I don't know if I can tell you. The Canon, y'see—"

"Forget it, for Christ's sake, forget it," said Father Conroy and moved quickly away.

Outside the door, he took the pipe out of his pocket, saw it was empty, and blew an angry blast through it. He looked out over the deserted graveyard, squinting into the sun, so that the leaning stones seemed to leap into life, crowded together like people. Christ, what a mess we get into, why don't you stop us, why don't you ever let us know what you want from us? I could have helped him out at the time, but I never even thought of it. I let him steal from the Canon, and now they're bound together like father and son. Is there nothing now I can do for him? Nothing he might want me for? If I only had his address!

Near his car, the little group of evicted drinkers was standing disconsolately by the wall, waiting for him to go.

"Men!" he greeted them as he opened the car door.

They saluted, then drew nearer, attracted by the quality in him which always seemed to draw the unwanted, the dispossessed.

"That was terrible harsh treatment Father Cullen gave ye."

"Ah, no, Father," one of the older men said. "Sure, at the back of it all, he's the best in the world. 'Twas only ye all had him fussed."

"All the same," he protested, tongue in cheek, "it wasn't as if ye were doing any harm."

"That's what I was saying." The man with the bottle had already had a fair sup. "Maurice himself, Father, would give a long spell below to be with us, giving him a good send-off." He emptied his glass, shook it out, and began to pour. "Ye'll have a small sup, Father?"

"I won't, thanks; it doesn't agree with me."

"Ah, come on, Father."

"But I'll tell ye what!" He fumbled out the empty pipe.

"If any of ye have an oul' fill, 'twould be most welcome."

"Sure, Lord, Father, if that's all ye want." The older man came forward, unbuttoning his tobacco pouch. "Ye must be a happy poor man."

"Indeed, yes," said Father Conroy as he filled the pipe.

"What more could I want?"

Chapter 6

And Lancelot at the ring rides well! Now, who the hell was Lancelot, he wondered, as he swatted away the phrase and knew it was circling out there beyond his reach, in mischievous orbit. Phrases sometimes hung around for days, tormenting him, then vanished as suddenly as they had come. Why hadn't he paid attention at school, learned the whole verse, as people like Mahon always did? One could kill a quotation stone dead, if one knew the line before and the line after!

Come on, Lancelot, he told himself, ride it well. He pulled his hat down over his eyes, crouched over the wheel of the Volks, and raked at the accelerator. He was back now within the parish boundary, riding the home range, big boss Conroy, the fastest gun in the outfit!

One of his less trusty hands was on the road before him, the postman wavering homeward on his daily round. At the sound of the car, the fellow pedaled over to the left, jumped off, and pulled his bicycle in toward the ditch in mock alarm. He waved, and Father Conroy drew up reluctantly.

"Lord save us, Father, that was a fair clip you were going!"

"Something for me, Tim?" He wasn't in the mood to be bantered. The fellow was settling himself for a long talk, peering into the car like a camel, to try to see where Father Conroy might have been. A camel's thirst he had too, as Father Conroy well knew.

"I left it up at the house, Father. One of them brown ones. Ah, sure, it didn't look very interesting – an oul' bill, I'd say." He waited until Father Conroy impatiently shoved the gear into first, then added, "Your uncle James was there."

"James?"

"He went off again, Father. Couldn't wait. Sure, he's like yourself, always on the go."

"You're sure he went away?"

"Oh yes, Father." And as the car moved off, he called, "He'll be back, though, you may be sure."

Father Conroy drove the car around by the side of the house and right into the yard, then shut the yard gate. The back door was on the latch; he locked it, in case James returned, and stood a moment, considering his own impregnability. Should he draw the curtains on the front windows? Maybe not. James would notice and, anyway, had probably seen all he wanted to see, with hands cupped against the glass.

In the kitchen, he sat down and rested his elbows on the table. There were still the day's visits to make; there was dinner to get, but here he was now, under siege, waiting for the enemy to make the first move. By God, he thought, leaning forward on the table and burying his head in his hands, I'm not in form for this. To tell the truth, I'm bloody well beat.

He thought of his bed upstairs, tempted to make the long journey up to it, to crawl into its rumpled warmth. But no, he had never yet lain down by day, not even for a cold or a bout of flu, and he wasn't going to run the risk of being surprised by James, wasting time on the flat of his back.

And Lancelot at the ring rides well! Bugger you, Lancelot! He sank his head defiantly down, spreading out his arms to cradle it. A few minutes' shut-eye and he'd be right! He felt his eyelids grow heavy and was just about to resign himself to sleep when he noticed the tip of a pound note protruding from his breast pocket. He shoved it back quickly, but the damage was done. He knew he could not sleep with that in there, waiting to be dealt with. Damn it, would he never get any peace?

There had been a key, once, for the cupboard door, but it had developed a will of its own, a mean way of evading him, of turning up in places where he was sure he had never left it. He had given up using it long ago and now wedged the door shut with a piece of folded cardboard.

Now even the wedge worked against him. It held the door like a claw, so that he had to brace himself against it and pull. The darkness within made him pause, just a second, before plunging his hand in. He groped quickly for the jar, the half-empty one, and when his hand touched one of the others, it blundered on, pretending it hadn't noticed. Suddenly conscious of the uncurtained window behind him, he stuffed the two notes in without taking the jar into the light. He pushed the door to, feeling the claw within take hold of it and hold it fast. His heart was beating a little more quickly as he stood back, dusting his hands together. He was slow to turn around to the window, though there was no one looking in and nothing there, only the trees and fields of his parish.

Back in the kitchen, he sank down at the table and tried to settle again into drowsiness. How much was in there? Not a great deal, no, there couldn't be. He had taken out most of it – one hundred pounds, or was it one hundred and fifty (he couldn't remember)

– the time Owen died, but Owen's widow, Marie, wouldn't take it. (No one could blame her, of course, for not wanting to have any more to do with the Conroys.) What had he done with that money? Had he put it back? It would be impossible ever to make a will unless he knew. Yes, if he ever did want to make a will, he would have to take the money out and count it, every penny of it, draw up some kind of balance sheet, calculate what was due and what was spent. That would be a major operation, a whole day gone, at least. And would it be worthwhile, for God's sake, for the little that was in it?

Anyway, why the hell should he make a will? To please James, who had something in mind for Jimmy? No thanks, Jimmy was well able to fend for himself. Who else was there? Tomás? Yes, Tomás was one man he might have left it to. Why hadn't he given it to Tomás, instead of the Canon's silver? Why had he let it lie there, buried at the bottom of his portmanteau? If he had only given it then, Tomás would be cabling to him now rather than to the Canon, writing letters, perhaps even coming home to him on a visit.

He glanced around the kitchen, startled at the thought of anyone coming to stay with him. Why, he demanded, why didn't I think of that? Even if I didn't give it to Tomás, why didn't I think of the others who needed it, of Owen? Oh, Christ, Owen!

But I mustn't bring all that up, not now. The money wasn't mine; it just came to me. I didn't ask for it, or even want it. It chose me, and because I didn't know what to do with it, I put it out of my mind and, like a potato left in the dark corner of a shed, it couldn't be stopped from sprouting.

Ara, nonsense! He shifted impatiently. She hadn't meant it to sprout. She hadn't meant me to keep it as a seed. She meant me to spend it as any priest, any man would spend it – a flutter on the horses, poker in a Lisdoonvarna hotel, or perhaps as she had suggested, just a new suit of clothes. She meant it to come out of the blue, a Godsend, to be flogged quickly and forgotten. That was the kind she was. For all her talk, she gave no more thought to that money than to whatever it was that brought us together.

His first visit to her house seemed more than casual; it was as if he were looking for her, as if he knew that she would be there. He was in London, waiting for a curacy to fall vacant back home, a young priest, raw as they come. Most of the time he spent in the streets around Victoria, sounding the tall, gloomy houses for echoes of Catholicism. One house he had tried several times. Although there was never a move of the yellowed curtains and no sign of life through the area railings, he suspected that someone within was aware of him. He was intrigued too by the barrow women in the street, the way they paused in their trading whenever he knocked at the front door, breviary in hand. The name of the place, the Glencullen Guesthouse, seemed to be a clue; it could have been Scotch, of course, aggressively Presbyterian, but that was a risk he was prepared to take.

One evening after dark he descended the area steps and knocked on the side door below. It was opened by a stout, red-cheeked girl of about seventeen, wearing an apron too small for her and bedroom slippers. When he asked, "Are ye Catholics here?" she shook her becurlered head but seemed unable to close the door on him. "Are ye Irish?" he demanded, and she shook her head again, then began to edge back, leaving the door still open.

"Who is it, Mary?" a voice called within, a strong, country voice, as Irish (as he told her later) as spuds and buttermilk.

The girl looked up at him, gave him a timid smile, then turned and fled. He moved well into the doorway and listened to the whispering at the end of the passage. The woman's voice was grumbling, "Oh, indeed you did, you gom!" Then she came into the passageway, stalking toward him, a big woman of about sixty, dressed in black, with a face that would put the fear of God in you. "Well?" she said, putting one hand on the door.

No "Father," he noticed, and said, mildly enough, "Don't blame the girl, ma'am. I had my foot in the door."

"Well, ye may take it out now, if ye please." And she began to push the door to.

He looked down at his threatened foot, as if it was an object for which he was only very remotely responsible. "It's me best pair of shoes, ma'am. Don't destroy them on me."

"Well, then!" she exclaimed, and she held the door a moment, at a loss. "Faith!" she sniffed. "If them are yer best!"

"I have a pair near as good, but they catch me at the heel. This way of life's a divil on them."

She was still held by him, but only barely. "What a time to come, anyway! Battering at people's doors that have no time for ye, or interest, ayther."

"It's a bad time for me, too. I'm due back for my tea this hour or more."

"Hmm!" She surveyed the foot that held them so uneasily poised. "Couldn't ye call back, then, some other time?"

"I could, I suppose, but I mightn't get this far."

"No, ye're dead right there." The door began to move in again, but he had seen a flicker in her eyes. Could it be amusement? He shifted his foot farther in. By God, he thought admiringly, she's a tough one, all right.

"What is it ye want, anyway?" she demanded. "Money, I suppose?"

"Well, no. Though I wouldn't refuse my rightful dues. I'd say it's a good while since they were paid out of this house."

"Not since I got sense."

"I'd say you never went short of that."

"No, mind you, I didn't," she said slowly, judiciously, and he realized he had one weapon at least, flattery. "But isn't it strange how I swallowed all yer talk, like the rest of them back home – novenas, and rosaries, and mysteries, and the divil knows what."

"I suppose, ma'am, you had no choice."

"Nor I hadn't." She looked at him at last with real interest. "You're right there, faith."

There was a silence. Father Conroy looked down at his foot, wondering whether it was safe to withdraw it. She considered the buttons of his waistcoat, as if counting how many were missing. "Well," she said, turning away with a hitch of her apron, "I'm going in, anyway, to finish me tea."

It was hardly an invitation, but neither was it a dismissal. He brought his other foot smartly in, and when she did not turn around, he closed the door and followed her down the stone passageway. He passed a half-open door, through which came kitchen smells. As he paused, wondering who was giggling within, she called out, "Come on!" from away in front. So on he went.

The passage led to a small room in which a gas fire burned.

As he followed her in, she cried, "Watch out! The mat!" He

halted in midstride, but was too late to avoid stepping on the mat. There was a loud pop, and the gas fire went out. She looked at him, shaking her head in contempt. "You would!" she said, then leaning past him, shouted down the passageway, "Mary! It's out again!"

Warned by the pop of the fire, Mary was already on her way with a box of matches. Stifling a giggle, she got down on her knees and lit the gas, while the woman stood over her, grumbling, "As clumsy as the rest of ye! I declare to God, 'tis a herd of heavy bullocks I do have, the way they do be trampling on that gas!"

Father Conroy looked at the girl, wanting some opening to talk to her, but she avoided his gaze as she rose and hurried out of the room.

"Mary?" he asked. "Is she...?"

"No," the woman snapped. "There's nobody Irish in this house, and any there is, they want to forget it." She lowered herself into the battered armchair, in front of a tray with a pot of tea and a plate of toast and jam.

"I see!" He looked around, at the old family photographs on the sideboard, at the portrait of Willy Redmond on the wall. "Easier said than done, I suppose."

She sucked impatiently at her tea and ignored him.

He had nowhere to sit. The other armchair contained a dog, one of those hairless terriers which can be mistaken for a cushion. "May I sit down?" he asked.

The woman uttered a grunt, at which the dog slithered sullenly to the floor. It lay on its belly under the table and watched him between its paws.

She bit into her toast. "Tsk, tsk," she said, glaring at him. "Hard as a rock! And the tea stone cold!" She swept up the tray and went out. He could hear her calling for Mary and giving orders for more tea and toast.

A dish of fruit stood on the sideboard, oranges and apples topped by a banana of unusual size – all artificial, he thought. Defying the dog's growls, he reached over and pinched one of the apples, to his surprise finding it was real. The door swung open before he could pull his hand away. "Ha!" She put her hands on her hips and looked at him, caught in that attitude of guilt. "Go on, so. Put it in your pocket. If you want it, take it."

"Thanks," he said, grinning in an attempt to make the best of the situation.

"Now!" she said, leaning forward to confront him. "Tell me why I should pay ye yer money!"

But, of course, she never paid him, on that or any subsequent visit. The phrase became a catchword; she used it whenever he called, which was not often – he had too much to do to have time for unpromising souls like hers. Only sometimes, weary of the reverent, evasive welcomes of the immigrant Irish, he made his way to her, to seek her minimal hospitality. It was a change from the fantasy life into which the immigrants would have drawn him, a life exemplified by the way the old parish priest drowsed over the Irish newspapers on Sunday afternoons, recalling his last holiday in Ireland, planning his next, living out his span in a cocoon of Irishness. There was no cocoon about her. And yet, the Glencullen was a refuge, more of a home to him than Rosnagree had been since his father died.

He noticed a few things about the house, though, sometimes a delay at the door, the whisk of a petticoat through the banisters, the giggling in the kitchen as he passed, but he was too innocent to draw any conclusions. Only when the other curate looked at him, with the affronted air which the English seemed always to turn on him, and said, "Good God, Father, you don't go *there!*" did he suddenly flush as at a revelation. And, though he muttered defiantly, "Why wouldn't I, man? Isn't she from the County Limerick?" he raged inwardly at the fact that she hadn't let him know, had let him walk into a rebuke from a supercilious Englishman.

Yet, he went to see her again a few times. It was not prudent, but he was young and impatient of the greatest of the clerical virtues. Welcomed grudgingly as ever, he sat in her room, drinking tea and carrying on the pattern of exchanges which followed, "Why should I pay ye yer money?" Although they could laugh, be familiar, he was never completely at ease there now, being too conscious of creakings above the ceiling, the distant sounds of baths emptying, lavatories flushing, of footsteps, voices on the stairs. He was always afraid of finding the suspicions of the prudent ones well founded.

When he was called back to a parish in Ireland, he never thought of going to tell her; he had too many official farewells to make, to his youth club, his footballers, his sodality members. He must have been some months in the new parish when he got the letter; it was unsigned, but he knew it could only be from her. "This is for yourself to spend. I know you'll get the best out of it, but, first, buy yourself a decent suit and not be going around like you had no friends."

Enclosed was fifty pounds in notes. It was the beginning of his hoard, carried in his portmanteau from parish to parish, from house to house and at last pushed into the back of the cupboard at Kilbride, where it continued to grow in the darkness.

Drowsily, he thought of the cupboard. What would it be like in there, among the jars, with the door wedged shut on him? He was in darkness, moving slowly forward, reaching out blindly with his hands. Something moved away from him, slithering, with an occasional sharp knock on stone. Why was he following it? He didn't know; he was trembling with fear, yet he had to press on, reaching out his hands toward it. For a moment, something white glinted just above his head, like a great eye rolling. He tried to scream, but the sound lodged in his throat.

Something warm, hairy, brushed against his hands. It moved swiftly, floating away from him, and now he could see that it was a horse's head silhouetted against the slit window in the stable in Rosnagree. His arm was around it, and he was braced against it, trying to force on the bridle. He felt his face pressed against the warm, sweaty skin and with rising excitement knew that he was beginning to master it. Slowly he forced its head back and felt the bit forcing its lips apart. It tugged away from him, trying to fling its head free, but he crouched down exultantly and threw all his weight against it. The sweat ran into his eyes and down his face as he felt it come slowly toward him. His feet dragged on the floor, but he knew it was coming. Then suddenly, three sharp thuds rang out. Startled, he let go his grip. Again they rang out, hollow now like hooves lashing against the wood of the stall. He sank down into the darkness.

The knocking was all about him, dazing him. He lifted his head a little and stared, unmoving, not sure where he was, why he was slouched at the table in his own kitchen. When the noise suddenly stopped, he leaped to his feet and rushed toward the hall. The knocking started again. He stood staring at the hall door, his hand on the wall to support himself. His left leg seemed to have lost all feeling.

The knocking redoubled in fury. He started forward, about to drag the door open and confront his caller. Then he was held by the thought that it could only be James. Stepping aside into the study, he peered out into the drive. Yes, James's car was standing there. He drew back, feeling rage well up within him. What could James want – only to snoop about, pass cutting remarks, offer useless advice. No, he was damned if he'd let James in.

He tiptoed through the hall, glaring at the door as if to defy the letterbox to open and expose him in flight. In the kitchen, he stood and listened to the knocking, wiping his forehead, which he found was damp with sweat. Christ, what a dream that had been! Must have been the rashers at the breakfast – probably sliced off a ham intended for Bat Cullen's dogs. His leg was still asleep. Well, never mind, a good walk would send the blood flowing back into it. A pity he hadn't asked Bat for some liniment to rub it with.

The knocking ended with a furious rat-tat-tat, and the footsteps shuffled quickly down the steps. That was James's shuffle, right enough; he was safe for another while. Then, in panic, he thought of the yard gate. He had shut it, all right, but had he locked it? If James pushed it open, he would see the car in the yard and know that the badger was holed up within.

Father Conroy slid back the bolt on the kitchen door, half-ran, half-tiptoed across the yard, and reached the gate as footsteps scrunched the gravel on the far side. Fumbling, he slipped the bolt across, then leaned against the gate in relief, as the latch lifted and rattled unavailingly up and down. That fixed ye! he thought, as he peered through a crack at a rim of black homburg turning below him. He noticed another crack in the door, lower down, just about the level of the hat, and realized that James's eye would, in a moment, be at it, peering in. Immediately he dropped to knee height, a painful stance, which, however, he held resolutely while he watched the lower crack for the white of an eye. This is how we've always been, he told himself, James and I, trying to catch each other out, but careful always to look through different cracks. Church and State, he chortled. Christ, I must remember to tell that to O'Hara. There was silence at the far side of the gate. James was still there, listening carefully; Father Conroy could hear the sound of breathing, becoming gradually more stertorous. Was James, too, doubled up, watching the crack for his eye? Damn it, he was getting cramp; he would have to move. Slowly, still painfully crouched to knee height, he edged away from the gate and along the wall of the yard. Only when he was out of James's line of vision did he straighten up with a groan of relief. And then he saw that young Gabriel, his Mass-server, had been watching him all the time from the garden path.

They stared at each other in silence. Father Conroy was the first to recover himself. He beckoned angrily. God Almighty, he muttered, have I no privacy?

The boy came forward warily. He gave a squeak as Father Conroy caught him by the shoulder and pushed him headlong into the kitchen. "Now! What ails ye now?"

"Granda!" was all the boy could get out, in his fright.

"Oh no," he groaned, "not again?"

"Yes, Father. He's took bad."

He would! thought Father Conroy, as he went raging up to his oratory to get the sacred oils. Trust oul' Kavanagh! He could imagine James's triumph when he appeared, flushed out of his den. Well, a sick call was a sick call. He would just have to own up, let James have his gloat.

At the back door he paused. The boy was running back the way he had come, scrambling over the wall at the foot of the garden, taking the shortcut through the churchyard. Father Conroy glanced toward the yard gate, then, hunching himself up in his coat, he hurried down the garden, making a detour to keep out of line with the crack in the gate. When he reached the shelter of the lilac tree, he scrambled over the wall. A chuckle broke from him as he dropped among the tombstones – a schoolboy's crow of delight at having bested the master.

The candle was lighted at the bedside. All was in order – the woman of the house had had several false alarms already. Old Kavanagh lay breathing shallowly. His eyes faltered open, and he smiled.

"I've seen you a lot worse," growled Father Conroy.

He had to stoop to hear the reply, above the murmur of the rosary from the next room: "Faith, I'm not done yet."

"You're not, indeed. With the help of God."

It was a neglected sacrament, he thought, as he touched eyes and ears and nose and mouth with the oil. People took it lying down; that was how they were taught to take it, as the last round-up, a pious suspiration to help them give up the ghost, stretch out nice and easy like so many fish fillets. He had always thought it was a sacrament for the living, that every sacrament was for the living, to make them stand up and get on with it. Living was getting on with it. Once you stopped getting on with it, you were no use to God or man.

The rosary was over in the kitchen. The family was standing up, one by one. Peter dusted the knees of his trousers. They weren't overcome; there was no crying; they knew the old fellow was doing his best and that, if his time had come, it had come.

He sat down with them for a cup of tea, casting a regretful glance at the blank face of the television set. The time passed pleasantly in talk, while Mrs. Kavanagh looked occasionally into the bedroom to keep an eye on the old man.

"I'd miss your father," Father Conroy said to Peter. "Why in God's name did you never learn all those songs off of him?"

"I don't know, Father. I never seemed to have the time."

"And what time had he, working till dark for the farmers?"

"Ah, 'twas different then, Father. I gave a few year in England at the building, and there was no time there – there was good money to be made. And even now, working on the roads, there's no time; when I come home, I have to help to put the kids to bed and do their sums for them. They had more time in the old days, more room in their minds. My father, now, could tell you the history of all the big families around. He could tell you about the Conroys, even, and they're two parishes distant from us."

"The great Conroys!" said Father Conroy heavily.

"That's right, Father. There was a time when a Conroy of Rosnagree could walk three mile down the bank of the Glendine river and he never to leave his own land."

"Happy days!" said Father Conroy.

"Yes, Father," Peter said, uncertain of Father Conroy's mood, and he blundered on to fill the silence, "Did he ever tell you how it got its name, Rosnagree?"

"The grove of the horses. I know all about it."

There was silence. Even the indefatigable Peter could see that the subject had been thoroughly dismissed. He said no more until Father Conroy rose to go. "Your uncle James passed us on the road."

"Too bad he missed me."

"Oh, he'll be here again next week. There's a meeting called of the party committee. We told him we wanted him here."

"He's not used to that kind of invitation."

"We're sick and tired of him, Father, and that's the truth. We're going to put him on the spot over the contract for the roads."

"Here?"

"Here, in this very room."

Father Conroy looked around the little room, with the turf fire in the grate, the red mantelpiece crowded with photographs and china dogs. Was this to be James's Waterloo? It seemed an unlikely place for the old warrior's career to end, in the comfortable glow of the Sacred Heart lamp.

Peter was looking at him, waiting for him to say something, a word of support. There was only one thing to say, give him the boot! Too long have you put up with him! And yet, thinking of that desperate knocking at his own front door, the words stuck in his throat.

"Father!" the woman called, gesturing into the bedroom. He hurried to the doorway. The old man was sleeping, his breast rising and falling gently, his face at ease.

"Put out that candle," he told her. "He'll be needing it again."

"God bless you, Father, I know he will."

Up the road homeward, he leaned tiredly toward thoughts of bed, the bliss of sleep. It seemed a long time before he reached the gate. He turned into the deeper darkness of the drive with what seemed a slow, wheeling, laborious movement. Suddenly light exploded in his face; it filled him, stretched him upward and outward, so that his first thought was a panicky, Christ, I'm dead! Then a car door slammed somewhere ahead.

"Ah, Father!" James's outline approached. "Isn't this a piece of luck? I thought I'd drop in and I passing. And here you are."

Blast you, I might have known you'd stay on, sit it out. And the shock you gave me! My legs are like water. However, he kept his voice steady and said, "I hope I didn't keep you waiting?"

"Not at all, Father; you couldn't have timed it better."

"Well!" he said. Well, what? What were they to talk about? James was waiting to be invited in. Well, make him work for the invitation! "I don't often have this pleasure, James."

"To tell you the truth, I only dropped in to give you a message from Mikie. He wants the pony."

"What pony?"

"Ah, now, Father, sure you discussed it with him. You wanted a trade-in, plus a little cash in hand."

"From you, is it?" Of course, it was! Another bribe for the beloved Jimmy. "Well, he must have taken me up wrong."

"I see. So there's no deal!"

"No, James, no deal." Not with you.

Well, that was that. There was no need for the invitation, after all. But James showed no sign of leaving. "I see you're doing great work in the garden," he said.

"You must have been here early, so."

"No, I just saw by the headlights and I coming in that you must have been cutting down some bushes."

"Ah, you mean the pyorrhea by the gate?"

"Yes, that's gone."

"And the erysipelas! Did you notice the pruritis gone too?"

"Ah, sure, I wouldn't know the official names. I'd know what they look like, though I'm no gardener." He looked suspiciously at Father Conroy's deadpan face. "Not like your father. He was a great gardener. He'd know what you were talking about."

Father Conroy shifted uneasily. He hated any reference to his father – his mother had made them so often, self-dramatizing her loss.

"He had roses," went on James, "and the big orchard at the back. And d'you remember the sundial he brought home from an auction somewhere? He was so proud of that! 'Twas set up in the middle of the garden with a sweep of gravel all around it, like they had in the big houses. But sure, he wasn't like a Conroy at all!"

"What d'you mean?"

"I mean" – the cunning little eyes searched Father Conroy's face for some way of softening the words, while still giving offense – "he wasn't grubbing after things like the rest of us. He thought he was above that."

"He was above it," Father Conroy burst out. "He was the only one of us who knew how to live."

"Oh, of course. That's what I'm saying." And he went on, as if aggrieved at being misunderstood, "Sure, wasn't he my own brother? And he certainly looked after Rosnagree well."

"Better than it was ever looked after, before or since. Are you going to come in?"

As they climbed the steps – the old man eagerly shuffling ahead – the phrase came buzzing in on a new orbit – And Lancelot at the ring rides well. Lancelot, my father.

Chapter 7

James seemed ill at ease. He had been set in the big armchair, hatless, like an egg in its cup, waiting to be topped. Prowling around him, Father Conroy turned suddenly to catch him out, then passed on, baffled by the anxious, shortsighted stare with which his uncle looked through him. What did the old fellow really want? The will – was he still snooping after it? Still trying to feather Jimmy's nest?

It took Father Conroy a while to realize that James was peering at the testimonial on the far wall, trying to read the curlicued inscription from the St. John Bosco Youth Club, Victoria: "To our dear Friend, Father Tom Conroy, we present this Address, as a Token of our Appreciation and Regard, on the Occasion of his Return to his beloved Ireland. Sensible of the Loss, etc."

"That?" Father Conroy waved toward it. "Just a lot of oul' plamás from some young people I knew one time."

"Oh?" James still peered anxiously.

"It proves that I was appreciated, anyway, if only in England."

"Oh, England?" James sat back, relaxed. What England thought didn't matter; local praise was the only kind he was jealous of. "That was a long time ago, Father."

"Some of it still holds good, maybe."

James said nothing. He had never been known to try his hand

at a compliment; his talent lay in cutting people down to size. "I was just going to tell you about Jimmy," he began.

"Oh, yes, so Jimmy's getting hitched!"

Only the swift darting of the eyes betrayed James's surprise.

They seemed to dart around to cover the back of his head, and finding their way blocked, to return to flash a warning, an intimation that there might be someone behind him, a nonparty man, a non-Conroy, some kind of interloper. Let's keep talking, the eyes said, just keep talking. "What d'you think of it yourself, Father?" he whispered.

"Oh, well" – Father Conroy took a chance on the fact that whatever Jimmy did, he would fall on his feet – "I'm pleased, naturally."

James thought the remark faint praise. "A decent, respectable family!" he said indignantly. "With a damn good business house there on the Square. The father took the other side in the old days, but sure, these things can't be helped. The young people nowadays couldn't care less which side their parents were on."

Their name? Father Conroy, knowing his bluff was about to be called, tried to guess their name. Why the hell hadn't Kate told him? She was as bad as the Donovans now, just as close.

"I'm surprised Kate told you," James went on. "Jimmy had them sworn to secrecy till it was all fixed up. I was let in on it myself only because Jimmy wanted me to have a word with the girl's father, which I'm glad to say was well worthwhile."

"I'm sure."

"I had to make over a tidy bit of business to Jimmy, the auctioneering end of things. Ah, well, 'twas time for me." He smiled coyly, put his hands together, then gave that warning dart of the eyes. "It should fit in well with the farm-machinery side of theirs. If Jimmy plays his cards right."

Ah, yes, now Father Conroy had it. The Burkes of Castlemore, the hotel and hardware place on the Square! It was a step up for a Donovan from the back of the mountain. Father Conroy smiled and murmured, "Don't worry! Jimmy never misses a trick."

"I take it, Father, you'll be performing the ceremony?"

"If I'm asked."

"Oh, you will be, Father, don't worry about that. Now, the question is, who can we have to assist? The Burkes, of course, will be asking the Canon – he'd be a first cousin of the girl's father."

"Then he can assist."

"Yes, but I dare say we could do with someone else as well, from our side." And James fitted his hands together and admired the blunt steeple his fingers made. Dare you, thought Father Conroy. Too bloody much you dare say! What you mean is that Father Conroy plus A.N. Other equals the Canon. "Don't take me for granted," he burst out.

The phrase had a familiar shape, as if he had made it himself a long time ago. Don't take me for granted! Yes, it fitted into its place, all right, the same phrase, with the same man, and it had the same ring, though everything else was different. James sat up straight then, a stumpy block of a man filling a kitchen chair. He had left off his Sam Browne belt, but he still wore the trench coat and leggings as proof of that national record, which began when he was taken by the Tans from his job in the creamery store and carried as a hostage on their raids through the countryside. (It was only after his escape that his military genius emerged. Although no one but Father Conroy seemed to wonder whether he had ever been within the sights of a British rifle, his feints and night maneuvers had terrified the Tans with visions of an unsleeping enemy on the prowl. Fabius Cunctator, Father Conroy had called him, with grudging admiration. But Fabius Cunctator had been caught out by Hannibal. No one had ever caught out Uncle James.)

One short, shining leg swung carelessly over the other, he sat, very sure of himself, of his uniform, of the new role he had won in public affairs, even of his place as head of the Conroy clan. "Don't take me for granted," Father Conroy had told him, across the still-to-be-furnished room. Just back from England, the young priest had been too late for the Black and Tan War, but just in time for a small, local conflict which was more bitterly personal and on which, as yet, he had not taken the side expected of him.

"You don't understand, Father." James smiled forbearingly. "How could you, and you away so long? It's not a question of wages. That might have been fixed easily enough – twenty-five shillings, thirty shillings a week, whatever it might be. No, what they're demanding from us now is our right to the soil. Imagine that! Here we are, giving them every thing – a free cottage, milk, potatoes, as much turf as they can cut – all for the bit of work they do for us. And now they come and grudge us our right to hold our own land."

"What land? I've no land. You've no land."

"Ah, for God's sake, Father, you know well what I mean. The right of the Irish farmer to his own land. We may not have any land, you or I, but 'tis in us, we were born to it."

"'Ireland summons her children to her flag and strikes for her freedom.' By God, strikes is right. The poor divils have their wages cut by ten bob a week as soon as ye get yer freedom."

Uncle James took out his pipe and began to fill it, slowly, in that public way which he was to bring to a fine art in years to come. He did not speak until it was in his mouth, ready to be ceremonially lighted.

"You heard, by the way, what happened in your mother's place the evening before last?" he said, as he swept the match aflame.

"I heard one version, anyway."

"The way those heroes of yours surrounded your mother's servant girl..."

"Ah now, James, Madge McGarr is a hardy old stager. She could take care of herself before they were ever heard of."

"They surrounded her, anyway, in your own yard in Rosnagree, knocked her down and brutally..."

"They asked her to join them, and when she told them to take themselves off to hell, her bucket of milk got spilled."

"They had her on the ground, and only for your brother Frank, God alone knows what they'd have done to her."

"I heard she chased them out of the yard and beat them over the heads with the bucket."

"To assault a helpless female and bear her to the ground! Even the Tans themselves never did a thing like that."

"I'd say, James, it was the first time Madge ever put bad thoughts into any man's mind."

"Father!" The pipe came out of his mouth and stared with him at the priest. "Father, I don't think your spell in England did you any good."

Father Conroy got to his feet. "Nice of you to call, James."

Uncle James sat there, refusing to move. "I'm not at all satisfied, Father, that you know your duty in this matter."

"And what's that?"

"To name the blackguards responsible, to point them out from the altar on Sunday. Your brother Frank will give you all the names you want, the ones from your parish here. It's a bad business, and it's looking worse – they say the red flag was raised in the town of Donore. 'Tis up to us now, the responsible people, to bring the country back under law and order."

"How would you define that, Uncle James?"

"What?"

"Law and order?"

James's pipe suddenly failed him. He looked at it a moment, then stuffed it into his pocket. "God damn it, I'll take this matter further."

"Where to?" Father Conroy smiled. "My mother?"

"Father, don't play-act with me, I'm warning you. I'll take it to your parish priest. I'll take it to the Bishop, if all goes to all."

"I thought he had you excommunicated for undermining British law and order."

"That was a misunderstanding, as you well know."

"Ah, yes, we're all to climb on the bandwagon now."

James got slowly to his feet. He patted the pipe in his pocket, as if to tell it, listen to that for talk!

"He'll be interested to hear that remark, Father."

"It'll be a change for the old man to know what his clergy is thinking."

"We'll see, Father, we'll see." And James stumped out and down the path to where his chauffeur was waiting with the official car.

"Don't take me for granted," he had told James. But it was he himself who had taken everything for granted, not least the common humanity of his own flesh and blood. He had not expected to find the beast in the name of Conroy.

He was hearing confessions in the chapel a few nights after Madge's bucket of milk had been spilled. Footsteps came hurrying up the aisle, and someone knocked on the door of the confessional. "Father!"

He closed the door on the penitent and drew back the curtain. A young man was in the aisle leaning breathlessly against the door, cap pulled down over his eyes. When Father Conroy pointed angrily toward the cap, he pulled it off quickly, revealing an unruly mop of red hair.

"You're wantin' in Glendine, Father," he gasped, "as soon as you can."

Father Conroy came out of the box, folded his stole, and turned to hang it on the hook. "Who are you?"

The young man was moving off a few impatient steps. "Ah, you wouldn't know me. I'm stopping with the uncle. I'm from away over beyond." And he gestured toward the east.

Father Conroy nodded. He was used to young men on the run, staying with their uncles. "Where are we going? 'Who is it?"

"Hassett, Father, Denny Hassett, the last house up the glen." Hassett was said to be one of the leaders of the laborers on strike. No doubt, he figured high in James's list of those involved in the Madge incident. "I'll get my bike."

"'Tis outside, Father. I sent a young lad up to your house for it."

Such hustling made Father Conroy suspicious. Was it a trap? Priests were being dragged into things now, the strike, the civil war down south. Suppose they wanted him as a hostage?

The bicycle was at the gate, a boy waiting in the dark to push it into his hands. The young man was already mounted and moving on ahead. Although Father Conroy was fit and well used to cycling, it was all he could do to catch up as the road wound upward. "What happened?" he called.

"I was abroad in the field, when I seen the trap going up to the house and the men in her. I made no delay, Father. I ran straight down to Fogarty's below on the road and got on the bike. Oh, please God, we'll be in time."

They were in the long glen, standing on the pedals to urge themselves faster up the steep road. It seemed to Father Conroy that he was not moving forward at all. Between one sharp bend and the next, the walls of the glen shut out the starlight on either side.

The road grew steeper, and they had to dismount. Half-walking, half-running, they pushed their bicycles before them, slipping and slithering in the ruts of the road. Father Conroy had to stop to ease a stitch in his side.

"Are ye right, Father?" the young man called.

"Wait," he shouted, "wait a moment."

It was very still – the only sound the rushing of a stream by the roadside. He felt closed in by the darkness, stifled by the lack of air between the walls of the glen. His collar choked him. He pulled it off and stuffed it into his pocket, then remounted and pressed himself forward up the hill.

A light appeared in the distance and disappeared again. The young man stopped. "Father, look beyond!"

The sound of the tumbling water seemed to grow louder.

The sky had lightened above the head of the glen – the moon was rising. He could see something moving on the gray hillside, down along the line of the walls.

"They're coming, Father."

"Who are they?" he whispered.

The young man raised his hand. A hoof slipped on a stone. A burst of a song was suddenly hushed. They could hear a faint murmur of voices.

"They have a share of drink taken," the young man said.

They pulled their bicycles into the side of the road, under the shadow of a thorn tree. A dark shape lurched up a moment against the skyline, then slipped out of sight. The sound of hooves drew nearer, the hum of rubber-tired wheels moving fast, the creak of swaying springs. Father Conroy made a move to go out into the middle of the road, but the young man put a hand on his arm to restrain him. He watched the faint gray of roadway between the walls ahead. In a moment, a deep, solid blackness filled it, over-topping it, so that he drew back, wanting only to hide from it.

It passed him by. The hoofbeats, the hum of wheels, the creak-ing – these were its only sounds. It might have been empty, a black, hollow mass swaying past him. As it disappeared into the darkness below, it struck a spark from the road. A man's voice murmured, and there was a low laugh. Then the sound of hooves died away, and in the silence he heard again the rushing of the stream.

"D'ye think they saw us, Father?"

He shook his head, relieved to think of it as "they." No, they could hardly have seen him under the thorn tree, but he wished now that they had. Why hadn't he called out, stopped them, demanded to know their business? Why was he shaking? Was he afraid? "Who are they?" he asked.

"I don't know, Father."

"But you saw them when they came."

"Yes, Father." The young man remounted and rode on ahead. "You wouldn't know them."

Lamplight spilled out through the open doorway of the cottage. A little girl stood there, her red hair tangled about her face. She had one hand on the doorpost, and she was peering in, afraid to enter. So absorbed was she that she did not notice their approach until they flung their bicycles against the wall. She looked around, staring out toward them, into the darkness. She backed away, then suddenly turned and disappeared into the room. When they entered, the top of her head showed just above the overturned kitchen table.

The floor was strewn with broken delph. Only one cup still hung on the dresser, where the flame of the oil lamp fluttered, unsheltered by a globe. A pool of milk lay on the stone floor.

Father Conroy hurried around the table to where a woman was kneeling. She looked up at him with terror in her face. Beside her a man lay, half on his side, his face to the floor. His back was bare, and his trousers hung loosely about his buttocks. Thin lines of blood ran this way and that across his back. The pool of milk, where it had spread this far, was tinged with red.

The woman began to scream. He didn't know what to do, but stood before her, helplessly staring down at her open mouth. It was the young man who lifted her to her feet and half-led, half-carried her into the other room.

Father Conroy knelt beside the man, not wanting to put his hand out, but at last he reached out and pushed the man over on his back. The trousers were soaking wet. He watched the eyes for a moment, then put his hand on the cold, sweaty skin of the chest. The heart was still beating.

The young man had come back and was looking at him, waiting for directions. He could think of nothing to say. It was the young man himself who went and brought back a blanket. Then Father Conroy thought of the act of contrition and bent down to whisper the words in the man's ear.

They lifted the man's shoulders and spread the blanket underneath and wrapped it around him. The young man went into the bedroom and came out dragging a mattress, onto which they rolled the body. Next, he blew the fire aflame and hung over it the kettle on its crane. He lifted the table upright and set on it a basin with soap and a towel.

Still kneeling by the mattress, Father Conroy watched these preparations. Himself unable to move, he was awed by the other's efficiency. At last he nodded toward the room within. "Was she here when they came?"

"Yes, Father."

"And the child?"

"Yes."

He got up at last and went toward the little girl in the corner. She looked up at him, then fled screaming into the other room.

"She thinks you're one of them, Father."

Father Conroy looked at him in surprise, then searched in his pocket and pulled out his collar. Clumsily, he fastened it onto the stud and closed it around his neck.

"It's not just the collar, Father."

"What d'ye mean?"

The young man looked away.

"Come on! Tell me what you mean." But he did not want to hear. He had a premonition which chilled him.

The young man knelt to blow the fire with a bellows. "I got a good look at them and they going in, Father."

Father Conroy waited. His lips were so stiff that he could hardly speak through them. "Who were they?"

The young man laid down the bellows, looked up, then looked away again. "I think one of them was your brother Frank."

What happened then? Father Conroy could not remember clearly; it seemed to be all confusion. There were sermons, speeches rather, from the pulpit. He had appeared once among the men in Donore, been cheered up onto a platform, looked down on a crowd from which red flags burst at a word. Yes, he had spoken against "them" – against James, against his brother Frank – against all of them, the class into which he had been born. He had been for – What had he been for? It all seemed so unclear now, what had seemed then so clear – the farmers stepping into the landlords' shoes, the new gangers taking over, while the people still broke stones.

It was talk that could not be ignored, nor was it ignored for long. The letter from the Bishop came in due episcopal course. No explanation was given for his transfer, but he knew, everyone knew, that he was being put out of harm's way. No place in the diocese was farther out of harm's way than the chaplaincy to the Sisters of Charity in Castlemore.

Looking back, it seemed a hole in his life, that period in Castlemore. It gained him nothing, lost him nothing. His duties were as light as his stipends. My stretch in Limbo, he would joke about it, not then, but long afterward, seven years in the land of Nod, to the east of Eden.

The flicker of revolution was soon quenched. The labor organizer fled with the fighting fund, and the laborers, most of them, went back to work on the farmers' terms. When, at last, under a new bishop, Father Conroy moved out to a country parish (everything forgiven, but with a faint shadow on his name, like the temporal punishment due to sin), he found that, where once the laborer had shared the farmer's meals as one of the family, now he was served at a separate table, beyond a closed door. The milk and potatoes he once got in addition to his hire were now measured out and paid for by deduction from his wages. It was all taken for granted, like a custom followed for generations. Only Father Conroy seemed to remember how things had once been, and, though he never directly refused an invitation, he contrived never again to sit down to eat at a farmer's table.

Uncle James, on the other hand, had no difficulty in forgetting what had happened. As time went on, he managed to persuade everyone with a vote to forget it too; in fact, he owed his seat in the Dáil as much to the support of the laborers as of the farmers. He offered himself to them all on election platforms, offered himself with such ferocious sincerity that it seemed as if he intended himself for public consumption. And in a sense, he did. The dignity with which he began to carry himself was that of a public sacrifice.

He learned the value of dress – a hard-brimmed hat and a long black coat, usually hanging open to disclose the waistcoat and gold watchchain. No one seeing him in this funereal attire could doubt but that politics was a respectable profession. As the community settled into its new mold, he established himself halfway between the family solicitor and the priest. He affected the heaviness of scholarship, especially when he appealed to the Gaelic past – our God-given heritage – a vast, rather gloomy hinterland which he had never had time to explore personally, but from which he had been brought certain useful souvenirs, old saws which he used in his speeches to emphasize that a good start was half the work, that order and precedence must not be ignored, and that certain promised schemes could safely be left in the hands of God.

Father Conroy had sworn never to give the man his vote. Yet, several times when he was tempted to vote for some harmless alternative, he found he could not pass the name, Conroy, on the ballot paper. All he could do was spoil his vote – a small gesture, which had as little effect on the fortunes of the country as his "Don't take me for granted" had had on the fortunes of the Conroy clan.

"Don't take me for granted." He said it obstinately, as if he were saying it for the first time.

The old man was not listening. With his face composed into its most solemn, public lines, he was gazing at… What could it be? The old standard lamp in the corner?

"What is it?" asked Father Conroy brusquely.

"I'm just admiring your lamp, Father. Fine piece of brass. Don't often see them now, except in the odd big house." He pressed himself forward, about to get up, the old auctioneer waiting to be asked his opinion on an interesting lot.

"An interesting lot, I suppose?"

"Yes." He subsided immediately. "What size bulb is that you have in it?"

Father Conroy shrugged.

"Looks forty-watt. It's not enough, Father. You'd need, I'd say, a hundred-watt at least, for fear you'd strain the old eyes. Look at me, now, never wore glasses in my life, never had a day's trouble with the sight, thanks be to God. That's one thing I never stinted on, Father. It's not worth it, putting in a forty-watt where you'd need a hundred-watt."

Father Conroy stared into the middle distance and said nothing, until at last the hundred-watt man began the long operation of putting away his pipe and tobacco.

"That was a very pleasant audience you gave me, Father, after all." He reached out, smiling, for his hat and gloves. He had the edge, all right. But what had he wanted? Surely he hadn't come about the pony? Or Jimmy? Or just for a casual snoop around?

He leaned forward, exaggerating the difficulty of getting up. "It's a long time, Father, since we had you at a family wedding."

"There haven't been any to go to."

"That's true." He was on his feet at last. "Ah, well, if Frank had only given his mind to it."

"For God's sake, how could he have brought a woman in there, to Rosnagree?"

"Ah, now, Father, you're very hard on your poor mother. You always were."

Was it true? Father Conroy had no wish even to consider the question. Flippantly he said, "Well, it's too late now."

"I don't know, Father." He allowed a small smile, man to man, understanding of lechery. "He'd make an attempt, anyway. And he might succeed, After all" – the smile widened, as it did

when he flung a gibe across the benches of a council chamber –
"the Conroys were never shy bearers, Father, those that could give
their minds to it."

Aha, James, thought Father Conroy, you never changed. You
could never resist the cut, however low. It was your weakness,
you oul' bastard, and you never knew it. With a less hasty
tongue, you might have made it as a Minister.

James pulled on a chamois glove, his face intent on it as he
snapped the button precisely. "Frank, of course, will be at the
wedding, Father."

Frank! Yes, of course he would be there. Would it be possible
not to meet? Hardly! It would be too difficult to slip away, after
saying the Mass and all. Say no more about the wedding, he told
himself; you're being watched. And then he thought, suppose my
mother comes too?

"And your mother too, Father."

"You think she'll be there?"

"Oh, she'll be asked, anyway, you may be sure of that."

"She won't come, of course." Not at her age, not when I'm to be
there, not when we have to speak to each other across all those
years of silence.

"I think she might, Father; I think she might. Frank, now, might
bring her, if he thought you'd like him to."

So that was it! The net, closing in on him again! His first
impulse was to evade it, as he had evaded it before, but he had
good reasons then, and he seemed to have none now. Jesus, he
thought, if I say no, this oul' bastard will stay arguing all night.
I'm tired. "I'll think it over," he said.

"Very good, Father. Sure, you can't do more than that. I may say she's…" He smiled, just a little, as if to point up the cliché in a companionable way. "… she's not what she used to be."

"I don't think any of us have changed much." Least of all you, James.

"We're none of us what we used to be, Father, and that's the truth."

Well, at least, he thought as he followed James to the door, he knew what the visit was in aid of. A peace mission, at long last, and James out to make a name as family mediator. If they wanted peace, of course they should have it: he couldn't very well refuse. Just to be sure, though, he said, "Has Frank actually asked you?"

James paused, cornered at the door. "Not in so many words, Father, but I'm quite sure he wants you to…"

"I'll think it over," said Father Conroy coldly. So the truce was only James's idea as yet. Yes, it would suit his book to have Jimmy fall in for Rosnagree, as well as for whatever might be squeezed out of his own will. Jimmy, the sole heir of the Conroys! It was on that basis, no doubt, that the marriage had been arranged, old Burke having driven a hard bargain. Well, Jimmy wasn't the only heir, thank God.

"What about my English nephews?" he asked.

"Who, Father?"

"The young Conroys. Owen's sons. The heirs to Rosnagree."

"What? What about them, Father?"

"Surely they've been asked?"

"Lord, no, Father." He managed a smile of derision. "Sure, we don't know anything about them."

"I'm not so sure about that," Father Conroy said, and watched James's smile fade. Of course, it was only bluff, but the remark would make James uneasy for some time. Already the old lips were repeating the remark, trying to test Father Conroy's exact shade of meaning.

But James wasn't finished peeling the visit, like an onion. In the hall he turned suddenly to say, "Tell me, Father, is the schoolhouse free on Thursday?"

"For what?"

James brushed carefully at his hat. "It's just a small meeting I'm calling. I'll be giving a bit of a talk, and then maybe we'll have a few questions afterward."

"I thought that was arranged for Kavanagh's kitchen."

James's eyes flickered. "You keep in close touch, Father."

"Because I'd prefer you had it there. Anything political…"

"Oh, it's not that, I assure you. Anybody's welcome. *Fáilte roimh cách*. In fact, I'd be very pleased if you'd come along yourself."

"What would I be doing at a thing like that?"

"A man like you would appreciate it, Father. The cut and thrust, you know, democracy in action. You'd be very interested."

"Thanks, but…"

"No, really, Father. You'd be at liberty to leave whenever it suited you, any time at all. And, of course, I needn't tell you the people would like very much if you'd open the proceedings with a prayer."

"With a prayer?"

"Yes, Father, a prayer."

That put him in a right fix. Could he refuse a prayer? "Don't tell me you're that worried about Kilbride?"

"Ah, no, Father." A big laugh. "We don't need the Man Above to support us in Kilbride. Just a little prayer, you know. *Bail ó Dhia ar an obair,* a blessing on the work, as they used to say long ago."

"I suppose such a sudden access of piety must be a sign of something."

"Aha, Father, we're not as black as we're painted. Well, I'd best be off. I'll see you there, then, on Thursday." And he went down the steps, clapping the hat on, like a lid on what he had won.

"At Kavanagh's," Father Conroy called after him. "You'll be meeting at Kavanagh's."

James barely paused, accepting the compromise. "Right, Father, but I'll see you there."

Back in the study, Father Conroy found himself facing an old photograph, of the family, on the wall. It had been taken soon after his return from England, outside his house, his first house in the diocese. He was standing in the middle of the family, arms folded in a proprietorial way. James stood to one side, rather sourly – there had been some trouble about making him take off his hat (his hair was noticeably thinning). Afterwards, Father Conroy had remarked, showing him the photograph, "And there *you* are, Uncle James, hat in hand, looking for my vote."

Yes, he thought, and forty years later, he's still looking for it, my family vote. I'll make him sweat for it.

Chapter 8

He found an envelope on the hall table when he turned around, secreted there like a cuckoo spit in the last moment of leave-taking. Even as he tore it open, he had an oppressive sense of what the message would be.

It was more than he expected, much more. He slipped out the new, neatly folded five-pound note. The letter (on Dáil stationery, of course) said simply:

> Dear Father Thomas,
>
>   Next Sunday, please announce: "Your prayers are requested for the repose of the soul of Hannah, dearly beloved wife of James Conroy, T.D., whose anniversary occurs about this time."
>
>   A small contribution is enclosed for Masses.
>
> Sincerely,
James Conroy

Dearly beloved? Well, maybe! One never knows. She had always moved in the background of James's life, below the stairs, in the shadows of the big kitchen. Had she been happy, out of the light? Maybe she had; maybe her dull metal had shone for James. Yet, for thirty years her anniversary had passed inexpensively, without qualms. How come it was suddenly worth five pounds?

He took out his Ordo. How many Masses should he say? There were plenty of vacant spaces in the week to come; Mass offerings were few this time of year, when seeds and fertilizers had to be paid for. He put James down for five Masses. Briskly, pleased at his own businesslike air, he patted the book back into his breast pocket. Then he stood a moment, irresolute, looking at the five-pound note still folded between his fingers.

So, once, he had stood, looking at a note in his hand, not knowing what to do with it. Five pounds? Hardly; such a sum would have seemed impossible in those days. One pound, perhaps? Or was it ten shillings? Trying to remember, he suddenly caught the smell of geraniums, an imprisoned smell, and remembered the airless front hall of Rosnagree.

"Ten shillings?" he could hear his mother's voice beyond the half-open door of the kitchen. "Would you mind telling me what you'd want ten shillings for?"

There was a low murmur as Frank replied, embarrassed, knowing that his younger brother was waiting outside the door. How old was Frank then? Twenty-eight? Thirty? He himself was twenty-six, home from England on holidays. He wanted to call out, "Frank, it's all right, I have it, let me give it to you!"

But his mother's voice went on, "The races, indeed! And what about the marigolds that ye were to thin? Are ye going to leave Petie and the young Higginses the run of the place?"

"They'll carry on all right."

"Don't I know the way they'll carry on, making a clean sweep when there's no one here to keep an eye on them." And then she lapsed into that tone of self-commiseration which always set Tom Conroy's teeth on edge. "Mother of God, isn't it a fright to have the minding of ye all."

But it wasn't true, he wanted to shout, it just wasn't true. Not about Petie and the young Higginses, who crawled along the drills with sacks tied about their knees, their hands scored with the warm, dry, reddish clay. They would all work the better, knowing that her tall, black figure might at any moment come accusingly from the copse at the end of the field. Come on, Frank, he wanted to call out, don't mind her. I'll give you the ten bob.

As if he could hear, Frank said, "All right, so, I'll go and ask Tom for it."

"Oh, indeed you won't. You will not, then, you'll do nothing of the kind."

And next moment he could hear her climbing the dark enclosed stairs to the room under the rafters where she had moved after his father's death. In the old days, it used to be Kate's room. Sometimes, on a wet day, when the rain was drumming on the slates just above their heads, Kate and Owen and he played hide-and-seek above the rafters. He remembered the rough planks barking his knees, the warmth behind the chimney where he hid, holding his breath, while he listened to them crawling nearer. He was conscious of the solidity of Kate's whitewashed room below, against which the wind flung itself like waves against the hull of a ship. It was exciting to be there, at the very center of the sheltered life of the house.

Now, his mother filled the room, during the long, sleepless hours of her night, with the moan of her prayers and pious ejaculations. He could not bear to go up there, knowing that the room must have changed since she moved into it to begin her long, tedious preparations for death.

So, listening to her footsteps on the bare boards, he could not follow her movements, could not guess where she kept her money, their money, the fruit of Rosnagree. Did she guess at his fear of her? Was that why she resented him so much? She could not bear Frank to be beholden to him, not even for ten miserable shillings. Remembering the sound of her footsteps treading so surely across the room above, he complained, I never asked her for anything. I never wanted a thing from her. And yet, she always wanted me to think that it was I who made her suffer. She made me her Cross.

Damn little cause she had; not even his full fees at the seminary did she have to pay – they were met to some extent, at best, by his grand-uncle in South America. No, he thought with satisfaction, he owed her nothing.

He went to the cupboard and pushed the note into the nearest jar, then turned away, brushing his hands together. Nothing he owed her. Nothing.

He came into the kitchen at Rosnagree, hot and sweaty, out of the glare of the sun. He was working with Owen at the hay, and he had come to refill the gallon can with tea. He knew from the guilty way she moved that he had surprised her, and searching the dimness of the room, he noticed that Owen's coat hung on the back of the door and that she half-stuffed some papers back into the pocket of it.

"I gave that fellow a list for the creamery," she murmured,

seeing his glance. "God knows what he did with it." (It was always "that fellow," never her son Owen, the heir to the farm, which she held only in trust.)

"I'll tell him," he said; "maybe he has it with him."

"Oh, sha, don't bother." She took the can from him hastily and went to the teapot simmering in the ashes. "I don't know what the blazes he does with things."

But he knew what she had been after. All that summer, Owen's girl, Marie, had been writing, sometimes two letters by the same post, and Owen used to wait on the road, for fear the postman would bring the letters to the house. Whenever he could find no excuse to get away, he sent Tom (home on holidays from the seminary) to waylay the postman and to claim for him the plump envelope with the English postmark and the careful, childish handwriting.

When Tom returned with the tea, Owen was in the middle of the sunny field, singing as he tossed the hay up into a cock. Tom went straight up to him and said, "Those letters of yours. Don't leave them around."

Owen said nothing. For a few moments he continued to toss the hay up in heavy forkfuls. Watching his face slowly redden, Tom wondered if his nose would begin to bleed as it used to in childhood tantrums. Sure enough, Owen stopped forking the hay. He wiped his nose, looked at the red smear on the back of his hand, and said, "She wouldn't read them."

"I don't know. Maybe not."

"I'd walk out tomorrow if she did."

"All the same," said Tom, "you'd better keep them in my suit-case." He did not need to add that they would be safe there;

both knew that she was wary of him, of some vengeful spirit in him which might be all too easily roused against her. So, all that summer, the girl's letters grew into a bundle beneath the theology textbooks which he should have been reading, but which he would not spare time from the work of the farm to attend to. He brought them back to college with him, never thinking of taking them out. They were never to grow anymore; a few weeks later, he had a letter from Owen under an English postmark:

Dear Tom,

I took the big step at last. I got a job at the building, and there's good money in it. Marie is well. She's going to finish her exams at the hospital, and then we'll be free as the air. Between us, we won't be long setting aside the price of a good place back home and enough to stock it as well. She's living in, this week, so we don't see much of each other, only a few hours before she goes back on night duty. God help us, I'm doing the cooking. It gives Marie a good laugh.

I hope you won't be annoyed that we went ahead. We couldn't wait any longer, whatever they thought in Rosnagree. I would have liked to wait till you could say the words over us, but that would be a whole year, and we were thinking in weeks and days. We went to a cousin of Marie's in the Birmingham diocese, and he didn't keep us waiting long. Anyway, I know we did the right thing.

Write soon and let me know what you think.

Your affectionate brother,

Owen

P.S. Any news from Rosnagree?

He was ordained a year after that and a few months later was working in his London parish. It was after Christmas, nearly two years after Owen's letter, that he got a few days' leave from his parish priest to go to Birmingham. He traveled up by an evening train, on his own all the way across the English Midlands. There was no one to meet him at the station, though Owen had told him he would be there. The big, blue-black buses went past in the deserted street, and the roadway shone wet and black under the street lamps. He stood outside the station, waiting for the bus to Sparkbrook, and for the first time since he had come to England felt the loneliness of exile.

The bus left him in a street of small, back-to-back houses of blackened brick. He turned off into Byron Street and then into Shelley Street and Wordsworth Street; it was impossible to see how one street differed from the other, and he found himself anxiously looking for landmarks to ensure his return, a glimpse of a factory chimney or the gleam of a railway signal between the rooftops.

Even as he turned in the gateway, he was hoping the house was not the one he was looking for. And yet, it looked Irish – the curtains pinned up unevenly, the old car tire where the bit of grass should have been; yes, already he knew the look of impermanent exile. The fat young woman who answered the door seemed flustered at the sight of him. Two small, half-dressed children pulled at her skirt, and she quelled them with a slap as she directed him up the uncarpeted stairs.

"But they're not in, Father; only the babbie, and he's asleep."

"Who's minding him, the baby?"

"I'm minding him." She took his remark amiss and added hotly, "Sure, what harm can come to him?"

"I wouldn't know, ma'am," he said civilly, "but I'd have thought one of them would be here to look after him."

"How can they, when they're both out working? Indeed, then, 'tis proud of them ye ought to be (for I can see by ye, you're a brother of Owen's). There's not a pair like them in this town, and that's a fact. They're so steady, Father, no drinking, no loud talk or carry-on; God love them, sure they never stir out when they're at home. Not like my own bucko, Father. The divil knows where he does be half the time, and to tell ye the truth, Father, I don't like to ask; 'tis no place I should know about."

"How long is Mr. Conroy here?"

"Near a year now, since just before the babbie came. Oh, 'tis a good house, Father, don't you worry about that; there's only respectable people here. Mr. Conroy wouldn't have had e'er a place to go only for me, and even if they do pay me a few bob for giving an eye to the babbie, sure, isn't it worth it to them?"

"Show me their room, if you please."

"Certainly, Father. And I'll send up one of the youngsters with a sup of tea to ye."

"Don't bother, thanks." And he pushed his way past her into the room, as she lit the gas light.

The cot was in the corner. He went over to it, stared down at the fair head, the round flushed cheek sunk deep in the pillow. She came across to draw up the rug around it, but he said violently, "No, leave him alone," and she looked at him a little frightened and quickly left the room.

He looked around, at the iron bed that sagged in the middle, at the linoleum-covered table, the mantelpiece with the photograph of himself on his ordination day, the gas stove, all so crowded together that one could barely thread a way through them to the door. Then he looked down again, and at the thought of Rosnagree he groaned, "Oh, Christ!"

The baby's fist lay exposed; he drew up the clothes about it, gently, and the baby sighed and moved its head, seeking warmer depths in the pillow. He looked around for someplace to sit down. There were two chairs drawn in to the table, but though he pulled one out, he did not sit; he felt that by doing so, he would be yielding to the domination of the room, like all those objects meanly crowded together. He moved to the window, drawn by the dark between the street lights, the spaciousness of the sky above; and just then, he heard quick footsteps in the hall. They pounded up the stairs.

The door flung open, and Owen rushed in. He came forward, put out his arms. "Tom. Thank God! You came at last."

Father Conroy half-evaded the man's rough hug. "All right! There!" He was disconcerted by the force of the greeting. The Conroys were usually so casual with one another. "Yes, I came. How are you?"

"I thought I could get off early. I wanted to be at the station – but sure, there you are!" The eager face, the smile, the brimming eyes – it was a quicker, more emotional Owen than he remembered.

Was it happiness? Of course, it must be. She made him happy (and, at the thought, his heart went out in gratitude to her); she made him happy, even in this place. Everything would be all right; this was only temporary, this room, a resting place. They would be moving on soon, with their baby. Weren't they both young, strong, keen to do well?

"Marie's working, I hear?"

"Yes, Tom, just for the present. Doing well too – she knocked down a fiver last week. And I'm getting a fair bit of overtime."

"You'll be moving on, then, out of here?"

"Oh, it's not too bad here, really. We're in it so little." He moved around the room, picking at the curtains, pulling the oilcloth straight on the table. He had lost weight. His cheeks had hollowed, his eyes seemed larger. "It'll do us till we have enough put together."

"Put together for what?"

"Enough to go back with. To Rosnagree."

Father Conroy stared, suddenly cold with apprehension.

"To buy the place, I mean. I'm not going back cap in hand, if that's what you were thinking. I'll offer her a good price, as good as she'd get from anyone else."

"But, for God's sake, it's not…" Not for sale, he meant to say. Rosnagree was not anyone's to sell.

"Not what?" Owen asked hotly.

"I mean…" How could he explain? That it was as unsalable as his family name. Owen would never understand that. To him it was simply land, cattle, trees, grass. "How d'you know she'll sell?"

"She'll sell, all right. I'll make her sell."

"But… you can't stay here that long, not with the child, not here."

"We're not moving anywhere else."

"But Marie won't want…"

"She'll stay here as long as I want."

"But you can't, Owen. Not in this… It's no better than a kip. Look, I'll go look for a place for you. Any place would be better than this."

"I don't want a better place." And he turned around slowly, rigid, eyes blazing. "I want this."

Father Conroy made his way to the table and sat down. He could think of nothing to say. He looked down at his hands, locked together on his knees, and was afraid to look at his brother.

Owen began to talk about his place of work, awkwardly at first, as if he wanted to fill the silence, then excitedly, as he described a ganger of whom he had fallen foul. The man was from a place down the country, called Modeligo. ("Think of that," Owen cried with derision, "Modeligo!") He had passed some comment on a trench that Owen had dug, that it wouldn't do, it needed leveling off. "But I didn't take him up on it," said Owen. "I played it cute. I went and leveled it, nice and quiet, without saying a word. Oh, I've learned the game, Tom, you didn't think I would, but I know how to let them ride me till the right moment. And that'll come! By Christ, it will! I'm only waiting for the day when I draw my cards. I'll make for him, that man from Modeligo, and I'll ram my knee into his belly, and I'll tell him, 'Next time you meet a man from Rosnagree—'"

He stopped suddenly and listened. In the silence, Father Conroy could hear his own heart beating; he stared at his brother's flushed face, waiting for the torrent of words to gush again from the half-open mouth.

The front door closed below, a quiet, authoritative sound, as of someone accustomed to closing it, making her house complete.

"Marie!" cried Owen. He rushed out of the room and ran down the stairs. A few moments later, smiling in triumph, he led her in, pressing her forward across the room toward Tom.

She came slowly, as if she wanted to hang back in the shadows of the door. Father Conroy was reminded of how she had hung back when she had been called out of class in the village school, and how the teacher had come down and pushed her out to the blackboard. What had she been ashamed of? Torn stockings? Broken shoes? Ringworm? He could not remember. She might have had many things to be ashamed of, coming, as she did, from one of the hovels in the muddy lane behind the church.

Perhaps she's in awe of me now, he thought. But no, her cool gray eyes considered him seriously, and he realized that she was the strong one. (Hadn't she won Owen so completely that he had been sick for the want of her?) On her depended the safety of the small household. And then he knew why she hung back. He could see it in her eyes, in the lines of her face. She was tired.

He touched his lips to her cheek and said, to hearten her, "That's a great little nephew you gave me, Marie."

She smiled at that and turned to the child. "You've seen him yourself, so?"

"Oh, a right little divil," said Owen as she picked up the baby. "As strong as a horse. He can rock the cot around the room after me, no matter where I go." He smiled up at the child in her arms, inviting Father Conroy to admire it too. The baby peered crossly down at them, its face moist and red from the pillow's warmth. It pursed its lips inward until the gums began to show.

"Oh, Christ," burst out Owen. "He's off again!" Impatiently, he waved her away. And only then, as she turned to lay the wailing baby down on the bed, did Father Conroy see that she was carrying her second child. He felt his heart contract with fear for them, for all the life imprisoned in this room.

*

Two years later, Owen was dead. The usual Conroy complaint – the heart that stopped suddenly in the heat of the day. Father Conroy was back in Ireland then, in his first parish. As soon as he got Marie's telegram, he asked the parish priest for the car and drove over to Rosnagree. In a field beside the road, he saw Frank strolling, driving in the cows, and at the same time keeping an eye out for passers by. He stopped the car, and Frank waved his stick, then sauntered over, vaulted the wall, and approached the car, smiling. In the back of the car, as they drove up to the house, he began to cry. Father Conroy left him there and went in to tell Mama the news.

She did not cry. She stared at him. Her mouth worked once as she swallowed, but she said nothing. He remembered a cock he had tried to kill when he was a boy. He had volunteered to kill it for her – he wanted to show her he could. Its beak opened and closed as he laid it on the rounded tree stump they used as a chopping block. He swung at it several times with the billhook, but he was so nervous that the hook merely sliced along the feathered neck, until, to his horror, the beak suddenly filled with blood. Impatiently she snatched the billhook from him and cut the head off with a single blow.

As she moved around, busily getting ready Frank's clothes for the journey to Birmingham, he watched her with the same horror. She seemed to him capable of anything. From that moment, he could never forgive her for Owen's death.

She brought the suitcase out to Frank, still whimpering in the back of the car. They whispered together for a few moments, and she passed something to him, probably his money for the journey. Father Conroy got in and without looking at her, drove off.

They caught the train to Dublin and traveled by night boat to Holyhead. They found Marie in the same house, the same room, awaiting them. The new baby was in the cot; the little boy was being looked after by the woman downstairs. All the evening and until late that night, strangers drifted in and out, men from the building site where Owen had worked, a few girls from Marie's hospital. The table was set with cups and saucers, and one of the nurses came up the stairs with a big teapot; her companions passed around the tea to the shy workmen, who stood around by the walls, awkwardly holding their caps in their hands.

The body lay on the bed, a white face and a slight molding of the clothes. Candles burned around it, and a big vaseful of dahlias wilted as the night wore on. One of the girls brought Father Conroy a cup of tea and a plate of sandwiches, but he waved them away; the thought of food sickened him. The men came up to him, shook his hand, and murmured words of sympathy, then left quickly, their feet clattering on the stairs, their voices suddenly loud in the street below. More people came; the room seemed to fill with them as they came, three, four, five at a time, sidling in through the doorway, blessing themselves hurriedly, heads lowered as they tiptoed forward to crowd together by the wall. The face lay on the bed; it seemed to be fining away already into the whiteness of bone. The thought struck Father Conroy that they might all be consuming it, breathing away its air, absorbing the warmth of its flesh. In terror, he pushed his way out of the room, groped his way downstairs and out into the backyard. And gradually, as he breathed in the darkness under the misty, distantly swimming stars, he managed to quell the nausea within him.

When he returned to the room, Marie and one of the girls were tidying up the tea things. Frank was sitting in the armchair, writing in a notebook which he put away in his overcoat pocket when he saw his brother approach. Father Conroy thought no more of the notebook till next day, when Frank consulted it before he paid the undertaker his bill at the railway station. Later that night, on the journey to Holyhead, Father Conroy returned to their compartment to find Frank, notebook in hand, drawing back from Marie. She seemed upset, as she turned to look out of the window. Frank put the notebook away hurriedly and they sat in silence, until at last Frank got up and went off to the dining car for a drink.

Father Conroy gave Marie several openings to speak, but she continued to stare sullenly out of the window. For the rest of the journey Frank stayed drinking in the bar, and they sat looking out into the darkness, which was broken only by the lights of small stations along the north coast of Wales. In the confusion of getting on board the boat, he forgot to ask Frank for an explanation of what was happening, and next day, when the funeral was over, it was too late – the chasm had already opened between him and his family. His mother had not appeared at any time during the funeral. And the Mass, the undertaker's bill, everything entered in Frank's notebook, had been paid by Marie out of the money which Owen and she had saved to buy back Rosnagree.

Several times afterward he wrote to her, offering her help, once even enclosing a substantial money order, but she returned his letters unopened. He did not blame her; damn good cause she had to forget the Conroys. Some years later he heard from a priest in Birmingham who had made inquiries for him that she had married again and gone to live in a seaside town in the south of England; he did not trouble her further.

It troubled him now, though, that he could not remember the names of her sons, Owen's sons, the only sons of the Conroy clan. Perhaps she had told him; if so, he had not taken note of them. It had seemed a small matter at the time, but later it seemed shameful that they should be nameless to him and to the family whose surname they bore. They would be in their twenties now, married perhaps, with children of their own. Did they know about him? Did they know about Rosnagree, which their father would have claimed for them and which now, barren of children, would soon pass into other hands?

Had they even heard its name? And if so, would they know what it meant – Ros na Graidhe, the Grove of the Horses? And even if they knew, would it mean anything to them, who had never seen the old trees on the hill behind the house, the grove which for generations had stood against the north wind and the east. It was in that grove that he had played with Frank and Owen and his sister, Kate. He knew its deep, green, soft-layered places, now primrose-filled, now swept with flurries of leaves. He knew its sounds; he had wakened to them on summer mornings, on stormy nights been held by them at the brink of sleep. It was all Rosnagree to him.

And to them? No, Marie would never have told them. How could she? It meant nothing to her.

But I'll see that they know about it; I'll make it my business to tell them. Because it's theirs, yes, theirs! Why shouldn't they have it if they want it? It's theirs, and Mama and Frank can't deny it to them if they come to claim it. I'll make it theirs.

Christ, Conroy, what are you at now? Rosnagree was never theirs and never can be. Nor is it yours, either, to dispose of. You once had the chance of it, when Frank was going to be a priest, but when he changed his mind, you chose to get up and go. That's your job now, to be a get-up-and-go man, so up you get and let's see you go. Enough of the mooning; get cracking now, quick!

What at? He consulted the mute face of his bargain clock – his glugger. It showed, as always, twenty minutes to ten. Time to say his Office.

And afterward? As he climbed the stairs to his oratory, he thought, well, afterward, there are lots of things to be done afterward; think out something to say for Sunday, get rid of that curse-of-God pony. (Why not call on Drewitt and tell him to take his bloody animal off the parish grass? Never know! Drewitt might change his mind about wanting it.)

And there was Farrell, that makeshift curate. Where was he? Why hadn't he shown up during the week for his weekly conference (as he called it) with his parish priest? About time the pup was brought to heel.

And so, just as the flourish of trumpets introduced the late news on television, Father Conroy knocked at the curate's front door and smiled his way in past the young housekeeper, who had just been washing her hair. Farrell half-rose out of the depths of his armchair and made a show of going to turn off the television, looking to Father Conroy for a sign that would allow him to leave it on. But no sign came: Father Conroy pulled a chair around and sat down, blocking the view. Resignedly, the curate rose and turned down the sound. Then, drawing his chair toward the big, glowing fire, he said, "You missed a good program there earlier, Tom!"

"What?"

"*On the Land*. I'm following the series. Liver fluke was on tonight. A fascinating thing."

"I'd say." Name of God, a townie like Farrell! Farming in the cozy little sitting room of his cozy little bungalow! He cleared his throat in a way he used to strike foreboding into the hearts of a congregation. "I didn't see you around lately," he said, giving the sentence just enough lift to mean, were you around at all?

"I called over twice, Tom, but you seemed to be out."

"I was out. Today."

"Ah yes, I thought you were. No matter, though; nothing startling to report." Seeing Father Conroy lower, he hurried on, "I was just thinking, Tom, we ought to get some classes started here for the Young Farmers. All that stuff – liver fluke and so on – it's not really getting through, now, is it?"

"Getting through to what?"

"What?" Farrell looked startled. "Oh, yes. Oh, I think, Tom, that the Young Farmers are coming along well. I'm going to suggest they change their meeting to this night every week. They can get a grant for a television set to watch the program down in the Hall. They could have great discussions afterward."

"Yes, the Young Farmers!" Most of them in their forties and fifties, unmarried, lazy, selfish as sin. They could put on a great show of enthusiasm at their meetings, as long as Farrell was present. As soon as he was gone, out came the cards, and the hands of poker or pontoon were dealt out. Sometimes the games lasted till morning. "A bomb under them, that's what they want."

"Ah, now, Tom, you're being hard on them; there's great stuff in those fellows. More discussions are what they need to get them thinking for themselves."

"Well, I suppose there's no harm in it…"

"That's right, Tom. I think it's a good thing."

"…to have a few more of us sitting around on our arses."

"I don't think…" Father Farrell hastily picked up the poker and began to stir the fire, to hide his reddening cheeks. "I don't think that's quite fair, Father."

"Never mind," Father Conroy said brusquely. "You're saying the first Mass on Sunday, then. What about Evening Devotions?"

"I'll take them."

"Right. Don't forget to mention confessions on Thursday for the first Friday."

"I know."

"You'd better enter it in the book, just in case. Also, the collection for the baptistry: they're still putting nothing in the box. Give them a few words about that."

Farrell said nothing. His eyes turned defiantly toward the television screen, over Father Conroy's shoulder.

"The collection," prompted Father Conroy.

"If you think it's important, of course I'll mention it, Father."

"What do you mean, if I think it's important?"

"I mean…" He took up the poker again and raked away.

He was spunky, but not quite spunky enough to face Father Conroy head on. "…in this day and age, I'm inclined to agree with the people about that project."

"In what way, may I ask?"

"That it's not all that important. Surely to God, we've enough spent on concrete blocks; it's not there the spirit is."

"Are you trying to lecture me?"

"I'm not. I'm just trying to say that I don't think you have enough respect for… for certain things that count."

"Such as?"

"For people, Father. After all, we're told now about the People of God, that it's in them the Church…"

"You are lecturing me."

"I'm not. I just thought I should tell you…"

"I don't want to know."

"No, you don't. But let me tell you something else, Father, that pony of Mr. Drewitt's—"

"What's that to do with you?"

"Mr. Drewitt was here with me twice this week. I know the trick you played him, a mean trick that a tinker would be ashamed of. And to make it worse, the man's not even a Catholic!"

"I have my reasons."

"I hope they're good, because there's going to be a right stink about this business."

"Listen, Farrell, if I want your advice, I'll come looking for it. And as for your People of God, it's out in the churchyard I see some of them every Sunday, instead of inside, hearing Mass properly. Yes, down on one knee on the gravel they spend their time, skitting and gossiping, aye, and even playing cards on the gravestones, that's how some of them hear holy Mass."

"I'm not denying…"

"No, because you can't."

"Father!" Farrell put down the poker and stood up, so suddenly that Father Conroy thought for a moment he was about to be attacked. Then, surprised, even disappointed, he realized the young man was holding himself back. "I think we should stop this now, before we go too far."

"You stop it. I came here to give you your instructions, since you didn't call to me for them."

Farrell turned away and said very quietly, "I don't think I'm free from blame. For some reason, we don't seem to be working together as we should to give the people what they expect from us, what they need. I've been thinking, for some time, that I should ask for a transfer."

"Go ahead."

The young man flushed violently. With a hot rush of delight, Father Conroy saw that his hands had begun to tremble.

"I will, then! I think you're a selfish, corrupt, impossible old man. You've been lying down on the job here for years, letting the place fall apart. But the people aren't fools – they'll cop on yet. And when I hear talk these days of the priesthood of the laity…"

"Priesthood, my arse."

"Stop it!" Farrell rushed forward, grabbed the lapels of his coat, and half-lifted him out of his chair. "Stop it, do you hear?"

Christ, watch this! Farrell's going to hit me! Come on, then, you young tipper, hit me! Here I am, open to you! Hit me, come on, hit me!

But Farrell flung him away, so suddenly that he was thrown back against the bookcase. Fighting for his balance, he saw Farrell go flailing away to the window and stand there, halted suddenly against the folds of the curtains. Weakly he groped his way back to his chair and slumped down into it.

"I know what you want," Farrell shouted. "You want me to lose my temper. That's what you've been after ever since I came here. Why? Will you tell me that? What have I done?"

Father Conroy sat, head on his chest, gaping at the floor.

What have I done, he asked himself, Christ, what have I done? He could hear Farrell's voice rising, as if cheated by his silence. "…a holy show, a laughingstock… even Drewitt and the pony…" To shut out the sound of it, he put his hands over his ears. Tears were running down his face. He couldn't stop them. Somehow it seemed impossible to take his hands away, to protect his face. He had to let the tears run, as they had never run before.

The shouting stopped. Farrell was offering him whiskey. He refused. "I've managed without it till now." And so, Farrell bawled his housekeeper up out of her bed to go and make tea; she brought it in her overcoat and curlers, looking in fright at Father Conroy as she put down the tray. Not knowing how to go, she waited and timidly asked, "Is the tea all right, Father?" "Grand," Father Conroy said, before he even tasted it. And, after she left, he added, as he wiped his face with his handkerchief, "I wouldn't like to be keeping that one in tea. She has a fine, liberal hand, God bless it. She'd pickle you in tea."

Farrell drove him home and at the door of his house began to help him out of the car, but he insisted on pulling himself out. Farrell shut the car door for him and said, out of the darkness, "Remember that man, Tom, that you sent us to see, up in the Bohernascorna Gap? We went up, all right, to see him, Dickie and I. 'Watch and Pray,' I believe you call him. A most entertaining character. He had us in stitches with his stories. We spent the whole evening there."

Father Conroy waited, peering into the darkness where his curate stood. "Well, what are you trying to tell me?"

"He seemed very much in awe of you, Tom."

"He's an old humbug."

"No. He told us about the way you go up to the Gap to see him, and the way you give him talks – as good as sermons, he says – to keep him on the straight and narrow. Oh, he thinks you're the greatest, Tom."

"Good night," Father Conroy said roughly and turned away.

"Would you do something, Tom? Would you go and see a doctor?" Farrell's voice came from the darkness.

"For what?"

"I think you should, Tom."

"Damn it, I've managed without them till now."

"All right, then, good night." Farrell moved away.

"Take my car."

"No, no, I'll walk. It's all right." And then the voice said hesitantly, "We'll forget about all that, Tom. It's a closed book."

"What?" he demanded. "What's a closed book? What the hell are you talking about?"

But Farrell's footsteps moved quickly away, crunching the gravel toward the gate. And Father Conroy turned to grope his way to his front door, somewhere, a long way, ahead.

He dreamed that night he was in a wood, rooted in one spot. A wind blew, branches threshed, the trees strained all around him. Leaves began to fall, slowly at first, then with gathering force, until a tempest of leaves rushed past him. They filled the spaces between the trees, moving with a strange sound, like the distant drumming of hooves. The sound grew louder and louder, until it seemed that the whole wood was on the move, galloping away from him. Then the sound died away into the distance, and he was left standing alone.

Chapter 9

When the first light came through the uncurtained window, he began his slow roll out of bed, eyes closed, mind slipping into its cogs for the long haul up out of sleep. At the cold touch of the linoleum on the soles of his feet, his right hand moved, jerking out the outline of the cross over forehead and chest. He was erect now, and the flinty light was forcing its way between his eyelids, shining into him. And he was still resisting it as he groped for his clothes.

Shivering, he pulled on his trousers, hopping on his good leg as he forced the other leg past the creases, which seemed to have stiffened with frost. The house was silent, no slam of the back door or pounding of feet in the hall. It was ten minutes after Mass time. What was keeping Gabriel?

As he put on his vestments in his oratory, he knew there was something he should remember. Someone to meet? Some message to pass on? What day of the week was it, anyway? He turned to where Gabriel usually knelt, but the boy wasn't there. Little tipper, he thought, I'll straighten his legs for him!

He tied the cincture about his waist and ducked down to peer out through the little window at the bullocks moving stiffly in the field, blowing their long breaths before them. A hardy day, by God! How was that pony keeping?

And then it hit him, what had happened last night. At first he shook his head. No, he had dreamed it, he couldn't have broken down – why would he do such a thing? In Farrell's house, my God, Farrell of all people? But as he drew the cincture tight about him, he knew that he had, yes, that he had broken down and cried like a baby.

He took up the chasuble and stood with it in his hands, about to drop it over his shoulders, to enclose himself in its black folds. Why, though? Why had it happened? What word or look had split the rock, made the waters flow? Name of God, what could have happened to him?

A whinny came from the outhouse in the yard below. That curse-of-God pony! Quickly he dropped the chasuble over his shoulders and reached for the tapes to tie it at his sides. Of course, the pony! Farrell had been shouting about it, telling him Drewitt was making threats, that there was going to be a stink. Yes, that was it. No wonder he had been upset last night – what business was it of Farrell's?

I'll give the bloody animal back to Drewitt, that's what I'll do. Get it out of the place, out of my mind. I haven't had a day's rest since it came, awake or asleep. As soon as Mass is over, I'll call on Drewitt and tell him to take it away. Or should I call? Wouldn't it be better to send a message, to send Gabriel? Yes, it would be more dignified. I might be tempted to give him a punch, shut his big gob for him.

But where was Gabriel? The little brat was late. And supposing Drewitt didn't really want the pony, after all? That was quite on the cards. Maybe I should go myself and find out how the land lies – make a deal, if there's a deal to be made.

The argument went on as he waited for Gabriel. To go or not to go? He saw to the cruet (Gabriel's job), filled one of the little jugs with wine from the bottle in the cupboard, went down to the tap to fill the other with water. As he turned on the tap, he heard the chapel bell go clang, clang, clang. What could it be? He stood listening to the panicky sound that made feet quicken in the last rush up the hill to the chapel. Christ, could it be Sunday? He rushed to the window and, sure enough, saw the bicycles stacked at the church gate, the men going in the door, and Gabriel in his white surplice, tugging on the rope. For the first time in his life he had forgotten Sunday Mass for his people.

The church was quiet, when at last, breathless, unshaven, unprepared, he swept out onto the altar of the chapel. A few reproachful coughs let him know they had been waiting a long time. Well, let them wait; too long had he waited for them, too long had they taken him for granted. Could he work that into the sermon? To shake them out of the trance in which they were settling themselves to "hear" Mass? And then he faltered at the steps of the altar, when he suddenly thought, God, I've no sermon.

No sermon, not even a note. He was not an improviser; his sermons had to be assembled, built like a bridge, each pontoon fixed firmly in place as he moved steadily out from the bank behind him. Yes, like a bridge over a dark flood of water. And it had to be built in broad daylight, in the fear that at any moment he would be picked off by some unseen sniper.

Not that there was much likelihood of a sniper in Kilbride! But the feeling had always been with him. Once, coming back from a holiday, he found he could not preach; the sermon just hadn't come. He never took holidays now, because he had to spend his Saturday nights walking around his parish. Saturday nights were always special. He didn't call anywhere; he knew the women were busy ironing shirts and scrubbing the necks and knees of the little ones; he knew each man was standing in his vest and trousers by the side table, a basin steaming before him as he peered into a clouded mirror and scraped off a six-day growth of beard.

It gave him a good feeling to know that all that was going on. And so, he liked to stroll around in the dark, to look at the lights of the houses, and get "the feel of his parish." He knew he was preparing himself, as they were. He was building his bridge for them.

And now he had no bridge, nothing for them. He tried to pick up a few points as he rattled his way through the Gospel. It was about the confrontation of Jesus and the Jews before the Temple: "Thou art not yet fifty years old; and hast Thou seen Abraham?" "Amen, Amen, I say to you, before Abraham was made, I am." Surely he could build on that? But it was going to be tough.

He took off his chasuble, folded it on the altar, and came down in his white alb to the altar rails. First he read the announcements, the death notices, something about a meeting of the creamery committee, a notice (that must have been handed in by the sergeant last summer and mislaid in the book) about cutting noxious weeds – thistle, ragwort, and dock. Could he work that into the sermon? He had a vision of hordes of thistle, ragwort, and dock converging from the highways and byways, trampling over fields sown with faith, in their big Garda boots. Steady now, he told himself, for God's sake, concentrate.

He laid the announcement book down on the altar rail. His arms were paining him, both arms. He reached his hands together, clasped them before him with some difficulty. He felt better with them clasped, as if he were closing some kind of circuit.

The people were watching him, no one coughing, all well above their usual level of concentration. Or were they? Hadn't they always watched him as sharply as this? Wasn't it the highlight of their week, that they looked forward to, believing in him, knowing that he would give them his best? He tightened his arms together and stiffened against the pain that ran through him, an iron hoop of pain that tightened his arms and chest. Christ, what was he to say?

A penny dropped into the candle stand by the altar rail, and the clunk of it echoed through the church. Watch and Pray was lighting a candle. His long, shaky arm reached up to the flames on the stand, nearly level with his face. He tilted the candle to let it take light.

All Father Conroy's frustration found vent, at last. "Sit down," he shouted, but the old fellow continued to stare along the line of candles, waiting for his own to take light, his face so intent, so immobile, that only the shine of his eyes made it seem alive. That blind serenity enraged Father Conroy. "Leave the candle alone, man. And sit down."

Watch and Pray looked up, startled, as if he had just been awakened by a voice from on high. Then he blew the candle out, dropped it back into its box, and scuttled back to his seat on his crooked legs.

Where was he? Noxious weeds, seeds of faith… Damn it, how could he be expected to preach with clowns like that interrupting him? He glared out at the congregation, challenging them to accuse him of dereliction of duty. They sat absolutely still, eyes fixed in front of them. Maybe they weren't with him at all? Maybe they were in their usual Sunday trance? He cleared his throat and began, "Today's Gospel, in case you didn't hear it, is about Our Lord's argument with the Jews, who refused to recognize in Him the Son of God, greater than Abraham and the prophets. 'If I say the truth to you,' he tells them, 'why do you not believe Me?' Well, why? Why was He so concerned about them? What did He want them for? Why does God want us to believe in Him?"

He stopped and looked around. Watch and Pray was murmuring the rosary to himself, fingers slipping along the beads at a great rate. The teacher was looking at his nails, comparing one hand with the other.

"There's only one answer," he said. But what was that? He remembered something about a wager – Pascal, was it? – that it was safer to believe than to take a chance on not believing. But that couldn't be it; there must be more to it than that; Pascal wouldn't have taken such a mean way out. Surely someone else must have tackled the problem and come up with a quick answer? Yes, the quicker the better, for now Watch and Pray had stopped shifting the beads; the teacher, all of them, were looking up at him with renewed interest.

His eye was caught by the big collection box on the porch on which a couple of young fellows were leaning casually. "Why d'ye want this church?" he asked. "Why do ye need that article of furniture down there on the porch, which some latecomers seem to think is placed there for their comfort? Now, I've spoken to ye before about that box. 'Tis all one to me whether ye fill it or not. 'Tis not my porch, nor my church. If ye want a cracked and gutterless porch, well, that's your problem." And then he added one of his throwaways, almost under his breath. "Ye're well used, God knows, to be the laughingstock of the parishes around."

As they stirred, some uncomfortably, some with irritation, he smiled a little, knowing that he had them to handle as he wanted. "Not that ye need ever be ashamed of the building itself. Your great-grandfathers put it up – God only knows how they did it, two years after the Famine. It must have been a change from hearing Mass in a smoky kitchen or around a slab of rock in a corner of a field. No, they didn't do a bad job, even if it is a bit damp and has the door on the windy side. I'm just wondering whether ye would have put up anything at all." He was really harrying them now. "Oh, yes, ye milk yer cows and fill yer churns, ye have yer breakfast, the bowl of porridge, the eggs and bread and butter, maybe the rasher and black pudding. Ye get yer Sunday papers and see that the Russians or maybe the Yanks have sent another rocket to the moon. What do ye want a church at all for?"

They were quite still, staring up at him with real interest. Go on, man, he told himself, you're doing fine. But what was he to go on about? Christ, he thought, I'm back where I started. Only now, I've brought in churns of milk, rockets to the moon. "All these things don't matter," he went on; "we have them, whether we believe or not. But each one of us has the choice of something more. No one can choose for us, and all we have to go on" – he lifted his arms to emphasize it, and the pain made him gasp – "is that Christ said, 'If any man keep My word, he shall not see death forever.'" And with arms still painfully extended, he turned around to grope for the altar.

The movement took them by surprise. They stayed sitting as he drew the chasuble with trembling hands up over his head;

then he heard the hurried rumble as they stood up for the Creed.
They moved into it as if in relief, taking over from him even as he
began the first verse.

"I believe in one God, the Father Almighty, maker of heaven
and earth and of all things, visible and invisible…"

How had he slipped up? Not even in his first sermon had he
made such a hames of it. As he freewheeled through the prayer,
his voice drowned by the crowd's confident singsong, he tried to
think of what he should have said – "Everyone that is of the truth,
heareth my voice"? No, not quite, but there were dozens of texts
that he should have called on; not called on – they should have
come to him unbidden, as they had once come. What was wrong?
Why could he not lift his right arm?

The crowd was nearing the end of the Creed now, turning
the corner into the straight, the finishing post within sight of
them ahead:

Together with the Father and the Son He is adored and glorified.
He it was who spoke through the prophets. I believe in one,
holy, catholic and apostolic church. I profess one baptism for
the remission of sins. And I look forward to the resurrection of
the dead and the life of the world to come. Amen.

They rumbled snugly into their seats, sitting back for the Offer-
tory, to let him get on with it. Well, he would get on with it, he just
had to get on with it, accepting the wine and water from the server,
keeping his hand in close to his side so that no one would know.

And get on with it he did, conscious of nothing but the effort of
lifting the chalice, of breaking the bread, of extending his arms in

the blessing. "The Lord be with you." When he left the altar at last, he felt the satisfaction of having survived, just barely survived, in spite of them all.

Mrs. Delany was frying rashers and eggs at the oil stove in the vestry. He unvested slowly, having difficulty with the alb until she came across and helped him. Thank God, she wasn't a talker.

His mouth was sour; he didn't feel like eating anything, but he let her go back to the stove and continue with his only cooked breakfast of the week. He knelt at the prie-dieu while she set out the things on the checked tablecloth, then he took his place at the table, and she set the cup of tea before him. Gradually he felt himself reviving.

It was his favorite hour of the week, when he rested after work well done. He liked the hot, strong tea, the chair, worn into comfort by generations of clerical posteriors. Above all, he liked the room, the way the light came through the diamond panes, which always shone – he never knew why, nor did he know why the walls always seemed so freshly yellowed; he would have been shocked to know the amount of time Mrs. Delany spent cleaning and distempering the place. It was her room, really, an extension of her neat, warm, well-scrubbed kitchen in the cottage down the road.

Now he watched her move, unsmiling but benign, from the stove to the table, setting out his breakfast before him, the porridge and the cream, and after that the plate of rashers and eggs, the toast and marmalade. When she finished serving him, she withdrew to her chair by the stove, where she always read a book while he ate. A devotional book, maybe? But no, it was a book from the public library, as he could see from the battered maroon jacket. For the first time, he wondered what sort of book she would read.

She looked up in surprise when he asked her, then showed him the cover. "I can't pronounce the name, Father."

The Brothers Karamazov, he read. Good God!

She leafed through it thoughtfully. "I read it before, but they don't change the books very often, and most of what they have is trash."

"But that's good, is it?"

"Well, yes, Father. It passes the time." And she found her place again and settled herself into it.

He sipped his tea and watched her, afraid that she might say or do something else to estrange his vision of her still further. Someone – Mahon, probably – had lent him a book by Dostoevsky once, and he had read the first hundred pages or so, then given it back, saying it wasn't good to disturb people with books like that. Yet, for seven years she had been reading while he breakfasted on Sunday morning, seven years she had sat here with her gray hair drawn neatly back, her chin on her hand, her eyes moving calmly behind her glasses. He had always thought of her as poor Mrs. D., the widow woman, and here she was, more complete than he.

She looked up suddenly at the sound of footsteps on the path. Knowing it was Father Cullen come for his weekly colloquy, she got up and put another cup and saucer on the table, then went back to her chair by the stove.

Father Cullen came in on a cold breeze. "Mornin', Tom. Mornin', ma'am." He pulled off his coat and sat down at the table, blowing on his hands. "How goes it, Tom?"

"Fine." Father Conroy moved his right hand to pour out the tea, then remembered and used the other hand.

Father Cullen looked at the bad hand, glanced up as if to speak, then looked away. "Hell of a night I had, up till all hours. Snow White had another litter."

"That's good."

"I'll keep one for you. A little fawn bitch, a beauty."

"No, thanks."

"Never too late, Tom. The sire has a touch of class – broke thirty seconds at Clonmel. Why don't you call over, anyway?"

Yes, why don't I? I might find out about Tomás, worm the address out of him. But would he give it? I wonder!

Father Conroy glanced at the woman. A pity she's here! I could have sounded out Bat now, taken him off his guard. Maybe I should go and see him, though. Maybe he wouldn't mind giving me the address, in which case I could write straightaway to Tomás...

Ah no, he thought, angry with himself. Bat promised the Canon to keep it to himself. It wouldn't be fair to put him on the spot.

"No, Bat, you won't tempt me," he said, shaking his head.

Bat stirred his tea, glanced again at the hand, and glanced away. "Heard you had a go at them again over the porch."

"Yes. What did you talk about?"

Bat fidgeted. "To tell the truth, with all the fuss last night, I didn't get a chance to prepare anything. I rubbed it in about marriage, though – you know, stop hanging around, get down to it, name the day. I usually do, this time of year."

"Mine was about faith."

"Faith?"

"More or less."

The woman hadn't looked up. Father Conroy watched her, ill at ease, wondering how much of these conversations she had been absorbing for the last seven years.

Bat planted both elbows on the table and came out with it. "Game ball, Tom?" he asked.

"What?"

He winked toward the window and lowered his voice. "Anything I can do?"

"No, I'm game ball." But he wished Bat would look away. For such a stupid man, Bat could fix you with a gimlet eye. "No need to worry."

"I just thought... You know how a fellow gets a bad patch." He winked again at the uncurtained window, and Father Conroy had the impression that the room darkened for a moment. "There's nothing for him then but the prayers. Keep up the oul' prayers." He gave another wink. Cripes, thought Father Conroy, is it my guardian angel he's winking at?

"Yes, Bat." He smiled in his most gentle, misleading way.

"You can't beat them, the oul' prayers. The rosary's your man. There's no better comfort in a bad patch. Tell us, Tom, d'ye say it at all?"

"What?" he said irritably. "The family rosary? No, I don't."

"There you are!" Bat turned toward the invisible being at the window and triumphantly indicated Father Conroy. "And tell us, Tom, why don't ye?"

"Because it wouldn't make one ha'porth of difference, that's why."

"Oh, God. Oh, Tom!" He seemed scared that his confidant

at the window might have overheard. "And your Office?" he whispered.

"Of course!" Father Conroy said indignantly. "Naturally, I say that."

"Still, if ye don't say the rosary…"

"Look, Bat, all that's wrong with me is a touch of sciatica, that's all."

Bat's eyes wandered in alarm over Father Conroy, trying to assess the real damage. "And the leg, Tom?"

"That was the kick…" But no, what was he thinking of? There had been no kick, apart from the one in his dream. "Oh, anyway," he burst out, "'Tis all right now."

"I'm going in to Castlemore on Tuesday. I'll take you in, and you can let Fogarty have a look at you."

"Fogarty? I wouldn't bring a dog to that fellow."

"As a matter of fact, Tom" – Bat flushed and raised his voice – "I'm bringing him one of the litter I promised him. And I may say, I couldn't think of a better man to bring a dog to."

"Oh, there's no better man," said Father Conroy soothingly, "but all I need now is a rub of embrocation."

"Then why didn't you say so before? Sure, I have the very thing out in the car. I use it on the dogs when they're going to the track. It's great stuff. You can see it soften up the muscles like melted butter. I'll try a little on you now, if you like."

"Ah, no, don't bother."

"Tom, I'm going to get it for you right now. What harm can it do you, anyway?"

Before Father Conroy could protest further, the jar of ointment was fetched in from the car. In a few moments his coat was off and his shirt sleeves rolled up. He resigned first his right, then his left arm to be rubbed with the tacky gray stuff. Under the warmth of Bat's hands it seemed to him that the pain began to fade.

"Now, then, how's that?"

He bent his arm carefully. "It's better, I think."

Bat screwed the lid on the jar and stood up. "Keep that stuff by you, and give yourself a good rub with it, morning and evening."

"Thanks, Bat. I'll face anything now."

Bat shook his head reprovingly as he took up his cup of tea. "Ah, but don't forget, Tom!"

"What?"

Bat bent nearer to murmur, "The rosary!" and smiled over the steaming cup.

I know Bat, thought Father Conroy, smiling too. And Bat knows me; yes, he does. I'm part of his world, like the seven dogs. I'll stay part of him, whatever happens.

Surprised, unnerved, he looked across at the chapel woman to see if she had guessed what was in his mind. She looked up at him calmly, only barely aware of him, and slowly turned a page.

I'm part of her too, he thought. Like Alyoshin, or whatever his name was, and all the other characters she reads about. I'll live on in her.

And as he looked from her back to Bat, still smiling over the cup, yet another phrase flew in from the past: "It seemed that to be known is to have life and continuance in other men's keeping."

Now, who the blazes had said that?

Chapter 10

He thought again of Tomás that evening. Even if he never got the address, it would be a relief to know what had happened to the boy. Surely the Canon couldn't begrudge him that bit of information? Besides, damn it, maybe Tomás would like him to know. If so, what right had the Canon, or Bat, to come between them?

I'll drive over to Bat, that's what I'll do. I'll put all my cards on the table and leave it to Bat to tell me or not to tell. Bat's a decent sort. Bat will tell.

Just as he got ready to go, he had a call from Joe Halpin. He groaned as he saw the confident figure come up the drive – next after Watch and Pray, Joe was the biggest cross he had to bear.

He was a strong, rubicund fellow of about forty years. He lived alone in a county-council cottage and sometimes did odd jobs for farmers, when they could get no one else. The trouble about Joe, Father Conroy had once remarked, is that he thinks manual labor is a Spaniard.

He wore a sheepskin jacket, bought secondhand at the horse fair in Donore. It was too small to zip up, so that a large expanse of hairy chest was left bare. More hair sprang out from under his cap. His eyes were gray and serious, set very wide apart; his manner, as always, was placid. He carried a duffle bag, out of which stuck a large packet of cornflakes.

"I brought you a piece of the Sunday paper, Father. There's a bit in it about dreams. Remember what you were saying?"

"No, Joe, I do not." God Almighty, what had he said to cause another visit, a further infliction? Was it safe to talk about anything with Joe?

"It do say here that Shakespeare and other great writers got most of their stories out of dreams. There was a man called…" He searched the paper for the name. "Coleridge, now, and I was wondering if you ever heard tell of him, because I had a dream once that was very like the one they do say he had."

Father Conroy took the paper firmly. "I'll have to read this at my leisure, Joe. Was there anything else you wanted?"

"Sure, no, Father, except that I have another post in view, and I'd be obliged to you if you'd do the needful."

Damn it, another reference! Father Conroy summoned up a smile. "What is it this time, Joe?"

He took the newspaper clipping that Joe gave him and searched it for the most likely post. "Curator of Manuscripts in Nottingham University"? Surely that couldn't be it? But yes, Joe's black fingernail was underlining the ad. "That's a post, now, that might suit me right well. A man could do some literary work in a post the like of that. I was reading in the *Sunday Express* about a grocer in Wales who kept a notebook under the counter and, begod, didn't he write three great novels, with no bother on him at all. Just filling in, like, between customers."

"You want the reference now?" asked Father Conroy gloomily.

"Straightaway, Father, if it's all the same to you. There'll be a lot of men putting in for a job like this, and I wouldn't want to be behindhand."

Christ, what a job I have, thought Father Conroy and, raging, he cleared a space on his desk and began to write. All the time, Joe kept talking about an article he had read in the *News of the World* about an attempt to force open a tomb to prove that some writer was really someone else, or that someone else's tomb was really the writer's – he could not remember which.

"Whisht, man," Father Conroy called in exasperation. "Will ye let me write the bloody thing!"

It wasn't too bad, as references went. Father Conroy watched Joe perusing it, chanting the words under his breath in the manner of the national school spelling class. "'Sober, industrious, Mr. Halpin is a young man who has never been known to start trouble. He comes of decent, respectable stock…'" Father Conroy flinched as he listened. "'A man of parts, Mr. Halpin has still to find the proper outlet for his talents. I have no doubt that when he finds it, he will make his mark…'"

God forgive me, thought Father Conroy, in despair. The leavings of our educational system, fit for nothing at fourteen but to chant his tables and spellings! What opportunities could he make anything of? No farmer called on Joe, except as a last resort; there was no man in the parish quicker to disable a tractor or put a milking machine out of action.

Joe looked up, eyes shining. "This is the best yet, Father." Carefully he folded it into the wad of literary clippings. "D'ye know, Father, I think I'll keep this, it's so good, and not waste it on that crowd in Nottingham."

And, as he went out the door, he called, "God bless you, Father.

You can handle a pen with the best of them." He hitched his duffle bag full of cornflakes up on his shoulder and went off down the drive, content for another week or two.

He was hardly out of sight when the Sergeant arrived to ask Father Conroy to come and settle a dispute. Father Conroy had no trouble in guessing who had started the dispute – another of his oddballs, Mrs. O'Flynn. They all come to me, he thought, the oddballs. They're all I ever get. Young Farrell gets the cream, the decent citizenry, the sane and the sober. About time I did something about it, gave myself an agonizing reappraisal, as Farrell would say, Maybe I need a new image.

One of his least favorite chores was to make his way up to the highest point of his parish, to the small farm where lived that most formidable parishioner, Mrs. O'Flynn, She was a woman whose eye he avoided even when he preached at her on Sunday. A former schoolmistress, she still spoke with the patience and precision of one addressing meaner intelligences than her own. At sight of him entering the farmyard, she would put down the bucket of mash and draw near, hitching her jersey higher on her impressive chest. Then, leaning upon the haggard wall, she would proceed to inform him, in carefully articulated English, of the shortcomings of his parish and of all in it, including himself.

While he listened, unable to get a word in edgeways, he watched her husband dourly hump great, steaming sprongfuls across the yard. And, all the time, he was aware of her pet ram that stood on the step outside the front door and stared down at him disdainfully. A ménage à trois, he had called it, and that flash of vengeful inspiration had been some consolation for all the trouble they caused him.

For, not only her manner, but also the candor with which she was afflicted occasioned neighborly assaults against her husband or herself. These led eventually to scenes in court, which were reported in shameful detail in the local papers.

A dispute recently about a boundary ditch had culminated in an attempt by a neighboring farmer and his two sons to impale Mr. O'Flynn on the points of their hay forks. Mr. O'Flynn, however, could still show a surprising turn of speed, thanks to his long experience of such situations. Charges and countercharges had been laid, and now another court case was pending, in spite of the attempts of the Sergeant to talk both sides out of it.

He was a big, silent man, the Sergeant, who patrolled his district in slow motion on a big bicycle. Shyness made him sweat easily, which was why he never prosecuted anyone (and consequently, it was said, had never been promoted). Now the thought of giving evidence in court in a case involving the O'Flynns threatened him with total dissolution. When he appeared at Father Conroy's front door, he took off his cap and wiped all over his head as he implored Father Conroy, for God's sake, to come up with him to the O'Flynns and see what could be done to effect a settlement between the parties.

"Go up yourself, so," said Father Conroy.

"Sure, it's not my place to do the like of that."

"It's not my place, either."

The Sergeant continued to wipe his head obstinately. He knew that anything he might say to Mrs. O'Flynn would be flung back at him in court. It was different for Father Conroy.

"It's *not* my place," raged Father Conroy. "I don't see why I should be dragged into it. Why don't you let them fight it out between themselves?"

The Sergeant said nothing. He had always found silence a powerful argument, even against the badgering of superior officers. Now, he watched it effectively answer Father Conroy's question. Father Conroy had to go, otherwise there would never again be any peace; the parish would be split in two while the case was hammered slowly all the way up to the Supreme Court.

When they reached the O'Flynns', the Sergeant waited discreetly outside in the yard while Father Conroy went in. The two O'Flynns were sitting in the middle of the kitchen, side by side, looking as if they had been interrupted in some private proceedings, a rehearsal of the court case, perhaps – she the prosecuting counsel, he the counsel for the defense. Between them sat the ram, its head on one side, an expression on its face which made Father Conroy say, after half an hour of fruitless argument, "I wonder, ma'am, would you mind putting that animal outside?"

"Dodo? He's not doing any harm."

Father Conroy looked at the ram. He was sure he would get nowhere while it sat there and stared back at him with, yes, the expression of a hanging judge.

"I'd sooner you put that animal out, ma'am," he said firmly.

"Put it out," said the husband, "when the priest tells you."

After a moment's defiance, she rose and led the reluctant Dodo outside. "Now," said Father Conroy, as she returned in a fury, "we can talk some sense." And indeed they did, for Mrs. O'Flynn was too furious to put up any coherent argument. As soon as the husband weakened, Father Conroy got up and went to the door.

"Come in, Sergeant," he called. "They're ready to talk business."

He left them to it. As he waited in the yard, listening to the Sergeant's soothing voice within, he filled his pipe with tobacco extorted from the Sergeant and stared at the sullen face of the ram. "Beat you, you bugger," he told it, as he lit up with a flourish. And while the ram stared back at him unwinkingly, he blew his smoke over the land to which he had restored once more the peace of Caesar.

It gave him satisfaction, of course, the role of guardian of the peace; it made him feel, as they drove down the hill, that Kilbride had need of him, as it had of the Sergeant sitting sedately by his side. Together they patrolled their plantation, like foresters in a dry summer, beating out the small fires that sprang here and there out of the heather.

But, damn it, he thought later, in the silence of his house, what use was it when all was said and done? What had he achieved? Preserved the Sergeant's quiet life, saved some lawyers' bills, made a truce for a few weeks – until the O'Flynns started another row. It was all as futile as the letter he had written for Joe Halpin, as futile as anything else he had done for Kilbride. In his whole life, in fact, had he ever done anything that was not futile, anything strong that would last?

And so, he began once more to think of Tomás. Was it too late? Too late, he amended hastily, to call around to see Bat? No, of course not. It was never too late to call on Bat. Ceremony was something that Bat would never know how to stand upon.

Calling on Bat was a daunting experience, though. As he got out of the car, a pack of hounds bounded around the corner of an outhouse and flung themselves upon him. Beating them off, he crossed the bone-littered yard at a quick shuffle, half-stooping to protect the calves of his legs. They circled him hysterically as he fumbled with the makeshift wire noose on the garden gate; then they swept in with him, snuffing at his heels, lunging through the bedraggled bushes on either side as he hurried up the path. To his relief, Bat appeared at the back door in a filthy apron and gave a high-pitched yap, somewhat like their own. Then they all swept together into the kitchen, where a great, black pot simmered on the range, lumps of meat bobbing about in it. The room smelled of straw and rendered fat.

With a perfunctory rinse of his hands under the kitchen tap, Bat put on the kettle for tea, then took up the half-chewed skull of something and flung it out the door to be pursued by the pack. He shut the door on them and came back to take several loaves of bread out of the bin, feel for the freshest one, and plank it down on the bread board.

Father Conroy did not wait for tea. He put his question without much ado and watched Bat's forehead wrinkle as if in pain.

"But d'you really want to know, Tom? You see, I told you the way I had to promise the Canon…"

"Fair enough," said Father Conroy and stood up to go.

"Ah, now, wait, Tom. What's your hurry? If ye must know, sure, damn it, ye must have some good reason, and I'm sure the Canon won't mind…"

"No, it doesn't matter. Forget it, Bat."

"I'll tell you what, then. I can't give ye the address but the Canon wouldn't mind if I showed you the photos he got."

"Photos? Did he send photos?"

"Ah, yes, he sends them often, every Christmas. Americans do that, you know. It's a business kind of thing, keeps them in touch with the trade." He bustled into the study, began to shuffle through drawers full of papers. Father Conroy crowded behind him. "Yes, here's one. I think it's the latest."

Father Conroy took it eagerly. The Christmas card was a family snapshot, set in a frame of holly and ivy. A man and woman and three, four, five children sat against a background of blue wallpaper. The face of one of the children caught his eye, a boy's face, Tomás' face, but with something different about it. The close-cropped hair, was it? No, of course not, that must be the son. And Father Conroy's gaze wandered to the face of the man.

"You'd hardly know him, I suppose," Bat said, watching. "I suppose he's changed a bit."

Yes indeed, changed a bit! Father Conroy would not have recognized the plump, smiling face under the balding forehead. A settled face! Christ, he thought, what a fool I am. Sure, this man is not Tomás, not any longer.

"He's in insurance, I believe," Bat said gently. "Put himself through college and all. There's great credit due to a fellow that does the like of that."

Father Conroy turned away.

"If you want the address, Tom, damn it, I may as well give it to you."

"No, I don't think I do."

"Don't mind about the Canon. I'll explain if he gets huffy…"

"No," burst out Father Conroy. "I don't want it."

He took his leave soon after, not waiting for the kettle to boil. Bat accompanied him to the car and stood in an awkward silence as he got in.

"You're all right, Tom?"

"Game ball."

"Don't forget, now, what I told you." He began his winking act again. "The spiritual reading, that's the most important thing, boy, the spiritual reading and the prayers. And most of all, the beads." Another conspiratorial wink. "The beads, Tom, the beads."

"Thanks, Bat," muttered Father Conroy.

As his car carried him away, he found that he was still holding the colored snapshot. He crushed it in the palm of his hand and flung it, raging, out the window.

Chapter 11

More moral support came next day, from an unexpected quarter. He was saying Mass in his oratory, when he heard a car come up the drive. "Qui es in coelis," he said, ducking down, but he was too late to see it draw up on the gravel beneath the window. There was a peremptory toot on the horn. Who could it be? "Sanctificetur nomen tuum."

The car door slammed. Hardly Farrell, and certainly not a parishioner, no, none of them would dare to summon him out so impudently. Who could it be? Gabriel's nailed boot was scraping at the floor, hinting willingness to rise and find out. Could it be Drewitt? He set his teeth and went on, "Adveniat regnum tuum, Fiat voluntas tua... Stay there, Gabriel!... in coelo et in terra..."

And slowly, with more ceremony than usual, he continued to the end of the Mass. He was listening, of course, for a knock at the door, but none came, no sound at all.

He descended at last, tantalized almost beyond endurance by the thought of Drewitt searching the parish lands for the pony, but yet having forced himself to fold away his vestments and say all his prayers. He opened the hall door with his most forbidding air and stalked out onto the top step. And then he laughed with relief to see Father O'Hara's car.

Father O'Hara himself was not to be seen. The drive was

empty. The land on either side, the whole countryside, looked spacious in the morning light, a clear, hard light reflected from white trees and hedgerows and frosty fields. The sun was rising, like a flat, cold orange above the hills. He began to walk eagerly down the drive.

Father O'Hara was leaning on a gate, looking out over the fields. His hair stood up in a white ruff on his big head. The fur collar of his golf jacket was turned up about his ears, so that he seemed like a burly old lion miraculously erect and smoking a pipe. Without looking at Father Conroy, he took a hand out of the pocket of his jacket and waved hello. He was contemplating his setter as it coursed over a distant field like a drop of red – no, not blood – some more quirky yet resolute liquid, like mercury.

"Hurry up, Tom," he called. "The whole morning will be gone on us."

"Where are we going, then?"

"We're taking the day off." He led the way back to the car and opened a door for Father Conroy. "Get in. Mind the lunch there in the basket. Elsie, as you see, has done us proud." "Ancilla mea," said Father Conroy suddenly, joyously mimicking Canon Fitzpatrick.

"Ancilla mea is right. Let anyone try taking her off of me."

"Sí réalt eolais na maidne í," hummed Father Conroy. "Agus drúcht an tráthnóna."

"What's that?" asked Father O'Hara, who was short on Irish.

"She's the morning star/And the dew of the evening."

"I'd nearly say you were right," said Father O'Hara. He put two fingers in his mouth and whistled. At the shrill blast across the fields, the deep drop of red rolled to a stop and seemed to freeze into the picture which held cattle and snowy trees and long stretches of amber sunlight.

"Lord God, what a powerful morning," said Father Conroy.

And it lasted; it lasted them nearly all day.

They drove away fast, making their getaway. As they crossed the parish boundary, Father Conroy eased his legs forward and reached in his pocket for his pipe. He looked straight ahead as he smoked, for once under no obligation to amuse; he was slowing down to O'Hara's pace of living, which made no demands, but accepted as conversation any reasonable silences.

The setter bitch stood on the back seat, head upreared between them. Around her drifted the smoke from the two pipes, puffed lazily, as from chimneys on a day without wind. She stared ahead through it, undisturbed by it, still panting slightly, tongue lolling. She was well aware of her importance to the expedition and of her ability to make it a success.

They put a good distance between themselves and Kilbride and found themselves at last on one of the hills overlooking the parish of Rosnagree. They parked the car by the roadside. While Father Conroy pulled on a pair of Wellington boots he found in the trunk, Father O'Hara got out and relieved himself against a low brier hedge.

"Isn't that a fine parish?" he declared as he slowly buttoned his fly. "No man could ask for better."

"I was born here," said Father Conroy, still busy with his boots.

"Oh, yes, of course you were. You know it all, so." And, as if this completed his satisfaction, Father O'Hara moved ponderously to get out the guns.

They set off, at last, heading along the brow of the hill.

The dog ran back and forth along the hedge and then broke through into the field beyond. They gave her her head for the first few fields, and she careered away in front of them, distracted by the wealth of scents and unable to settle to anyone. The day was still cold; the breeze had freshened from the northeast, and small white clouds moved across the pale blue sky, now and then obscuring the sun. Shadows went flying across the countryside below. The men blew into their hands as they walked; when they crossed a stubble field, the straws snapped underfoot like twigs. The earth was frozen so solid that their heels seemed to ring on it.

The dog coursed a little ahead of them, stopping briefly with paw upraised, then continuing her search along the headlands of the fields. Sometimes cattle followed her close, moving in little rushes, their stupid bullock heads breathing out resentful, steamy clouds at her heels. She moved on unaware of them, blind to everything but the scent she had chosen to follow.

They walked in silence. Father O'Hara held his gun carelessly poised, yet he was intent on every sign that the dog made. For all his weight, he moved in a predatory way which had its own grace. By comparison, Father Conroy looked awkward; his hat and heavy belted overcoat, which reached to his shins, gave him the appearance of a large black bird hiding a crippled wing. His leg, indeed, was giving him trouble as he scrambled through gaps in hedges and stumped over hardened hoofprints in gateways. But it was not that which ailed him (he was conscious of it as no more than a handicap which had to be overcome). What disturbed him was the sound of his father's voice, heard suddenly after half a century. He could not remember when the words had been said, but he could hear quite clearly his father say, "Yes, driving in the cows, boy, across a field of white clover, before the world's awake."

He looked down at the frozen fields of Rosnagree and tried to remember what had gone before or after those words, but the countryside below gave him no help. Yet, he recognized every landmark, sharpened, magnified by the whiteness around it. He could even see in the distance, like the opening of a cave, the wood which sheltered the house where he was born. It was the country-side of his boyhood, and he was moving around its borders, shut out from it. So complete was it without him, so disembodied did he feel, that he expected any moment to see his own figure drift painfully across it, a black shape in hat and drooping coat.

He roused himself to fire the first shot. The dog had worked her way through a plot of kale, when a pheasant burst out into the headland, well out of range, and ran for the ditch. As it suddenly rose, he swung his gun and fired. The dog looked back at him in surprise, and Father O'Hara chuckled quietly as the bird volleyed away up into the sky. Yet, he was glad he had fired. He had been afraid of that landscape, which had its own existence apart from him, its own sequence of time, under the shifting light of sun and clouds. The shot had served to establish him again, to anchor him in the world of Father O'Hara and the dog.

"Easy, Tom, easy!" Father O'Hara was saying. "We'll get our chances yet."

The next bird rose out of the stubble; he watched Father O'Hara bring it down with ease. "See now!" said Father O'Hara as he thrust it into his bag and wiped his hand on the grass. "Easy does it!"

They circled the hill without further success. Hunger at last made them set a course across the fields toward the car. Father O'Hara took the lunch basket out to a log by the roadside and opened the packets of sandwiches and the thermos flask of chicken broth. The dog sat on her haunches, head on one side, watching them. Occasionally they peeled off a sliver of meat and flung it to her. They ate in silence, watching the breeze move in the hedge, stirring the twigs and old leaves.

Father O'Hara blessed himself when he was finished, and got out his pipe. Father Conroy, too, got out his pipe, and together they sat a long time on the log, smoking. The dog began to fidget in the briers, complaining a little, and watching her, Father O'Hara said, "You didn't move out much lately, did you?"

"Move out where?"

"To Cullen, or Mahon, or any of us."

"What for?"

"Well, because—" He made a soothing noise to calm the dog and, as she ceased her whining, said, "Why don't you come over on Ascension Thursday, Tom? I'm having them all in."

Father Conroy said nothing, and after a pause they began to talk about Father O'Hara's holidays – a topic often discussed in the diocese, since Father O'Hara was one of those who like to submit their decisions for general approval.

He was thinking of going to Lourdes again. "The ideal spot," he said. "I often think, of all the places where Our Lady might have appeared, she could not have chosen any place better."

Father Conroy nodded, but he was thinking of the time he had been there, long ago, as chaplain to a pilgrimage of elderly Children of Mary. It wasn't so much the commercialism that disturbed him, the tons of pious junk that filled the stalls in the streets; he could take that – one had to, in this day and age. It was the crutches, hanging like stalactites from the roof of the cave, the candles moving in rivers of light down the great stone terraces of the basilica. It was the way people knelt for hours before the grotto, waiting.

One night, as he walked by the river, three girls came toward him from the grotto with their candles still alight, tall girls with Spanish faces. Linking each other closely, they passed him in silence. The girl in the middle was being supported by the other two; her head was bent, and she seemed to be crying. He stopped, looking after them as they passed into the darkness under the trees, and heard a fit of sobbing, so wild and passionate that the sound stayed with him all night. He was glad to be shut of the place and had no desire ever to go back to it.

"I don't think there's any experience to equal saying Mass there in front of the grotto," said Father O'Hara. "There's something… Oh, I don't know." He sensed perhaps that he wasn't getting across. "The wine with every meal, too! Gives one a new slant on life! And it's worthwhile taking a trip over toward the coast. I've always thought that Basque cooking is out on its own."

"Is that so?" said Father Conroy. How could one eat and drink with that desperate sobbing in one's ears? But people did. They learned to live with all that naked faith. Good people, priests like Phil O'Hara! I should have learned to live with it. Damn it all, it was my job to learn to live with it!

"Oh, yes," sighed Father O'Hara, "what they can do with fish!" And he knocked the dottle from his pipe.

They got up and began to move downhill from the high fields

which they had walked in the morning. Father Conroy said, "I might, Phil. I might come."

"One o'clock, then. Make it earlier if you like." And so, the arrangements for Father Conroy's last day were settled.

They passed sheep grazing on a slope. The bleating of the new lambs sounded deafening, as if they were penned in a room. One of the lambs had only just been born; its coat was still pink, and there was blood on its hindquarters. They stopped a few moments to watch it rise trembling to its feet. Then they passed on in silence.

The sun was dropping toward the west, and the countryside below rearranged itself in new, deeper patterns as the light slanted more shallowly across it. The colors came up like velvet brushed against the pile. Across one of the green, low-lying fields below the dog moved in a soft, red billowy roll.

"God!" said Father O'Hara, "but 'twas a powerful day!"

Near the bottom of the hill, they passed through a field in which was a rath – a mound raised by some ancient people – now overgrown with ash and hawthorn. Father Conroy remembered it well; he had helped harvest barley once in that field. Now the field showed signs of neglect; there was a deep-green boggy patch at its center, covered with clumps of gray rushes tipped with rust. Yet, one could still see the wide pathway to the rath that had never been plowed. The barley had been carefully sown to avoid the rath and the path approaching it.

The dog's head came lolloping into sight over the tops of the rushes. Gradually she began to circle in more tightly toward the path, her friskiness gone in a sense of purpose; she came into the open, stretching herself forward in long, careful strides.

"Now, Tom!" murmured Father O'Hara.

As the dog pointed herself at a clump of scutch grass, Father Conroy moved forward, raising his gun. Suddenly, out of the clump of grass, broke a hare – so big that it seemed impossible it could have fit into so small a "form," but had risen somehow out of the ground.

"Go on, Tom!"

Father Conroy took aim. The hare's great, elastic bounds were taking it out of range.

"Damnation, man, why don't you fire?"

Father Conroy lowered his gun.

"You're not superstitious, surely to God?"

Father Conroy made no reply. As they moved out of the field, though, he looked back and reluctantly, as if he had to make some explanation, he said, "Strange how that strip was never plowed."

"Waste of good land," grunted Father O'Hara.

"Hungry grass."

"Ah, nonsense! In this day and age!"

"I helped harvest barley once in this field when I was a lad. The old man who owned the place told me why the strip was never plowed."

"Those old pishogues!" Father O'Hara growled down in his throat, "They're died out now, those yarns, and no harm."

"I saw…" Father Conroy began, then decided not to go on. A wind among the barley shocks! It had risen suddenly in the air, a cone of black seed and whirling straw. Slowly it moved around the field among the watching harvesters, then, as if guided by some force within it, made its way in the direction of the rath. It left the ash and the hawthorn bushes dusted with straw and seeds. We laughed at it, thought Father Conroy, but we didn't go into the rath after it. What were we afraid of? The still, small voice that never came?

"I don't go for them at all," Father O'Hara said vehemently. "The electric light put a stop to that sort of oul' talk."

"It meant a great deal to the old people. It answered something for them."

"You'll always get an answer, Tom, from superstition. The easy answer."

"There may be a good basis for it, though." The hungry grass, for instance. The phrase brought him all the way back to early childhood. Who had told him about it? Or had he made it up himself – how the grass where a famine victim fell was infected for all time with his hunger, how anyone crossing it began to die, denied nourishment from the food he ate. "Only a people who know what famine means would have thought up hungry grass."

"Come on," said Father O'Hara. "The light is going, and we've a lot of ground to cover yet."

Father O'Hara brought down his second cock easily, and soon afterward another bird, which Father Conroy had missed. They were drawing near to a long, low farmhouse, with its whitewashed outbuildings set solidly about a yard. Above its blunt, smoking chimney, the sky was green and the first stars were shining out. It was very still. In the solitary fir tree beyond the house, pigeons were grumbling as they settled in for the night. Tree and house had darkened till they were almost one, the last shape of the day.

"Let's go in," said Father Conroy. With every step he took, his strength seemed to drain out through the soles of his feet, and there was nothing in him to replace it. His gun hung in a lump across his hollow forearm. I'm beat, he told himself, but aloud he said, "I used to know the old man here."

"He's a long time gone now, faith. A grand-nephew of his has the place now. A fine lad he is, too. He got married lately to a girl from the town, a great little worker, though you'd never think she'd be able for it. We'll go in, all the same. It's a house you'd be at home in."

A milking machine was thumping quietly in a building off the yard. The light was on in the byre, and as they passed, an elderly laborer came stooping to the doorway and peered out at them. He recognized Father O'Hara at once but had to be told who Father Conroy was.

"The Lord's sake! Sure, is it yourself, Father Tom? Faith, but you're the last person I'd expect to see in these parts. You never came near us for years."

"Are they in?" Father O'Hara motioned toward the window, from which light poured out through a gay chintz curtain.

"No, Father, you're out of luck."

"Off gallivanting, I suppose?"

"Into town they went, to do some shopping, and I'd say, Father, they wouldn't need persuading to stay on for the pictures or a dance. The young people nowadays! 'Tis they do have the time."

The priests began to move off.

"But go on in, let ye. There's a pot of tea inside that I'm just after wetting five minutes ago. The missus baked a cake of soda bread – 'tis wrapped in a cloth – and there's shop bread in the bin if you'd sooner have that. Let ye go in and make yerselves at home." And as they still hesitated, he added, "The boss would have my life if I let ye go without bite or sup."

The kitchen was in the thatched part of the house, a spacious room brought up to date with cheerful wallpaper. The old, wide hearth had been bricked in and a modern anthracite stove installed. Beside it was a pen in which lay a lamb, head erect, ears nervously pricked. A bright checked cloth covered the table in the middle of the room, beside which were set two newly painted white chairs.

Father Conroy pulled one of the chairs around to the fire and drew off his boots to warm his feet. Father O'Hara poured out the tea and brought it to him – it was very strong and sweet – with a thick cut of soda bread, so warm that the butter melted on it.

"A fine place," said Father Conroy at last.

"'Tis. Snug."

"No children?"

"There's one on the way." Father O'Hara shifted on his hams and said with satisfaction, "I married them myself."

Good man! Father Conroy was tempted to say, but looking at Father O'Hara's face shining benignly in the firelight, he merely shifted into a more comfortable position and murmured, "Ay, 'tis a snug place."

"Oh, a fine place, surely."

There was more Father Conroy wanted to say, but he did not know what. His empty limbs were filling up now with drowsy well-being. He felt too comfortable to move, and yet, there was some question hovering on his mind. He looked around the room, noticed a pair of slippers which had been scuffed off near the door to the room above. She must have small feet, he thought; they were fancy slippers for a farmhouse, with red roses on them, and they were fairly new, no doubt a wedding present. The room door was slightly ajar; yes, it was the bedroom, he could see the bedpost inside. Did they have a feather mattress? There were so few of those left in the country (a traveling salesman, a proper rogue, had collected them all, exchanged them for mattresses of fiber). But they'd probably have a feather bolster anyway, of the old sort. Yes, they'd lie there and leave the door ajar, so that they'd have the light from the fire.

Oh, here, what am I doing? Prying like that; God, I ought to be ashamed of myself. He looked uneasily toward the door, as if the couple were indeed in there, in the warm firelit dark. What was I going to say? Damn it, I was going to say something. He fetched up, to his surprise, a deep sigh.

"Lord, Tom, what's that in aid of?"

Hastily Father Conroy said, "Imagine them going off to the pictures!"

"Oh, well now, why wouldn't they? They're a hard-working young couple, and they're stuck here, day in, day out. Why shouldn't they break out now and then?"

"You'd think…"

"What, Tom?"

"… they'd have everything here."

"Oh, I don't know. I like a good picture myself. I fancy a good Western, I must admit that. John Ford, now, I'd cross Ireland to see a John Ford. He's my man."

Father Conroy let his question lie wherever it was; he was too comfortable to dig for it any further.

The roll of a laden churn in the yard brought Father O'Hara to his feet. "We'll fall asleep here," he said, buttoning up his coat. "Come on, and we'll go away."

They called good night to the old man and took the road back to where they had parked the car. The wind had dropped; there were no clouds, and the stars shone brightly. The dog moved along inside the roadside ditch; they could hear her rustling in the briers and splashing through ice-laden pools. After the warmth of the house, the night stretched immensely around them. They shivered a little in the cold.

Just before they reached the car, something moved ahead, a black shape between the hedges. Footsteps sounded faintly, but the shape did not seem to be coming any nearer. They quickened their pace and then found that it was indeed coming toward them, but so slowly as hardly to be moving. They could hear, as well as the footsteps, the tapping of a stick.

The figure was small and hunched. It was an old man, head bowed almost to his chest. They bade him good night as they passed, but he made no reply. The dragging footsteps and the tapping of the stick continued behind them. Looking back, Father Conroy said sharply, "Who's that, Phil?"

"I don't know from Adam. An old tramp, maybe, on his way down to spend the night in the hay barn below. Deaf, the poor fellow."

As Father Conroy looked back, the question nagged at him again but still wouldn't form itself into words. He stood thinking, as Father O'Hara got into the car and opened his door from within. What could it be? There was the whirlwind that passed through the barley field. The bloodstained lamb on the hillside. The warm farmhouse and the slippers with red roses. And now, the old man tapping his way downhill in the dark.

Were they small, individual explosions in his mind, or was

there some fuse that ran between them, from one to the other, so that they detonated into… into what? What question could it be?

"Wake up, Tom," called Father O'Hara, and chuckled as Father Conroy started and hastily climbed in. "You're coming, so, on Ascension Thursday?"

"Yes, I'll come."

That was one certainty, at least.

Chapter 12

There was suddenly a great deal to be done – things he had let slip, all kinds of affairs to be settled. Ascension Thursday loomed ahead, when he would come face to face with his peers. Everything had to be ready by then.

Yet he himself did nothing. The things he had let slip, all the affairs to be settled, presented themselves before him with their own solutions. He was simply called on to be a witness to what had already been decided, in the same way as he witnessed marriages determined independently of him by fate, or rather by the claims of land or money or by the more mysterious workings of the spirit or the glands. And so, uninvolved, he found himself present at the two meetings called in the parish during the week.

Two meetings in Kilbride! The parish suddenly came to life, not only to life, but to a realization of its own existence. The last big meeting in parish memory was in 1932, the year Dev came tumultuously to power. There had been a meeting before that away back in the 1880's or 1890's – something to do with Home Rule, or was it the Land League – no one was quite sure. Kilbride slept like a hedgehog between meetings, but its winters lasted a generation or more.

The private meeting of James Conroy's supporters was the first to be held. James had not called it, but he handled it as if he had. As he came in, the men sitting around the Kavanaghs' kitchen stood up, even the most sullen of them. (They stood, not for him, but for Father Conroy, whom he ushered in before him.) He laid a black leather box on the table; it lay there for the rest of the evening, tempting the men's wary eyes to stray to it, away from the business of the meeting. He sat on a kitchen chair on the outskirts of the crowd, having ushered Father Conroy into the armchair (which had been intended for himself), right next to the glowing coals.

James's first step was to seek out possible allies and set aside the neutrals. He did this by smiling at the men, one by one, and inquiring after a new house or water supply or byre, thereby reminding all present of the state grant he had obtained for the embarrassed client (the grant would have been obtained anyway, without his intervention, but he had never let that fact be appreciated in his constituency). When, at last, the first angry questions assaulted him, he listened calmly, looking through the papers in his briefcase as if the answer were somewhere in there, if only he could find it. When the voices grew louder and his statement of the case had been greeted with derisive laughter, he went back to search in the briefcase, as if there were more there he had not said. At last, when the meeting threatened to get out of hand, he looked up suddenly at Father Conroy and, as if bringing up a matter of the utmost moment, said, "Tell me, Father Thomas, did you ever take a trip by plane from Dublin Airport?"

Father Conroy paused in surprise, as he mopped his face. "No, James, I didn't." And because he was sweating in the hot seat intended for James, he asked irritably, "What's it got to do with this carry-on?"

"Did you, Mr. Toomey?" James asked the old teacher in the corner. Toomey looked up, as startled as a boy caught napping in class.

"I was never up in an airplane, Mr. Conroy."

"Any of you men?" He looked eagerly out over the company, encouraging them to try to show a bit of interest. And as they began to shake their heads, he went on, "Because I did. Yes, I took a day trip lately from Dublin Airport. As luck would have it, I passed over the parish here and looked down, and I said to myself, 'There's Kilbride now, down below!' And d'ye know what I'm going to tell ye?" He held them for a moment on the hook. "I never saw the parish looking better, no, never in my life saw it looking neater, more prosperous! I must say it's a credit to ye all."

They waited. Surely there was more to come! But no! Smiling benignly, he had gone back to search in his briefcase. And though they tried, they could not climb again to the heights of indignation from which he had dislodged them; their petulant questions offered no foothold.

When the talk flagged and the danger was past, he emerged from his briefcase and reached behind him for the black leather box.

"I want ye all to stand up," he said.

They stared at him in alarm.

"Come on now, don't be shy! I want all yer photos, every one of ye, in a nice group that ye can frame. Stand up, there, you, Pat."

And gradually, with much pushing and shoving, he got them all grouped, the older men sitting sedately in the chairs, with arms folded, the others standing self-consciously behind. All the time, he exclaimed about the wonders of the Polaroid camera.

"'Tis a marvelous yoke. The best gadget yet. It takes the Japs! Oh, 'tis they have the brains."

They suffered their photograph to be taken, none of them being able to express what they all felt – that his capture of their image gave him a hold over them.

While he held up his hand for silence, they waited tensely for the photograph to be hatched inside the camera. As soon as it was ready, he flipped it out and handed it to Mrs. Kavanagh with a flourish. "There now, ma'am! That's a little keepsake for ye. To remind you of the pleasant evening we passed under this hospitable roof!"

He handed the camera over to Pat. "Now," said he, "you must take one of me." He moved into the chimney corner and turned to pose for them, his thumb hitched in his waistcoat, above the heavy gold watch chain.

"If only we had a gun!" muttered Father Conroy. There was a laugh, which was stifled almost at once, at sight of him, staring solemnly into the camera. How could they laugh at him? He was so much stronger than they; he put himself so fearlessly at their mercy.

Soon afterward, still mystified, sullen, exasperated, they filed out. They could not even refuse to return his cheerful good night.

"Well, that's that!" he said to Father Conroy as he got into his car. "It went very well, yes, it went splendidly. A public man has to get out among the people. Keep in touch!"

"You forgot the prayers," murmured Father Conroy.

"Ah, yes, I did, mind you. I forgot the prayers. That's not like me now, to do that." He looked down a moment, fiddled with the medals on his chain. "I'll tell you, Tom, between ourselves, it may be my last appearance."

"What do you mean?" Was James – (yes, say it!) – was James on the way out too? Sick? Afraid? The poor man!

"I'm retiring."

Was that all? Father Conroy turned away impatiently. James had been threatening to retire for years.

"I am, Tom. Now, there's no use in trying to make me change my mind, because I won't do it. I think it's time for the youth to take over. Amn't I right, now?"

Father Conroy nodded. Still, it wouldn't be the same, bastard and all as he was, it wouldn't be the same without a James Conroy. All those years, not (as James himself said) of service to the community, but of getting the better of the "other fellow" – what were they for? Father Conroy remembered pictures of James breathing over the shoulder of the poll clerk, trying to check the "other fellow's" votes, ready to pounce on one which had the stamp missing, of James bending down, head cocked, to count the bundles of fifty ballot papers as they were placed on the table – all pointless as regards the final result, but showing the man's concentration on every detail of his profession of winning votes. There were dubious stories, too – the illiterate old woman, for instance, who was held by two of his men outside the polling booth and made to repeat his name over and over, so that when she was at last pushed in to vote and the presiding officer began to read over the names for her, she rose, like a trout, to the name of Conroy. What was it for, all that dedication? "Is it for Jimmy? For Jimmy to take over?"

"You've got it, Tom! The boy's made for it, just made for it. I thought of bringing him along tonight, but I thought, damn it, if things go against me (I didn't think they would, but they could have), if they go against me, he'd have a better chance starting off on his own."

Father Conroy muttered, jealously, "Why shouldn't he start on his own?"

"Why not indeed, Tom? But you know yourself, merit is sometimes overlooked in this country, even by the best people. All things being equal, a little push does no one any harm. Anyway" – he reached for the car door and began to pull it shut – "I know you'll do the needful, Tom. You know" – one eye narrowed, very slightly – "when the time comes!"

He drove away, filling the car like an old and battered potato – a seed potato, which, given the usual conditions of soil and climate, would not, could not, be prevented from sprouting.

The second meeting was, as Father Conroy said, a horse of a different color. He had nothing to do with it, but he knew that Farrell had been working on it for a long time before it was broached to him. His public attitude to "this traveling show" was one of amusement. Seeing the poster in the village shop, he quizzed it up and down with his nose, affecting extreme shortsightedness for the benefit of the shopkeeper and the farmer's wife at the counter.

"Are you interested in the future of Kilbride?" he read, spelling it out slowly, syllable by syllable. "Has your parish got a future?"

"Ah, Father Farrell!" he murmured, shaking his head sadly.

"You're wasted here! 'Tis selling soap on television you should be!" And he went on to read, "Come to the meeting on Wednesday next to hear the Apostle of the Save the Small Farms Movement, Father McEvilly in person."

"Stars of screen and radio will attend," added Father Conroy.

He tossed some small change to the shopkeeper. "An ounce of plug for the our pensioner here!" While he cut and rubbed the plug, he went back to reread the poster. "The future of Kilbride," he mused. "Well, well! It's a class of a carnival, so?"

"Ah, no, Father," said the shopkeeper, an earnest, beefy man in shirt sleeves. "Ye see, it's this committee that Father Farrell wants to set up…"

"I see. Ah, well, I thought there might be clowns and fortune-tellers and such-like."

He lit the pipe with a match from the shopkeeper's box and began to move with an exaggerated hobble toward the door. "And forward, though I canna' see," he intoned, puffing the smoke before him, "I guess and fear."

With Father Farrell he adopted an air of bewilderment, as if the whole thing were too much for him, especially since it had been sprung on him at such short notice. "I don't know," he muttered, scratching his neck, to the irritation of his curate, "I don't know what I'm supposed to do. Sure, won't you have all the big shots up there on the platform? What d'you want me for?"

"You'll have to be up there, that's all!" the curate told him curtly. "It's expected of you." His eyes were heavy; he had been working late for weeks, getting questionnaires out to each household, writing to councilors and Dáil deputies, badgering the county-council officials to ensure that they would be present and up on the platform.

"But what do I do?" Father Conroy asked plaintively. "I'm no good to sing."

"Sing?" The curate glared from bloodshot eyes. "What d'you mean, sing?"

"I used to be good at th' oul' step dance. Or even the soft-shoe routine," said Father Conroy. He hitched up the knees of his trousers and shuffled a few steps back and forth before the incredulous eyes of his curate. "D'ye think they'd like that?"

"Ah, Father, for heaven's sake!"

"I wonder, now, why it's called a routine? That's an interesting one, now. You'd think nothing would be routine to artistes and show people. But there you are! They have routines, just like the rest of us."

Father Farrell contained himself. He could not spare time to tangle with Conroy now. Besides, he sensed something in Conroy's clowning which warned him not to go too far – some of the fault was his own for keeping Conroy in the dark so long. "I'm afraid I must go, Tom," he said, with a glance at his watch. "I've a lot of things to attend to."

He must have attended to them well. Father Conroy was astonished by the number of cars that went past to the schoolhouse on the night of the meeting, most of them bearing the registration numbers of neighboring counties. A Garda patrol car was parked at the crossroads, and the guards were directing cars onto parking places well beyond the schoolhouse. Drewitt's big car went past; even the quality was in attendance. Father Conroy turned his head hastily away, thinking of the pony.

The public house was packed with men getting into good form for the meeting. Their heads and shoulders seemed to be wedged together behind the yellow blinds. Out on the porch, latecomers were gulping down pints of stout that were passed out to them over the crowd.

In the schoolhouse, the women were waiting. The girls settled in little groups on the small benches; they giggled and shoved each other as the boys eyed them silently from just inside the door.

Father Conroy went up the room to the table where a group of solid men, including two county councilors, had already installed themselves in chairs. Father Farrell was calling on the other men at the door to move down the hall to their places. At sight of Father Conroy, he broke away from the group and came hurrying forward. "Why don't they come in, Father?" he demanded. "For God's sake, we must get them in. We can't keep him waiting."

"Keep who waiting?" asked Father Conroy, at which the curate brushed impatiently past, leaped down off the stage, and went running down the hall, clicking his fingers to summon some of the youths by the door.

A stranger in black, who had been sitting with his head resting on his hands, looked up at the exchange. "Father Conroy, is it?" He got to his feet deliberately, as if counting the cost of each movement. He had not looked so big, sitting, but now Father Conroy realized with surprise that he was overtopped by several inches. A dour-looking brute, he thought, looking up at the long, brooding, fanatic's face. Then Father McEvilly smiled, and his large dark eyes shone with a cautious humor.

He put out his hand and said, "Forgive me for not calling on you before the meeting. I've been driving all day and thought I wouldn't make it in time."

"That's all right," said Father Conroy. "Kilbride obviously thinks there's plenty of time in hand."

Father McEvilly spread out his hand in a curious gesture; it intimated – well, that's the situation, if you're willing to put up with it. And at once Father Conroy felt he was being impelled to do something, to take some positive action, such as rushing out straightaway to drive in his flock, just as Farrell had done. Yes, the man was a pusher; there was no doubt about that. He's not going to push me, though!

"I'm new to this part of the world," said McEvilly. "You have good land here compared to where I come from."

"I wouldn't call it good," Father Conroy replied, and to his annoyance again evoked that gesture, this time meaning, you could make it good if you wanted to.

What's the fellow's own place like? he wondered. Maybe he should stay at home there, help them reclaim a few boggy acres from the snipe and the curlew, instead of traipsing around the country peddling his cheap remedies.

"I'm glad you're giving me this opportunity, Father," said McEvilly.

This time Father Conroy tried the gesture. All right, it meant, I'm giving you the opportunity; let's see what you can do.

McEvilly looked at him sharply and seemed to get the message at once. He smiled suddenly. "I won't raise any false hopes. I can promise you that."

The men were coming into the hall quickly, Farrell somewhere circling behind them, snapping at their heels. Heads down, faces hidden by their caps, they came in, and avoiding the eyes of the priests on the platform, darted into seats near the door. "Come on up, men," called McEvilly. "Come up. I didn't drive half the length of Ireland to talk to the wooden benches."

He's got a neck, thought Father Conroy, ordering people around like that, my parishioners. That's my job. And he got down off the platform himself and angrily called the men forward.

Farrell was in the doorway with three county-council officials, the County Manager, the Chief Agricultural Officer, and the Chief Engineer. He was trying to direct them up onto the platform, but they were looking around for seats as near the door as possible. They huddled together, glancing anxiously around to make sure there was no press photographer present. They had been unable to refuse to come. Now they were alarmed lest they seemed to lend too much weight to the proceedings.

"Leave them alone, Father Farrell," called Father Conroy. "Don't you see they're not here!" And as the curate went with him toward the platform, he said, from the side of his mouth, "It was their unofficial, ineffable presences you were dragging up onto the platform. 'What meat is on them?'"

The platform party was taking up its position behind the table. As Father Conroy was guided by Farrell to the chair in the middle, he muttered under his breath, "Damn it, you didn't tell me I was chairman! What d'you want me to say?"

On his right sat Father McEvilly and the two councilors (there to claim any political benefits that might be going). On his left sat Farrell, and beyond – God, how had he got in on the act? – his nephew, Jimmy, shooting long white cuffs out of a charcoal-gray suit. Yes, Jimmy himself, like a bank clerk as he spread a sheet of paper out before him and selected one of the pens from his breast pocket. Was he taking over from old James? Already?

"Now, Father!" whispered Farrell.

"D'ye want all these buffs to speak?" he whispered, leaning

sideways to confer seriously with the curate, the senior man with the very much junior.

"Yes. No, I mean, not the councilors." Poor Farrell was sweating, his eyes protruding with the strain. "Sorry, Father!" He drew a sheet of crumpled paper from his pocket. "I should have given you this."

ORDER OF SPEAKERS

– The Very Reverend Thomas Conroy, P.P., opens the Meeting.
– Rev. Father Robert Farrell, C.C., introduces the Guest Speaker.
– Father McEvilly speaks.
– Questions, Resolutions, Election of Committee.
– Vote of Thanks to Guest Speaker, proposed by Mr. Jimmy Donovan of Slievenalua, County Councillor; Treasurer, Total Abstinence Association; Member of G.A.A. County Board; Chairman, Young Farmers' County Committee.

Father Conroy studied the list as if it were a document of great moment.

"Now, Father!" urged poor Farrell again.

How was he going to start? As he rose to his feet, buttoning his shabby waistcoat, he launched out in the only style he knew would give him his place in the affairs of the evening, the style of one of those on the benches by the door, one of themselves! In fact, he seemed more one of "them" than anyone else present, so limited, so poor in wit, so anxious did he seem to follow what was going on, to know why all these important-looking people had descended on Kilbride to take its people in hand and show them what to do. For his part, he implied, he was prepared to sit back and listen gratefully to all the advice these important people had to offer, and he hoped that every man, woman, and child here present would do the same.

As he sat down to enthusiastic applause (they knew where they were now; they had someone on their side), he felt himself raked by a sharp glance from McEvilly. Now, what's he beefing about? he wondered. Does he think I said something wrong? Somebody here has got to speak up for the poor man in the cap! Why shouldn't it be me, who have never had need of a platform from which to talk down to them? In fact, I shouldn't be up here at all; I *am* the poor man in the cap.

Father Farrell was already in full flight. "This ministering angel," was one phrase Father Conroy caught. Surely he wasn't referring to McEvilly? But indeed, it seemed as if he was, for McEvilly, to do him justice, was passing a hand down over his face, rather wearily, as if he had been embarrassed by this sort of gush many times before.

If only the man had looked more prepossessing! He kept his head down as he rose to his feet, giving an immediate impression of sullenness. Then he threw his head up, screwed his eyes to look up at the naked bulb hanging from the ceiling; he cleared his throat and finally glowered at a point somewhere just above the heads of the men standing in the doorway.

"People of Kilbride!" He had a voice like a cross-cut saw; it overrode all the fidgety little noises in the room. One felt that nothing could stop it, not even when it snagged sometimes over a word, as if tearing at a knot or a nail. God, what an ugly voice, thought Father Conroy; what an ugly man! But there was, almost at once, dead silence in the room.

"… the fact that you asked me to come is enough for me. It's a start; you know now there's something wrong in Kilbride, and to those of you who don't know, or won't admit it, I say – look around you! Yes, look around! What d'ye see? What's wrong here?"

He gave them a moment. Father Conroy looked down at his people. Si monumentum requiris, respice! What was wrong? What did the fellow mean? The old people were looking around, stiff-necked, in their respectable way, eyes bulging to left and then to right. Watch and Pray was in the front seat, fingers jerking on the rosary beads, lips pattering out the prayers. He, for one, wasn't worried. Only the children nudged each other and stared frankly around.

How quiet they were, even the children! Yes, the children! The old people! Even as McEvilly began to speak again, Father Conroy at last got the message.

"A whole generation missing!" said McEvilly. "The generation that carries us forward, that takes a chance on the future."

God, yes, of course! How could those old ones take a chance on anything? The slump of their shoulders! Their downcast heads! They knew what it was to take a beating. The candles for the wake were already stored at home, on the top shelf of the kitchen dresser.

Politicians, priests, public men – all blather about emigration, but this is it, going on for years, a dry rot in the floorboards under-foot. Why didn't I notice it had gone so far? I say Mass on Sunday, turn around to preach to them; how could I have been so blind?

They were looking at McEvilly, hardly breathing, trying to see themselves as he saw them, a whole parish looking at itself for the first time. Only the small group of teen-agers by the wall shifted, raised uneasy faces to the speaker, then glanced at each other, as if afraid of what might be in each other's minds.

"I bring you no magic formula," the ugly voice told them. "Anything you want to do, you'll have to find out yourselves the way to do it. All I came here for was to tell you to look at yourselves, to ask yourselves the question, am I making good use of the life God gave me? Or am I just sitting here, waiting for the life to come?"

Even Watch and Pray got that one. He stopped fingering out the prayers and stared with mouth half-open. Did he make good use of the life God gave him? Who in the parish did? As Father Conroy searched the familiar faces, he felt a spasm of pain grip his arm and shoulderblades. It folded him back, breathless, in his chair. God, he thought, what a place to get this! Here I am, on the rack before them all. He gritted his teeth and held in his pain, so well that the others on the platform did not take their eyes off the speaker to glance at him.

The spasm went as quickly as it had come. He lay back weakly, his cane chair creaking with the strain. Am I making good use of the life God gave me? Jesus, I'm trying to hold on to it, that's all. A trickle of sweat ran down the side of his nose; he got out his handkerchief to mop his face, to wipe all around between collar and neck. It was the heat, that was all; the windows were all shut. Yet he could not summon enough energy to call on one of the men to open them. The meeting would be over soon, with the help of God. McEvilly's mouth opened and closed soundlessly. He seemed to be annoying the three men from the council – the Chief Engineer was scribbling in a notebook, while the County Manager fed comments out of the side of his mouth.

A committee was being formed. Father Conroy watched help-lessly as a few of the more solid farmers rose when called upon to take office. They were taking the parish out of his hands; that's what they were doing. And he could only sit here, unable to move! Who was this fellow, anyway, this black stranger ordering his people about? What right has he to interfere? I hate him for being here. I hate his voice and the way he flings out his hands. I hate him because he can do things and I can't.

Something was wrong. After the first volunteers (primed beforehand by Farrell, of course), nobody else rose to offer himself. Farrell looked panic-stricken as he read out the vari-ous station areas of the parish. The hall became quite silent; the people were aware that a decision about their future was to be given or refused. Even McEvilly put his head in his hands and glowered down the hall.

Then, slowly, Watch and Pray rose to his feet. There was a titter at the back of the hall, but the old fellow remained standing, leaning forward out of the school desk, like an old thorn tree, with his hat clamped on his head and the gray hair in wisps around his face.

"Will I do, Father?" he called, and when a great laugh burst out, he grinned and turned around to his mockers. "Sure, God is good. He'd send someone better if He could."

"Put down his name," McEvilly said. Then, sternly, he called out over the laughter, "How many young people do we have here between the ages of seventeen and twenty-one?"

He got them to stand up, which they did, one by one, reluctan-tly. When nine or ten were standing, he said, "Now, those of you who don't want to serve on the committee may sit down."

Some stood; some tried to sit, then rose slowly again. They looked around in confusion for their elders to direct them; they had never been called on for a decision before.

"All right," McEvilly said quickly; "Come up to the platform, and Father Farrell will take your names."

Oh, you clever bugger, thought Father Conroy; you've got them where you want them. And it was so simple. All these years I've been sitting here, and I could have done it, I could have had them organized just like that. Why didn't I? Why didn't I even think of it?

While Farrell took over the organization of the committee, McEvilly slumped down in his chair. This was only one meeting of many; it came after one, before another, with long journeys between, across an emptying countryside, finding his way in the dark to obscure parishes where the rot had set in. What drove him, forced him to sit, head resting on his fingertips, dominating crowds of strangers with the force of his will? Father Conroy stared at him, as if his pose would reveal an answer.

Jimmy had risen to propose the vote of thanks. He had an inattentive audience. The people were excited, eager to get outside to discuss all that had happened, but Jimmy was not to lose his opportunity.

"I'm not going to propose a vote of thanks. I don't see why I should." He paused to let that silence them. "I'm not going to thank anyone, even Father McEvilly for all the miles he's come tonight."

Father Farrell was staring down the hall, tapping his hand on the table in agitation. This was terrible, an insult to the guest, the great McEvilly. There was an embarrassed murmur from the crowd. Father McEvilly smiled to himself, the only one to see what was coming.

"This meeting should never have taken place. It's a reflection on all of ye that ye should have to come together tonight to save the parish of Kilbride. What have ye been doing here all these years?"

Father Conroy kept his head down. Jimmy's getting at me, he thought. I'm the one who was in charge. He means, what was I doing? Head still lowered, he glanced around. No one looked at him, yet they must have noticed the gibe. Were they avoiding him, careful not to involve themselves until the charge was pressed home?

Jimmy pulled slyly at his cheek and smiled; he had all the attention he wanted. He wasn't blaming anyone in particular, he said, he hadn't been doing all he should have been doing himself, in his own parish. However, if a certain course were adopted – with the support of the people, of course – he would, please God, have the opportunity to devote himself to the interests of not only Kilbride but of every parish in the county which was in the same predicament.

Here we go, groaned Father Conroy; break for the commercial. And indeed, Jimmy did pause to let the whispers throughout the room break into a burst of applause.

So Jimmy was running for office. And party politics had still to be fought. Father Conroy glanced at Farrell, who looked upset, and at McEvilly, who stared stony-faced down the hall. Well, it was their fight; it was up to them to keep the politicians' paws off the committee. Good luck to them; it's got nothing to do with me.

Yet, as he listened to his nephew's speech, Father Conroy sank his head in shame, trying not to think of what was being said, not to hear the applause for such stolen gems as, "When the history of Kilbride comes to be written, this will stand out as our moment of decision, our finest hour," and "Ask not what Kilbride can do for you, but rather what you can do for Kilbride!" Wild and heartfelt applause greeted this last flourish as Jimmy sat down. The meeting, thank God, was over.

Father McEvilly clapped very briefly, then went down to gather the new committee together. He spent a long time among them, questioning, listening, making jokes, a different man altogether from the dour speaker he had been on the platform. The young people crowded in, eager to be assigned their tasks. Already they were becoming conscious of themselves as a group with a certain power to be wielded.

When the hall was cleared, the priests and official visitors were transported to Father Farrell's house, where tea was being served. Father Conroy found himself penned in a corner by the three wise men from the county council, who stood sipping tea while they listened to old Toomey, the schoolteacher.

"Covered in evergreens," Toomey was saying. He sat on the pouf, clasping his knees to him. All his features drooped; even his glasses, the sole support of his face, slid occasionally down his nose and had to be pushed back with the tip of his finger.

"Yes, but you can't have—" the Chief Agricultural Officer protested.

"All the hills clad in virgin forests of spruce and pine. And little villages in the clearings, such as you get, I'm told, in the Black Forest of Germany. We'd have charcoal plants too, and plastics, for which I understand timber is the primary raw material.

The logs could be floated down the larger rivers to vast sawmills, such as you get in Scandinavia and in the eastern states of Canada. Or is it the western states?"

"The eastern, I think," said the Chief Agricultural Officer, "but tell me—"

"No matter, I think it's both. In the river mouths, we'd set up shipyards for the manufacture of fishing boats. Oak, of course, has historically been the timber most favored... but I'm sure that pine..."

"Look," the Chief Agricultural Officer interjected, "I can get you Sitka spruce at a special rate of five shillings for five hundred, if you'd take on the job of organizing a planting scheme."

"Sitka spruce?" said Toomey. "Sure, how do we know that's what suits us here in Kilbride? Soil and climatic conditions, they're very important, you know, they'd have to be gone into very carefully."

"They have been."

"Ay, but not in Kilbride. And anyway, who's going to give us the land? No, gentlemen, let's face it, our first and most basic impediment is climatic. Progress in Kilbride is impossible until we take steps to ensure that not only do we get the weather we're entitled to, but that we seem to be getting it. I'm referring to the biased weather forecasts we're continually being given on the wireless."

"In what way, Mr. Toomey?" asked the County Manager, a tall, stooped, rather humorless man with dyspepsia. "I mean, I don't recall—"

"'Tis a disgrace the way the man on the wireless always mentions centers of low pressure around this part of the country. Sure, 'twould put anyone off coming here. Now, if we didn't have this climate business always thrust in our faces, we'd be an ideal mark for the tourists. You see, gentlemen, if we had the tourists coming to Kilbride, why, we could lay out a village green, a pitch-and-putt course, do the place up, build a decent pub, plan a whole new… a whole new…"

"Dispatch center," said Father Conroy, unable to stomach any more.

"I beg your pardon, Father, I'm referring to the tourist trade."

"Dispatch center!" repeated Father Conroy. "For sorting and labeling of emigrants. We'd also need a reception center for handling the new settlers."

"What? Ah, now, Father, I'm serious."

"So am I," snapped Father Conroy, as the County Manager and staff tried on dutiful smiles. "What we need at the present time is a change of population. We need to bring in a complete new race of people, Germans for preference. We need to move the present lot out, lock, stock, and barrel, every mother's son of them."

"You will have your joke, Father."

"I'm not joking at all, Mr. Toomey. We're here long enough, that's what's wrong with us. We're tired of the place, we need a change. Sure, even the motorcar can't keep going, unless you change the sump oil."

"Hee, hee, Father," tittered the County Manager. "You're hardly suggesting you can change us as easily as the sump oil of a car?"

"Why not?" Father Conroy confronted him savagely. "Stalin did it. He couldn't wait generations for the idea to sink in."

"Ah, now, Stalin, Father!" The Chief Engineer shook his head, then backed away as Father Conroy swung on him. "You don't mean to say we'd bring the communists—"

"We'd bring peace, that's what we'd bring. We've no quarrel with the French or the Poles or the Dutch. We'd even pull with the Russians. We'd have Europe eating out of our hands, man, if we were planted in the center of it."

"I think, all the same, Father" – the fat, priest-handling councilor had joined the group and was breathing hard at Father Conroy's shoulder – "I think you'd be sorry to leave our Kilbride."

"I would not then. I'd know that new German homes were springing up all over the parish, healthy as mushrooms. Besides, they'd have left places like Dachau and Belsen behind them. I bet we could find plenty of fuel for those old gas ovens."

They were silent, looking at the ground.

"Plenty of deadwood," said Father Conroy, "like us."

The County Manager coughed and extended his hand. "Well, Father, we must be off. It's been very interesting." And with some haste, bumping together in the doorway, they made their departure.

Yes, he had shifted them, all right, but when he looked around, the room seemed as full as ever of people who could be dispensed with. They were all facing toward the table at the far side of the room, where McEvilly was sitting, eating a snack. Over their heads, he got a glimpse of McEvilly's knife raised to emphasize some word. Well, there was no point in staying. He had heard enough oul' chat for one night.

On his way out, he was accosted by a stranger, a burly fellow of about forty-five, dressed in the houndstooth tweed jacket and cavalry-twill trousers of the gentleman farmer. He was sipping tea and surveying the company with a rather superior air.

"Well, what did you think, Father? What's your honest opinion?"

"Of what?"

"Of the great man, Father? He was in fair form tonight, but I've seen him put on a better show."

"Father McEvilly, you mean?"

"Ay, that's what I'm saying. I've heard him now, oh, I suppose ten or twelve times. I drove sixty miles to hear him tonight. I follow him up, you might say. And d'you know what I'm going to tell you? I don't honestly think he's learning anything; I mean, when you take into account all the experience he's had."

"Learning what?" asked Father Conroy coldly.

"Well, now, Father." He put another spoonful of sugar in his cup and stirred with relish. "I'm by way of being a speaker myself. You know what I mean – I won the Young Farmers' cup for debate two years running, and I train our own team – I say all this without boasting, just to show that my opinion on the subject is worth something." He sipped his tea, as if there were no more to be said until this information had been properly digested.

"But you found the meeting interesting?" prompted Father Conroy.

The fellow finished his tea and laid the cup and saucer down. "Moderately so, Father. McEvilly, as I said, was in no more than fair form, but that young fellow, Donovan, Jimmy Donovan, he's a flyer."

"You liked him?"

"He'll go far." He hitched his thumbs in his waistcoat pockets and lifted himself up and down on his toes. "Being a grand-nephew of old James Conroy won't do him any harm. And, of course, a meeting like this is a godsend for a young fellow who wants to show off his paces."

"And what d'you think the people of Kilbride thought of it?" asked Father Conroy mildly.

"Of what, Father?"

"Of this act they put on tonight?"

"Oh, 'tis time for them to do something. Sure, 'tis a terrible hole of a place. Who'd stay in it the way it is?"

"I do."

"Begod, Father, I'm sorry… I didn't know… I thought you were a stranger here, like myself."

"I'm the man, you could say, who's responsible for the way it is."

"Oh, no, Father, I'm sure no one would say…"

"But you could say it!"

"No, I couldn't, I wouldn't… I think, Father, if you'll excuse me, I've a long way…" And as he bolted for the door, he threw back over his shoulder, "I'm very glad of the pleasure. Delighted, Father."

By God, thought Father Conroy, I'll clear this bloody place yet. He moved toward the table around which the priests and important visitors were talking animatedly. Phrases like "pilot area," "tractor co-op," and "soil survey" hung in the air about him. Through a gap between their heads, he saw McEvilly seated at the table, stirring his tea, his long face darkly brooding. Beside him, a loud-voiced secondary-school teacher from Castlemore was talking about morphology. "Oh, 'tis a science all its own, you know. It's fascinating to discover why one parish decays, while the one beside it forges ahead."

Father Conroy moved quickly away and stood, biting his thumbnail. What was this, anyway? Why were all these people passing judgment on his parish, on him? A bloody postmortem, by Christ. What right had they to come here?

Across the room, McEvilly looked up, gazed at him, and smiled as if to say, "See what I have to listen to!" Father Conroy slowly nodded his head, and McEvilly lowered his eyes to brood again.

He's a man I'd like to talk to, but there's no chance of that – he's moving on early tomorrow. Anyway, what would we talk about but maybe a pig-fattening cooperative or a knitting industry or putting more land into beet? He wouldn't know what I want to talk about.

And what's that? I don't know myself. It could be that the pigs, the knitting, the beet would do very well to talk about. He looks like a man who'd know *why* you'd want to talk. And damn it, I'd like to know what it is that drives him, on and on, from parish to parish, meeting to meeting – what doesn't drive me. I'm a priest the same as he is. I've attended to my duties, never missed a Mass, been there for confessions, for baptisms, for the last sacraments. I took trouble with my sermons, and I preached – what? Was it what I should have preached? Yes! "For the Jews ask for signs, and the Greeks look for wisdom, but we, for our part, preach a crucified Christ…" I, for my part, that's what I preached, a crucified Christ.

And that's enough, he thought later, as he lay in bed. It's what I was ordained to do. The lights of a car, coming from the curate's house, swept along the ceiling, then left the room darker than before. "'I have nothing on my conscience, yet I am not thereby justified.'" If Saint Paul knew that he had not justified himself, why should Father Tom Conroy, parish priest of Kilbride, consider that he had?

Footsteps went past on the road, somebody walking there in the darkness, confident of his home ahead. Should I have been hired at all, he wondered. Why the hell wasn't I left as I was, in Rosnagree, plowing in the lower field, down by the river?

He had been at it all day, preparing for the winter wheat, and now the evening was drawing in and he was looking ahead between the horses' heads, wondering whether he could manage another drill before dark. He whistled to himself as he followed the plow through the damp, darkening earth. Beyond the bare hedge, the river flowed past, deep and silent. He called to the horses, and they swung around, their breasts touching the hedge. The plow lurched over the ruts of the headland. "Whoa," he shouted, and as the horses stopped, he wiped his forehead with his sleeve and looked back up the field, still undecided whether to go on or to finish up.

Somebody was coming toward him, down the line of the last drill. He could see only the face, a white blob floating over the dark surface of the field. It startled him for a moment, not only its appearance at that twilight hour, but also the feeling that he had not, as he had thought, been alone in the field. Then, as it drew nearer, he saw with relief that it was Frank.

With relief and then with apprehension. He had never seen Frank at home before during the winter term, not since Frank had gone away to school ten years before. Why should he be here now, walking the furrow in his black clerical clothes? Why should that face, floating in the dusk, carry a premonition of change, of the end of the old life in Rosnagree?

Yet, Frank was smiling, and his air was jaunty, as he said, "Hullo, Tom, you didn't expect to see me back?"

"What's the matter? Is there something wrong?"

"Oh, no, nothing wrong." He came closer, smiling. "I'm back for good."

"Back here?"

"Yes, where else?"

"But what about—" About Rosnagree, which my father intended for me? What about the priesthood he had intended for you? It was then, without thinking, that Tom Conroy gave his answer, an answer to a call that had never been made. He levered the plow over the headland and flung it on its side against the ditch. "Well, then," said he, as he rubbed his hands clean on his trousers, "I may as well give it a try myself."

Frank understood at once. He stared, a little frightened. And no less frightened, Tom began to untackle the horses. On the way home by the river path, the horses plodding beside them in the dusk, the chains jingling, Frank laughed and said, "You're joking, Tom."

"I'm not. I'm going to give it a try."

Why not? Or rather, why? He did not ask himself. He only knew, as he led the horses into the darkness of the stable and heard their hooves clomping on the concrete behind him, that there was no going back. Rightly or wrongly, he had enlisted, and now he must march.

And I'm still marching, he told himself. He turned restlessly in bed, keeping within the narrow limits of his own warmth; yes, at least I'm marching. But where to?

Chapter 13

Yes, he had stepped into Frank's shoes; it was as simple as that. He never asked himself why he did it; at the time, it seemed the necessary thing to do.

But later on? Surely he must have wondered sometime whether he need have done it? Surely during those years at the seminary, when he walked around the track with his classmates (boys two or three years his junior, who regarded him with a mixture of sympathy and amused apprehension) – surely he must have asked himself why? But no, he could not remember having done so; he had been so maddened by their attitude, so impatient of that sedentary plod around the track, that all he had wanted was to break through the routine of the seminary to what lay within.

Soon he had no longer any need of their sympathy. The secondary-school course which they were completing was attacked so fiercely by him, swallowed up so completely, that it seemed (as one of his classmates put it) that he had been craving for the stuff all his life, that Cicero, Vergil, Euclid, and the rest were meat and drink to him. So quickly did he catch up on the younger boys, so far did he outdistance them, that at the end of his first year he was called to the president's room and told that he had been recommended for admission to Maynooth.

"Maynooth, Father? Ah, no."

The president looked up.

"Yes, why not? Mr." – a glance at the papers before him – "Conroy."

"Ah, not me, Father. Thanks very much."

The president became interested. His manner warmed a little at such humility.

"But we've chosen you, Mr. Conroy. We want you to go."

Conroy tried his yokel act, a bashful twisting of the fingers. "Sure, I don't know, Father. You'd have to get a degree and all that."

"Yes, of course." The president was pleased – he had a batch of degrees from Maynooth himself. "That's why we want you to go."

"Ara, no, Father. I don't know…"

"Oh, come now, Mr. Conroy. From what your professors say of you, I'm quite sure you're capable of doing credit to yourself and to us, that is, if you continue to apply yourself with the same diligence you have shown here up to now."

Conroy shook his head ruefully. "No, Father."

"Why not? What's the matter, young man? Are you so lacking in spirit? Why, this is a challenge which I should have thought an ambitious young man would leap to take up!"

Conroy fidgeted. "I'd just… rather not, Father."

"But, Mr. Conroy, you can't possibly refuse. Don't you realize that a place like this…" He spread out his hands, laying the place flat, then hastily restored it. "…dedicated, as it is, to ideals and high standards, insofar, of course, as our resources allow, cannot possibly offer you the tradition, the breadth of vision, the… ah, style, which a great university…"

"I'm sorry, Father."

"You're trying me, Mr. Conroy, trying me very hard."

"I'm sorry, Father, I didn't come here for... for what you're saying."

"And for what, pray tell us, Mr. Conroy, did you come?"

With a shuffling of feet, a twisting of hands, Conroy muttered, "Ah, sure, I just came to be a priest."

The president flushed deeply. He stared up at Conroy's face, as if he could trap those deadpan features into some flicker of malevolence or mockery. But Conroy looked down at him in surprise and managed a timid half-smile.

"Very well, Mr. Conroy," the president said, "we'll make alternative arrangements. Will you be good enough to find Mr... ah, Peter Mahon, and ask him to come to me? At once!"

Conroy's refusal to go to Maynooth won him a peculiar place in the life of the college. It added to the apprehension with which the students regarded him. "A hard man," they called him, half-admiringly. What would he do next? They awaited his fate with pleasurable dread.

To the faculty, Maynooth men all, teaching for their sins in a provincial establishment from which all the intellectual cream had been skimmed, his refusal was insolent, a slap in the face for them and for those abiding values by which they judged St. Declan's. How were they to handle him?

Nothing, of course, was discussed officially, because it was not admitted that there was any situation to discuss. For want of a better policy, he was ignored. And so, during his years at Declan's, he got away unreproved with certain remarks, with a general attitude of prickly independence for which a man less in evidence than he would have been expelled.

How had he endured it for six years? He remembered it as a drafty place of long green corridors and cold rooms where he had studied always, it seemed, with frozen fingers and blankets wrapped around his legs. Yes, it was cold: the chill spread outward from the staff, inhibiting even the most innocent of friendships.

Had he never thought of leaving? Once, a group of students was standing in the handball alley, talking about one of their fellows who had just "chucked." As Conroy joined them, a wag turned to him and said, "Hey, Tom, any hope of your chucking?"

While they waited for his answer, he held out his hands and examined the palms carefully. "Where else could I go now?" he asked. "What else could I do? To dig I am not able, to beg I am ashamed."

No, he had never thought of leaving. In fact, he rather got to like the place. He discovered that he had a mind. He crammed everything into it – he thought that was what his mind was for, and he was never told otherwise. Knowledge gave him power. Even parodied, as he delighted in parodying it, he used it to win the applause of his fellows. They discovered in him how much they wanted relief, even the relief of being scourged by laughter. And he, more than anyone, knew how to scourge the lazy-minded and the prig.

About his own spiritual life, it was felt that he had great, dark depths to hide. His silence on the subject was regarded as significant. So too were the occasional remarks he passed, however offhand, even crude, like the answer he gave the pious young first-year student who accosted him one morning with the remark, "Tom, I had a really wonderful meditation this morning, thanks be to God."

"Ah, yes." Conroy looked at him with great understanding. "Nothing like a good crap first thing."

Some of the faculty, those more practiced at divining spirituality, had their doubts about him, but no one was prepared to put him to the test; they were mindful of his success in tweaking the nose of authority. Once, for instance, at one of the marathon viva voce examinations, which they took so solemnly, when the professor announced the theme on which he was expecting to discourse, Conroy calmly corrected the quotation, in Latin of an almost insolent perfection. The professor started, glanced at his colleagues, and when they, unable to help, looked away in embarrassment, he began to check hurriedly through the pile of books before him.

"Allow me, sir," said Conroy. And frowning, with tongue slightly protruding, he soon ran the quotation to earth.

"As you say, Mr. Conroy," said the professor, drawing the book from him, "and now, perhaps you would let us have the benefit of your observations without further delay?"

He retaliated later, in class, when Conroy gave a somewhat free interpretation of a scriptural reading. "Mr. Conroy, of course," he told the other students, "will always insist on improving upon the commentary." And he passed on to the next question, as Conroy smiled, accepting the rebuke as a compliment.

What bastards they were! Yet, he had not thought them bastards at the time, as poor Mahon (now one of them) did not seem to him a bastard now. He had accepted them, as the young fellows in Declan's still accepted Mahon, as part of the system. And he had accepted the system; yes, he had made it his own, mastered every detail of it. In the process, he never considered that *it* might have mastered him, made him its own.

Or almost its own. As a student, he had had to wear Frank's overcoat. It was not a good fit, and the top button could not be fastened across his chest. He never bothered to get the coat altered; during all his years in the college, he wore it swinging open, however cold the wind. Like the coat, the system had never fully enclosed him.

He remembered the coat on the day of Jimmy's wedding, when Frank walked back into his life as casually as if he had walked out of it only the week before. He was well into his sixties, yet he seemed as young as Father Conroy remembered him. Perhaps this was because, in his weathering, he had become more of a type than a person; he had the well-stored look of a certain type of unmarried Irish farmer; his whole manner betokened a dedication to the here and now, an unshriveled confidence that the fullness of life still lay ahead. The black, tight-breasted student's overcoat could no longer have contained that pagan plumpness.

After twenty years of estrangement, he shook hands easily. His first words were, "Well, Tom? And how's the world using you?" While the wedding couple posed for the first photograph in the vestry, he sought the first gamy kiss from the bride. Fumbling shamelessly, he won it from her as she bent to sign the register. Then, while Father Conroy doffed his vestments, he turned to chat to the altar boys. "So you're a nephew of Patsy Burke's, now," he exclaimed. "Well, well!" And on he went to trace the Castlemore line of the Burkes, as if the history of the bride's family had suddenly become the most important thing in the world for him.

Father Conroy was thinking of the coat and of the peculiar smell that had always hung within its folds. Maybe it was the smell of geraniums that Frank had carried with him into the vestry and that brought to mind again the enclosed, stuffy front porch of Rosnagree.

"What d'ye want a new coat for?" his mother had said. "Is Frank's not good enough for you?"

He got up from the suitcase he was packing and put on the coat. In silent protest, he stood before her with his arms hanging stiffly out from his sides.

" 'Twill do you the while you'll be there," she went on, not looking at him. "When Frank wasn't suited there, why d'ye think you'll be?"

Slowly he began to take off the coat.

"It only needs the buttons shifted," she said, seeing his face. "I'll do that for you."

"No," he burst out. "I'll wear it as it is."

Yes, that smell had always tainted the memory of home. The inquisition of the young scion of the Burkes went pointlessly on. Nothing big had ever upset Frank – he attended so well to the little details of life. He looks ten years younger than me, thought Father Conroy; no, twenty years younger at least. He's never carried any burdens since Owen's death, nor any burdens before that either. He's never carried anyone's burden, least of all his own.

As he knelt at the prie-dieu to say the prayers after Mass, Father Conroy caught the altar boy winking at a companion and pocketing the pound note that Frank had slipped him.

"Well, isn't the world a small place," Frank said. "Fancy Patsy Burke's brother having a big lad the like of you!" And with practiced hand, he squeezed the boy's neck. The boy squirmed in feigned delight, unconsciously aware that every payment demanded some service rendered.

Well, it wasn't much of a service, thought Father Conroy, a feel here and a squeeze there. Frank had settled for the small pleasures of life.

The mindless stream of questions continued at the wedding breakfast. Seated glumly beside the bride, Father Conroy could hear Frank, on her other side, quiz the Burke ladies about the history of their hotel. The old waiter delayed more and more often to join in until at last his arm was laid familiarly along the back of Frank's chair. Name of God, what gem of knowledge did Frank always expect to come up with? There was no doubt that they were a respectable family, the Burkes. Their hotel was a respectable house, patronized by the older type of commercial traveler. There wasn't much else to say about it, except that it gave a right good spread, not like the flashier hotels uptown, which often gave several wedding breakfasts the same morning – champagne uneasily buoying hotted-up broiler chicken, ice cream, and tinned fruit. The Burkes, at least, knew how to cater for people from the country.

Damn it, though, there was no need to trace their history back, as if they were royalty. That only implied how much the Conroys had to gain by the match.

For, of course, the object of both families at the reception was to show how little each had to gain from the alliance. On both sides were people of substance, Castlemore business people with useful political pull on the Burke side, strong farmers on the Donovan (or rather, the Conroy side – for Uncle James sat like a reigning chief beside the bridegroom). To balance Father Conroy, the Burkes had brought along Canon Fitzmaurice, a very distant relative indeed, but of indubitably traceable connection. His senior position in the diocese was nicely calculated to offset Father Conroy's closer relationship with the groom. And, by virtue of that seniority, he it was who would open the speech-making and, of course, stress the advantage of marrying into the Burkes.

How like Frank, though, to be quite innocent of these matters! Not innocent so much as insensible! It did not matter two hoots to him what happened to the Conroys – signs on, he had never married, though, God knows, any girl should have been glad to walk into a fine place like Rosnagree. She would have had to cope with his mother, of course, but still, if he was a man at all, he should have faced up to that problem. No, he had let himself be imprisoned in Rosnagree, with the smell of those geraniums.

It had seeped into the food, the smell; Father Conroy could taste it more strongly with each mouthful. It flowed into his saliva, soured his tongue and the back of his throat. He chewed but could not bring himself to swallow. Some of the people around him were already finished the course. Christ, how was he going to get through the heap on the plate before him?

He felt a hand laid on his arm. The bride was looking up at him. "I think you must be out with us, Father!"

"Out with you? I'm not, indeed."

No, of course not. Yet, she was right; he was making no effort, had made no effort all day. She was a lovely girl, too – much too good for Jimmy – with her level blue eyes reproaching him. Did she know that she was being bought, a Conroy acquisition worth so many votes?

"You're looking very cross, then." She smiled, but a little

anxiously, and he realized that she was keyed up with the effort to make the day go well. He reached out and touched her hand where it lay on the table. And, though she smiled at him, he could feel her tremble slightly.

"I'm having a good old time, behind this poker face."

"I don't think you are," she said, a little too definitely, for she flushed and turned back to her plate.

He remembered the biggest day of his own life, his first-communion day. It began with the fuss of being bathed by Kate in front of the kitchen fire, of being dressed in his new suit, cut like a man's by the village tailor. Kate led him into the slow, self-conscious procession of children up the aisle. On he moved, slowly approaching the altar, nearer to it than he had ever been before, so near that the forest of votive candles shone in his eyes. His hands were joined on his breast, the hands into which, later that afternoon, new shillings were pressed by uncles and aunts when his father brought him visiting. In strange houses of distant cousins, he played stiffly, in his new clothes, with children he had never met before.

Home then, they came in the pony and trap, he full of jelly and cakes and sweets, his father singing as they drove into the yard. Then, suddenly, at sight of the house, of his mother in the doorway, the day broke in a frightening tempest of tears.

His mother's angry face followed them into the hall. "What's the matter with that child?" As his father carried him up to bed, he heard her call, "It's spoiling him you are!"

His father sat beside him for a while, bewildered, asking, "What is it, little man, tell me?" And all he could do was to shake his head, unable to understand, himself, what it was he had wanted of the day. What had he wanted? What more could he have had?

Laboriously, he plied his knife and fork, gathering enough for a mouthful. The waiter passed behind him, removing the empty plates. He tried to catch the man's sleeve, but his movement was somehow too slow, and he found himself left with the heaped-up plate still confronting him. Resignedly, he loaded the fork and began to lift it to his mouth, but at the tainted taste of his tongue, he felt his body revolt. He got to his feet and blundered past the backs of the chairs toward the distant door. A long corridor stretched before him. He ran down it, stooping forward to the men's room. The lavatory was cold. He leaned his head over the bowl and supported himself with his hand against the wall.

Come on, Conroy, he told himself in self-loathing, can't you perform, you fool! But he couldn't. He waited there with his head bent over the bowl. The rough concrete wall pressed down against his hand, as if it were about to overwhelm him. Oh, Christ, he thought, what are you waiting for? Do it now, if you must!

But nothing happened. The chill of the cubicle entered into him, and he began to laugh. A nice place you picked! he said, sobbing for breath.

There was no sound, nothing but a tap dripping with a slow, ponderous rhythm. And gradually, the feeling of queasiness subsided. He dried the sweat from his face and thought of escape. But no, how could he go? He was needed – they were counting on him to speak. He would have to stick it out to the end.

No one noticed his return. They were listening to a high-pitched, disembodied voice, which he couldn't place. He felt as if he no longer existed for them, as if they were people in a picture and he were outside the frame, trying to break in. He put his elbows on the table and sank his face between his hands, trying to think, to concentrate. He heard a low groan, and to his surprise, realized it came from himself. People suddenly leaned forward to peer at him; some of the girls tittered. The bride whispered close in his ear, "That's not fair, Father! Suppose the Canon does that when you're speaking!"

He nodded, looking down at the tablecloth before him, as if he had been deservedly chidden. His plate was gone – well, thank God for that. There was nothing before him but a glass of orange squash. He reached out for it, then stopped, realizing that the toast had not yet been given. Great God, a speech! Yes, he would have to follow the Canon. What was he going to say? He forced his attention out onto the people sitting silently around him, composed again in their picture. Couldn't he stay out here on his own? Maybe they didn't want him breaking in on them?

The girl's hand pressed his arm. She had a nurse's casual, friendly pressure; he liked it. She nodded her head, inviting him to listen.

"...the holy feast of Cana..." the voice came through at last. Who else but the Canon sprinkled his wedding-breakfast speeches with allusions to Cana, as if to show that marriage wasn't too bad, after all, since Our Lord hadn't condemned it.

He glanced at the girl – what did she want him to hear?

She was looking down at her hand with the ring on it. At his glance, she looked up and smiled at him. Happiness is near, she was telling him, almost within grasp. Don't spoil it.

So what was he going to say?

The Canon was moving on from the Holy Family. "This young man, who, I may say, is of well-known stock, is linking himself today with as old a family as there is in the county. The Burkes have been settled here in these parts since the first De Burgos, or (as they became in Irish) De Búrca, came with fire and sword. They numbered bishops among them, I might say, Stephen de Burgo, and later, nearer our own time, Most Reverend Dr. Matthew Burke, renowned for his piety among the men of the generation before mine. I remember him myself, when I was, you might say, a child in arms. Then there was Father Aidan, the great preacher and Prior of the Franciscan Monastery (to which our family has been a patron for generations). He, too, of course, has gone to his eternal reward. I must not let the occasion pass without reference to my own beloved father, one-time mayor of the town which I am now proud to have in my spiritual care. Many others of the connection held positions of honor in church and state, but I have said enough to indicate the importance of this occasion for the young couple here and indeed for all of us. And now, bearing all this in mind, may I wish them every happiness and God's blessing on them both."

Father Conroy joined briefly in the respectful applause. When it died down, attention shifted to him, but he sat on, unable to collect his thoughts. The irritation with which the speech had filled him was checked only by his anxiety not to hurt the girl.

"Go on, Tom!" Frank nudged him. "The Conroys!"

At that, he rose slowly, buttoning his jacket. His first sentence welled up with delightful ease, to be uttered with a self-deprecating smile, hands outstretched toward the people, as if to say, Look at me! What am I doing here at all?

"Sure, I'm only a poor, simple yob of a country priest," he said. In the silence, somebody laughed. Somebody else clapped. Then, as the bolt went home, there came an outburst of delighted applause. Father Conroy looked around him, as if mystified by what he had done. He had them now; even the Burkes were laughing in spite of themselves. Already, the next devastating sentence was forming in his head. He gave a sidelong glance of triumph at the Canon, then checked himself at sight of the old man's crestfallen face. Damn it, he had gone too far. He hesitated, aware of the girl's anxious face, upturned to him. You're spoiling the day for her, you mean bastard!

They were silent as they waited to savor the next sally. Blast them, anyway, what were they waiting for? A spectacle? Well, he was going to disappoint them; he was going to put them in their places. But how could he, without adding to the Canon's shame, the girl's anxiety?

He hesitated, face downcast, frowning with the effort of concentration – and he felt the big moment pass. He had lost them.

"I haven't anything to say," he told them slowly, "beyond joining with the Canon in wishing these young people God's blessing on their marriage." And abruptly he sat down.

After a pause, they began to clap. I've ruined it after all, he told himself. I should have told a few jokes, anything to keep it going. He saw that the girl was looking down at the tablecloth, not smiling. Yes, I've ruined it.

To his surprise, Frank stood up. It wasn't his turn to speak – Uncle James should have come next – but Frank stood there confidently, a moist glow in his apple cheeks.

"After all that talk of the great Burkes and Fitzmaurices, not to mention the Conroys" – he paused to let the laugh of anticipation go by – "I'd like to say simply that no bishop or mayor or canon or Dáil deputy ever gave half as much pleasure to the eye as the handsome young couple who are sitting among us here this morning."

That's the line, Father Conroy thought; that's what I should have said.

"And since credit should be given where credit is due, I suggest that we owe particular thanks to the glamorous young lady on my left, whom I've just discovered is the mother of the bride. Mrs. Burke has provided" – he continued over the applause – "has provided a twofold delight for the eye…"

A bit flowery, thought Father Conroy; don't overdo it now! As if he had heard, Frank moved on to take up the Canon's reference to the marriage feast of Cana.

"…and after all, what a right good hooley they had at Cana! Six water jars, two or three firkins in each, that's six twenties – one hundred and twenty gallons of wine! It's all right, Canon!" – he waved as the Canon gestured angrily – "I'm not trying to lead astray the members of the Total Abstinence Society; I just want to point out that Christ started his ministry at a feast where everyone was having a good time. There was a danger the party was going to fall flat, but he made something great out of it. I wouldn't worry about that abundance of wine. Didn't the prophecies say, 'Behold, the day will come when the mountains shall drop sweet wine and all the hills shall melt'?"

Good, thought Father Conroy, that's giving it to them. "And the plowman shall overtake the reaper and the treader of grapes him that soweth seed." How's that for a marriage text? How's that for speeding the pulse, for sending the blood to the head in a spray of red corpuscles, for shifting the sleepy old Adam out of his niche?

Because that's why we're here, God damn it – canons, Dáil

deputies, farmers, shopkeepers, respectably bedded ladies of Castlemore – we're here to pop these two into the warmth of the marriage bed.

And we know it; we won't admit it, but we know it. Observe our bodies slacken into the chairs, our faces soften with food and drink, our eyes grow hazy as we drink in the excited tenor slurry of Frank's words. We're slumped together, all of us, in the depths of a big family bed. Observe Frank bending over to whisper in Jimmy's ear, his arm on the young man's shoulder. And the girl, even the girl, catches the reflected warmth of our flesh, only on her it's like sunlight, the smell of heather…

Oh, Christ, he thought, as he shifted angrily, don't torment me now!

Nobody looked at him; nobody noticed his movement. Am I the only one aware of this? This fleshliness? Maybe I am; maybe it's that bloody imagination of mine; yes, damn it, that's all it is, exciting me with bad thoughts about the girl in the high-necked, maiden-white dress. Relax, man, relax! Let yourself drift along with the rest!

And drift he did, eddying tiredly with them as they moved out into the sunlight for the photographs.

The speeches were over, that of the plump young priest whose comical eye made everyone laugh, even that of Uncle James, who half-rose from his seat to murmur drunkenly that he had never enjoyed a wedding as much, that it was far better than his own had been, in fact, that he felt this was his own.

Urged by the photographer, the crowd moved out. James pawed at Father Conroy and slopped whiskey over his waistcoat. "By God, Tom," he burst out, "that's the first decent drink I had for years. You don't know what it is to be watching your tongue, knowing there's a dozen around you waiting to cadge something off you, ready to down you if you don't give them what they want." He freed his arm to take a big gulp from the glass. "Well, they can bugger off for themselves now – I've nothing for them. I'm free, Tom; I'm going to spread my wings."

"Drink that up and come on out."

"Yes, yes, I'm coming. Here, give us your arm – this oul' table has stretched itself. It's hard to get around it. I've nothing to give, Tom, and I've nothing to get. Not like yourself, who has to soldier on!"

"You're not done yet with your soldiering."

"I am, Tom, I am." He hung heavily on Father Conroy's arm as they moved with the crowd down the dark corridor toward the bright patch of green. "Never again will I have to listen to some jackass trying to threaten me with his vote. Oh, no, Tom, my soldiering days are done."

The light hit them as they emerged and stood a moment, dazed, holding each other. Then they were urged forward into the crowd, brushing against shoulders, thighs, arms, as Jimmy pushed them into the center places. "Hurry up, now, Uncle James, there's a big cloud coming up."

They stood where he left them, blinking in the sunlight, held up by the press of people about them. The bride had been seized by some young men, cousins and friends, who carried her past on their shoulders and ran across the lawn. She beat at their hands, laughing, pleading to be let down. They enthroned her on a rockery, her train stretched out on the stones below, and flung themselves down around her to face the photographer. Then, whooping, they picked her up and came rushing back toward the main group. Jimmy stood watching them, smiling, alone. He glanced up at the cloud, now almost on the sun, estimating whether they would make it in time.

"There's only one thing," Uncle James was murmuring; "we've got to make sure that boy gets his foot on the rung."

Held tightly in the crowd, Father Conroy could only nod and say, "Ah, yes, Jimmy!" If I took my feet off the ground, he wondered, would James and the rest bear me up? Would we fly away, the whole swarm of us, before the cloud crosses the sun?

"Yes, Jimmy!" said Uncle James with satisfaction.

The photographer lifted the camera and took aim. Jimmy glanced upward, then composed his face in a smile. The camera clicked, and then, a fraction of a second later, the cloud touched the outer rim of the sun. It was a good day for the Conroys, after all.

And so it remained. Hours later, after songs, dancing, much drinking, Father Conroy found himself at the railway station, still imprisoned among them. From windows along the train, heads peered out to watch them gathered noisily at a carriage door. All the confetti had been thrown. The young men and the bridesmaids waited restlessly for the train to be off, impatient to get back to the dancing and drinking, to the fun of the day, from which they were temporarily leashed. The bride stood by the carriage door, one foot on the step. A flushed and moist Frank held her with his arm around her shoulder. She looked back at Jimmy, aloof behind her, then caught his hand and impatiently made him mount with her to the step. Frank still clung to her, his arm trailed about her hip. Even when she disappeared within, he stayed looking up, his hand still outstretched.

The plump young priest was talking to two big handsome

matrons with black brows and creamy complexions. One of them leaned capaciously forward to say, "Ah, yes, Father, sure, I've often admired you on the links, your style, I mean," and then she glanced under her brows at her sister.

"Did ye?" He pressed nearer, eyes damp and shining. "Did ye like my style?"

And the sisters pouted at each other and laughed as they drew in closer to him.

Father Conroy backed away, not knowing where to look. Christ, this was terrible! He had to get out of here. Sweet Jesus, they were all at half-cock! He turned and began to force his way out, jostling and shoving through the crowd. He heard the bride call his name, but kept pushing through them, conscious that they were penning him in, suffocating him.

Then, suddenly, he was free of them and hurrying away down the long stretch of empty platform.

The diesel's hooter blared, and the train began to pull out. He heard a wild outburst of cheering, but he did not look back or stop until he reached the steps down to the street. There he took out his handkerchief and wiped his face. And as the chill street wind struck him, he realized with a shudder that his clothes were stuck to him with a communal sweat, which made him feel unclean.

Ned Foley was in the yard when he reached home, standing like a statue that had always been there, with cap tilted back and eyes raised to a pointless hole in the sky. He came to slowly, drawing the cap down to its proper angle in salute.

"It's the pony, Father. Mr. Drewitt has been in to Father Farrell, and he says that if ye don't…"

"Take it away!"

"Ah, now, Father, ye're not going to…"

"Take it to hell out of here. I'm sorry I ever laid eyes on the thing."

"Oh, well, then!" He pushed up the cap in protest. "Will I take it now, so?"

"Do. This instant."

And so, a few moments later, hooves clomped across the cobblestones of the yard and softened on the grass verge by the gateway. Father Conroy waited by the back door until the sound dimmed into the distance; then he lifted the latch.

A can of milk and a basket of eggs had been left on the kitchen table. He stood looking at them, wondering should he make tea, but the effort of filling the kettle seemed too much. He drank some milk out of the can and felt in his pocket for a handkerchief to wipe his mouth. There was a wad of paper in his pocket, which he drew out and opened with some premonition. It was an envelope containing two five-pound notes, nothing else, no note of explanation, nothing to indicate who had slipped it in there. Could it have been James? Blast him, he should have known that I wouldn't want anything for a family wedding – but, of course, he did know; that was why he slipped it in my pocket. Well, here it is. I've got to put up with it.

As he searched in the cupboard for the jar, his hand encountered a bundle of papers. He drew them out and found that they were letters loosely held together by an elastic band. He slipped out the first one, blew the dust off it, and unfolded it, carefully, because it cracked along its folds.

Casa Cural,
Los Hatos.
February 1, 1920.

Los Hatos! Uncle Joseph, the Conroy emigrant! Now, why had he kept the letter? There must have been some good reason, because he had never believed in hoarding things out of sentiment. He saw that the letter was addressed, "Dear Frank." Of course! The old man had never really grasped the fact that he had taken Frank's place in the seminary six years before. So now, in the year of his ordination, he was still being addressed in Frank's name! That must have seemed a joke at the time – perhaps that was why he had kept the letter. Some joke! Who was it on, on Frank or on himself?

He shut the cupboard door on the money. Well, now, what should he be doing? It was still daylight – the evenings were stretching, each, as his father used to say, three steps of a cock longer than the last. He was tired, and there seemed to be nowhere to sit down. The place was littered with papers; even the armchair was filled with them. A pity it wasn't dark; he could have gone to bed. Well, why not go up? Lie down for a spell, have a little rest.

He began to climb the stairs, slowed down by the strangeness of it, going to bed in daylight. He pulled the curtains and began to undress, conscious of the sound of a tractor in a distant field, of voices passing on the road.

The sheets were cold, and he turned sideways, drawing up his legs to conserve his meager store of warmth. Sleep seemed far away. His mind went back to the wedding, to the girl, the way she had knelt before the altar, eyes lowered as she murmured the words after him. He had looked down at her eyelids. They were a nice shape, rounded. Was it the same pleasure one got from breasts, looking at them? At the way they pressed against the top of the prie-dieu, tight under the white lace. And now, loosened in some hotel bedroom...

God! He turned over violently in the bed, feeling for his breviary, but it wasn't there. He had left it downstairs in the kitchen. He should get up and go down for it, but he could not make the effort; his mind, sharpened though it was, could not drive his sluggish body. He lay there and deliberately sought for something he could direct his mind toward, not a prayer, because that did not always work, just something ordinary he could concentrate on. Cold! Yes, that was it.

What was the coldest thing he remembered? A memory floated up, forgotten till now. He was a child, about five or six years old, and he was lying on his side in a bed, a thick featherbed, the visitor's bed in Rosnagree, which he and the other children sometimes used to bounce on. Uncle Joseph, the old priest, was in the room, preparing to undress. He smiled at this, remembering his surprise when the old man took off his jacket and he saw that everything was not black underneath – in fact, that his uncle wore a striped shirt like his father's. Underneath the shirt was a woolen vest. The boy watched the old man peel it off. Below the sunburned circle of skin around the neck, the skinny body was almost transparently white.

Lying there, watching the old priest pull on a nightshirt and kneel to say his interminable prayers, the boy felt he had discovered something he should not have known. Excited, he wanted to speak to the old man, to ask him – what? Whatever it was, the silent figure knelt at the bedside, head in hands, and at last the boy dozed off and was only vaguely aware of the sudden coldness in the bed, as if all the warmth in which he had been cocooned were being drained away. Even through his sleep, he had been conscious of the cold all night.

Was the old man aware of him? Of course not. And yet, that scene, so long forgotten, must have forged some link between them, so that, later, when he got those vague and wandering letters, addressed to Frank instead of to him, he had kept them, knowing that they had indeed been meant for him. Yes, he remembered now the feeling of affection which they had aroused. That was why he had put them carefully by – he had thought of the old priest remembering the small boy staring wide-eyed at him from the bed. Why else would they have been written so trustfully? Why else would they have been written at all?

Why didn't I ever write to anybody like that? Because I never needed to. I was among my own people. I was secure. Warm. Or was I? What is warmth?

He remembered a night he woke up to hear the wind tearing at the brittle Scotch pines along the edge of the wood. The rain beat against the window under the eaves, and lightning flashed in the room, so that the shape of the bed and chest edged through the blackness that followed. Yet, he lay calmly watching (though he must have been crying earlier or he wouldn't have been in that room, in his parents' bed, with his father's arm about him). Yes, that was warmth, that was security, well-being, warmth.

Father Conroy drifted into sleep. With his legs drawn up, he slept in his own foreshortened area of warmth, while the light deepened into dusk and the distant tractor fell silent.

He had a disturbing dream. He dreamed he awoke with the knowledge that there was someone in the house, moving about downstairs.

He sat up in bed, listening, but could not hear a sound, and though he was not afraid of a thief, he felt the utmost reluctance to move. Only when he got out of bed and switched on the light by the door did he realize that he was not in his own house, but was back in his room in Rosnagree.

He moved silently out onto the landing. His hand groped for the switch, and as the light went on, he thought how strange it was that they should have electricity laid on and that he should know where the switches were. He went down the dark, enclosed stairs, switching on another light there. And so into the hall, with its smell of geraniums. The parlor was empty. Everything looked strangely sharp under the unaccustomed brightness of the light. He turned away toward the kitchen door, which stood ajar on the darkness within. It was in there, whatever it was! There was nobody else in the house, but himself and it.

He was trembling now, facing the door. At last, reluctantly, he moved into the doorway. He reached in for the switch, but it seemed to be farther in, well within the dark. In he moved, reaching fearfully forward, his body drawn from him by something more powerful than he had ever known, its trembling now a regular pulsation which he tried vainly to quell. He knew there was something there, someone, some flesh his own should know, but though he kept blundering forward in mounting horror, he never reached it.

He awoke to find himself trembling violently. He drew the blankets about him and lay still, trying to calm his fear, to stop his trembling. And then he felt a warmth on his stomach, a long-forgotten, shameful warmth, spread from navel to thighs.

In disbelief, he touched his hand to the place and withdrew it instantly as it encountered the warm slime of his seed. Oh, Christ, he moaned. He flung the clothes back and got out on the floor, where he swayed dizzily in the icy darkness. Oh, Christ in heaven, pray for me! And then his knees gave way, just as he was about to will himself to kneel, and he was on the floor, crying, sobbing, "Jesus protect me, save me! Oh, Jesus!"

Gradually his body returned to his control. He got up, switched on the light, and dressed himself. Downstairs, in the kitchen, he found his breviary and began to read, but the phrases skidded away before his eyes, their Latin surface unbroken. At last he put the book down and said the "Our Father" slowly and with intensity. That calmed him, so that he was able to put on the kettle and make himself a pot of strong tea. He cut a thick slice of the homemade bread and ate it as he drank. Only then was he able to finish his Office. He was only just in time – it was but a few minutes to midnight.

All the time as he read, his mind was on what had happened, not on the wet dream itself (for he had often had to reassure anxious young men in confession about such things), but on the circumstances which had brought it on – the empty house, those lights switched on one by one, the treacherous darkness which had overwhelmed him. What was the meaning of it? Or had it any meaning? Was it sent to fill him with guilt and terror? Then surely it must have had a meaning, a purpose apparent to, yes, to the malicious power that sent it. He must have done something wrong, to lay himself so open to it. But what? Christ, what have I done?

With his Office said, there was nothing to occupy him in the kitchen. He went into the study and moved around, trying to tidy the papers on his desk, making bundles of them, only to find that there was no place to put them but on the mantelpiece or in the armchair. The curtains were not drawn; the room lay open to the darkness. He should go back to bed; all this tidying needed a clear head, and it would he better to leave it till the morning. Anyway, what was the purpose of it?

He stopped tidying, but he could not leave the room; he was held there. He looked around him. What was he meant to do? Then he noticed that he had left the cupboard door ajar. His money was in there; he did not know how much. Not very much – how much, he just did not want to know. And yet, someday he should take it out and count it. He stared at the door, half-open on the darkness within. Yes, someday he would have to take it out. But not now, not just now. Come on, he told himself, leave it, get off to bed with yourself. You're in no state to count it now.

He turned away, still reluctant to leave the room. On the pile of papers on the desk was something familiar, ah, yes, the letter from Uncle Joseph in South America. He picked it up, glanced quickly down it, and as he did so, felt the familiar ring of the phrases. He had been young when he read it – just before his ordination – yet he must have taken it in well, perhaps been struck with compassion for the old man thinking of St. Brigid's Day in Ireland, the first day of spring.

Or was it familiar because now he knew himself what the old man had meant, "Why, then, should my own mean so much to me now, and these people nothing? That's just one of the questions which keep my night's sleep from me. So little light is given to us." He thought of the thin, white body with the neck burned brown above the ring of the collar. Had he answered the letter? Perhaps he hadn't, being too busy with the preparations for his ordination. But what could he have said? What could stop an old man "pondering over problems that will never get anyone anywhere"? As easy cure the wind on the stomach; yes, he remembered that, and the damn tortillas. My God, yes. What could he have said that would have killed the taste of those damn tortillas?

He stopped suddenly at the last paragraph, at the reference to the money enclosed "to help you over these last couple of terms and to lighten the expenses of your mother. I'm sorry it's not more. I haven't helped you as I should have, all these years in college." Slowly he put the letter down, folding it carefully along its creases. Yes, he thought, but of course that's what I must do. I must get all that money out and give it to someone of the family. That will have to be done. I'm going to clear it all out, not now, in the morning. I'm going to close up that cursed hole for good and nail the door shut on it.

But who is there to give it to? Jimmy? No, he could see Jimmy looking up at the sun, smiling, confident of the camera's click. No, not Jimmy. Not Frank, either – he would fritter it away. And there was the time when Frank had sat in the railway carriage crossing Wales, with his little notebook, keeping account of the expenses of Owen's funeral. No, not Frank.

Owen was the only one who should have had it, the only one I would have wanted to have it. But it didn't come to me in time, and then, when I offered it to Marie, she refused it, rejecting (and no wonder) all that came from the Conroys. But what about… yes, by God, that's it, what about her two sons, my nephews, Owen's two sons, whom I haven't seen since they were babes in arms? Aren't they entitled to it? Aren't they the ones who should have had Rosnagree?

It was crazy; he knew it even as the idea took possession of his mind. It was as crazy as Owen's idea of saving enough from the wages of a builder's laborer to buy back Rosnagree, yet, it gave him strength to step forward and shut the cupboard door. The thing to do was to find them, those two Conroy heirs, but that wouldn't be too difficult. England would have to be searched, but England wasn't that big, and it was thickly veined with Irish connections. Possibly their mother still had relatives in Castlemore, they wouldn't take long to trace, in which case he could be on his way tomorrow. It was crazy, of course it was crazy, and yet—There was a new vigor in his step as he went up the stairs to bed.

Chapter 14

Next morning, it did not seem so simple. What good would the money be to them now? Each of the young Conroys was probably settled already in the station of life he had chosen, perhaps married, with children. Was it right to unsettle them now?

And yet the money was due to them. It was the measure of what the Conroys owed them. Or was it? Surely they were owed more, much more? What money could compensate for the loss of Rosnagree?

Well, then, why shouldn't one of them have Rosnagree? That would solve all the problems at a blow. Yes, one of them would follow Frank, would use the money from the cupboard to buy stock, fix up the house and outbuildings, restore everything to what it had been in the old days. And if he was married, why all the better – the future of the family would be secure.

But first, it would be necessary to come to an agreement with Frank, or rather, with Mama (for, though she no longer held the pursestrings, she had never formally made the place over). Would he go see her? Yes, he would; he wasn't afraid. How could she possibly refuse him? When, though? Why, the sooner the better, today, now, while the mood was on him. It would be a relief to see her and to get the whole business over and done with before someone, anyone of them, God forbid, should die. Frank had mentioned that she was not well. There was no time to lose.

He cut himself a hunk of bread in the kitchen. Quickly he buttered it and took it out with him to the car, losing no time. He was just getting in, munching away, when a voice hailed him from the gateway.

"Padre!"

Oh, no, he groaned, Drewitt! In the midst of death, we are in life! He held the door open, resignedly looked around.

"Just a moment, Padre!"

"I'm going out, Mr. Drewitt. Couldn't you call again?"

But Drewitt kept coming grimly on. The blue pinstripe of the city gent made him look small and purposeful, like a bluebottle. Jodhpurs and tweeds had done something for him, after all.

"That pony," he gasped, catching hold of the door and yanking it open. "That pony you sent me, Padre..."

"Yes, what is it?"

"Look!" He produced his right hand from under his coat and shoved it in Father Conroy's face. Gray-faced but triumphant, he waited as Father Conroy inspected the bandages.

"Tut, tut, Mr. Drewitt, what happened?"

"The pony! I was trying to saddle him when he backed me into a corner of the stable."

"He bit you? Oh, Lord!"

"He attacked me, damn near killed me. I seem to have caught my hand on a nail in the floor."

"On the floor? My God! He knocked you down?"

"No, he did not, but how the hell d'you think I got away? Damn near killed me, he did. When can you take him back, Padre?"

"Take him back, Mr. Drewitt?"

"The sooner the better. Mrs. Drewitt is extremely upset. I shouldn't be surprised if he kicks that door down."

"Well, he's not mine, Mr. Drewitt. I'm not responsible for him."

"Oh, but you told me when I took him…"

"You didn't have to take him, Mr. Drewitt."

"You assured me that he would be suitable for Mrs. Drewitt. You mentioned her constitutional. I distinctly remember you using that expression."

"Did I?" He tried to pull the door shut, but Drewitt had it by the handle. "Anyway, I told you he had no mouth."

"No mouth?" Drewitt's voice peaked. "If this is your bloody Irish idea of a joke, Padre…"

"I'm telling you he had no mouth. If you have any complaints…" He tugged suddenly at the door, and Drewitt, who was doing a little dance of rage, was too late to stop it closing. "If you have any complaints, Mr. Drewitt, I'd suggest you take them to the tinker."

"What tinker? What are you talking about?"

"The tinker who made him what he is." And Father Conroy rolled up the window. Smiling and nodding in answer to Drewitt's mouthings, he raised his hand in benediction as the car moved forward.

At least Drewitt had taken his mind off the ordeal before him. He drove into the yard of Rosnagree and stopped a moment in the car, wondering how best to take her. The place had grown heavy with greenery; it lay quite motionless in the hush of midday. Banks of fuchsia, not yet broken into flower, piled up against the stable wall as if they had tried and failed to reach the roof. A trellis sagged under the riotous growth of a rambler rose. Thick carpets of ivy on the walls gave the house a dim look; it seemed to have retreated a step from view, become a reflection in a dark glass.

Even the stones of the yard were green. There were no fowl, no animals, no trespassers of any kind. The grass bore the fresh marks of tires; Frank, no doubt, was on the wing. Ah, well, that wouldn't make things any easier. For he was suddenly afraid of opening the gate under the briers, of going up the overgrown path to the front door. And when he did so, it seemed to take him a long time, as if the house were moving back before him.

The door stood half-open. He heard a woman's voice within, humming a pop song that was being flogged on the sponsored programs. He pushed open the door and entered the gloom of the hallway. The smell of geraniums came at him, like something in a nightmare which he expected but hoped not to meet. He stopped, thinking he could still retreat if he wanted to. Then the kitchen door opened and a young girl came out. She stopped humming at sight of him. Her mouth fell open. It was moist, red, enlarged with lipstick. She was very young, not more than twelve, wearing a dress which she seemed about to burst out of. She brought a big red hand to her mouth.

"Oh, Lord, Father, you gave us a fright." A cheeky slut, by her eyes, the way she invited a smile at her distress. "Frank's gone to the races in Mallow."

Frank, she called him! Who the hell was she? Good God, could she be a McGarr, another generation of them abreeding in the cottage by the front gate?

"Where's Mrs. Conroy?" he demanded. He wasn't going to discuss Frank and his whereabouts with a one the like of her.

"She's above in her room, Father. I was just going up to see would she be wanting any breakfast."

"Any breakfast? Hasn't she had it yet?"

"She won't take it when I bring it. She has to be in the mood."

"I see," he said, staring at her keenly, "So she's very troublesome, then?"

"Ara, no, Father, she's no trouble. Sure, ye'd blow her off the back of yer hand. There's not a pick on her, the poor oul' thing."

Thing, yourself! he thought, furious that a McGarr should be able to talk like that, so brazenly. Damn Frank, anyway, for his lack of pride.

The stairs was clean, though, and the bed so white that the old woman looked lost in the expanse of it. She didn't see him at first. She was gazing toward the window that was open to the sunny air. There seemed very little of her beneath the clothes; most of her was head, and most of the head was eyes – the same sharp, close-set eyes which met his in mirrors. He had never thought till now that perhaps he resembled her.

He stood by the foot of the bed, and after a while she looked down at him and said, "Ah, there you are." She patted the bed by her side. "Sit down, sit down. You'll have to sit on the edge of the bed. That one took the chair."

"There's a chair over there."

"That one took the chair."

Was she blind? Or deaf? Or both? He looked at the chair, doubting it himself, then slowly lowered himself onto the edge of the bed. Out of the corner of his eye, he glanced at her and saw that she was staring directly at him.

"Well?" she said.

He tried to think of how to begin. Something about the girl downstairs? That might only annoy her – not that he would blame her, with a young slut of the McGarrs in control. And yet, to give credit where it was due, the place was well looked after; the ceilings that sloped down to the eaves were freshly whitewashed; along the wall, the big chest of drawers gleamed with polish. Even the brass handles shone on the trunk in which she used to keep her best clothes. He wondered if they were still there, the clothes, and what would happen to them.

"Well?" she asked testily. "Did you get them?"

"Get what?"

"The seed. Isn't that what you went into Maloney's for?"

"Oh, yes," he said, confused, "the seed."

"And the colter. You got the colter!"

Trust Frank, he thought. The same old Frank, sneaking off to Mallow races.

"Anyone would think you were making it," she commented. And she loosed the shaft in the way he remembered, tossing her head to give it greater impetus. God, wasn't she a hard woman!

"I'm not Frank."

She said nothing. The clear eyes stayed on him, but their expression did not change. Was it blind she was? Or deaf?

"I'm not Frank," he said, more loudly.

She had heard him, all right. Her eyes stayed on him with a distant, unfocused look, but her fingers twitched on the sheets. Why hadn't Frank told him the way she was? Mama couldn't come, was all he had said, she's not too well. Could he possibly not know? Or was it that now, when he had the freedom of her purse, that he did not care?

"Can't you see me?" he murmured at last.

She nodded. He was sure she couldn't, that she just would not admit a need to wear glasses.

"How did you get here from the station?" she asked.

"I came by car."

"Oh, yes, you got a car at the station."

What station, in God's name; what was she talking about?

"I suppose you left the family there?" My God, worse and worse! But she went on, "You had a right to bring them. Not her, but the little fellows. How many is this there are? I forget."

He remembered his joke about the last bishop, poor old John Francis, who in his dotage had taken Father O'Hara for a large materfamilias. The joke was on himself now, on him with a vengeance.

"Two," he said, "two boys."

"God bless them, 'tis a pity you wouldn't bring them." And she murmured, as if explaining why to herself. "It's desperate quiet here now."

"Next time," he said. God forgive me, I'm a blackguard to the bitter end.

"Ay, do, when they'll be off from school. I'm going to sow a bed of scallions as soon as the weather takes up. You used to like them in the evenings, with lettuce and soda bread, yourself and… and…" Her voice trailed away.

We used, indeed we used. On summer evenings, when we'd come back late after footing turf, we'd go out to the kitchen garden she had made and we'd pick a handful of scallions, wet with dew, and a head of lettuce from the dark under the tree. Then we'd dip a jug in the churn beside the fuchsia hedge, and we'd bring it in, still warm and dripping. And she'd be cutting and buttering the soda bread for us.

Keep up the blackguarding, boy, keep it up quick! "And how's Tom?" he asked.

She stared at him as if she hadn't heard. He had to say the name again: it sounded strange, his own name. "Tom?"

She shook her head. Her face puckered, as if she were going to cry. Oh, Christ, no, he thought, don't let her cry. I couldn't bear that.

But she did not cry. She looked straight before her, her face still puckered; she seemed to be summoning up some memory buried way down.

He got to his feet. Should he go? Get the hell out before his blundering caused any more trouble? He stood up, trying to make up his mind.

Through the window the sun shone on the bawn field, where a few hens scratched at the beaten clay around an abandoned harrow. His father had taught him hurling there; on summer evenings after supper they had moved about the field, pucking the ball back and forth to each other across the white clover. And she? She had watched them from this window, leaning against the sash, as she rocked baby Owen to sleep and the shadow of the wood stretched across the field.

What had she thought as she watched him chase after the ball and lift it with his hurley? Yes, what had she thought of him? He had to know.

"Tom!" he said fiercely. "What about Tom?"

She smiled. "I'd like to have seen the two little lads. 'Tis a pity you didn't bring them." Baffled, he sat down again on the edge of the bed and watched her. "Frank wanted them here that time, but sure…" She lapsed again into silence, then shook her head. "Your father wouldn't have it."

"He was dead!" he burst out. "He died when I was nine!"

"Oh yes." She nodded. Her eyes lifted slowly, searching for his face, and she said, in her old voice, "None of ye did what he wanted ye to do."

What you wanted us to do! That's what you mean. It was you who kept him by you, referring all things to him, justifying your tyranny by his assent from the shades. And yet, we didn't hate him. At least, I didn't. Christ, wasn't that a miracle, that I never grew to hate him!

"He was a fine man!" he said, with his voice raised.

That seemed to penetrate to her. She shifted uneasily. "He never knew what he wanted. I often tried to tell him, but I couldn't, for fear he wouldn't take it from me." She lapsed into a silence. "He was foolish, like—"

"Like Tom!" he said triumphantly. She looked up quickly.

"Who is it?" she whispered.

But he didn't want to hear any more. He got up quickly, and she looked startled when the bed creaked. Over her head, he lifted his hands. "In nomine Patris, et Filii et Spiritus Sancti…" he whispered, and remembered the morning he had touched her cheeks with his hands, his palms that had been bound together in the sacrament of ordination.

"Who is it?" Her head turned, eyes wandering in search of him. But he couldn't bear to stay any longer. He was afraid of what would happen when those eyes would find him.

On the way down the stairs, he paused to blow his nose angrily.

The girl came out into the hall and smiled up at him. "Won't you wait and have a bite to eat, Father?"

"No, no, child, I must go."

"But I have the kettle on."

"No!" And to atone for his rude shout, which startled himself too, he dug his money out of his pocket and showered it into her hand. "There now, buy yourself some sweets."

And as she stood there, staring into her hand, he slammed the door shut, afraid of that voice now calling from upstairs, "Who is it?"

The sun was shining. Birds flew out from the bushes. He stopped halfway down the path and looked back. He should have stayed. He should have listened to whatever she might have had to say, her explanation for all the past that had come between them. But hadn't he left it too late? He looked back at the house. The windows were dark, their small panes reflecting the overgrowth of twenty years. He imagined he could hear her voice still faintly calling, "Who is it?" How could she have recognized him, when she had never known him? It was too late.

As he hurried to the gate, he saw a big clump of brambles in the middle of what had once been the garden. Pulling aside some of the briers, he could see that the pedestal was still there, and the brass dial, now black, which had once measured out the hours of sunlight. If nobody knew it was there, it would just crumble away under the weight of the brambles. And who would know, after she was gone, and Frank, and the place altogether sunk in greenery?

A half-hour's work would clear the brambles away, just one half-hour with a billhook and a strong arm to wield it. But whose?

It would have to be the arm of someone who cared, of a Conroy. Yes, there was no other way out of it; he would have to go to England and bring back Owen's son. There was still something to be saved out of the past.

Chapter 15

The journey passed quickly. Large stretches of it he was anesthetized against – Dublin, for instance, a gray, unfriendly place (like most country people, he felt more at home in London), then the deck of the mail boat and the long night journey across England. He reached London early in the morning.

He sat a long time in the station cafeteria over a cup of tea and a cellophaned packet of sandwiches. A bent, old attendant, muttering to himself, loaded a trolley with soiled cups and plates and mopped the table around Father Conroy's saucer, as if it was a thing that had grown there overnight.

While he waited for the Eastbourne train to leave, he decided to ring up Marie. He felt a need to make his purpose more real. Besides, he was accustomed to drop in on people without notice, and it occurred to him that she might not, after all, be there.

The phone was answered by a man's voice – to his surprise, for he had not considered her husband till now. He explained who he was, but the slow, north-of-England voice kept repeating patiently, "Who? I'm sorry, but I can't quite catch… Who is it, please?" And then with relief he heard it say, "Just a moment," and Marie's voice took over, "Who's that speaking?"

It took him aback, the very precise Englishness of it; a hardwon precision, he realized.

"Father Conroy," he said. There was a long pause, and he thought, my God, she's not going to see me. He looked out in despair into the cafeteria, where the old man was taking away his cup and saucer and sweeping the cellophane into the trolley. And then she answered, "Who?"

"Father Conroy." And he added, knowing himself to be pleading but unable to stop himself. "You remember! Tom! Owen's brother!"

"Oh! Oh, yes, of course!" But no welcome, no surprise, even.

"I'm in London, I thought of calling out to see you."

"Oh, do. Yes, that would be nice. Let us know whenever you're free."

"Well..." Damn it, he couldn't back out now. "I'm free today."

"I see. Would you like to come for tea?"

For tea! It seemed an infinity away. How was he to spend the time waiting?

"We have an Irish priest here, I believe. Father Delaney. I'll ask him in too. We don't often have anyone from the old country drop in on us now."

"Marie!"

"Yes?"

"I wanted to talk to you."

"To me?"

"Yes. About the family."

"The family? Oh, your family?" She laughed easily. Was it possible she felt no rancor? He could not believe it. "How are they?"

"Fine."

"Your mother?"

"Yes."

"And your big brother, Frank?" Did she remember Frank with his little notebook? Keeping tally of the funeral expenses?

"Marie, it's your family, your two boys. I'd like to meet them." What were their names? Quick, for God's sake! "Would that be possible?"

"Oh, I suppose so. Ian – he's the younger – is staying here at the moment; he drove over from Aldershot yesterday. He's a real home-bird, our Ian. The other… I suppose you don't remember their names?"

"No."

"Paul is practicing here in Eastbourne. Gynecology, luckily enough – his own keep arriving, like Christmas." She paused, a small chilly moment. "Irish fashion! Do you want to meet *them* as well, the mob?"

"No, I don't think I'll have time." It didn't look so good. And she sounded a pain. Probably didn't practice either, married in a registry office and aggressive about it. However, he was committed now; there was no backing out. "As a matter of fact, I was thinking of going down this morning, if that would be all right?"

"Just a moment." There was a conversation off the phone, and he could hear her say, "Yes, this morning." Then she came back again with, "Sorry, Bill was just going shopping when you rang. That will be all right."

"Right, Marie." He didn't know how to break off.

"He'll meet you at the station," she went on. "He's not a Catholic, but don't mind that; he rather likes priests. These English, Father." There was what sounded like a suppressed laugh, a whispered "Stop it!"; then into the phone she said briskly, "See you then, Father. You'll be here about twelve." And she rang off.

He stood outside the phone booth, looking toward his empty table. If he sat down again, he was lost; he must go on, not thinking about the possibility of failure. He had a couple of hours to fill in before the later train; he filled them in just walking about the streets, coming back occasionally to sit in the waiting room. On the train, he dozed his way out of London, then fell asleep at last. Wakening at Eastbourne, seizing his old portmanteau, which had come with him on his first missionary journey to England, he realized he had forgotten to shave.

Not that it mattered. What difference did it make how he looked, when his purpose was going to startle them so much? To reclaim one of the lost Conroys for Rosnagree! So outrageous did it seem, so reckless his hope, that he laughed as he stood on the platform of Eastbourne station. By God, he'd show them!

But he grew subdued after meeting Marie's husband, who introduced himself simply as Bill. Sitting back in the lovingly looked after old Wolseley, he listened to Bill's chat and watched glimpses of the flat, gray sea go past between the pastel-washed houses and the banks of orderly flowers. Bill was small, neat, a freshly laundered old man with the manner of a dapper school-boy. His affability seemed calculated, and Father Conroy thought of it as a barrier, which he would have to break through. Yet what Bill was saying assumed that they were already intimate.

"Mahzie's chest, you know" (his northern consonants were bathed in a throaty, confidential warmth, like Vap-O-Rub) "— we call her Mahzie (Mah-zie, you see) – her chest has never been very strong. So when I retired, we thought things over for a while, went into it very carefully, and at last decided to come south. No, she's had no trouble since, touch wood. You know, Father, most of the time I tend to forget she's Irish, but then, my goodness, she does something all of a sudden, like producing you, if I may say so, out of a hat."

Father Conroy grimaced, looking straight ahead.

"To think, until a few hours ago, I had no idea she had a brother-in-law, a priest! That's what's so Irish about her."

"I don't think that's particularly Irish."

"Oh, yes, Father. It is, and I think it's marvelous. You know, things just pop out; you never know what to expect. It was just a little worrying when I was on the urban council back home. About religion, for instance. I'm C. of E., of course, in moderation, but I must confess I was shocked at what she'd say about people of her own denomination. I didn't like it; it caused bad feeling and wasn't at all good for business. However, we've got on very well, considering, and since we've come south, she occasionally even goes to Mass. You'll be able to discuss all that with her, Father. I'm sure you'll find it very rewarding."

But it was Bill who found the encounter rewarding, as he did everything relating to Marie. He stationed himself behind her, one hand on the back of her chair, like a well-groomed watchdog, everything about him suggesting intelligent interest and a complete lack of understanding.

But why? Marie did not look as if she needed a watchdog. She did not face Father Conroy so much as confront him. Her voice was even clearer than it had seemed on the phone, no Irish hesitancies left in it. She was sure of the facts she had chosen to live with, and so far, Father Conroy had not established his claim to be one of them.

How, he wondered, had she so emphatically put it out of mind, Frank and his little notebook, all that miserable past? Damn it all, why should it still grieve him, who had lost so much less? How could they sit there, explaining to him about Eastbourne and why they had decided to come south, as if it were the only big decision of their lives?

Seated in an old armchair, a buttress of comfort, he looked around him as if the answer were somewhere in the room. The mantelpiece and occasional tables were crowded with knick-knacks and photographs – a small faded one of Owen, lost among the studio portraits of stiffly smiling children, of grave young men in uniform and academic robes. Could the Conroys have counted for so little? Even when the talk began to range back over the past, it was always the post-Conroy period they talked about. The watchdog, he felt, was no longer necessary. And he was wasting not only their time, but his own.

Footsteps sounded briskly in the hall. "Ian!" said Marie, and shifted her bulk around, beaming herself on the door. Father Conroy looked up in renewed hope.

He was a Conroy – that could never be denied – a Conroy to the life. He had the features, blended, made smooth as they had not been for Owen, for any of them, least of all for Jimmy Donovan. His body was finer – long and slim, with good bones set off by the sweater and close-fitting jeans. He carried a tennis bag, which he shifted adroitly from right hand to left as he came forward to shake hands. While his uncle was being explained to him, he swung the bag gently against his thigh and looked polite.

A cool card, thought Father Conroy; let's try him with shock tactics. "I remember seeing you bathed once, young man."

There was no smile, just a mildly incredulous look.

"In a tin bath, on the kitchen floor," Father Conroy went on.

"You didn't, Father," said Marie. "That was Paul you saw."

Blast! The young fellow gave him a cold look, as if to say, who's this head case, anyway? Where did one go from here? And then Father Conroy saw that Marie had flushed and was pursing her lips. So there were some tender spots in those hidden years that might be probed! That gave him some encouragement, when she got up and went into the kitchen to get lunch.

"You're the lad that's at Aldershot, aren't you? How long are you there?"

"About two years." A shrug. "Long enough."

"Your service must be nearly up, so?"

Ian looked blank.

"Your national service, isn't that what you call it?"

The young man appealed mutely to his stepfather, as if to say, you explain it, for God's sake!

Bill hastened to oblige. "I don't think I told you, Father. Ian's a regular. Very young, too, but he was in the first six out of the Staff College. I have the photograph here. Where is it, Ian?"

And grudgingly, Ian handed over the photograph from the side table.

The British Army! Father Conroy looked at the rows of young faces that looked sternly back at him from under the lines of horizontally peaked caps. Name of God, what chance was there? What kind of a cracked old fool was he? He put down the photograph gently and began to rise to his feet. Get yourself out of here, he told himself, while you still seem halfway sane.

But lunch was ready, and Bill had him by the arm. "Of course,

Father, there's no national service now. We haven't had it for, oh, how many years, Ian?" He was touched, amused, bubbling over with solicitude as they took their places around the table in the dining room. Poor Father, he was obviously thinking, buried so long in Ireland. No telly, no papers, no post even. Just a great, shabby, green shrubbery with the mist hanging over it! You stupid oul' bollox, thought Father Conroy, and glowered down at his plate.

"Paul must be delayed," said Marie, bustling in. "Let's start without him."

"National service," chuckled Bill. "Fancy that!"

"Ian's been through the Staff College," she said sharply. "Fifth, wasn't it, Ian?"

Yes, she was vulnerable, all right. But how was that going to help? There was no future in Ian. That was plain to see.

"He's always been keen," Bill bumbled happily on, "as long as... as we've been together. You know, the Scouts, the O.T.C., that sort of thing. The Army seemed the natural thing, and luckily I managed to get him into Wellington."

Father Conroy looked at the young man opposite, already starting on his steady, purposeful way through the largest helping of roast beef and Yorkshire pudding. How much Conroy was in him to be reached?

"Nearly time for him to settle down," Bill went on. "Right, Father?"

"Nonsense," Marie said.

"I don't see why he shouldn't..." Bill began, but when she glanced at him, he ended with a murmured, "... think about it."

"He's time enough," she said, and made it quite definitely the last word.

Father Conroy let the silence lie for a moment. The young man ate stolidly, as if the conversation had nothing whatsoever to do with him. Oh, a cool card, right enough! But Father Conroy knew that there was an opening somewhere near, if he could only find it.

"Ah, well," he offered, "no use in rushing him, I suppose. But, on the other hand—" He chewed slowly, swallowed, and said, "You don't want to be putting him off."

"Putting him off?" Marie lowered her knife and fork. "How do you mean, putting him off?" She leaned her elbows on the table, confronting him. "I may say, Father, that young people are very welcome in this house. We like them to feel at home, and, as you know, many parents don't bother these days. We believe they should meet in the home atmosphere."

"Of course," Father Conroy hastened sternly to confirm. Catching Ian's hostile eye he decided to gamble on a long chance. He gave a slow wink and held his breath while he waited for the result.

It worked so well that he could hardly believe it. The young man looked down at his plate, and a flush rose in his cheeks. Poor fellow, thought Father Conroy, he's only half-hatched. He knows it, though; he's waiting for deliverance. What a pity he had never been told of his right to an Irish farm! If only there were more time! Yes, it would take time for the idea to sink in.

Bill was staring in a startled way from Ian to Father Conroy. He must have caught the wink. Don't bark now, old watchdog! Father Conroy's look warned. Aloud, the priest said, in a deep, churchly tone, "Oh, well, Marie, these things we must leave in God's hands." And he let a doubtful silence fall on the subject.

The phone rang as they sat over coffee. It was Paul, to say he could not make it but that he would like to meet his uncle later, sometime in the afternoon. Unfortunately he could not invite him home ("Just as well!" murmured Marie), so he suggested that they meet for tea in the foyer of the Palace Hotel.

"What a good idea!" said Bill, rubbing his hands excitedly as he came back to the table. "So now, Father, I suggest that I take you on a little guided tour of the town. We'll drop in at the Palace for tea and then come back here for supper. How's that?"

Father Conroy demurred; he wanted to start for home that evening, and his train was at five o'clock. However, when he learned that Ian was not coming with them, he said that yes, perhaps he might come back.

"I won't say good-bye, Tom," Marie told him at the door. "No." Hesitantly he put out his hand to Ian, who stood behind her. "So I'll be seeing you later, then, Ian?" The young man said nothing, but glanced at her; she gave no sign. Well, thought Father Conroy with sinking heart, if he's still tied to the apron-strings, what chance has he of being allowed to claim his ancestral land? Slowly Father Conroy withdrew his hand. "I don't know, Marie," he pleaded. "Still, there's lots of things we haven't got around to yet."

"What sort of things?" She paused, about to close the door.

"Oh, you know, the old days."

"They're past, Tom." She laughed harshly. "Don't you people know that yet?" And firmly she eased the door shut on him.

Father Conroy and Bill set off in the Wolseley. "It all fits in beautifully, Father," Bill enthused. "Mahzie has to have her rest at half-past two, whatever happens. It's her trouble, as I mentioned before. She'll perk up no end once she has her rest."

Father Conroy, too, would have liked to doze by the fire in the stuffy sitting room. The rigors of the night's traveling by boat and train were coming against him. With a great effort he tried to follow the meanderings of the voice beside him, to look at what was pointed out to him, the mounds of municipal flowers, solid as pincushions; the steps of hotels, rising in long, stately, out-of-season terraces; the few gulls slanting in the cold air above the promenade. What had it all to do with Rosnagree?

Suddenly, he was not quite sure how, they were in a great, deep-red hall, whose walls rose up into a high-windowed dimness. And they were crossing it, for a long time, making no noise, toward a big open fire of blazing coal. Lying back in an armchair, the glow of the fire on his face, he watched a tall man in black come floating toward them across that floor that was as soft as the heathery scraw of a bog. "Buttered scones"; yes, there was some talk of buttered scones, and he nodded, then let his head sink down on his chest. He knew it was just a moment of rest and that soon he would have to stir himself again. Every moment now was precious.

He heard music somewhere; it came to him, muted through many corridors, across empty lounges. What was it? Violins? A Viennese waltz? Straining to hear, he became conscious of the ceaseless, complacent voice at his side. "…in a private ward… so there she was on night duty… a thank-you letter… I never expected…" What was he talking about? "And then, at last…" Yes, Marie, it must be the story of Marie and himself. "Appalled,

Father, yes, really appalled. Those two poor children..." Yes, it was the whole story, and he was enjoying it so much, telling this priest. Wasn't that what priests were for, listening to other people's stories, living by proxy?

Father Conroy shifted impatiently. The big grandfather clock in the corner said a quarter past four. Where was Paul? Why wasn't he coming? Already their waiter was returning, bearing aloft their faintly steaming tray. The fellow had said he would be here at four.

His gaze wandered on, drawn by a man and woman at the head of the staircase. They were standing there, very erect, looking out over the hall, aware of but not looking at the people below. The man bent his head slightly to speak to the woman, and she smiled, raised her head, then deliberately, arm in arm, they began to descend, pausing a little at each step, as if to make sure that each small advance made its proper effect. As they came into the level of light, Father Conroy saw that they were old, extraordinarily old. Yet, the man's hair was still black; it was combed from a central parting and fell, long and straight, around his white, shrunken face. Two button-eyes gleamed on either side of a small, hooked nose. His clothes had an antique cut, the coat tight and long, almost like a frockcoat, the white of the shirt high about his neck. The woman's face was set in a smile, self-absorbed, misty as the makeup she wore. The outlines of her real face seemed no longer there.

As they descended, conversation ceased in the lounge. Several waiters drifted to the foot of the stairs and stood waiting in a submissive row. One of them fell in beside the couple, and, holding himself very straight, as if on guard, began the long, soundless progress toward a table in the far corner of the lounge.

Bill leaned forward excitedly. "You saw them, Father? You know who they are?"

Father Conroy could just make out the two white faces in the dimness of the corner. Deliberately he looked away. He bit into a scone and began to chew with his most nonchalant air, closing his ears to what Bill was saying. But he could not keep it up; the scone had no taste. Worse, as it disintegrated in his mouth, it seemed to spread its sharp, metallic flavor right through him, so that he felt a slow movement of bile in his stomach. He took a drink of tea, but that seemed only to flood the bile upward into his throat. He got to his feet quickly. Bill was saying, "... for years, Father, in exile..." Then he was striking blindly across the hall in the direction of the cloakroom.

He was just in time. As the fit of retching passed and he leaned, trembling, over the bowl, he had a vision of a bare, brown, treeless country which he had never seen before. Across it, two figures were approaching him, two ancient figures, straining forward toward him, clutching each other, quite naked. A spasm went through him; his head shuddered violently. After it had passed, he felt cold and empty. And as he filled a glass to wash the taste from his mouth, he knew for certain that he was going to die.

The knowledge must have shown in his face. Bill looked up at him when he returned to the table and then looked quickly away. Yes, Bill knew. Bill, at last, had met something with which he could not cope.

So, it was true then. Please, God, don't let it happen to me here, not in England. Let me, at least, get out of here!

"More tea, Father? That must be quite cold."

"No, thanks." He lifted the cup but could not drink. How was he to get away? He looked around for some excuse; he couldn't just get up and go.

The old couple had finished their afternoon tea. Even before they rose to their feet, the waiters had appeared at their side. The slow procession back to the stairway began – before a great, unseen audience, she smiling out of her unreal face, he very stern yet condescending. Behind them, attending every movement, the three waiters moved, their only real subjects. Paid, too, thought Father Conroy, and you may be sure, damn well paid. He laughed suddenly, out loud, and Bill looked at him, shocked.

"Na flatha fá raibh mo shean roimh éag do Chríost," he said, putting down the cup of tea, untouched.

"I beg your pardon, Father?"

"A bit of Irish! Gaelic!" What had put it into his head? Egan O'Rahilly, back there in the seventeenth century, what made me think of you? Or you of me, maybe, you surly old poet of a broken world! *I'll stop now. Help I'll not call out for. Soon I must go to join them, that sweet company of men, the princes who bore my seed before Christ's birth.*

He got to his feet. "I must go, Bill."

"But he may still come, Father. Paul is often…"

"No, I must go. I must get the five-o'clock train."

"Mahzie's expecting you!" Bill paused, as if that should be sufficient to induce Father Conroy to stay. When no reply came, he said, "Are you – I mean, are you sure, Father, that you're feeling all right?"

"I'll do. Yes, I'll do fine." But would he do? For the long journey home, which was a whole night away? Impatiently he said, "I must hurry. I must get that train."

*

He did not miss it. He made sure of that. In a panic, he urged Bill to the station and ran onto the platform. But when he was on the train, and later, on the far side of London, when he was on the boat train to Holyhead, the wheels began beating out his message for him. "I'll do, yes, I'll do, I'll do, yes, I'll do." And he closed his eyes to it, trying to keep out any tremor of doubt. The night was before him, the width of England and North Wales, then the Irish Sea.

He sat, sometimes dozing, sometimes starting awake. The light was dim. It seemed as if the compartment were diffused into the darkness outside. So too were the faces of his fellow passengers; he was never quite sure how many of them there were within – so many of them seemed to be riding outside the train, over the fields and hedgerows. There were a couple of Irish laborers; he noted the boots and the heavy, belted overcoats. And there was a fat, elderly woman in tweeds, with blue hair, who talked all the time to a girl in school uniform, several times mentioning Bordeaux. Once he heard the girl murmur, "It's very dark in here."

"That's because the lights aren't fully on, my dear," the woman told her. And again the woman said, "Ah, the tea, you didn't like the way they made tea. But, my dear girl, you should have had coffee!" And again, "A daughter of Dr. Doyle's, who goes to the Sacred Heart, your age, yes, she can speak three languages. But, of course, the Sacred Heart!"

And Father Conroy, watching the girl's listless face, wondered whether she thought the world was like that great, fat bitch. And of course, it is! he thought. Or is it? At once, the wheels seemed to catch the question from him. "It is, or is it?" they said. "It is, or is it?"

He dozed, their mockery in his ears, conscious now and then that the people were shifting about him, their faces drifting out into the darkness and as pointlessly drifting back again. He hardly noticed the transition to the boat at Holyhead. A Welsh porter took him, stumbling, through the Customs and up the gangway to the First Class. At sight of his ticket, however, the man muttered something, picked up the portmanteau, and escorted him brusquely down to the steerage.

His bunk was in a half-empty dormitory. He shoved the portmanteau underneath it and turned straight in, fully dressed. People came pushing past in the narrow passageway, their baggage brushing against him. A child was crying. A door opened for a moment farther down the corridor and a voice bawled out a song; then the door slammed to. There was a continual shuffling of feet, a whispering all around him, but the most persistent sound of all was the ring of heels on the metal plates overhead. Up and down, back and forth, those iron heels went, and in trying to picture someone pacing up there, he dropped off to sleep.

Yet the sound persisted. He recognized it now as the clatter of his own footsteps; he was descending the fire escape of St. Declan's in the dark, conscious of his fellow students sleeping within. However lightly he trod, the sound he made could be heard all over the quiet college, and at last, impatiently, he went thundering down the iron rungs, past the black windows, to the ground. He knew where the path was, but to enter it was like wading into a stream, which brought him on and on till he reached a wall, towering above him. He felt his way along the rough stones, fearful of something after him that he could not see – was it a dog following silently in the darkness of his tracks?

In panic, he heaved himself upward and was on top of the wall, straddling himself over it, letting himself down into the abyss on the far side. Slowly he lowered himself, with his toes now unaccountably bare, scratching vainly for a foothold. He hung there by his arms until he was about to scream with the agony of it, but he knew he must not make a sound. At last he could bear it no longer. Still silent, he let go and dropped down into the darkness.

He did not notice the shock of landing, for, at once, he was a small boy running into a wood. He blundered through bushes, stumbled into holes that were hidden by drifts of leaves, and as the trees closed about him, he stopped, gasping for breath, to look back the way he had come. But he could not see; the trees were all around him, and there was no sound but his own breathing.

And then he was standing outside a cottage, watching the smoke of a newly lit fire rise from the chimney. He was cold, hungry; his arms hung stiffly by his sides. He moved to the front door and knocked timidly. There was no answer. He knocked again and after a while stooped to look in the window. A fire glowed on the hearth, but there was no movement within. Everything was still, as if the people were waiting in silence until he went away.

It was daylight now, and he was walking fast, as if he knew what he was making for. The trees thinned out into a clearing, and he hurried forward, thinking he had reached the edge of the wood; but again they thickened, and he had to push his way through furze and briers, and he was far from what he was searching for. Then, suddenly, he came upon the stream.

It was not easy to follow. The ground sloped this way and that; the stream ran, looping back on itself, sometimes disappearing beneath the brambles, so that he had to search for it by the sounds it made. An evening mist filled the wood, and still he followed the stream as it ran over rocky patches of ground, dropping fast in little waterfalls which shone in the gray light. At last the trees thinned away and he saw what he had been looking for, the dark flood of the river far below. It was almost night when he reached it. He stood for a long time watching its dull shine as it swept past him out of the dark and into darkness again. He no longer felt the cold or the hunger or the stiffness in his arms. But as he watched, the shine slowly faded, and he knew that it was time to go, yes, to go home to Rosnagree.

He set off upstream, and around a bend saw before him a bridge. It was an old footbridge, its timbers gapped and the farther section of it no more than a wooden rail hung over the river. He took the first steps on to it, and stopped when he looked down and saw the water flowing blackly beneath him. As he clung to the rail, a sob tore itself out of him, surprising him, because he hated to cry. He gripped the rail tightly and stumbled back to the bank. There he flung himself down, trying to stop the sobbing that hurt inside him.

But the pain would not stop. And gradually, as he lay there, he realized that he was not alone. He lifted his head. There were voices near, the growl of a dog. Quickly he scrambled up and was about to run, when, close in front, tall black shapes moved along the riverbank toward him. "Hold him, there!" a voice called, and he stopped, held from escaping by the ordinariness of the tone and the words. A match was struck. As it guttered in the hollow of a hand, he glimpsed what he thought was his father's face under the peaked cap. Relief flooded right through him, so great that he felt quite weak after it. And even when the match light flickered higher and he saw that the face was not his father's, the relief remained.

"Who are ye, at all? What are ye doing here?"

"I got lost," he said quickly, eager that the men should not go away.

The match went out. "D'ye hear that? He got lost."

"L-l-lost from wh-where?" the man holding his arm said. His voice was younger; that fact and the stammer gave the boy confidence to say firmly, "From Rosnagree."

"The Conroys', is it?"

The boy nodded, though he could not be seen. He felt a lump of pride in his throat that the Conroys should be known of, so far from home.

"A Conroy from Rosnagree," the older man said loudly. Was the younger man deaf? Possibly, because all he said was, "You've no c-coat on."

"I lost it."

"Lost it?" The older man clicked his tongue. "Lost his coat and all."

The restraining hand was gone; the boy was free now to escape, yet he continued to stand there, unwilling to move away from the hidden company about him. For though the darkness was complete, he was clearly conscious of the two men, even of the dog snuffing somewhere near. All at once, a warm, heavy weight descended on his shoulders, draped itself around him. "No," he protested.

"G-go on. Put it on ye!"

And from then on, he seemed to lose control of his limbs.

He moved drowsily in the warmth of the coat, as if he were floating along, buoyed up within it, through the darkness of trees. And at last he seemed to float into the dimly lit kitchen of a cottage, and sway there, as if he might be drawn out again on a retreating tide of darkness.

The younger man was kneeling by the fire, fixing sods of turf in the ashes, and he himself was seated on a sugán chair, the coat still wrapped about him. He looked around him, at the dresser of delph, the little red Sacred Heart lamp that cast a circle of light up on the black rafters. The older man had taken down the oil lamp from the wall and was trimming the wick. His face, bent intently over the flame, was familiar, and the boy realized that it was his own father's. Yet, when the lamp hung back on its nail and the man turned to him, the boy was not so sure. No, he thought, how could it be? His father was in Rosnagree. This man lived in the cottage, and the young man was his son.

The man moved to the middle of the room and pushed up his cap to scratch the top of his head. "I dunno," he said. "Would he blow the fire for us?"

The young man looked up from where he knelt at the fire. He seemed the more certain of the two, for he addressed the boy directly and asked, "Would ye blow the f-fire for us?"

The machine was by the bench in the chimney corner. The boy sat down by it and began to turn the wheel. The flames licked around the sods of turf and then crept upward in long, narrow tongues. Still the boy kept turning the wheel, slower now, more drowsily, so that he was almost asleep when the old man called out, "Come on, son, let ye sit up to the table."

And to his surprise, he found himself leaning his elbows on

the bare table. He had a saucerful of sweet tea between his hands, and he was drinking from it, as the men did. He knew he should be drinking from a cup, but this was the way the laborers drank at home, and he did not want to seem different. The men spoke little. The older man kept his head down, cutting the meat on his plate with his big clasp knife and mopping up the gravy with a hunk of bread. When he had finished, he pushed the plate away from him, blessed himself, and put on the cap which he had left on the table beside him. Then he looked at the young man, inviting him to take the initiative, but he was still busy eating.

"Would he stay with us?" he asked at last.

"W-would ye stay with us? You could l-look after the place for us."

"I'd rather be out with ye."

They both laughed at that.

"We do be w-working at the forestry."

"Ye'd be too young yet," the older man said.

"Ye'd be af-fraid of the trees."

And they both laughed again.

The boy felt too warm and full to answer. He put his hands under his head, propping up its sudden, heavy weight. His cheeks were roasting on the palms of his hands.

And then he was in a bed, a high bed with a soft, thick feather mattress into which he was snugly sunk. The door into the kitchen was half-open, and he could hear the murmur of voices there, the scrape of chairs on the flags of the kitchen floor. The rosary began with the son's voice, saying, "Our F-Father, who art in heaven, hallowed be thy name, thy k-kingdom come, thy w-will be done…"

And as the boy lost consciousness, Father Conroy awoke.

He lay stiffly on the hard bunk, searching for some clue to where he was. The light was very dim. As he pulled himself up, he felt the edge of the bunk shuddering beneath his hand. Around him, in the lower berths, people lay, each a mound of brown blanket, very still. There was no sound from them, and for a moment he felt he was the only one alive. Then the throb of engines pushed its way up out of the silence, and he thought, God, yes, I'm on the mail boat, going home.

He looked for his portmanteau, but it was not there; he had had it coming into the customs shed. Had he brought it on board? He sat, trying to think – there was scarcely air to breathe, and he felt his vest stuck to his back. His breviary was in it, and his leather Mass kit, which he had had since his ordination day. God, he couldn't lose them! He'd be lost without them! What should he do? Go up and find someone to report to!

Quickly he got out and stumbled past the half-lit rows of bodies. The companionway was empty. He hurried upward, drawn by the light that had begun to dilute the globes of faded yellow that hung around each electric bulb. Cold air blew in his face as he stepped over the threshold and turned into the shelter of the afterdeck. The sun's light fell on him through the clear air; he imagined its distant warmth on his face. To the southwest, the mountains of Wicklow were on the horizon. He knew their shapes, their dark, misty blue, deepened here and there in places which the sun could not yet reach. The warmth was on his shoulders now, sinking into every pore of his body. He was weak from it; he could not move, not even to raise his eyes from the mountains, drawing steadily nearer, with the gulls circling against them like tiny seeds of white.

Snatches of his dream still hovered in his mind. There had been a voice with a stammer, and he remembered that he himself had had a stammer in his first years at the national school. One day, when he was on his way to school, he had flung his schoolbag through a gap in a hedge and gone wriggling in to find a hidden place beside it. He remembered his dismay when he could not find the schoolbag in the breast-high corn. Just like his portmanteau, which he had lost in the *tellonaria*. In the *tellonaria*? He groped toward the source of that long-forgotten phrase and, for once, came triumphantly upon it. *Origen*! The pilgrims on their journey through life! The customhouses, where their goods were stolen or mislaid, so that when they reached their destination at last, they had nothing left. He too had started out with his schoolbag and now he had divested himself of everything. Even the tools of his trade were back in Holyhead, probably in the hands of her Majesty's Customs!

But surely he had found the schoolbag, after all? Yes, he must have found it. Wasn't that the day he mitched from school, and his father came upon him in the corner of a field of barley? There he was, trapped as the reaping machine came rattling nearer, drawing with it the voices of the laboring men. His father parted the tall grasses of the headland and found him there, waiting, crouched on the ground like a hare in its form. His father was shouting – what, he could not remember, but he could remember the pain of being the cause of that anger. And he had answered, with his head bowed in shame, "Because I'd s-s-sooner be here with you!"

What had happened then? Had he been beaten? Had his father looked at him, speechless, and turned away? He could not remember. He did not know whether it had turned out happily or not, and now, no one would ever know. He had kept it buried too long in his memory. Soon it would be buried with him forever in the darkness of the clay.

But, no, he did not believe that. He could not believe it.

It would be remembered; somehow it would live on, every detail of it fresh and clear to a new generation, the children of light. Yes, he thought, looking up into the sun, whose bright particles showered him with their sharp, glinting edges, "Et claritas Dei circumfulsit illos." Claritas Dei, the light of God.

The mountains were nearer. The sun was picking out white specks that were walls and gables of houses. A gull came sailing overhead. He watched it lifting above the masthead. He too felt bereft of weight, as if at any moment he would be blown away like a dandelion seed by the wind of the ship's passing. He smiled, looking down at the black sagging overcoat that clung to him, ballasting him. Only for the coat, he would float upward; yes, he thought, chuckling, thaw and resolve myself into a dew, a great hazy smoke scrawled Adieu in the sky over Dublin. There would be questions in the Dáil about it, of course; Deputy Jimmy Donovan would rise to his feet, and with the voice and gesture of his old uncle, ask the Minister if his attention had been drawn to the activities of a certain firm of doubtful repute (i.e., which had not contributed to party funds), whose advertising was disturbing the minds of decent citizens and was a slur upon the national image.

All right, then, Jimmy boy. Since I'm one of the family, make it worth my while and I'll advertise what you like. Drinka Pinta Dieu? Give every Man his Dieu?

"Farewell, my aged parayents," he sang, dragging the words out in a ballad singer's nasal drawl,

> To you I bid adieu.
> I am crossing the wide ocean,
> All for the sake of you.
> And if ever I return again…

I feel great, by God. Only for this oul' coat! Damn it, I'll take it off me.

And so he did, folding the coat over his arm and standing with a waiting expression on his face as Ireland floated toward him. And as the arms of Dun Laoghaire harbor opened to receive him, he felt that he might, at any moment, dissolve upon the sun-warmed deck.

Songs, phrases, welled up in a miraculous spring within him as he moved through the Customs. He got onto the train for Dublin, nearly bursting with the effort to keep them suppressed. At Kingsbridge Station, he walked up and down the platform as he waited for the train to the southwest, and felt neither cold, nor pain, nor hunger. When the outer suburbs of Dublin, the streets and streets of council houses, fell behind, he got up, unable to abide any longer the sleepy faces of his fellow passengers. Like fish gasping on a strand, he thought, and began to move along the train.

In the bar, he met at last someone whom he felt he could talk to. The man was swaying back and forth in front of the bar, waiting to be served. His old coat hung open, his belt dangled over his belly, his cap was down over one eye, and his trousers looked as if they had been slept in. He was looking around him, unshaven, drunken, benevolent, an Irish Paddy on his way home from England with lashings of money hot in his fist'. "I love the fields," he announced as the train lurched him forward to give him a glimpse of the rich Kildare pastures flying past. "The grass, th' oul' bullocks!" He straightened up, saw a ticket collector approaching, and took a careful step forward, hands out like a boy about to trap a butterfly. "I love the lads in C.I.E." The ticket collector evaded him and passed hastily on. "Jesus, I even love the Govormint. Up Dev!"

"Good man, yourself!" called Father Conroy, who had hunched himself over a cup of tea in the corner.

The man waved a hand hazily in his direction. "Won't be long now, Mac. The Curragh of Kildare, then on to Maryborough, and in no time we'll be home." He lifted a hand, as if to shush an audience into silence, and sang:

'Tis not the leavin' of Liverpool
That grie-ee-ves me,
But, my darlin', when I think of thee.

"Will ye have a drink?" asked Father Conroy.

"I will, bejasus." He peered toward where Father Conroy's voice had come from. "And the blessings of the Lord Jesus be upon ye, whoever y'are. Now, if them C.I.E. bastards would only come out from their cubbyhole and serve us!"

"Bang on the counter!"

"Bang on it! I'll put my fisht through…" And then he saw the priest's collar. "Oh, Jesus, oh, sorry, Father. I never saw who was in it."

"Bang on the counter."

The fellow hesitated, then raised his fist. Just then a young waiter put his head round the hatch and said, "Well? What is it now?"

"Give the man what he wants," called Father Conroy.

The waiter gestured toward the man incredulously. "Him, Father?"

"Give him what he wants, I said." Because we're up here toge-ther, Paddy and I, we're up here, way up above C.I.E. bastards and bullocks and fields and Dev. We can see them all below there, creeping around, not knowing how funny they look.

Yes, funny! The waiter came along behind the counter, slim in his white jacket, carrying his oiled black coiffure indignantly, as if he were balancing it aloft. And Father Conroy laughed.

"Somethin' for yerself, Father?" the man sang out, as the large glass of Paddy was pushed before him.

"No thanks, Mac. I have all I want." And Father Conroy paid the sullen waiter and turned back to his cup of tea.

The man laughed exultantly as he took up his glass. He raised it to Father Conroy in salute. "To hell with poverty, Father. We'll kill a hen!"

And, watching him down the drink, Father Conroy too laughed. The bullocks, the fields, Dev, C.I.E., this drunken oaf – he loved them; yes, he loved them all. Even old sourpuss, as she led her niece past to find a table farther on – he loved her too, and the niece, poor girl, who had been finished in Bordeaux.

Affectionately he waved to them. And laughed when the old lady glared at him and hurried her charge quickly on, so as not to be scandalized by the sight of the drunken priest.

He was home by midday. The silence in the house was disapproving. Where have you been, it said, gallivanting again? The clock in the hall looked at him, hangdog, and he screwed up his face at it, mimicking its expression. I'm breaking out, he told all the sullen furniture, clearing off. Too long have I looked after ye, cared for ye, mothered ye! Now, yez can shift for yerselves! "With me bundle on me shoulder," he sang, "Sure, there's no one could be bolder…"

Me bundle! Yes, he had a bundle, all right, but he wasn't going to bring it. He flung open the door of the cupboard, daring it to come out, but it sat there like a badger in the butt of a barrel. Well, he'd bait it! He'd find its match, to drag it out by the scruff of the neck. Who, though, who?

He had to be quick. O'Hara? No, he was too used to handling money; he'd spend years disposing of it conscientiously. Bat Cullen? God love him, the shock would kill him. No, he wanted someone who would attack it like a terrier, half in panic, half-delirious, who would spend it fast, to put it out of mind and memory. Someone like Mahon.

He hesitated a moment. Ah, no, not poor Mahon, Peter the celestial plumber. But that was the very reason. It would have to be Peter Mahon. Nobody else believed so implicitly in the system; it would be no trouble to him to pull the chain and swish it all away. There was no doubt. Peter Mahon was the man.

He began to laugh, thinking of Mahon's face when the Bishop

would read him the letter. Yes, it would have to be done formally – a letter to the Bishop and all – otherwise, Peter would try to sidle out of it. But what to say?

He cleared a place on the table and began: "My lord, I most humbly request that in the event of my…" "departure," he was going to say, and paused to consider how his absence would be officially noted. "Conroy, yes, he departed." "Emigravit ad coelum," they used to say in the old parish records. "Sealed with the seal of faith, sleeping the sleep of peace."

And then, impatiently, he wrote, "…death, that Father Peter Mahon, my fellow student and…" What else? Friend? He had hardly spoken to the man in his life; still… "…friend," he wrote, "be asked to administer my effects. I give him full power to dispose of all as he thinks fit. I have complete confidence in his discretion." And you can say that again!

He snatched his head, thinking out some nice, flowery phrases that would irritate his lordship, then scrawled his signature at last. But, just as he addressed the envelope, he thought of the post, that it was already gone.

The post already gone! How was he to put in the time waiting? Blast it, he thought, sitting down at the kitchen table, suddenly disconsolate. He could belt into town and get the post there, but what then? He couldn't return here to… to sit down and wait. What the hell was he to do?

He noticed the calendar on the wall, with the ring around the date. Of course, O'Hara's dinner! Well, he could go along there, why not? See Mahon there too, maybe even speak to the fellow, see what fist he was likely to make of the job.

He stuck the envelope in his pocket and turned to go. In the hall he turned and looked around. The clock still looked at him, hangdog, and he pushed at it playfully. Damn little he'll get for you, he told it.

What happened to a place, though, when you left it? Did everything stay suspended in space, waiting for you with the same expression till you returned? It was a question he had asked before; it had that dimly familiar feel to it. Of whom, though, had he asked it? His father? Perhaps. He could see his father smiling and saying, "Does it stay the same? Sure, how do we know, once our back is turned?"

And now he was driving fast along the road, whose every twist and turn he had known as a boy. Beyond the wood, over the bridge, O'Hara's house came in sight. He could see a figure in black in the garden, moving between the trees, Mahon as sure as God. Well, maybe they would find a lot to say to each other. Maybe they were intended to be friends, after all.

He got out of the car and looked up at the house, from which came the sound of voices. Clamor gentium, the third stage of a good meal! What came before that? Yes, the tooth-work – stridor dentium. Well, they must be taking both stages together. And first of all, there would have been silentium; he had missed that stage. Hadn't he had enough silences in his time?

He slammed the car door shut and hurried up the path. On his way, he turned to look for Mahon among the trees, but Mahon was gone. Only the gardener was there, the old man, head bowed, scything away. And Father Conroy plunged forward into the laughter and talk with an eagerness he had never known, not even when he drank the wine and broke the bread of life.

About the author

Richard Power was born in Dublin, Ireland, in 1928. An exchange scholarship took him to the United States in 1958 for two years of study and teaching at the Writers' Workshop at the University of Iowa. He returned to Dublin and became a civil servant, but at the weekends and in the evenings he wrote: stories, essays, and plays, in Gaelic and in English. His masterpiece, *The Hungry Grass*, was first published in 1969. He died suddenly a year later, at the age of forty-one.

More from Apollo

NOW IN NOVEMBER
Josephine Johnson

> *Now in November I can see our years as a whole. This autumn is like both an end and a beginning to our lives, and those days which seemed confused with the blur of all things too near and too familiar are clear and strange now.*

Forced out of the city by the Depression, Arnold Haldmarne moves his wife and three daughters to the country and tries to scratch a living from the land. After years of unrelenting hard work, the hiring of a young man from a neighbouring farm upsets the fragile balance of their lives. And in the summer, the rains fail to come.

BOSNIAN CHRONICLE
Ivo Andrić

> *For as long as anyone could remember, the little café known as 'Lutvo's' has stood at the far end of the Travnik bazaar, below the shady, clamorous source of the 'Rushing Brook'.*

This is a sweeping saga of life in Bosnia under Napoleonic rule. Set in the remote town of Travnik, the newly appointed French consul soon finds himself intriguing against his Austrian rival, whilst dealing with a colourful cast of locals.

THE MAN WHO LOVED CHILDREN
Christina Stead

All the June Saturday afternoon Sam Pollit's children were on the look-out for him as they skated round the dirt sidewalks and seamed old asphalt of R Street and Reservoir Road that bounded the deep-grassed acres of Tohoga House, their home.

Sam and Henny Pollit have too many children, too little money and too much loathing for each other. As Sam uses the children's adoration to feed his own voracious ego, Henny becomes a geyser of rage against her improvident husband.

MY SON, MY SON
Howard Spring

What a place it was, that dark little house that was two rooms up and two down, with just the scullery thrown in! I don't remember to this day where we all slept, though there was a funeral now and then to thin us out.

This is the powerful story of two hard-driven men – one a celebrated English novelist, the other a successful Irish entrepreneur – and of their sons, in whom are invested their fathers' hopes and ambitions. Oliver Essex and Rory O'Riorden grow up as friends, but their fathers' lofty plans have unexpected consequences as the violence of the Irish Revolution sweeps them all into uncharted territory.

DELTA WEDDING
Eudora Welty

The nickname of the train was the Yellow Dog. Its real name was the Yazoo-Delta. It was a mixed train. The day was the 10th of September, 1923 – afternoon. Laura McRaven, who was nine years old, was on her first journey alone.

Laura McRaven travels down the Delta to attend her cousin Dabney's wedding. At the Fairchild plantation her family envelop her in a tidal wave of warmth, teases and comfort. As the big day approaches, tensions inevitably rise to the surface.

THE DAY OF JUDGMENT
Salvatore Satta

At precisely nine o'clock, as he did every evening, Don Sebastiano Sanna Carboni pushed back his armchair, carefully folded the newspaper which he had read through to the very last line, tidied up the little things on his desk, and prepared to go down to the ground floor...

Around the turn of the twentieth century, in the isolated Sardinian town of Nuoro, the aristocratic notary Don Sebastiano Sanna reflects on his life, his family's history and the fortunes of this provincial backwater where he has lived out his days. Written over the course of a lifetime and published posthumously, *The Day of Judgment* is a classic of Italian, and world, literature.

THE AUTHENTIC DEATH OF HENDRY JONES
Charles Neider

> *Nowadays, I understand, the tourists come for miles to see Hendry Jones' grave out on the Punta del Diablo and to debate whether his bones are there or not...*

A stark and violent depiction of one of America's most alluring folk heroes, the mythical, doomed gunslinger. Set on the majestic coast of southern California, Doc Baker narrates his tale of the Kid's capture, trial, escape and eventual murder. Written in spare and subtle prose, this is one of the great literary treatments of America's obsession with the rule of the gun.

THE LOST EUROPEANS
Emanuel Litvinoff

> *Coming back was worse, much worse, than Martin Stone had anticipated. When he got into the boat train at Liverpool Street, with English newspapers and periodicals stuffed under his arm, the usual drizzle falling from the grimy London sky, he'd told himself this was just a business trip...*

When Martin Stone returns to Berlin after the war, he knows his homecoming will be a painful one. For he is a Jew, and he is back to seek restitution of his family's fortunes. First published in 1958 after Litvinoff's own visit to the city, *The Lost Europeans* portrays a vibrant, flourishing Berlin, underlaid with an ever-present sense of sin and rot.

HEAVEN'S MY DESTINATION
Thornton Wilder

> *One morning in the late summer of 1930 the proprietor and several guests at the Union Hotel at Crestcrego, Texas, were annoyed to discover Biblical texts freshly written across the blotter on the public writing-desk.*

George Marvin Brush is a travelling textbook salesman and fervent religious convert, determined to lead the godless to a better life. With sad and sometimes hilarious consequences, his travels take him through smoking cars, bawdy houses, banks and campgrounds from Texas to Illinois and into the soul of 1930s America.

HISTORY OF A TOWN
M. E. Saltykov-Shchedrin

> *Despite their insuperable firmness of character, the Glupovites are a spoilt and extremely coddled people. They like to see a friendly smile on the face of their superior, they like to hear from his lips an occasional witty pleasantry...*

Regarded as one of the major satirical novels of the 19th century, Shchedrin's farcical history of Glupov (or Stupid Town) follows the bewildered and passive Russian peasants for hundreds of years as they do what they can – in a sluggish way – to live with the violence and lunacy of their tyrannical rulers. A harsh criticism of Tsarist Russia, this novel is strangely pertinent to today.

THE STONE ANGEL

Margaret Laurence

Above the town, on the hill brow, the stone angel used to stand. I wonder if she stands there yet, in memory of her who relinquished her feeble ghost as I gained a stubborn one...

Hagar Shipley has lived a quiet life full of rage. As she approaches her death, she retreats from the squabbling of her son and his wife to reflect on her past – her ill-advised marriage, her two sons, the harshness of life on the prairie, her own failures and the failures of others.